BY SUZANNE BROCKMANN

TROUBLESHOOTERS SERIES
The Unsung Hero
The Defiant Hero
Over the Edge
Out of Control
Into the Night
Gone Too Far
Flashpoint
Hot Target
Breaking Point
Into the Storm
Force of Nature
All Through the Night
Into the Fire
Dark of Night
Hot Pursuit
Breaking the Rules

SUNRISE KEY SERIES
Kiss and Tell
The Kissing Game
Otherwise Engaged

OTHER BOOKS
Heartthrob
Forbidden
Freedom's Price
Body Language
Stand-In Groom
Time Enough for Love
Infamous
Ladies' Man
Bodyguard

BREAKING THE RULES

SUZANNE BROCKMANN

BREAKING THE RULES

A NOVEL

BALLANTINE BOOKS • NEW YORK

Published in the United States by Ballantine Books, an imprint of The Random House Publishing Group, a division of Random House, Inc., New York.

BALLANTINE and colophon are registered trademarks of Random House, Inc.

Library of Congress Cataloging-in-Publication Data
Brockmann, Suzanne.
Breaking the rules : a novel / Suzanne Brockmann.
p. cm. — (Troubleshooters ; 16)
ISBN 978-0-345-52122-4 (hardcover : alk. paper) — ISBN 978-0-345-52124-8 (ebook)
1. United States, Navy, SEALS — Fiction. 2. Government investigators — Fiction. I. Title.
PS3552.R61455B75 2011
813'.54 — dc22   2011000561

Printed in the United States of America on acid-free paper

www.ballantinebooks.com

9 8 7 6 5 4 3 2 1

First Edition

For you, my readers

ACKNOWLEDGMENTS

Thanks, as always, to the usual suspects—the team at Ballantine, including my editor, Shauna Summers; my agent, Steve Axelrod; and my patient family: Ed and Jason Gaffney; Melanie, Dawson, and Aidan; and my parents Fred & Lee Brockmann.

A special shout-out to Scott Lutz for being an early-draft reader.

A huge thank-you to both the real Kathy Gordon and the real Nicola Chick. Your generous donations to The First Amendment Project are deeply and sincerely appreciated!

Thank you to the fabulous team at Advanced Physical Therapy in Sarasota: Casey, Lijah, Molly, Pam, and their fearless leader, Kitty Devine. Thanks for getting me back on my feet—and for enduring an author on deadline in the process!

Big thanks to *New York Times* Bestselling Author Brenda Novak for all her hard work raising money for diabetes research. For several years, I've participated in Brenda's enormous annual online charity auction. It's personal for Brenda, and now, after bringing Ben Gillman to life, it's become personal for me, too. Visit www.brendanovak.auctionanything .com and help make a difference.

Last but certainly not least, I want to thank *you*, my readers, who trust me enough to follow wherever I will take you, and who continue to give me permission to write the stories of my heart.

As always, any mistakes I've made or liberties I've taken are completely my own.

BREAKING THE RULES

CHAPTER
ONE

I t happened so fast.
The IED—a car bomb, had to be—went off in the middle of the busy neighborhood.

One minute Izzy Zanella was letting Mark Jenkins use him as a sounding board for the pros and cons of putting in an offer on a house before he and his wife, Lindsey, sold their condo—which was ridiculous, because Izzy had never owned property in his thirty years of life and wasn't likely to change from being a renter anytime soon. But that was probably why Jenk was bouncing his thoughts off Izzy—because said thoughts would, absolutely, bounce.

Of course, their Navy SEAL teammate and resident pain in the ass Danny-Danny-bo-banny Gillman had never owned property either, but he had an Opinion with a capital O on the subject—and that O stood for boring. Dan had spent most of the morning dourly warning Jenkie to not even *think* about buying anything in this craphell market—not until they had a buyer for the condo locked in.

Jenk, however, was in love—and not just with his adorable yet kick-ass wife. He was in love with his entire life, including Lindsey's whoopsie-daisy pregnancy. It had just happened, or rather, they'd just found out about it. And even though they had nearly eight full months before Baby Day, Jenk really, *really* wanted to buy what was, without a doubt, his idea of *the* perfect house, particularly since it sat three perfect houses down from the equally perfect home of SEAL Team Sixteen's former CO, Tommy Paoletti, whom Markie-Mark still loved nearly as much as Lindsey and their fabulous life.

And Izzy had to admit that living down the street from Tommy, who had a more-the-merrier policy to his almost-weekly cookouts, would be pretty flipping great.

Jenkins didn't want to hear any more of Gillman's doom and gloom, which was why he was walking next to Izzy and saying, "If it turns out we can't sell the condo, we can always go to Plan B—"

Which was when the world went *boom*.

Izzy went from nodding his agreement to soul-kissing the street and inhaling rancid water from a puddle that was part yak piss, part toxic sludge.

He rolled over to do a quick head count of his teammates and encountered Dan Gillman, who was doing the exact same thing, his hand on Izzy's leg—the better to shake him with.

"Zanella, Christ, are you all right?" Gillman asked, far more urgently than Izzy would have expected, considering that Izzy's main reason for finding Dan such a royal pain in the ass was the fact that Dan thought *Izzy* was the world's biggest load. And he'd come to his opinion about *that* long before Izzy had gone and married Danny's little sister, Eden, which had, inarguably, made things even more awkward.

In the best of times, they were frenemies. In the worst, they gave in to their animosity, at which point one of their fists usually ended up in the other's face.

And it was usually Danny's fist and Izzy's face. Although they'd definitely vice versa'd it a time or two in the recent past.

Izzy had to spit out the yak piss before he could do more than nod, but then he remembered that it wasn't too long ago that Dan had had the unnerving experience of witnessing a Marine who'd been standing a few scant inches away from him get hit by shrapnel from a similar explosion.

The kid had bled out in a matter of minutes, despite Dan's frantic attempts at first aid.

"I'm fine," Izzy reassured him. Their SEAL teammates—Jenkins, Tony V., and Lopez—were all fine, too, thank God.

In fact, Lopez was so fine, he was already running toward the smoke and flames. Izzy scrambled to his feet and followed, with Jenk, Tony, and Gillman hot on his heels.

They'd been a mere four blocks away from the former marketplace that was the bomb's ground zero, and as they approached, the chaos increased.

More than one bus was on its side. Other cars were flipped upside down, one of them burning.

Civilians were everywhere. Crying. Bleeding. Some of them were running away, some not doing much of anything but lying, dazed, where they'd fallen, slapped down by the blast's giant invisible hand.

The United States Marines, God bless 'em, were already on the scene, a female officer coolly and efficiently taking command of the rescue effort—getting the injured people out of the vehicles, evacuating the surrounding buildings, putting out the fires.

Izzy's ears were still ringing, but he saw what Lopez was doing with the hot Marine lieutenant's blessing. He was creating a first-aid station for the injured, right there on the sidewalk.

Sirens were wailing in the distance, emergency vehicles coming from every direction. But the streets were filled not just with people but with rubble and smoke, and holy shit, the front of an entire row of buildings, including his favorite shawarma stand, had been blown to hell. And the crater from the bomb had made the street here beyond the marketplace impassable every way but from the north.

Help was coming, but it wasn't going to arrive soon enough.

But Lopez was a hospital corpsman—the Navy equivalent of an Army medic—and he was focused on saving the lives that he could. Normally soft-spoken, he was using his outdoor voice to inform any other medical personnel on the scene about his makeshift triage area.

It was then, as Izzy was pointing out Lopez to an ancient woman who was half carrying her bloody and dazed nearly-elderly-himself son, that he noticed Mark Jenkins was looking a little pale. The height-challenged SEAL was holding his right wrist tight against his side, as if he'd jammed it bad when he'd forcefully come into close personal contact with the street.

"Y'okay?" Izzy stepped closer to ask, exactly as Dan, too, came over and inquired, "Jenkins, are you hurt?"

Jenk shook his head in a mix of both yes and no. "Help me find a piece of wood for a splint."

"Shit," Izzy said as he helped Danny sift through the rubble of what used to be that restaurant. "Is it broken?"

The owner had survived, thank God, but he was sitting now among the debris, stunned. "Hang on, Mr. Wahidi," Izzy called to the man. "I'll be right over to help you."

Everything was either too big or too splintered or too full of nasty-ass nails.

"A brace," Jenkins corrected himself as he bent to pick up a piece of what had once been a sign for tea. "I meant a brace. Son of a *bitch*."

His wrist was definitely broken.

He turned another more greenish shade of pale, his golly-gee freckles standing out on his nose, because he'd jarred his arm trying to measure it against that piece of wood.

"Maybe you should sit down, bro," Gillman suggested, which was stupid. No way was Jenkins going to sit down and surrender to a relatively mild injury when there were so many more severely wounded people to assist.

Of course, maybe Dan only meant it, like, *Maybe you should sit down for a sec, bro, because it is going to hurt like a screaming bitch when we belt your arm to that splint.*

But any mention of giving in to the pain would have pissed Izzy off royally were he in Jenk's tiny boots, so he took charge. "He's fine where he is," he told Dan, told Jenkins, too, because the man looked like he needed encouragement, and adding to Dan, "Don't bother with your belt."

Izzy found his spare bungee cords in his vest pocket and pulled out a couple. Those little suckers were useful, even when the SEALs weren't up in the mountains. They would work better than a belt to keep Jenk's broken arm supported by that piece of wood.

The wood, however, left much to be desired. So Izzy tossed Dan the cords, reaching down and untying his own bootlaces, even as he told Jenk, "I say go for it. Buy the house of your dreams."

As he'd expected, Danny objected, which was good. Jenk needed a little distraction. "And hold two mortgages if the condo doesn't sell?" Dan said.

"Sure, why not?" Izzy quickly stripped off his sock. It was a little soggy and extremely aromatic, but it would do the trick.

Dan was sputtering. "Because . . . it's insane?" But he saw what Izzy was doing and held out his hand for the sock and covered the piece of wood's ragged end with it, even as Izzy jammed his bare foot back into his boot.

"No, it's not," Izzy told Jenkins as he took the sock-covered wood from Dan and tested it against his own hand. Not great, but much better. Uncovered, that slice of raw wood would've scraped the shit out of Jenkie's palm. His sock gave it at least a little bit of padding and protection. "Because if you don't sell it, you can rent it. That's a great Plan B, my brother. You know, my lease is up in a month. I could be your tenant."

Jenk and Lindsey's condo was much nicer than his current place— which stupidly still reeked of memories of Izzy's too-short marriage to Eden. Although how that could be, Izzy didn't understand. He'd been married to her for . . . what? A week? Damn, he'd only made love to her once—but it had been in his bed, in his bedroom, in his stupid, stupid apartment, on their wedding night.

It had been an event of momentous importance that Izzy still dreamed about—both feverishly at night and in unguarded moments during the daytime, when his thoughts wandered off to a fantasyland where wishes came true.

Not only was Eden uncommonly beautiful with her big brown eyes and lustrously dark hair, her flawless smooth skin, heart-shaped face, that sensual mouth that was quick to smile. But she also got Izzy's

jokes. She spoke his language. She was funny and smart and courageous, and yes, a little bit crazy. Reckless. Unafraid to dance to a different drummer.

All that, plus a body that didn't quit...?

Back when they'd first met, Izzy'd fallen in lust with her at first
sight, and solidly in love within the first five minutes they'd talked. But
she didn't stay in San Diego for long. She left almost immediately, to
visit her Army sergeant father in Germany.

But then, six months later, when Eden had resurfaced back in
the States, she'd been six months pregnant and in dire need of a
knight in shining armor. So Izzy'd married her, even though there
was no way on earth that baby she'd been carrying could have possibly been his.

But he didn't care. He just wanted to be her hero.

And to get into her pants. Which he'd done after marrying her.

But then she'd miscarried, lost the baby, and run back to Germany.
And spent the past ten months refusing to see him.

Even though he'd gone all the way to Europe to try to see her,
more times than he could count.

"Jenkins has a two-bedroom," Dan pointed out. "What are you
going to do, get a roommate?"

"Ooh, Dan," Izzy said. "Great idea. We could finally live together."
He held the splint out so that Jenkins could put his wrist against it. This
was the part that was going to hurt, but Jenk nodded for them to do it,
just get it over with. He closed his eyes.

But it was Danny who made the choking, gagging sounds as they
got Jenk as patched up as he was going to be—at least until he returned
to the base and saw a doctor.

But Izzy couldn't resist pushing it, even though the last thing he
wanted was Danny freaking Gillman for a roommate. "Seriously, Dan,
if we split the rent it would be pretty cheap. You're not going to keep
bunking in the enlisted quarters, are you, now that you and Jenn are
tight? What are you going to do when she comes to San Diego to visit?
It's time you moved into big-boy housing."

"Go fuck yourself," Dan said, genuinely pissed. Apparently Izzy had trod on a hot button. Interesting. Was it the mention of Jennilyn visiting or just the mention of Jennilyn?

"I've found that I'm a little shy," Izzy said, "for such blatantly public displays of self-affection. Besides, I like to be wined and dined before I have my way with myself. I'm an old-fashioned kind of guy."

"Old-fashioned," Dan scoffed. "Is that the excuse you use to convince yourself that you're not a shithead? *I'm old-fashioned, because back in the eighteen hundreds men regularly took children as their brides...*"

She wasn't a child, Izzy stopped himself from saying, because he was *not* going to talk about Eden anymore. Not with anyone—and especially not her asshole brother. That part of his life was over and done. In fact, as soon as he got back to San Diego, he was going to ask the senior chief for some help in finding a divorce lawyer.

But Dan was into tit-for-tatting, and since Izzy had stumbled onto one of his hot buttons, dude now felt compelled to jump with both feet onto Izzy's.

In the past, Izzy would have risen to the bait and their conversation would've gone a little like this:

Dan: *At the end of the day, you're the one who was banging a seventeen-year-old.*
Izzy: *She was eighteen. And I didn't bang her.*
Dan: *Oh, excuse me. You made beautiful, tender love to her. That's right, I always forget. It was the four hundred and seventeen guys that came before you that she banged.*
Izzy: *Don't you say that shit about her—*
Dan: *She used you, man. She uses everyone. Why don't you just face the truth and move on?*
Izzy: (throwing a punch) *Why don't you go fuck yourself...?*

"Y'okay?" Izzy asked Jenk instead as the other SEAL experimented with the splint, cautiously moving his arm. Dan was watching closely, too.

And this time when Jenk nodded, it was a solid *yes.*

At that, both Izzy and Dan turned in a unison that couldn't have been more precise had it been choreographed, and they went in separate directions—Dan toward Lopez, and Izzy toward Tony V.

It was clear that they didn't need a debate or a discussion to agree they'd already spent far too freaking much time together today.

Although the good news was that neither of them was walking away with a bloody nose.

Of course, there was still a lot of daylight left.

NEW YORK CITY
THURSDAY, APRIL 16, 2009

Jennilyn LeMay was having a day.

It had started when she got to work and realized that she'd gotten the mother of all runs in her pantyhose, and that she didn't have a spare pair in her desk drawer.

She'd only had time for the quickest trip to the drugstore on the next block over, but that proved ineffective. Unbelievably, they were completely out of queen-size in every color and every conceivable brand, as if the place had been descended upon by a drove of bargain-hunting opera singers. Best Jenn could find, way in the back behind the tube socks, was a pair of thick white tights that were labeled both queen-size *and* petite—clearly designed for two-hundred-pound height-challenged nurses, rather than giantesses like Jenn who weren't quite six feet tall if they both lied and slouched.

No doubt about it, as far as her hopes went for—quite literally—covering her ass, the fat lady was singing.

While wearing seventy pairs of pantyhose.

The store clerk helpfully went to the same rack that Jenn had already searched before informing her that they still had plenty of size large—maybe that would work. She then turned and looked at Jenn, squinting slightly as she appraised her, adding, "Probably not."

And yes, lady. You got it. There *was* no way in hell that Jenn was going to be able to squeeze herself into plain old regular large. And thanks a billion for the pre-coffee esteem-bludgeoning judgment.

Sticking out her tongue and announcing, "My super-hot Navy SEAL boyfriend likes me just the way I am," seemed a little childish. Especially since she'd been cautious about referring to Dan Gillman as her boyfriend to her friends and family—let alone acquaintances.

It wasn't that he didn't fit the definition. He sent her an e-mail every day, when he could. Usually it was brief—*Too tired to say more than hey*... was a common one, along with *Thanks for the package*, and *Dreamed about you again last night, wild woman*... But sometimes he wrote her long, intimate e-mails about his highly dysfunctional family, about adventures he'd had growing up, about his plans for the future, about the unjust oppression of women that he witnessed every day, about a myriad of things that mattered to him.

And she e-mailed him back, also every day. She sent packages to him, too, sometimes as often as twice a week.

And yes, the first and only time they'd met they'd shared some ridiculously excellent sex along with a whole lot of intimate pillow talk. That, too, worked with the standard boyfriend/girlfriend definition.

But when Dan had suddenly gotten all *I love you*, after helping to save Jenn's life, well...

She'd needed to be certain that it wasn't just a heady mix of adrenaline and hormones talking, because she knew that she wasn't his usual type. So she'd sent him away, telling him that if he were serious about their relationship he could prove it by coming back.

Of course, days later he'd called to tell her that he was heading overseas, into one of the war zones. He couldn't tell her where and he couldn't tell her when he'd be back, but she knew from what he didn't say that he was going to Afghanistan.

There was no time for her to fly to California, to see him off. He was leaving immediately.

Jenn had cried for a week, torn between knowing that she'd done the right thing, and regretting that she'd wasted the little time they might've spent together.

But that still didn't make Dan her boyfriend.

So she said nothing to the store clerk. She just left, hoseless.

There was another drugstore a mere three blocks away, but Jenn had no time to go there. She had a conference call that she had to take at 9:15, and another at 10, so she'd hidden her bare, winter-pale legs beneath her desk and hoped she wouldn't be required to leave the office before her day ended at 8 p.m.

It wasn't an unrealistic hope. As New York State Assemblywoman Maria Bonavita's chief of staff, Jenn spent most of her time in their New York City office using phone, e-mail, and fax to put out the little fires that sprang up in the course of a day.

But unfortunately today's fire wasn't little, and it required a face-to-face with some rightfully frustrated and angry constituents. And since Maria was in Albany, Jenn's had to be the face they put out there. Because although her title was chief of staff, she was also Maria's *entire* staff, not counting the unpaid college interns. There was no one else to send.

So Jenn took her larger-than-large unhosiered legs, and her be-spectacled face that Dan claimed was "cute" despite her Amazonian size, and headed for the boarded-up building that had served as a homeless shelter for veterans before the grease fire in the restaurant next door had done its damage.

It had happened months earlier, in the coldest part of the winter — which had been devastating for the men who filled the shelter to capacity every night.

But there were problems with the insurance payout, as well as safety issues, that kept the place locked up tight. The shelter's organizers, led by a Vietnam veteran named Jack Ventano, had come to Maria's office for help after weeks of runaround.

She was trying to get them the assistance they needed to get their facility up and running again. But it wasn't happening fast enough. And now Jack had called, demanding that Maria come take a tour of the place, to see firsthand the mold that was starting to grow on the water-damaged walls.

Jenn had just gone into a CVS that was halfway to the shelter, and was searching the overhead signs for the hosiery aisle when her cell phone rang.

It was Mick Callahan, a detective with the NYPD, and a friend of Jenn's.

She answered as she continued to scan and finally just made a choice to go down the narrow aisle to the back of the store. "Hello?"

"Maria needs to get her ass down to the Vet Center," Mick said in his gravelly, native New Yorker's voice, without proper greeting or ceremony. "ASAP."

"She's upstate, but I'm already on my way," Jenn told him.

"Hail a cab," he told her. "And Mary, while you're at it. You're definitely gonna need divine intervention for this one."

She stopped, directly in front of a display of L'eggs. They had both her size and the color she'd hoped to find. Alleluia. "What's going on?"

"About seven of the vets have broken the lock on the door," Mick told her grimly as she grabbed a pair and headed for the checkout, up front. "They've gone inside, with several crates of supplies. I think they're going to lock themselves in until they get some action. We've been ordered to get them out, forcibly if necessary, but I've convinced the lieutenant to give you a chance to get down here and defuse the situation, but the clock's ticking. Jenn, seriously, you need to be here. *Now.*"

"I'm on my way." There were seven people on line and one slow-moving, half-asleep cashier, so Jenn sighed and put the pantyhose in a clearly designated dump basket near the exit before going out to the street and hailing a cab.

LAS VEGAS

Eden Gillman Zanella stood in the shadows of the shallow wing, just offstage, and tried to calm her pounding heart.

This was no big deal.

She just had to walk out there and do this exactly the way she'd practiced. If she got this job, she'd be bringing home somewhere in the neighborhood of two hundred dollars a night in tips.

And even though working at the Burger King for minimum wage was more dignified, it would take her months to earn the same kind of money that she could make here in a week.

Dignity was overrated, anyway.

And the female body was just that—the female body. Yes, she'd be the first to agree that hers was exceptionally nice-looking. She couldn't take any credit for that—it was an accident of birth.

True, she'd worked it, hard, to get back to her pre-pregnancy weight, even in the aftermath of losing her baby. And she'd had to get a tattoo to hide the scar from the C-section that had saved her life.

But she'd had a beautiful mother and a drop-dead handsome father, which didn't necessarily mean Eden had to be exceptionally beautiful. But luck had been on her side, and she was.

She had a classically beautiful face, with even features, big brown eyes and long, dark lashes. Her skin was smooth and clear, and she had thick, dark, shiny hair that fell halfway down her back.

Of course, while a pretty face and great hair were valuable assets, they weren't as important as the body she'd won in the genetics lottery. Tits and ass. It always came down to that bottom line, at least for men. And hers were world class—they had been ever since puberty hit.

And after years of getting leered at wherever she went, she was now on the verge of getting *paid* for the very same thing.

Mostly the same thing.

The song that had been playing—some generic 1970s disco— finally faded out and there was a smattering of applause from the crowd of losers and lowlifes who were out there getting wasted on a Thursday morning at eight o'clock.

The woman—billed as Chestee von Schnaps—who'd been on that stage came stomping off in disgust. "Four fucking dollars," she said, to

no one in particular. "The morning shift is bullshit." She stopped to
put a finger practically up Eden's nose, oblivious to the fact that she
was still mostly naked, with breasts that were nearly the size of basketballs. "You—new girl. Make sure that cocksucker Alan gives you breakfast. You work this bullshit shift, you make sure you at least get fed, you
hear me?"

Were those things real?

"You hear me?" the woman repeated, and Eden nodded, even
though Alan hadn't said a thing about meals. This was not a woman
with whom anyone would dare to disagree.

"I'm Nic. What's your stage name?" she asked, appraising Eden.

Her stage name. Instead of admitting that she didn't have one yet,
Eden blurted out the first thing that came into her head. "Jennilyn
LeMay." It was her brother Danny's new girlfriend's name, and right
from the first moment she'd heard it—in an e-mail from her other
brother Ben—Eden had thought it sounded like a stripper name.

The large-breasted woman seemed satisfied with that information,
because she nodded and stomped away.

And okay. Now Eden was in a panic, because the CD that she'd
given the DJ had started, which was her cue to take the stage.

She'd always thought she was well endowed, but compared to the
twin basketballs... Holy crap. This audience was going to look at her
and laugh.

"Go!" someone whispered as they put two strong hands on her
back and pushed her out from behind the curtain.

Where, oh sweet Lord, she froze.

She'd thought, with the lights, that she wouldn't be able to see the
audience, but they were lit, too. And she realized that Alan, the manager who was considering hiring her, had told her as much. *It's the eye
contact that'll get you the biggest tips*, he'd told her, when offering her
pointers.

"Dance," someone shouted, because she was just standing there,
gaping at them, as her life all but flashed before her eyes.

All the crap she'd been through, all the garbage, all the pain. And Izzy, who'd married her when she was pregnant, even though he wasn't the father of her child... *Don't think about Pinkie, don't think about Izzy...*

But she couldn't help thinking about them both—the baby and the lover that she'd lost. What would either of them think to see her here, now? But Pinkie was dead, and Izzy was gone.

Eden could see Alan in the back, in the DJ's booth, shaking his head in disgust.

"Get off the stage," someone else yelled.

She was blowing this. She needed this money. And it really was no big deal. She'd been putting on shows for men ever since she'd realized that if she washed her face and wore one of those silly dresses that her grandmother bought for her, her chances of being bought an ice cream rose exponentially. What was she, three, when she'd learned that? This was just a variation on that exact same theme.

She could see a man in the audience who could've been the brother of Mr. Henderson, her high school chemistry teacher, who'd let her know that a visit to him at home could significantly raise her grade for the semester. And there, at another table, was a man who had the same sleaze and smarm level as Mr. Leavitt, the sanctimonious father of one of her many high school boyfriends. He'd disapproved of his son dating her, but had turned around and propositioned her one night when he'd "accidentally" bumped into her at the video store, where he damn well knew that she worked.

And, there. Over there was a look-alike for John Franklin, who, at nearly four years her senior, had pledged his undying love before taking her virginity in the back of his car when she was only fourteen. He'd immediately dumped her—laughing because she'd been stupid enough to believe him.

This place was crawling with predators, with men who wanted a piece of her—and not the part that held her brain. But they weren't just in here, they were outside as well, scattered across and around and all over the world.

And she would have to put up with their unwanted attention and inappropriate comments while she worked for slave wages at BK or Micky D's, or even just walked down the street.

Or she could get rich off of them, working here, taking advantage of the fact that she had the ultimate power. She had what they wanted, and they could look, but they could not touch. Not unless they wanted to slip a five- or, no, a *ten*-dollar bill into the elastic strap of the red satin thong she'd bought just yesterday, as an investment for her and Ben's future. And even then, they had to watch their hands because the bouncers would kick their asses out of there if they even so much as copped a feel. No, if she so much as *claimed* they'd copped a feel.

She had the power. And she liked having it. She always had. She'd just had to learn not to trade too much for the proverbial ice cream—and never, ever confuse need and lust with real love.

She'd tried real love once—or she thought she had, and that had ended horribly. *Don't think about Izzy, don't think about Izzy . . .*

Money—she had to think about the money. She needed money—lots of money—and she needed it fast, in order to get Ben out of their stepfather's odious grasp. And here, at D'Amato's, with the stage and the lights and the men in the audience with the hungry eyes, she had the power to get it.

Eden forced herself to breathe and to not think about Izzy, or Pinkie, or even her little brother Ben as she walked to the front edge of the stage and called to the DJ. "I'm sorry, Vaughn, will you start that again?"

The DJ—a big black man—glanced at Alan, the manager, who was still shaking his head.

So Eden spoke directly to the predators who'd come there to see women get naked. "I'm a little shy," she told them, looking from one to the next, to the next, to the next, and on and on, around the room—eye contact. She was good at that. She made her voice a mix of sweet-young-thing and girl-gone-wild. She was good at that, too. "This is my first time. You guys all want to be here for my *very* first time, don't you? Will you help me out and ask Vaughn to start the music over?"

And now they were shouting at Vaughn, but they didn't need to, because Alan was already on board, looking at her and smiling. He gave Vaughn a nod.

And this time? When the music began?

Eden danced.

And when she left the stage, it was with a hundred and seventy dollars in tips—ten-dollar bills only.

Not bad for a bullshit morning crowd.

And needless to say, she got the job.

CHAPTER
TWO

D an was helping a pair of very young and very female Marine privates get the wounded off the toppled bus. One of them was inside, pushing a frightened woman and her wailing two-year-old out of the window and into the other marine's arms.

That second private—blond and cute in a Heidi of Wisconsin way—handed the child to Dan, who was on the ground. She then scrambled down herself to help with the woman, who was no light-weight.

The civilian was bleeding from a gash on her forehead, but she seemed more concerned with keeping her headscarf on. Her little boy was terrified, though, sobbing as he stood waiting for her, his arms out-stretched.

"Your mommy's going to be all right," Dan told him, trying various dialects, but the boy didn't stop crying even when his mother clasped him tightly in her arms.

"You should see the medic about your head," the blond marine tried to tell the woman, pointing over to where Lopez had set up his triage, where the first ambulance had finally arrived, bringing medical supplies. But it was clear she didn't speak English. The marine—the name S. Anderson was on her jacket—looked at Dan. "I'm sorry, sir, can you tell her—"

"I'm not an officer," Dan told her, then used his rudimentary language skills to point to Lopez and say *doctor.*

The woman nodded and thanked them both profusely, her boy's head tucked beneath her chin.

"But you're a SEAL," S. Anderson said as she scrambled back onto the bus. "There should be some form of address for SEALs that trumps *sir.* Maybe *Your Highness* or *Oh, Great One?*"

She was flirting with him, marine-style, which meant she was already getting back to work.

And Dan wasn't quite sure what to say. *I have a girlfriend that I really love* seemed weird and presumptuous. After all, if S. Anderson had been a man, he might've said the same thing, and Dan would've laughed and replied, "*Great One* sounds about right."

Except S. Anderson's smile was loaded with more than respect and admiration. There was a little *Why don't you find me later so you can do me* mixed in there, too. And Dan didn't think he was merely imagining it.

The sure-thing factor was flattering, as it always was, and the old pattern that he'd run for years kicked in, and he found himself assessing her. Her uniform covered her completely, but it didn't take much imagination to see that although she was trim and not particularly curvaceous, she was curvy enough. She *was* cute, freckled and petite and—Jesus, what was he doing?

But then there was no time to bitch-slap or otherwise chastise himself, because a gunman opened fire.

The first shot took down the Marine officer who was running the rescue effort, and the cry rang out, repeated by all of the military personnel in the area. Dan shouted it, too: "*Sniper!*"

Jesus, the civilian woman and her child were in the middle of the open marketplace, completely exposed.

S. Anderson saw them, too, and instead of diving for cover inside of the bus, she jumped back down to help him help them. Dan could hear her, just a few steps behind him as he ran toward the woman, shouting, "Run!"

But the woman had heard the shots, and she'd crouched down to shield her child, uncertain of which way to escape.

Because there was no cover anywhere near, and nowhere to run except...

"Go!" Danny shouted, thrusting the child into S. Anderson's arms, pointing to the blast crater. If they could get to the edge of that gaping hole in the road, and slide down to the bottom and then hug the rubble and earth...

The woman shrieked as her child was ripped from her, but his plan was a good one, because she immediately followed, no explanation needed.

He tried to shield her with his body, tried to get her to run a zigzag path that was similar to the one Anderson was taking with the little boy. But the woman's mission to reach and protect her child was so single-minded, it was like trying to push a freight train from its tracks.

From the corner of his eye, as he ran at the woman's top speed, Dan saw Lopez and Izzy pulling the fallen officer to cover onto the patio of what, in happier times, had been a hotel.

But then Dan saw Izzy turn to look out at him in disbelief. He heard the other SEAL shout his name, and Dan realized that the slap he'd just felt in the back of his thigh had been a bullet.

And Jesus Christ, that was his blood exploding out through the front of his pants from the exit wound. And sure enough, his leg crumpled beneath his weight with the next stride he took. But they were close enough to the crater for him to push the woman the last few feet, down into Anderson's waiting arms.

But Dan was still six feet away, with a leg that not only didn't work but, holy shit, was really starting to hurt. He had to crawl, pulling himself forward, his hands raw on the rough debris in the street, because he was *not* going to do this to Jennilyn. He was *not* going to come home in a coffin.

But he saw all the blood, and he knew he was dead. There was no way he was going to survive, even if he made it to cover. The mother-fucker with the rifle had hit an artery. Dan was going to bleed out before that sniper was taken down, and there was nothing anyone could do to save him.

But he didn't quit because he didn't know how to quit. And then he didn't have to quit, because something hit him hard in the side, and he realized with a burst of pain that it was Izzy, singing at the top of his lungs, "Oh, the weather outside is frightful..."

The freaking idiot had run all the way across that open patch of gravel and debris. He'd dived, as if sliding into home, right on top of Dan, and they'd tumbled together down into the blast crater.

But it was too late.

And wasn't this just the way it would happen? The last face Dan would see, the last person he would speak to before leaving this earth...

Was Izzy fucking Zanella.

The SEAL had stopped singing—thank you, God—and his face was grim as he rolled Dan onto his back; he ripped another of his stupid bungee cords from his vest pocket and used it as a tourniquet around Dan's upper thigh—as if that would help.

"What can I do?" Anderson asked as, in the background, the little boy continued to wail.

Izzy glanced at her. "Apply pressure at his groin. Help me slow the bleeding."

"Zanella..." Danny tried to get his attention, finally grabbing the front of his vest. "*Zanella*—"

"Hang in there, buddy," Izzy said, using his knife to tear Dan's pants to get a better look at his wound. "You're going to be okay." But Anderson blanched, in contrast to Izzy's reassurances. "We're going to get you to the hospital—"

"No, you're not," Dan said. No one was going anywhere with that shooter out there. Dan could hear the report of his rifle, again and again. "Zanella, you gotta tell Jenni for me—"

"No, no, no," Izzy said, interrupting him. "You're gonna tell her whatever you want to tell her yourself, bro. That sniper is toast. We've got the fucking United States Marines on our side. Am I right or am I right, Anderson?"

"Sir, yes, sir," she said.

"They're gonna take him out—"

"Not soon enough," Dan interrupted. He could feel himself getting cold. Ah, God, Jenni...He reached to grab Anderson's arm, because he had to make sure Jenni knew, and Izzy wasn't listening. "She didn't believe me," he told the woman. "Jenn didn't. And I need her to know—"

"Gillman," Izzy said sharply. "Listen to me. You fucking stop bleeding, do you hear me? You can do this. Use your brain for something other than being an asshole. Lower your heart rate and tell yourself to keep your blood away from this leg."

"Zanella—"

"*Do* it, goddamn it." Izzy turned to Anderson. "Keep applying pressure, Private. I'll be right back."

Izzy launched himself up and out of the blast crater, keeping his head down in a crouch as he ran back toward Lopez and the medical supplies.

He could hear the ping of the bullets, see the geysers of dust they kicked up as the sniper tried for him and missed.

And missed.

And missed again, suckwad motherfucker! Hah!

He slid into the cover provided by the ornate wooden deck of what once had been a fancy hotel restaurant, where patrons could dine on two levels. There'd probably been a tent to protect the upper level from the sun as the good folks of this town had had their business lunches.

Back during the time when the people of Afghanistan had both businesses and lunches.

But right now the wooden deck made it possible for the wounded to be cared for without risking death or injury to their caregivers.

One of whom was Lopez, who helped him to his feet. "Holy Jesus, Son of God," he said in Spanish as he saw the blood on Izzy's uniform.

Lopez was covered with blood himself, from trying to save the marine officer's life. Trying and failing, which sucked royal ass.

"It's bad," Izzy confirmed, telling Lopez what he didn't want to hear, yet already knew. "Dan needs surgery. Now. Bullet nicked his femoral artery."

"Fuck." It was not a word that Lopez used often, in English or in Spanish, but it fit the situation.

"I need a clamp," Izzy told him as he was already moving toward the medical supplies, "and some morphine and some bags of blood—he's O—and IV tubing. A needle—you know, all that shit."

Lopez was shaking his head, even as he rummaged through his equipment. "We don't have blood yet," he said as he gathered up everything else, scooping it into a bag for easy transport. "Or even any plasma extender. But if I can—"

"You're not going out there," Izzy told his friend.

"Yeah," Lopez said. "I am. I'll use the clamp—"

"Not good enough. *I'll* use the clamp." Izzy took the bag from him. "Danny needs blood, Jay, and I'm O, you're not. Give me the tubing—and two needles."

Lopez silently—but swiftly, bless him—added what Izzy needed to the bag.

And Izzy dashed back out into the sniper's kill zone.

Luckily for him, the dickweed was a relatively crappy shot.

New York City
Thursday, April 16, 2009

"This isn't the way to do this, Jack." Jenn stood her ground even as the big man took a step forward, on the verge of invading her personal space with the crutches he'd needed to get around since 1968. She held his gaze, too, refusing to let it waver, not even to glance behind him at the small crowd of other intimidating-looking men who'd gathered grimly to support him. Some of them had pulled back their jackets when she'd first arrived, to let her know that they were armed. And wasn't *that* just great? "You know that the assemblywoman—"

Jack Ventano interrupted her. "Isn't getting this done."

"It takes time," Jenn told him. "There are laws—"

"There should be laws," he agreed, "insisting that the men and women who serve our country get the care and the support that they need, instead of—"

"You *know* we're on your side."

"That's not enough, and *you* know that."

Jenn was silent then, because he was right.

The big man pushed his gray hair back from his face, revealing the edge of the long, rough scar he bore on his forehead. He'd gotten that in 'Nam, at Khe San, he'd told her once, when she and Maria had taken a tour of the shelter, back when Maria was running for office. He'd lost most of his leg in the same battle. But worst of all, he'd lost his best friend, a man named Tom Terwilliger—which was why this shelter bore Terwilliger's name.

Lost. What a funny euphemism for it. As if Tom and Jack's leg had both been accidentally misplaced.

"Maybe, this way, we'll finally get news coverage," Jack told her now.

"Maybe," she pointed out, "you will. Fat lot of good that'll do you, serving time upstate, in jail."

"Won't be the first time I have a temporary vacation in Ossining," he said with a smile that softened his harsh, weather-beaten features. "And if it helps this place get rebuilt..." He shrugged. "I can do the time standing on one hand."

"As soon as I walk out that door," Jenn warned him, "the police are coming in. If you or anyone with you kills a cop...Your trip upstate won't be temporary. And this place will never open again."

"No one's going to kill anybody," Jack reassured her.

"You can't promise that," she said.

"Yeah," he said, and the expression on his face was almost apologetic. "I sort of can. The police aren't coming in, because . . . you're not going anywhere."

Jenn laughed, but then stopped as the men behind Jack moved between her and the door. This was just perfect. "So what am I?" she asked. "Your hostage? For the love of God, Jack. We're *friends*. Friends don't hold friends hostage."

"*Hostage* is such an ugly word," he said. "But yeah. If that's how we have to do it." He shrugged again. "We were kind of hoping it would be Maria. Thought it might give her a positive bump in the polls. A win/win . . ."

"No," Jenn said. "Nope. No, Jack—" Her cell phone rang. "Think about what you're on the verge of doing. If you keep me here against my will? That's a felony." She checked her screen—it was Maria. "This is the assemblywoman," she told him, holding up her phone. "I'm going to take her call, and when I'm done? We're all going to walk out of here together. We're going to go get some coffee, and we're going to figure out a way to get you news coverage without a crime and a victim and a trial and a jail sentence." She looked around at his buddies. "Jail *sentences*—plural, gentlemen."

They seemed uneasy at that, looking to Jack for confirmation.

She turned away from them as she opened her phone and put it to her ear. "Maria?"

"Jenn." Maria had on her pure-business voice. Terse and to the point. "Where are you?"

"I'm over at the shelter, with Jack and some of his guys," Jenn reported. "We're just about to go to Starbucks." She glanced over at where Jack was now being questioned by his men, and raised her voice a little. "My treat."

He shook his head but two of his buddies seemed to like the idea. Jenn let them work on Jack as she focused her attention on Maria. "Where are *you*?" she asked her boss and longtime friend. "Because we could use you down here. These guys need a solution and—"

"I'm still in Albany," Maria cut her off. "Jenn, you need to go into the ladies' room or somewhere private. Immediately."

"That's...not possible right now," Jenn said. The facilities had been over near the kitchen, where the blaze had done the worst of its damage. "I'm kind of in a meeting with Jack. We're actually inside the shelter."

"Pass him the phone," Maria ordered.

"I don't think that's a good idea," Jenn lowered her voice to say. "Whatever you've heard, I've got the situation mostly under control." Or she would have, if she could continue to appeal to Jack's honor, his down-to-earth sanity, and his strong sense of right and wrong. Friends *didn't* hold friends hostage, and he knew it.

"Damn it, Jennilyn," Maria said in a rare burst of temper. "Pass. Jack. The phone."

"Jeez." Jenn turned back to Jack, holding her cell phone out for him. "The assemblywoman apparently wants to talk to you quite badly."

He took it. "This is Jack Ventano." He was silent then, just listening, frowning in response to whatever Maria was telling him, glancing over at Jenn and then away, down at the floor. He finally spoke. "She's going to want more information." He paused again, listening, then, "Okay. Yeah, I'll...Yeah. No, it's bad timing, but when is it ever good timing for...Yes, ma'am, we'll get her there. I'll have her call you back in just a few."

He hung up the phone, handing it back to Jenn, even as he turned to his posse. "Let's get those boxes out of here. We're standing down and moving it out. We'll fight this fight another day."

There was grumbling among some of his men, but the two who'd wanted Starbucks leaped to gather up their supplies.

Jack gestured toward the door as he told Jenn, "Let's go."

She hesitated for only a second or two before she followed him. "What did Maria promise you?"

"Nothing," he told her as he led the way out the door.

There was only one police car out there. But on second glance, Jenn realized that Mick Callahan's unmarked car was also double-parked in the street. He was leaning against it, and as he saw her and Jack emerge from the former shelter, he pushed himself up and came to meet them.

Jack, meanwhile, was giving orders to his guys. "Take the stuff back to my place. I'll meet you over there in about an hour."

Now Jenn was really confused. "I thought we were all going for coffee."

Mick didn't greet her. He just nodded to Jack, talking over her—which was hard to do because she was so tall. "I got it from here."

But Jack shook his head. "I'm coming, too. She'll have questions that I can maybe answer."

Mick, always such a hardnose with something of an oppositional personality, was actually nodding in agreement as he reached to open the back door of his car. He put his hand on Jenn's shoulder as if to usher her in, but she stopped.

"Guys. What's going on?" She turned to Jack. "Whatever Maria has planned, she didn't share it with me. Where are we going?"

"Jennilyn," Mick answered for Jack, "just get in. Then you can call Maria back and she'll, um . . . Explain."

"Honey, she wants you to be sitting down," Jack said, his brown eyes warm with concern and compassion. "So go ahead and sit, and I'll tell you."

And just like that, the world lurched, and Jenn knew with a horrible certainty that something terrible had happened. She lowered herself into the backseat of the car, looking from Jack to Mick and back, as God, Jack nodded and said the words she dreaded.

"It's about Dan Gillman."

"Oh God," Jenn heard herself say as all of the air left her lungs. "Oh no. Oh, please don't tell me—"

"He's been badly wounded," Jack said, which wasn't as awful as the words she'd thought he was going to say.

"Wounded," she repeated. Badly, he'd said. "*How* badly?" She fought the urge both to cry and to throw up. Neither would help her—or, more important, help Dan.

"Maria didn't know," Jack said, handing his crutches to Mick as he pushed her over on the bench backseat so he could sit beside her and take her hand. "But she told me he's a SEAL, and honey, SEALs are fighters."

Jenn nodded. Dan. SEAL. Fighter. Yes. Oh God. "Where is he?"

"Maria didn't know much," Jack said as Mick put his crutches in the front seat and climbed behind the wheel, signaling and pulling out into the traffic. "I guess she's got a friend whose husband is a chief in Dan's team...? She was the one who called Maria."

Jenn nodded again. "Savannah," she said. Savannah was Jenn's friend, too. It was her connection to SEAL Team Sixteen that had brought Danny into her life. Please, dear God, let him be all right...

"Maria's trying to get more information," Jack told her. "In the meantime, she figured you'd want to go home and maybe pack a bag, so you'd be ready to go, in case they send him somewhere a little friendlier than where we think he is right now."

Jenn nodded again and dialed her cell phone, calling Maria back, praying that from here on out, the news she received would only be good. "He's a fighter." She repeated Jack's words back to him just before Maria picked up her phone.

"Jenn," she said. "Are you sitting—"

"I already know," Jenn cut her off. "Jack told me. Danny's hurt. Please, just tell me what else you know."

"They're flying him to Germany," Maria told her. "Savannah's finding out where. She'll call you. She wants to buy a plane ticket so you can... But I don't think that's a good idea. Not yet. Not until..."

"What aren't you telling me?" Jenn asked.

"Jenni, he's still alive, but—" She cut herself off again. Whatever that *but* was going to be, she substituted it with, "He's strong."

"You need to tell me everything," Jenn said.

Maria exhaled hard. "I know. It's just...he lost so much blood," she said. "One of his teammates ended up doing a battlefield transfusion, and nearly died himself, because of it. Jenni, it's a miracle that Dan's still alive at all. If he didn't have the friends that he has... This would already be a very different phone call. As it is..."

Dear God. "Was it an IED?" Jenn asked, because it was clear Maria had gotten at least some details.

"Indirectly," Maria said, and her word only made sense when she added, "Dan was assisting with the civilian casualties after some kind of car bomb went off, and a sniper started shooting. He was hit."

"So he's been shot," Jenn said, meeting Jack's steady gaze, "someplace where he lost a lot of blood. In his chest or—"

"It was his leg," Maria told her.

"His leg," Jenn told Jack, unable to keep herself from glancing down at his empty pant leg. Oh God.

"If something goes wrong with the surgery," Maria said, "or if he's too weak to be operated on...He could lose his leg. And that's one of the better-case scenarios. I really think you should wait before you go anywhere, Jenn."

"I don't want to wait," Jenn said. "Tell Savannah yes, please buy me a ticket. Tell her thank you."

"Jenni," Maria started.

"I want to be there," Jenn said. "I need to be there when he wakes up, especially if...God, most people don't get that chance. I'm going to be there."

"Jenn, he might not wake up."

"But he's strong," Jenn reminded her. "He's a fighter. Just tell Savannah. I can be at the airport in an hour."

Danny *was* strong. He *was* a fighter.

But all young men and women who went to fight wars were strong. They were all fighters. And sometimes, despite that, they died anyway.

Jenn looked at Jack, who was still holding her hand.

And sometimes they lost their legs.

LAS VEGAS
DATE UNKNOWN

For too many years, there was no such thing as no in Neesha's world.

Dissent was not allowed, not without punishment.

Years ago, when she was first brought to this awful place, punishment meant an empty belly and nothing but a hard, cold floor to sleep upon, a faucet for water, and a bucket for her waste, while locked in a tiny, empty cell. That was often all it took among the other new girls to turn a no into a yes.

But in those early days, Neesha preferred the hunger, the bucket, and the cold floor to the pain and humiliation that came when the men—the clients or visitors, they were called—held her down with the weight of their bodies and jabbed themselves between her legs.

It was wrong, and she would *not* do it ever again.

And she screamed and cried, which frightened the visitors, and kept them from touching her. It also made the tall man with the florid face who was her new lord and master angry, so he locked her again in that cell.

The hunger made her cry, but she still said no. And then a fellow worker, a girl who was older, saved part of her meals to share. She furtively passed the morsels through the tiny window in Neesha's door. And so she put up with that hard, cold floor for nine whole days and nights of no, with only twinges of hunger instead of great, yawning pain.

But the tall man—Mr. Nelson—he must have found out about the food, because the kind girl vanished. Neesha hadn't seen her again, not even once in all of the years since.

It was then that Mr. Nelson brought Neesha and her no into a beautiful room—more beautiful than she'd ever seen before in her entire short life—where a magnificent meal was set out on a huge table.

He'd left her there, and Neesha, still hungry, had eaten her fill, filled, too, with hope that her grandfather, a man her mother had spoken of with such affection and respect, had somehow managed to find and rescue her.

But when a man came in, while he was, indeed, old enough to be her grandfather, he had a face as pale and a head as bare of hair as the moon. His eyes were not like Neesha's or her mother's. They were blue and flatly ugly, as if his soul had already left his body.

And although she hadn't yet learned to speak any American, she knew what he wanted from his gestures.

When she gave him her emphatic no, he smiled. And he didn't just take what he wanted anyway, like the other men before him, hands trembling and even weeping while they'd kissed her, before she'd learned that her piercing screams would scare them away when simply sobbing wouldn't.

Instead, he took while he beat her, and he laughed with delight even as she screamed. And then he took some more in ways that were meant to hurt her, until she lay naked and bleeding, too stunned to cry, on that beautiful floor.

The man washed himself after, whistling as he did so, and then he left.

Women came in then, but they weren't warm like her mother had been, back before she'd fallen ill and died. They cleaned Neesha and bandaged her as best they could, but they did it without any comfort or kind words. In fact, they spoke to her sternly. *You reap what you sow.*

And then they brought her back to her cell, where she wept until she fell asleep.

The door didn't open for three very hungry, very sore days as she lay on the floor, curled up in a ball. And when it finally did open, it was once again Mr. Nelson who stood there, looking down at her as she trembled and wept with fear.

And he took her, carrying her because her legs wouldn't hold her. He brought her back, not to the beautiful room, thank God, but to a separate bathing room, where the cold, angry women again washed her clean.

They braided her hair in a way that made her look even younger than she truly was, and they gave her a new dress and delivered her back to Mr. Nelson, who led her to the smaller room where she'd first lived and served the visitors, before she'd dared to say no.

A man was in there, waiting. His hungry eyes filled with tears as he saw her, because he, too, knew that what he wanted to do was wrong because she was just a child.

There was food laid out in there, too. It was nowhere near as sumptuous as the feast she'd had three days before. But it was hot and it smelled good and it would fill her belly and give her strength. The bed in the corner was soft and warm. Neesha knew that, as well.

And although she didn't speak Mr. Nelson's language and he didn't speak hers, he made it clear that it was her choice. She could go in.

Or she could say no, and go back to the room where the men wouldn't kiss her and lick her with their tremulous mouths, touch her almost reverently with their trembling hands, but instead would hit her and bite her and laugh while she screamed.

Neesha went inside.

And she never again said no.

Not until years later.

Until the day it happened.

Until the day that Andy, the fat daytime guard, had clutched his chest and fallen, gasping and wheezing, to the ground, leaving her door unlocked and open as he shuddered and shook.

Neesha stepped through the door and around him and quickly slipped from the wing of the building where the children were locked in their rooms. And because she'd just had a visitor who'd wanted only to watch and touch himself while she bathed and then put on the clothes and makeup of a much older woman, she was able to fade back and then pass, unnoticed, through the women's wing, where the guards were there only to keep visitors from going where they weren't wanted, instead of keeping the workers from escaping.

And then there it was.

An unguarded, open door.

It led to an outside that wasn't part of the small, caged, inner courtyard that she had come to know so well during her long years imprisoned here.

Neesha stepped through that door, marveling at a sky that stretched out to the horizon, at a sun that shone full strength upon her upturned face, a sun that was not weakened by a screen.

But there wasn't time to stand there, stunned by the possibility of her newfound freedom.

She was in a parking lot, outside of a long, low, adobe structure, and she quickly lost herself among the rows of cars, ducking down to hide from anyone who might come looking for her.

And they would come. Mr. Nelson. Or the guard named Todd.

And if they found her? She would be punished.

Of that Neesha had no doubt.

CHAPTER
THREE

They met, after school, in the coffee shop at the mall, because Eden didn't want her mother or stepfather, Greg, to know she was back in town.

And it was crazy, but she honestly didn't recognize her little brother when he first walked in. Ben had grown—a lot—since she'd seen him last. He was now taller than she was. And while he'd always been skinny, he was now razor thin, as if he'd been stretched on a medieval torture rack.

But the biggest change was to his clothing and hair. He'd always been a kind of geeky, dorky little redheaded kid, but now he was dressed like a Hollywood vampire, in black jeans, black T-shirt, clunky black sneakers, and a black overcoat that actually billowed behind him when he walked.

Eden had to admit the effect was striking. With his hair down to his shoulders and dyed a relentless, unforgiving midnight black, and with heavy eyeliner around his eyes, with the remains of black fingernail polish peeling from his chewed fingernails, the look accentuated his pale complexion and his blue eyes.

Both of which he'd gotten from his father, an Air Force officer their mother had hooked up with briefly after Eden, Dan, and their older sister Sandy's father, Daniel Gillman the second, had moved out for good.

Because they were only separated but not divorced, and because the Air Force captain was both married and a total son of a bitch, when Eden's mother, Ivette, got pregnant and Ben was born, she put Daniel Gillman the second's name down on the birth certificate, in the slot that said *father*.

Which had led to a lot of shouting and name-calling when their divorce finally went through, and paying child support became mandatory.

But Ivette had tried to pretend that then-five-year-old Ben was the result of a night she and Daniel had spent together when he'd returned to Fort Bragg, and she'd gone up to see him in Fayetteville. Daniel had been pretty drunk at the time—it was no wonder he didn't remember any of it.

Of course he didn't remember it, because it hadn't happened.

But because Ivette was not only a loser, but was also drawn to men who were losers as well, and because Eden's father was a son of a bitch, too, he didn't think about the damage that his words might do to a child when he used Ben with his blue eyes and red hair as Exhibit A. He didn't need a paternity test, he'd shouted, because there was no way a child this ugly, scrawny, and fair-complexioned could possibly be his.

It had been Ben's first meeting with his estranged "dad," and all of his fantasy expectations had been cruelly dashed.

As he grew, he continued to see himself only as ugly. Try as she might, Eden hadn't been able to change his mind about that. Because, bottom line, he wanted the same brown eyes and thick, dark hair that she and Danny and Sandy all had. He wanted to be a full, not a faux Gillman.

Eden stared at Ben now, dumbstruck. As she forced herself to greet and embrace this exotic stranger that her little brother had become, she wondered if he realized just how handsome—movie-star worthy, in fact—he was going to be in a few more years, when he filled out.

"Thank you for coming to Vegas," he said as he hugged her in return. "I would've just left home, the way you did, but..."

"Your diabetes," Eden said. He'd eventually run out of insulin.

She felt him nod. "I'd have to come back home. Or die."

His voice was different, too—it was now deeper than hers. It had always pissed him off, the way he'd often been called "ma'am" when he'd answered the phone.

Eden's voice had always been unusually low and husky, even when she was a child, and she'd turned it into a game—a contest—so that Ben would stop feeling bad. She would pitch her voice even lower to try to get the people who called to address her as "sir." Ben, in turn, had to *try* to get people to call him "ma'am," and whoever scored the most number of hits during the week got to choose the TV shows they'd watch on Saturday mornings, when their mother was sleeping late with whichever husband or boyfriend was currently sharing her bed.

Ben always won, but it didn't matter. Eden had always let her little brother choose anyway.

But those days were long gone. No one would mistake Ben for a "ma'am" ever again. Unless, of course, he threw away the Goth look and dressed in drag. That could work. He was going to be *that* pretty.

"How are you?" he asked as he hugged her. "Eedie, I'm so sorry about the baby."

Eden closed her eyes, refusing to go back there, but knowing it didn't matter. Whether she focused on it or not, for the rest of her life, she was going to walk around with an empty space in her heart. "Yeah, that sucked. Let's not talk about it."

"I didn't want to not say anything," he told her. "Not just about the baby, but, well, about Izzy, too. He was cool. He, um, came looking for you after you, you know, left."

"He did?" She pulled back to look up into her little brother's eyes.

Ben nodded. "He gave me his e-mail address and his phone number and, um, some money. A lot of money, actually. Three hundred dollars. He said I should hide it where no one would find it—it should be my emergency fund."

Eden stared at him. "Three *hundred*...?"

Ben nodded again. "He said that you told him you were worried about me, but that you were in a place right then—on account of

Pinkie dying—where you had to focus on taking care of yourself. He said if I needed any help, for any reason, that I could call him. If you hadn't e-mailed me and told me you were coming back...I don't know. I think I would've done it. You know. Called Izzy."

Great. All she needed was Izzy showing up. She could picture him, striding into this coffee shop in his cargo shorts and clunky boots, ready to save the day. Lord help her... "But you *didn't* call him, right?" Eden verified.

"No." Ben paused. "So what happened? That e-mail you sent me last year, right before you got married...It sounded like you really liked him."

Eden just shook her head. She hadn't come all this way to talk about her problems. Not that Izzy Zanella was her problem any longer.

She forced a smile and changed the subject. "So this is weird—you being so tall. You were so sure you'd be four foot eleven forever. I told you you'd grow."

Ben gave her a crooked half smile at that. "Yeah, I get these spurts and...It's been expensive. Always needing bigger clothes?" He gestured to himself. "This way, it's like a uniform. A pair of black jeans and a few T-shirts and I'm set—until I outgrow 'em."

"But that's not the only reason you dress like that," she pointed out.

"No," he agreed. "It's a multipurpose outfit. It really pisses Greg off. For a while I had a denim jacket that some asshole wrote *faggot* on the back of, so I added the words *Yes, I am a*...and I wore it everywhere. Until Greg burned it."

Eden looked up at him. "Are you really sure that you're...You know."

Something changed in his eyes, and she knew that she'd just made a blunder.

"Sorry," she quickly said, but he spoke over her.

"Gay," he said. "You're allowed to say the word. And yes, I'm very sure. Don't tell me that's a problem for *you*, too?"

"Don't be stupid," she said, far more sharply than she'd intended. But then she realized that being spoken to sharply was exactly what he needed in order to erase that defensive, wary look from his eyes. So she kept going. "*Stupid* would be a problem. Gay is..." She realized that she'd automatically lowered her voice to say that word, *gay*, so she started over. "Gay is not." She said it even louder. "Gay is not a problem. If Pinkie had been gay—if Pinkie had lived...Lord, Ben, what I wouldn't give for Pinkie to be alive and gay."

She felt her face crumple, felt her eyes well, and Ben hugged her again. And it *was* weird that he was bigger than she was, that his arms were long enough to wrap around her, instead of just around her neck. But he didn't just look, feel, and sound different, he *smelled* different, too.

And as he started to murmur, "I'm so sorry," Eden cut him off, pulling back to look at him through narrowed eyes.

"Do you *smoke*?" she asked him. "*Ben*..."

He looked abashed. "Sort of," he said. "I mean, yes, but not really."

"Grandpa Ramsey died of lung cancer," Eden reminded him.

Ben shook his head. "I don't," he said. "Inhale."

Did he *really* expect her to believe him? "If we can pull this off," Eden said, "and you're living with me? You are *not* smoking in my house. Read my lips. *Not*."

"No," he said. "I know. It's really just...It's a prop," he said, gesturing to himself. "Part of the...persona. I really don't inhale. I just light 'em and..."

Okay, so maybe she did believe him—which meant that he was still a dork inside. Which was a relief. "Then you'll have to keep your *props* out of my house."

Ben laughed at that, but his smile was twisted. "You want to know something funny? In Greg's house, I'm allowed to smoke, but I can't be gay."

"Our house. I meant to say *our* house," Eden corrected herself as they both sat down at the little table where she'd been filling out a job application. "And screw Greg. In his house, I couldn't be me, either. He's a creep."

There was a "Help Wanted" sign in the window, and applying for a job was a way to use the table without having to buy anything. Expensive coffee and pastries weren't in Eden's strict budget.

Besides, she needed a second job—a cover job so that she didn't have to tell Ben where she was really working—and this place, with its Internet café and public computers, would be perfect.

She glanced at her brother. "How's Ivette?"

He shook his head. "She's been working nights for a while—some new job. I haven't seen her that much."

"Sandy?" she asked about their older sister.

"She went back in."

To rehab. "That's good," Eden said.

But Ben shrugged. "It was that or jail."

"Who's got the kids?" Eden asked.

"Ron's mother, because, well, Ron *is* in jail."

"That's good," Eden said, both about Ron's mother and Ron's being in jail. Sandy's ex-husband was a twisted son of a bitch who drank even more than Sandy did, and the kids wouldn't have been safe with him. "His mom seemed ... nice."

"She lent Ivette and Greg some of the money they needed to send me to brainwashing camp in June." His smile was a twist of his lips. "She donated it to the church. I'm a church project—send the gay kid away to teach him how to be straight—how about that?"

"No one's going to send you anywhere," Eden told him. It was the reason she'd come back to this godforsaken place.

"Can we really pull this off?" Ben asked, the anxiety in his eyes making him look eleven again. And in a flash, she was back in New Orleans, at the Superdome.

Back then, she'd failed him. This time, she wouldn't.

"We can," she told him with far more bravado than she felt, because so much of her plan was riding on their brother Danny-the-magnificent—the Navy SEAL. Who *still* hadn't answered her latest e-mail. She had no idea what she was going to do if he told her no, or to go screw herself. To avoid that scenario, she had to make sure she paid him back every penny she'd ever owed him, *before* she asked him to make this new sacrifice. Which was why she was debuting tonight as D'Amato's newest stripper. "I'm going to get you out of here, Boo-Boo, I promise. California will be better. You'll love living in San Diego."

Her use of his childhood nickname made him smile, and again she was struck by how handsome he'd become. But oh Lord, while she was certain that living in San Diego would be better for Ben, she wasn't convinced it wasn't going to be hell on earth for her. Living on edge, near the Navy base in Coronado, afraid that any moment she might run into Izzy or one of his friends . . .

But unless she could convince Danny to transfer to the East Coast, she was going to have to make it work. She *would* make it work. For Ben's sake.

Because he was going to that ex-gay camp over her dead body.

"While I'm doing this," she told Ben, pointing down to her application, "use their computer and jump online. I need to find a place to live. Preferably a furnished sublet, dirt cheap, month-to-month lease. It's got to be big enough for you to be able to crash there whenever you want, so make sure it's a one-bedroom not a studio." He stood up, his chair scraping across the floor, but she stopped him with a hand on his skinny wrist. "And it needs to be far enough from Ivette and Greg's so that they don't stumble across me. Got it?"

Ben nodded, and they both got down to work.

LANDSTUHL, GERMANY
FRIDAY, 17 APRIL 2009

Jennilyn was there.

At first, Dan thought he was dreaming.

It was a really vivid dream, though. It was so real that he actually smelled her—the sweetness of her shampoo and that lotion she used to keep her hands soft. It brought him instantly back to her tiny New York City apartment, and those few days they'd spent, locked in there, together. Alone.

Most of the time, they'd been alone.

And naked.

And he was going to go with that—his memories of the last time he'd made love to her, and just float away again for a while, wrapped in the warmth and safety of a pain-free place filled with pleasure and lightness, when he heard her voice.

"No, that's okay," she said, as clearly as if she were standing next to him. "I don't mind seeing it. I'd like to. I'd...like to be able to help him take care of it, so..."

He felt the coolness of air on his nether regions, and then Jenn's voice said, "Oh," as if she'd been holding her breath and had exhaled it all at once.

She was holding his hand in his dream, he realized. Her grip had tightened, and it felt so real and solid, he almost didn't want to wake up because he really liked the fact that she was there. He tried to tighten his grip on her, afraid she would slip away, but for some reason, in this particular dream, his arms and legs felt heavy and uncooperative. He really had to work to do it.

But then she said, all in a rush, "Oh, my God, I think he just squeezed my hand. Dan...Danny, are you awake?"

"I'm awake in my dream, but my eyes won't open," he tried to tell her, but the words didn't come out very clearly. In fact, it sounded more like a moan.

"Are you hurting him?" he heard Jenn ask, her voice sharper. "Does he need more painkiller?"

Then another voice: "Honey, he's got plenty in his system. Trust me, he doesn't feel a thing."

"No one's hurting me," he tried to tell Jenni, but again it came out slurred together, and it reminded him of the monster singing "Puttin' on the Ritz" in *Young Frankenstein*, which made him laugh.

"Shh, Dan, it's all right. You're all right," Jenn said, her voice so sharp and clear even though she was whispering. He could almost feel her breath against his cheek.

And even though he knew it might end this dream too soon, he forced his eyes to open.

And there she was. Jennilyn. Gazing down at him with such concern on her face and tears brimming in her seemingly average but in truth astonishingly pretty brown eyes.

"I'm okay," he told her, laboring over each word to make it come out relatively clearly, since she obviously didn't like his *Young Frankenstein* imitation.

Her tears overflowed and she used the hand that wasn't holding tightly to his to reach behind her glasses and impatiently brush them away. As far as dreams went, this one sucked. Making Jenn cry was something he tried his hardest not to do.

But she was pretending she wasn't crying, so he went with it.

"Hey," he said.

"Hey," she said, too. "Welcome back."

"Where've I been?" Dan again took his time with the question, also noting that they weren't in her apartment, and that she had her clothes on, which was a shame. It had been months now, and the only time he got some was in his dreams.

He couldn't figure out where they were. There were lights that were too bright overhead, and he had to squint to keep his head from exploding. This certainly wasn't the enlisted men's barracks, in San Diego, where he kept a locker and sometimes crashed at night, when friends like Lopez, Jenkins, and Silverman tired of him surfing their living-room couches.

"You've actually covered quite a lot of ground over the past few days," Jenn told him.

It was then that he noticed she wasn't the only woman standing next to the side of his bed. There was a blonde on his other side, pulling a blanket back up and over his legs, and activating a blood pressure cuff that squeezed his arm.

A nurse, which meant—shit—he was in a hospital.

"I'm not dreaming, am I?" he asked Jenn, who shook her head.

No.

She'd come all this way. Wherever he was, he knew it wasn't Manhattan. Her being here involved air travel and time off from work.

"Is it bad?" he asked as he suddenly remembered. The car bomb. The sniper. The woman and child. The blood exploding out of his leg...

His leg...

But he lifted the blanket and saw that it was still there—heavily bandaged at his thigh. And great, he had some kind of catheter tube coming out of his dick, which bothered him far more to look at than any bandaged or unbandaged wound ever would, so he put the blanket back down so he wouldn't hurl.

"You're okay," Jenn was telling him as more tears spilled from her eyes. "Your waking up was the last big hurdle."

"I'm sorry I scared you, baby," Dan tried to tell her, fighting the sudden nausea. But the best way was to close his eyes, which gave his body some kind of disconnect signal, which he then had to fight in order to stay awake.

She leaned over and kissed him, her mouth soft against his, her fingers gentle in his hair. "It's okay if you go back to sleep now," she whispered.

"I'm glad you're here," he tried to tell her, but he was back to sounding like Frankenstein's comical monster.

"It's okay," Jenn said again. "Everything's going to be okay."

And he surrendered to the darkness.

Las Vegas
Monday, April 20, 2009

The boy who wore makeup was in the shopping mall again.

Neesha pretended that she didn't see him, didn't notice him.

So many people stared at him—she knew what that was like. She got stared at sometimes if she didn't find a place to wash up or clean her clothes in the sink. Sometimes she just got stared at because she looked a little different from almost everyone else in this city.

But now, today, the boy who wore black liner around his eyes and black polish on his fingernails was watching her, and the ice of fear slipped through her.

Maybe he worked for Mr. Nelson or Todd. Maybe he'd been sent to bring her back.

But he didn't look the type. He didn't look old enough, either, even though he was quite tall.

Neesha could feel his gaze upon her and she forced herself to stay seated even as he pushed his own chair back and stood up. She sat even as he began to walk toward her. If she had to, she could run.

He shifted slightly, as if he were going to walk right past, but then, at the last moment, when she was sure she was safe, he stopped.

And despite her resolve to not look at him, she found herself doing just that.

He was beautiful, with pale eyes the color of the open sky and skin that was much lighter than hers. "You don't really work here, do you?" he said.

She pretended to not understand. "I sorry," she said, making her voice higher pitched and singsong. "I not much speak American."

He reached a hand into his pocket, which made her heart race, until he pulled it back out—and held out a bill with a giant five on it— as if he wanted her to take it.

"Just in case you ever get tired of eating other people's leftovers," he said.

She didn't know what leftovers were, but just the same, Neesha couldn't take it from him. If she took his money, she would be indebted. She shook her head.

"Look," he said, "I've seen you. You find a group of people, usually a family with little kids. And you offer to clear their trays as if you work for the food court. But this is a self-serve place. You're supposed to bus your own trays—throw out your own trash. But little kids, they don't always eat their entire Happy Meal, do they? So you throw out the garbage and eat what's left."

She didn't say anything. She didn't look at him.

"I've seen you do it," he said. "It's pretty freaking brilliant. I just thought you'd maybe want...something fresh to eat sometime."

He was still holding out that bill.

She reached for it. Stopped. Looked up into those eerie eyes. "For this, I will *not* give blow job."

The pretty boy laughed his surprise, but then stopped. "Oh, my God, you're serious," he said as he sat down in the chair across from her and lowered his voice. "You're like, twelve. Are you...? Have you *really*...?"

"I'm sixteen," she told him, giving up her pretense of not being able to speak English well. After so many years, her accent was barely noticeable, too.

"You look twelve."

Neesha shrugged. "I'm short."

"I'm Ben," the boy said. "And I don't want a blow job." He caught himself, smiled. "That's not really true. I *do* want one, who doesn't? But...not from you. Trust me."

It didn't make sense, and she *didn't* trust him. "Then why do you give me money?"

"Because...you look like you need it more than I do. I've seen you here for about a week now, and you're always wearing the same thing." He looked down at his own clothes. "Of course, I'm one to talk. But I'm doing it as a statement. You're not."

He pushed the money across the table toward her and withdrew his hand.

Neesha found herself looking down at it. Wanting to take it.

Wondering what was the catch.

There was always a catch.

"When did you run away?" he asked, and she looked up at him, worried.

Ben smiled, which made him look like an angel, come down from heaven. "It's not really that obvious. I mean, I know because I pay attention. But you really *should* get different clothes. Maybe just a few other shirts. The Salvation Army sells stuff for two bucks a bag. Do you know where that is?"

She shook her head, and he told her, but the address was meaningless. She knew only a few streets and not by their official names but by their landmarks. She'd learned to speak English by watching hour upon hour of TV back when she was a prisoner, after they'd taken away her books and papers and pencils. She'd learned from watching and listening, but she hadn't learned to read it. Not yet, anyway. Not well enough to handle street signs.

"If you go there," he told her, "you just have to be careful. Sometimes cops hang out, looking for runaways. Make sure you tell the ladies behind the counter that you're looking for clothes for your sister's birthday. And that you're the same size. That you're twins. That way they won't flag you or ask too many questions."

She pushed the bill back toward him. "I can't," she said. And she couldn't—take his money, or his advice. As much as she would've loved to have a whole bagful of clean, fresh clothes, she couldn't do it.

She started to stand up so she could walk away.

But he stood up, too, far more gracefully. He pushed his chair in and backed off.

"I'd run away, too, if I could," he told her. "My stepfather is a son of a bitch, and my mother's invisible. School's a nightmare, and ..." He shrugged. "It doesn't matter. In a few months I'm moving to San Diego, to live with my brother and sister. Either that or ... I don't know, maybe I'll be dead. One way or another, it'll be an improvement. See you around."

And with that, he walked away without looking back, leaving that five-dollar bill on the table.

So Neesha picked it up, and put it in her pocket.

CHAPTER
FOUR

I love living in Germany, don't you?" the Army nurse asked Izzy as they sat at the corner of the bar.

In truth, Izzy fricking hated fricking Germany. It was where his soon-to-be ex-wife Eden had run after her baby had been stillborn. She had a friend here—Anya Podlasli—who gave her room and board in exchange for help with child care. And every time Izzy had gone to try to see his wife, old stern-and-disapproving Anya with her tightly, Germanicly pursed lips, had turned him away.

The last time had been the final time, except now here he was, unexpectedly back in Germany, not far from where Eden was living. The urge to go visit her for one *final* final time was strong. Especially when the training exercises he'd gotten caught up in after his release from the hospital had ended a full two days before his flight back to Coronado and his next assignment as a BUD/S instructor. Whoo fricking hoo. Still, everyone had to take a turn, and it was his—spurred, no doubt, by the recent supposedly irresponsible behavior that had put him into the hospital, true, but had also saved Eden's brother Danny's life.

Not that Izzy had done what he'd done for Eden's sake. He'd done it for himself and for Dan, and because sometimes rules needed to be broken.

And okay, yeah, he was a liar. He'd done it for Eden, too, because he knew she'd already had too much pain and loss in her life, and try as he might, he couldn't make himself stop caring about that, and about her.

But he *could* make himself accept the fact that his marriage to her was over, so instead of hopping a train and trying to see her one *final* final time, he'd put on some civvies and left the base. When he got off the bus, he'd started walking until he hit the first bar.

And when he'd found this one, he'd walked in and then found the first seemingly available woman and sat down beside her.

Love Germany? Sweetheart, he was counting the minutes before he could leave.

But telling this woman that wasn't going to get him laid. And that was his goal here, tonight, wasn't it? Sex with a convenient stranger, to pull him out of the purgatory in which he'd resided since Eden walked out of his life.

"I haven't ever really lived here," Izzy told the nurse. Damn, he'd already forgotten her name. Sylvia or Cindy or . . . Cynthia. That was it. A pretty name for an equally pretty woman, with her red curls and blue eyes. She was dressed down in jeans and a T-shirt, sneakers on her feet—which should have been a warning to him. She wasn't here trolling for a one-nighter, in her fuck-me shoes. She really was here for just a glass of wine. "I only drop in briefly, for visits."

"You're not stationed here?" Her disappointment in that news was almost palpable, and Izzy watched the integer for this evening's poten- tial orgasm count nosedive back to the solid zero it had been for most of the past year.

But it wasn't disappointment he was feeling, it was relief. And that pissed him off. He didn't want to not want sex. He didn't want to feel as if his getting in a little recreational happy-fun was wrong—for any rea- son. But most of all, he didn't want to look at a perfectly acceptable beautiful, sexy, and intelligent woman like fair Cynthia and think *why bother trying* simply because she couldn't hold a candle to his soon-to- be-ex-wife.

There was a lot of room between his current state of not having any sex at all and the unearthly bliss of being sent into sexual orbit via Eden. And the sooner he moved into that as-yet-unexplored territory between the two, the better.

So even though Cynthia was giving him all of the classic pre-shut-down, *this won't work because you're not stationed here* signs, he pushed aside his feeling of relief and went for it, firing the biggest gun he had in his possession.

"I'm a Navy SEAL," he told her, and yes, her body language immediately changed from *I have to go find my friends* to *What friends, I never had any friends.*

So he embellished, heavy on the lighthearted flirtation. "We only come to Germany to let you and the doctors check the stitches we give ourselves. And to give you pointers to use in the OR."

She laughed at that, and her eyes sparkled. She really *was* quite pretty. But not even half as pretty as Eden, of course.

Fuck.

"And how *are* your stitches?" she asked. "Wait, don't tell me—you need me to check them for you. Privately, of course, because you're bashful."

"I am." Izzy made himself flirt back. See, he could do this. "But alas, this time I have none for you to check. I was here because I donated a little too much blood to a teammate out in the field. I needed a major resupply of my own."

She sat back in her seat. "Oh, my God," she said, her flirtatiousness instantly gone, her eyes wide. "*You're* the one...? I heard about you."

"Uh-oh, that's never good," he said, going for the laugh and getting it.

"But it was in a good way," she corrected him. "You saved your friend's life. I was in awe when I heard what you did."

"In awe, like, you couldn't believe someone could be that stupid?" he asked.

She laughed again at his *stupid,* and agreed. "Stupid, but heroic. Even more so because you knew what you were doing. SEALs are a lot of things, but their stupidity usually doesn't come from ignorance. So I'll go with heroic. I'm glad I got to meet you."

"And to think," Izzy said, "you could have met me a few weeks ago. What a shame you didn't kick down my door to give me a sponge bath when you had your chance."

She laughed again. "Because Army nurses—unlike Navy SEALs— *always* get to choose their assignments."

"Then it was bad luck that kept us apart," Izzy said, sighing melo-dramatically.

"Bad luck and Major MacGregor," Cynthia agreed as she laughed, adding, "But... good luck that we both came here tonight."

"Sharing a drink," Izzy mused, holding out one hand, then putting out his other, as if weighing the options. "Being given a sponge bath..." He shook his head. "Sorry, not quite the same thing."

Cynthia's eyes sparkled again as she mimicked him with her hands. "In the hospital, on duty," she said as she held out one, then added for the other, "In a bar, with the whole night free..."

He was in like Flynn.

And weird that he should think that. *In like Flynn* was actually a reference to Errol Flynn, the movie star of the 1930s, who was so dashing and daring it was perceived that no woman would ever turn him down. Dude had been so freaking hot that that expression still lived on, halfway around the world from Hollywood, and well into the twenty-first century.

And okay. It wasn't as if all Izzy had to do was hold out his hand, and this woman would take it and lead him home to her place. He was going to have to work for it. But there was work and there was work, and this job wasn't going to be difficult. Like most women, she just wanted a little effort on his part. She wanted him to make her laugh. She wanted a little substance along with the spark of attraction.

Which he was already delivering, as well as another drink. As he caught the bartender's eye and motioned for another beer for himself and a glass of wine for the lady, he supposed that *in like Flynn* had hung around so long because it rhymed. If the guy's name had been Errol Floyd, he probably would have been forgotten.

As Cynthia accepted a refill of her wine with a smile, as she picked up the long-stemmed glass and took a sip, Izzy knew that it was weird that he should be thinking about the origin of an expression like *in like Flynn,* instead of inventorying the number of condoms he had on his person and imagining this woman's long, graceful hands and elegant lips on his body instead of that wineglass.

None. He had exactly zero condoms on him.

Because, truth was, he'd come to this bar tonight with no intention of actually getting any. And he may have been in like Flynn with Cynthia-the-nurse, but he absolutely couldn't imagine going back to her apartment and then having to talk to her afterward.

He could imagine the sex.

That was easy to do. And if he could've just stood up and pulled her into some random back room and, without further ado or conversation, nailed her and then walked away, he might've done it.

Maybe.

But maybe not. Because he liked her.

And she wasn't here for a casual encounter, the way he was. She was looking for a boyfriend.

"It was really nice meeting you," Izzy told her as he paid his tab and pushed away his untouched second glass of beer and climbed down off of that bar stool. "But I've got to go."

She was completely confused, so he tried to explain. "I can't do this," he told her. "The timing's wrong. I'm leaving in a few days and . . . you don't want that, and . . . I don't either."

Cynthia stopped him with a hand on his arm. "The timing's never right during a war."

And great. Now he'd moved, in her eyes, from hero to superhero. He couldn't have delivered a line more perfectly designed to convince her to break her rules if he'd tried. And sure enough, she was ready to write him a permission slip for a completely no-strings encounter—

which should have given him cause to have to work to keep his happy dance completely hidden from her view.

Instead he felt a wave of panic—and then of both shame and anger. Because he didn't want to go home with her. In fact, the way she was touching him made him feel claustrophobic, and he shifted so that her hand fell away.

But goddamnit, he didn't want to spend the rest of his life pining for someone he couldn't have.

So when Cynthia reached out to touch him again, when she said, "Hey, have you had dinner? Because I've got some chicken I was going to grill, back at my place…" When she gathered up her purse and jacket and gestured for him to follow her out the door…

Izzy didn't say no.

LAS VEGAS
MONDAY, MAY 4, 2009

The house was quiet when Ben came home from school, and he made a point to close the screen door behind him as quietly as possible, since that was one of his stepfather Greg's pet peeves.

Close that door like a human being, not like the wild animal that you are, boy…

Mondays sucked more than usual because Greg wouldn't drink on Sundays, and although he was a mean drunk, he was still plenty mean when he was sober, and his going without made him crazy, too.

And his Sunday self-prohibition extended until Monday at 5 p.m., at which point a stiff drink or five were finally allowed, according to the Rules of Greg's World. Greg compensated for Monday's hellishness by sleeping away as much of the day as possible.

Ben usually stayed away most of Monday, because waking Greg up would get him hit or spat on, which was disgusting.

It was hard to know which was worse—Monday afternoon or

Monday night, as crazy slid into a drunken mean that was wide awake into the wee hours of the morning.

He'd only come home to pick up the clothes he'd found last night, while rummaging through a box of Sandy's things that had been shoved into the attic. There were a whole pile of shirts from her pre-childbearing years that she'd never wear again, and Ben had tossed them into the washing machine so they wouldn't smell musty when he gave them to the runaway who hung out at the mall.

He moved noiselessly down the hall to his bedroom and grabbed the bag that he'd put them in, then swung into the kitchen to scrounge for a snack or at least a small glass of OJ to keep his blood sugar level and . . .

The letter was open and on the counter, addressed to Mrs. Ivette Fortune. It was from the Department of the U.S. Navy, and—holy shit—they were writing to inform her of their failed attempts to contact her via phone and e-mail regarding her son, Petty Officer First Class Daniel Gillman, who had—God, no!—recently been seriously injured.

But the letter didn't provide details and—*fuck*—it was dated April 20. There was a phone number to call for more information, along with a request for his mother to update her contact information, should they need to get in touch with her regarding Dan's condition.

Like, if he died.

It was May fourth, and Dan could well already be dead, the letter containing *that* information already wending its way to Vegas. The room spun and Ben's stomach heaved and he lunged for the fridge, yanking the door open. He grabbed the container of orange juice and drank straight from the bottle.

And got slapped on the back of his head, which sent the orange juice container flying and made him smash his nose into the closed freezer door.

"What'd I tell you about acting like a human being in my house?" said the man who'd just hit him so hard his teeth had rattled. "You drink from a glass, boy. God knows what kind of diseases a freak like you brings home!"

Yeah, he'd woken up Greg.

There was a smear of blood from his nose on the freezer, but that was the least of his problems as he turned and picked the letter up off the counter.

"You clean up this mess," his stepfather was saying, but Ben interrupted him—something he rarely did even though he'd long since given up on trying not to rock the boat.

"Is Danny all right?" Ben demanded. "What did they say when you called?"

"Is that letter addressed to you?" Greg tried to swat the letter out of Ben's hand, but Ben pulled back. "I said, clean up—"

"It's not addressed to you, either," Ben countered. "But whatever. I just want to know what they said when you called..." But as the words left his lips, he realized his mistake. He'd assumed that Greg had been as anxious and worried as he was. "You didn't call." He sidestepped Greg's pathetic attempt to get back that letter even as he moved toward the dirty white phone that hung on the kitchen wall. He picked it up and... Of course. There was no dial tone. What a surprise.

"Phone's out again," Greg said, as if that were the phone company's fault, not his. "Now you give that to me and clean up this—"

Ben hung up the handset with a crash as he stepped out of Greg's reach again. "Phone's *out*, because you didn't pay the fucking bill with the money my brother sent you. Did you pay the rent? At least you paid the rent, right?"

"Don't you dare use that language in my house!"

"It's *my* house," Ben shouted. "The only reason the rent gets paid is because Danny sends it every month—for *me*."

"Don't you raise your voice to me, boy!"

"He could be dead—right now!" Ben got even louder as he moved to the other side of the kitchen table. "And I know you don't give a *shit* about what that means to my mother and me. But here's a newsflash for you. If Danny's dead, he can't send home that money. Have you thought about that?"

And in a newsflash of his own, he realized that Greg *had* thought about that. But he'd thought about it in terms of the insurance payout Ben's mother would receive if Danny died. He didn't say as much now, but his answer was all over his ugly face. Besides, he'd joked about it in the past, plenty of times. *Maybe the kid'll step on a landmine and we'll have the money to start up that restaurant you've been talking about for years...Heh heh...*

"You probably spent the afternoon praying that he dies," Ben whispered.

"It would serve you right if he did die," Greg spat as he hit Ben with a slap that stung his face and spun him into the wall. "It wouldn't surprise me one bit if God punished you for your sins by—"

Ben had had enough. He lowered his head and threw himself forward with a roar, and he hit Greg in the chest with his full weight, which wasn't much, but was more than he'd ever done before.

Normally, he'd just cower and take his beatings.

But now they both went down onto the floor, right into the puddle of orange juice, with Greg kicking and scratching and slapping as Ben tried to keep that letter with its phone number out of the wet, even as he desperately tried to get away.

"I'll beat you, boy," Greg was screaming, showering him with spittle as he grabbed hold of Ben's hair and pulled. "I will beat you within an inch of your—"

Ben elbowed him in the stomach, doing some kicking himself to get free.

His knee must've collided with Greg's balls, because his stepfather screamed in pain and then started retching, finally letting go of Ben, who scrambled to his feet. He jammed the letter into his pocket as Greg curled, rocking, into a ball. If he'd known it would be that easy to win, he would've fought back years ago.

He had time to open the refrigerator and sweep his entire supply of insulin into a plastic shopping bag. He took the OJ carton, too, because he was still feeling pretty majorly out of body. He picked up the bag of clothes for the girl at the mall—there wasn't time for him to pack anything for himself, which was a shame. And then, as Greg was starting to make more intelligible sounds, Ben went out the front door, letting the screen screech and slap behind him, in one final *fuck you*.

LANDSTUHL, GERMANY
MONDAY, 4 MAY 2009

This was a bad idea.

Cynthia the nurse lived in a small apartment without a roommate, which meant the collections of teddy bears and Hummel figures and look—a Hummel figure teddy bear—were all hers.

What was she, ten? No, apparently not. There was a multitude of birthday cards artfully arranged on an end table that sat between a matching sofa and chair—both perkily, neatly floral-printed. *Big Three-Oh* one of the cards said in a cartoon bubble coming out of the mouth of a...wait for it...teddy bear. Yeah. The others were more Hallmarkie. *Love and affection for my darling daughter on this special day* kind of stuff.

There were a dozen of them. Two from her mother, one from her father and stepmother, the rest from aunts and uncles and cousins and friends. It was pretty impressive—the size of her support team. Impressive and nice. A lot of military personnel, himself included, didn't get even one card on their birthdays.

The apartment itself was impeccably clean and neat, and looked like something out of a Pottery Barn catalog. Everything had a place where it belonged, and the artwork on the walls was in perfect harmony with the beflowered furniture.

Of course, maybe she'd rented the place furnished and none of this was hers.

But the tidiness was all Cynthia—no doubt about that. There was no clutter anywhere. Not even a small pile of mail or a book out and open, spine up, on the coffee table. No sneakers kicked off while she watched TV and...Come to think of it, there was no TV.

She'd gotten a phone call right after unlocking the door and letting him in and he'd given her privacy by hanging here in her little living room while she bustled into the kitchen to start cooking dinner.

Izzy now wandered over to a small collection of DVDs and CDs that sat on a shelf beneath the bears. Her music was limited to classical. She had a lot of Wagner operas, which was alarming since it was just about *the* only form of music that would make him bleed from the ears while going blind. But the Wagner wasn't half as alarming as her DVDs. She had only seven—probably to watch on her laptop—and all were foreign art films, with a heavy emphasis on dramas about suicidal Scandinavians, shot in the dark of a northern winter.

"Why don't you . . . um. Do you want to take a shower?" She poked her head out of the kitchen, finally off the phone.

"Oh. Thanks," Izzy said as he moved toward the kitchen, where something was smelling very, very good as it cooked. "But no, I'm good." He stopped short. "At least I think I'm good." He did a quick pit check, but then realized . . . "Unless it's a thing, like you need me to shower . . . ?"

"No," she said far too quickly, which made him know it *was* a thing—she definitely liked men to shower before she had sex with them.

But that was okay. Clean was fine. It was good.

"How about we both take one after dinner?" he said, and her relief was nearly palpable.

The kitchen was all a maddeningly cheery yellow—and again, everything freaking matched. The only thing missing was a sign saying ZANELLA, LEAVE NOW, BEFORE YOU MAKE A TERRIBLE MISTAKE.

"That sounds . . . nice," she said.

Nice? Was she kidding? But no, she was just nervous. That made two of them.

"So," he said, searching for something to say. "You collect bears."

She smiled. "It's silly, I know, but my cousin's kids started sending them to me and . . . They get me one wherever they go."

"That's nice," he said, and God, now he was doing it, too. But it was true. It *was* nice. This apartment was nice. Cynthia was nice. Her family was nice. Nice, nice, nice.

"Have you lived here long?" he tried.

"Four—no, five years now," she told him as she handed him a glass of wine that she'd poured for him. She *was* lovely, with a body that filled the T-shirt and jeans she had on in a very satisfying way. "I was here for two years before I finally got my things out of storage. Thank God. That was hard, living out of suitcases..."

"For me a suitcase is a luxury," Izzy said, taking a sip. Damn, it was so sweet he nearly gagged.

"That's terrible," she said. "You must get so tired of it."

"No, actually," he said. "It's the way I...like to roll." Seriously? Had he just said *like to roll*?

But she was giving him hero-worship eyes again, and he knew that the shower-after-dinner thing was optional. She was ready and willing to do him right here on the kitchen table.

Of course the wine she was chugging was probably adding to her super-friendly *do me even if you're grubby* factor. She poured herself another healthy glass and drank about half of it in one fortifying gulp as she turned to stir what looked like a mix of onions and mushrooms that were sautéing in a pan on the stove. The chicken was cooking on one of those little George Foreman grills, plugged into a power adapter to make it compatible with the German electrical system.

Lettuce and other vegetables for a salad were out on the counter and Izzy said, "Oh, good, let me help," mostly in an effort to put down that god-awful glass of wine.

"Oh, thanks," she said. "The knives are—"

"I got it," he said, already finding one—it had a yellow handle, natch—and reaching to take a cutting board from where it hung on the wall. He started to cut up a pepper.

"Whenever the teddy bear count gets to ten," she told him, "I take them over to the soldiers at the hospital. The kids send me about one a week, so it doesn't take long."

"That's nice," Izzy said, mentally wincing at his word choice as they fell back into an awkward silence. It was then that he noticed a framed photo of what had to be Cynthia, pre-kindergarten, with her parents. "Are you an only child?"

"I am now," she said. "My little brother died in Iraq, back in 2003."

Ah, crap. "I'm sorry," Izzy said.

"It's been...hard," she said. Understatement of the century.

And Izzy put down the knife, because come on. There was no way he was going to have sex with this woman and walk away. Which meant there was no way he was going to have sex with her, period, the end, because walking away was a given.

"So," he said as he turned to face her, leaning back against the counter. "I saw the birthday cards and, um, I'm just kind of thinking, you know, turning thirty can be kind of hard for some people. Traumatic, even. Some people go a little crazy. Do things they normally wouldn't do..."

She laughed. "Well, that's me. Because I never do this." She looked up from stirring what had become a very decadent-smelling sauce to smile ruefully at him. "Never."

No shit, Sherlock. "I can understand you wanting to get yourself a birthday present," Izzy told her. "And as far as presents go, I'm pretty exceptional." He'd meant it as a joke, but she didn't laugh. Terrific. "I mean, only if you go for that kind of one-night-then-good-bye thing. I really meant what I said about that. That wasn't code or some kind of doublespeak for *maybe I'll stick around*. Or *maybe I'll call you in a few days*. Because I won't. Not a chance. I'm coming off of a fabulously, devastatingly broken heart and...On top of that, I've got a strong hunch that we're actually pretty incompatible. And as long as you're getting yourself a present, well...I would've thought you'd know yourself a little better." He straightened up. "So I'm thinking I should just let myself out, if that's okay."

"Wait." She took the pan off the burner and caught his arm before he could leave the kitchen. And again, just like back in the bar, he had to really work to resist the urge to pull free. "You're just...So sweet."

"Hardly," he said.

"No, you are," she said, and she stood on her toes and kissed him.

She tasted like that wine and he pulled away. She only thought she knew what she wanted. "I gotta go."

Izzy let himself out and ran down the stairs to the street.

He walked all the way back to the base, cursing himself with every step he took, for being the pussy that he was.

Because, God, his stomach hurt from still wanting—always wanting—Eden.

LAS VEGAS
MONDAY, MAY 4, 2009

The boy who wore makeup—the one named Ben—was in trouble.

He staggered slightly as he came out of the shop that sold absurdly expensive coffee, and he sat down right on the floor, just out of the busy stream of mall traffic.

Neesha moved closer, eating the McFlurry that had been left behind by an impatient woman with three extremely ill-behaved children, and it was only then that she realized Ben was crying.

That wasn't good.

She'd watched the relentless dance between the young people who spent most of their afternoons and evenings at the mall. There were two types—shoppers and walkers. The shoppers came in with a destination in mind, and left soon after, carrying heavy bags of clothing and merchandise.

The walkers were shopping, too, but not for anything that could be bought with money or carried away in bags. They were shopping for power. They were there to reinforce that power, and to be entertained by those who were weaker than they were. They traveled in packs, surrounded by the more moderately powerful who worshipped them, and they all kept constantly moving, searching for their prey.

And it wouldn't be long until one of the packs spotted Ben sitting there.

Crying.

The weakest of the weak.

As Neesha ate her McFlurry, she knew that she should cross the stream of foot traffic to Ben, to tell him he was in danger. But that five-dollar bill he'd given her still made her leery.

But then he looked up and saw her. Wiping his eyes on the sleeve of his shirt, he pulled himself to his feet. He had two plastic bags with him, and as he wove his way through the ladies with baby strollers, he held one of them out to her.

Of course she was already backing away.

"This is for you," he said, his words surprising her completely. He didn't try to come too close, which wasn't a surprise. He knew she was skittish. He just set the bag on the table that she'd moved behind so that something was between them, and then he backed off.

"It's clothes," he said, when she didn't move toward it. "One of my sisters'. It was her stuff. She's kind of gotten bigger, so . . . I washed it so you'd have something clean to wear."

"I'm not giving you a blow job," Neesha said.

"He doesn't want one from you, shortcake, he wants one from me." The boy who startled them both was taller and broader than Ben. He was older by a few years, too. And he was surrounded by three of his minions.

The pack had arrived.

But Ben didn't look away from Neesha. He just briefly closed his eyes. "I'm having a really bad day, Tim. My brother is a Navy SEAL, and I just found out he's been injured in Afghanistan, so back off, okay?"

She didn't know what that was—a Navy SEAL—but the pack leader did.

"A SEAL?" he said. "Yeah, right. Wait, don't tell me—he's gay, too."

Gay she knew. She'd watched plenty of episodes of *Will & Grace*. And she knew that some men came to the prison where she'd been kept, to entertain themselves not with girls or women, but with other men.

"Just leave me alone," Ben said wearily. "Or kiss me on the mouth and pledge your undying love, because this is getting old."

That was not the way the prey addressed the powerful, and the boy named Tim was not happy about that. But a mall security guard had noticed the tension and was heading toward them, which made the pack shift and shuffle their feet, impatient to be off.

And Neesha shifted, too, because she worked very hard to keep the guards from noticing her.

Ben understood, because he pushed the gift he'd brought toward her and whispered, "Go."

On impulse she gestured for him to follow, because the pack was moving, changing, too, heading toward the counter where delicious-smelling cookies were sold.

She could only assume they tasted as good as they smelled, because no one ever didn't finish one of them.

And Ben hefted the other bag he was carrying and let her lead him toward the sanctuary she'd found some weeks ago. A place where packs of kids and men seldom went—the mall's maternity clothing store.

But halfway there, out of sight of both the guard and the pack, he stopped her. "This is going to sound like bullshit," he said, "but do you still have that five dollars I gave you? I had a fight with my stepfather, and my wallet must've fallen out of my pants. I don't have any money and my sister's not at work—she works at that coffee place? She told me she'd be on for this shift, but she's not there and . . . See, I took the insulin from my refrigerator, but I didn't take any needles, but there're needles—and a phone—at my sister's apartment, and I really should've just gone there, but I thought she'd be here at work and . . ." He took a deep breath. "Bottom line, I'm freaking out because I think my brother Danny might be dead. I have to get over to my sister's apartment, but I'm feeling really sick—I have diabetes, so it happens sometimes—and I don't think I can walk that far. Even if I take the bus, I'm not sure I can get there without your help, and I definitely can't get there without that five dollars to pay the bus fare."

Neesha looked at him. She didn't understand half of what he'd said. Insulin? Needles? Diabetes she'd heard about. She'd seen commercials on TV. *Find the cure!* And she understood a dead brother and a missing sister. She also got *I'm feeling really sick*, and she could see for herself that Ben was struggling, even just to stay up on his feet.

So she dug the five-dollar bill he'd given to her out of her pocket and held it out for him.

"Thank you," he said, taking it from her and pocketing it himself. "Bus stops at the lower level, center entrance."

He faltered and she moved toward him, to keep him from falling. And they walked that way toward the escalators, her arm around his waist, his around her shoulders. He was heavier than he looked, for someone so skinny. But she was stronger than *she* looked, so it was okay.

And for the first time since she could remember, she was being touched by someone who didn't want sex from her. At least she hoped that was true. She found herself praying she wasn't wrong, that this wasn't some kind of trap. That she would go with him and... "You smell like oranges."

"Yeah," Ben said. "I know."

CHAPTER
FIVE

Ben sat on the floor of the little hallway between Eden's bathroom, bedroom, kitchen, and living room as Neesha cleaned his puke out of the bathtub.

"You really don't have to do that," he said.

"The sooner it's gone, the sooner it'll stop smelling so bad," she said.

"You could just leave," he pointed out.

She stopped swishing the water down the drain and looked at him, her little-girl face wary and alert. "Do you wish me to leave? Now that you're all right...?"

"No, I'm just saying," he said. "You're going above and beyond. I'm just... Thank you. That's what I'm trying to say. Most people find a reason to leave when I puke like that. They get grossed out."

"You didn't do it on purpose," she pointed out. "Some people stick their finger down their throat and do it on purpose."

"You mean, like being bulimic?"

She shook her head. "I don't know what that is."

"It's when you make yourself throw up after you eat so you don't gain weight."

She was amazed. "*You* would do this?"

Ben laughed. "Ew. No. What planet are you from, anyway? And what other reason would someone have to make themselves throw up,

besides not wanting to get fat? I mean, I guess maybe if they accidentally swallowed poison, or too many sleeping pills..."

Neesha turned off the water and dried her hands on one of the towels hanging on the wall rack. "For some," she told him, "it brings sexual pleasure."

And now it was Ben's turn to gape. "Seriously? To make themselves
puke? While they're...?"

"Or to be... puked on," she said. "Is that right, *puked*?"

She was asking about the verb tense and he nodded. "That's just
wrong." He stopped himself. "And okay, just because *I'm* not...
I mean, there are people who would say that being gay is wrong. So
maybe I shouldn't judge. I mean, if everyone involved wants to be
involved... Although please note I'm not volunteering anytime soon."

"But if not?" she asked. "What if someone doesn't want to... be involved?"

Ben sat up. "Neesha, do you have some kind of weird boyfriend, or
maybe it's your mother's boyfriend...?"

"My mother's dead," she told him. "She died a long time ago,
when I was eight." She took a deep breath, and let it out in a rush before she went on. "And after she died, I was sold to a man who brought
me here and... I was kept... locked up and... It was bad."

Ben stared at her, his heart in his throat, praying that she would
laugh or at least smile and say something like, *Wow, look at your face.
You actually believed me, Mr. Naive...*

But she didn't. Instead she said, "A few weeks ago, I ran away. I escaped. But I didn't know where to go for help and... I'm certain
they're looking for me."

"Wow," Ben said. "Okay. Wow. Neesha, if this is a joke—"

She looked at him. "You think I'm trying to be funny?"

"I don't know," Ben said. "Are you? I mean, it's the twenty-first century. People don't sell other people anymore."

She just looked steadily back at him.

"You said you're sixteen," he started.

"Eight years," she said. "Three months. And thirteen days. That's how long I was there. It got easier keeping track after I learned to count in English."

Ben still couldn't wrap his brain around any of it. "So you were, what? Some guy's slave? Did you have to, like, clean his house and, I don't know, pick his cotton?" Even as he asked the question, he knew he was way off base.

And even though she didn't speak, he saw the answer in her eyes, and in an echo of her earlier words that now rang in his head. *For some, it brings sexual pleasure.*

She turned away abruptly.

"Wait," he said as he pushed himself to his feet and followed. "Neesha, if this is true, you have to go to the police."

"I can't."

"Why not?"

"They'll send me away," she said fiercely. "I'm illegal, okay?"

"Oh, shit," Ben said.

"I shouldn't have told you anything," she said. "Promise me you won't tell anyone!"

"Neesha, I don't think—"

She picked up her bag and started for the door.

"Wait, okay?" he said again. "I promise I won't tell, if you don't want me to. I just don't know how I can help, without at least talking to my sister."

Or to Danny, who would definitely know what to do. Except he could well be dead. Please, powers of the universe, don't let Danny be dead . . .

"Why don't you stay, for a little while?" Ben asked, looking up from where he'd crouched with his head between his legs, to counter the wave of dizziness. "My sister'll come home eventually. You can meet her. And if you want to . . . We can tell her. But only if you want to."

Neesha stood there, uncertain.

"Okay," Ben said. "I'm not going to tackle you to the ground and make you stay. So . . . If you want to go, go. If you want to stay. Great. I've got to check my blood again, and maybe have a snack. You're welcome to have something, too. Or you could take a shower if you want. Wash your hair. But only if you want to, okay?"

Neesha nodded. And put the bag down. She was going to stay.

When the bigger conventions came to town, headliners came in from out of town to take the main stage, even on a Monday, leaving the newer girls like Eden working the poles on the edges of the room.

Still, the club was in a good location, and when those predominantly male-populated conventions arrived, it stayed packed pretty much 24/7, with the biggest lull being the hangover hours between 4 and 7 a.m.

At seven, things picked up again, because the club's restaurant served a convention special breakfast, and the combination of bacon, eggs, and bare breasts was too good for some men to pass up.

Today, Eden had worked a double shift—late night and daytime—because one of the girls had called in sick, and the place was jumping.

She didn't mind. It put her that much closer to her goal of being able to pay Danny back all that money that she'd borrowed from him through the years. That was her master plan. First, pay her older brother back, and only then ask him to step in and help her gain custody of Ben.

Danny was significantly older. He had a steady job. True, it was in the military, which meant he went TDY—temporary duty, usually overseas—at the drop of a hat. But that was a good thing, because there was no way in hell he would want to live in the same apartment as Eden for any longer than he had to. He hated her.

But her plan would work, because Danny *didn't* hate Ben. And since he wasn't an idiot, he'd quickly see that setting up their little brother in an apartment with Eden would be far better than subjecting him to Greg's abuse until he turned eighteen.

Unless, of course, Dan was in agreement with Greg, and thought Ben would benefit from being sent to one of those brainwashing, ex-gay torture camps...

In which case, Eden would be on her own.

Or not. Because she was still married to Izzy Zanella. And she suspected—no, she *knew*—that he'd be ready and willing to come to her rescue. He was that kind of a man.

The reliable kind, who liked playing the hero.

Eden had thought she'd spotted him this afternoon. There'd been a tall man with military-short hair and rough, craggy features sitting and watching her with his face in the shadows as she feigned ecstasy while caressing the pole.

At first her heart nearly stopped, especially when he stood up and proved to be extremely similar to her ex-husband in height and weight. But he didn't move toward her. He was only going to get another drink from the bar, and as he stepped into the light, she saw that he wasn't Izzy. He wasn't even close. But she spent the remainder of her time fantasizing about it—what she would do and say if Izzy did walk through those doors.

He'd be affronted and upset. And jealous. *Put your clothes back on!*

She'd be coolly dignified. *I don't take orders from you.*

We're still married, you know.

No, *we're not*, she'd tell him quietly. *I looked it up online. We're separated. By mutual agreement. And I'm glad you finally showed up because now we can start the proceedings for the divorce.*

I'm still in love with you, he'd say, but she would just laugh, because she knew it was a total lie. He'd never been in love with her. For some reason, he felt responsible for her. Indebted. And okay, maybe it wasn't *for some reason*, but for a very specific reason, in that she'd all but jumped him on the night of her eighteenth birthday, for a very intense session of revenge sex.

Despite her efforts, they hadn't actually had *sex* sex of the full penetration variety, but they'd gotten close. And they'd certainly both made each other come, right there on the sofa in Izzy's living room.

She'd been playing with fire at the time—she knew that now. But back then, she'd been focused on cutting her ties with her jerk of an ex-boyfriend, who'd ditched her at a Krispy Kreme.

Was it the smartest, most prudent thing she'd ever done? Definitely not. Did it help her feel less miserable and unloved? Ditto. But it had happened and she couldn't turn around and undo it.

Eden knew that Izzy, however, carried around a lot of guilt about that encounter. Her age—several minutes older than she'd been the day before, when she was still only seventeen—and the fact that she was the little sister of one of his SEAL teammates were both huge problems for him.

But he'd always found her attractive and irresistible—she knew that, too. He wasn't the only one. He was smoking hot, tall and solid, with the kind of body most women only ever dreamed about seeing in the flesh.

The second time they'd collided, six months later, she'd been pregnant as the result of being roofied by her ex-boyfriend's lowlife drugpusher boss—and wasn't *that* an episode in her life that she wished she could rewind and erase. But she'd soon realized that she wanted to keep her innocent child, and Izzy had come to the rescue and married her so that she and Pinkie, her unborn baby, would have health care and a roof over their heads.

He'd married her not merely because he liked being a hero, but also because he'd wanted to have sex with her. He was actually willing to marry her to get some, guilt-free.

Some hero.

Still, he was smart and funny—irreverent as hell. He always knew just what to say to make her laugh. He was not just a Navy SEAL, he could also sing better than anyone she'd ever seen on *American Idol*.

And when she was with him, she'd felt safe.

So of course, she'd walked away after she'd miscarried, after Pinkie had died and left her completely alone again.

She'd done a lot of crazy things in her life, but none as crazy as the things she'd done in those months immediately following Pinkie's untimely death. Postpartum depression, her German friend Anya had called it. It was natural, and it would pass. Except it didn't, not for a good long time. But then it started to fade, and she no longer felt crazy but just plain sad.

And now, after a few more months, her sadness had faded farther away. And from the distance that time had provided, Eden was able to see that, in addition to grieving Pinkie, she'd also been mourning the loss of Izzy.

The bus let her off at the corner and she took the back entrance into the apartment complex, heading through the center courtyard to the stairs, glad finally to be home, and grateful that she didn't have to go in to the coffee shop until tomorrow night, after tomorrow's daytime shift at the club.

The barista thing was her backup job—the one Ben knew about. The one she'd tell Danny about when the time came to contact him. She worked there an average of two four-hour shifts a week, usually at times when the other workers—mostly high school students—were unavailable.

As she opened her apartment door, she found herself face-to-face with a very startled young girl—maybe eleven or twelve years old—with a distinctly Asian background. She was maybe Hawaiian or Filipina.

Eden double-checked the number on the door—214. Yes, this was definitely her apartment. And that was the same crappy furniture inside, that had come with the sublet, not to mention the plethora of Buddha statues that sat on every available surface ...

"Ben, there's someone here!" the little girl called, her eyes never leaving Eden's, and Ben appeared from the little alcove kitchen.

"Where were you?" Ben asked, then turned to the girl. "It's okay, it's my sister." He turned back to Eden. "You were supposed to be at work."

"I *was* at work," Eden said, before she thought it through.

"No, you weren't," Ben said. "I went to the mall and you weren't there."

Oh, crap. She took her key out of the lock and closed the door behind her. The girl, meanwhile, still looked as if she couldn't decide whether to hide, fight, or flee.

"I was...at my other job," Eden said, using the little girl as a diversion to give herself time to think. "Who's your friend?" *What other job? Cleaning, but what? She'd already told Ben that cleaning houses had been too dangerous—going there alone...*

"This is Neesha," Ben said. "What other job?"

"Neesha who?" Eden asked, softening her words by smiling at the girl.

"I have to go now, Ben," Neesha said, clearly freaked out by Eden's sudden appearance. *What was she afraid of?*

"I'm sorry," Eden said, setting her shoulder bag down on the floor by the door as she continued to stand in front of it, blocking the girl's way out of the apartment. She directed her words at Ben. "But I really need to know who you're inviting over here, when I'm not around."

"I'm gay, remember?" Ben said.

"Yeah," Eden said. "But she's, like, twelve, and the last thing we need is—"

"She's sixteen," Ben told her, holding out what looked like a letter.

Eden took it and... "Oh no." *We regret to inform you...* But *Danny wasn't dead. He was only injured. Please, please, God—if there was a God—let Danny be okay...*

"Yeah," Ben said grimly as she looked up at him. "The letter must've come sometime over the weekend. I only saw it after school today."

"Did Ivette call this number?" Eden asked.

"She hasn't been home in a week. She's pulling double shifts and..." Ben laughed his scorn. But Eden could see beneath it to his terrible upset. "Greg let the phone get shut off again. I kind of—"

"You should sit down," the girl interrupted. "You need to tell your sister—"

"I'm fine," Ben spoke over her. "Eed, I thought you were getting a phone installed."

"I got a cell instead," she told her brother as she dug for it in her purse. "It was cheaper." She opened it and began punching in the phone number on the letter.

"Ben gave himself a shot," the little girl announced, "that he said might make him puke, and it did."

Eden looked up sharply at that. "Glucagon?" she asked. "Ben, your levels were that low . . . ?"

"I'm fine," he said again. "Now. But I was light-headed and I was trying to have some orange juice, and then Greg hit me, and Eed, God, I hit him back. And then I didn't have a snack, and I didn't have any money because my wallet was gone and I made it to the mall, but you weren't at work, like you told me you'd be. But Neesha was there, and she helped me get home . . ."

Ben was trying not to cry, and Eden put her phone down and her arms around him. "Okay," she said. "Okay. It's going to be okay, Boo-Boo, even if Danny's dead. It's going to suck and we're going to be sad, but we'll get through it. We'll be okay."

Ben kept fighting his tears as Eden pulled him over to the junky, stuffing-leaking sofa-bed that she'd covered with a sheet, and sat down beside him. "I don't want him to be dead," he said.

"I don't either," Eden said, as fighting her own tears made the back of her throat ache. "But if he is, we'll be okay. Whatever happens, we're going to be fine."

"I can't go back there," Ben told her. "I kind of kicked Greg's ass." He laughed, but it was more of a burst of emotion than true amusement, because it sounded quite a bit like a sob. "He's already planning to open a restaurant with the insurance money."

Oh, Lord. "Define *kicked his ass*," Eden said.

"I didn't kill him," Ben said, with a roll of his eyes. "I didn't even really kick his ass. I just wanted to. I kneed him in the nuts and he started screaming. I got away and . . . I left."

That was good. All they needed was Greg in the hospital—and a police warrant for Ben's arrest. Although, truth be told, he'd be safer in the juvie system than in that terrible ex-gay camp.

"He hit me first," Ben said, clearly thinking along the same lines.

"Did your friend witness it?" Eden asked, just as she realized that the girl was gone. She'd slipped out the door while both Eden and Ben were distracted.

Ben shook his head. "She was at the mall. And great. Neesha left. I was going to ask you if she could stay here, at least for a little while." He must've seen the great big no on her face because he quickly added, "She's in trouble, Eed. She's living in the streets and... She made me promise not to tell anyone, and to be honest, she didn't actually *say* what happened. It was kind of more implied, but some really, *really* bad things have happened to her, starting when she was little and..."

Eden closed her eyes and took a deep breath.

"Her mother died and it was awful," Ben continued. "And now she has no place to go."

"Ben," Eden said. Neesha may have had no place to go, but she was right up there on the top of the list labeled *Problems Eden Didn't Need.* "I know how much you still miss Deshawndra—"

"This has *nothing* to do with her."

Didn't it? Ben's best friend, Deshawndra, and her grandmother had died as a result of the flood after Hurricane Katrina. And this was the first time since her death—at least as far as Eden knew—that her brother had even made an attempt to reach out to another person even remotely close to his own age. But it was clear he didn't want to talk about that.

"Okay," she said. "Let's rewind a bit. Have you tested your blood sugar levels again, after injecting the glucagon?"

Ben nodded, relaxing, if only slightly, at the change of subject. "It's good."

"Show me. I want to see it," Eden said, standing up. Ben's last reading—and the time it was taken—appeared on the meter's tiny screen.

"Wow," Ben said. "Trust me, much?"

"You *are* my brother, right?"

"Half brother."

"Half," she said, "is close enough. Come on. Where's your meter? After I'm convinced I don't have to take you to the hospital, I'm going to make that call, find out what I can about Danny." Please, heavenly Father, let him be okay... "And you've got to call Ivette at work—let her know you're safe, you've got a place to stay, but you're not coming home."

"It's in the kitchen," he called after her. "And I don't have Ivette's phone number at this new place she's working. I only have her cell."

"Then call her cell," Eden said.

"So when were you going to tell me that you got fired from the coffee shop?"

Eden looked back at Ben. "I didn't," she said, then lied effortlessly, like the full Gillman that she was. "But I did get a second job. A cleaning job. I clean offices and clubs, after hours—with a whole team of, you know, other women. It's kinda nasty, but the pay's good. And I'm safe."

Ben bought it, hook, line and sinker—which was a ridiculous expression to use in the desert.

She checked the meter—he *was* being honest with her—and then she got her cell phone, and, bracing herself for tragic news because it had been that kind of a decade, she dialed the number on the letter.

LAS VEGAS
MONDAY, MAY 4, 2009

Neesha didn't need to take the bus back to the mall.

It was easy enough to walk, since this time she wasn't supporting a boy who was nearly half again her weight.

She didn't know a lot about diabetes, and Ben's explanations as he stuck himself with a needle didn't help educate her all that much further. But still, it was clear that he was ill. That couldn't have been an act, nor was his puking into the bathtub.

Still, going into that apartment with him, even though her heart was pounding...? And then, actually *telling* him even the little that she'd told him...?

It was a huge step for her. And a necessary one, ever since she'd determined that she would not be able to get the help she needed on her own.

She'd decided, weeks ago, that she needed to find a friend. Someone she could trust—and would trust—with her very life. She'd been cautiously increasing her contact with one of the ladies who worked at the library before Ben dropped into her life.

But Ben's sister, who bore the name Eden, was an entirely different matter. She was younger than Neesha had expected, and was far more beautiful than Neesha had expected. And that, plus all of the glittery, exotic costumes Neesha had found in the lower drawers of Eden's bedroom dresser, convinced her that Ben's sister worked in the sex trade.

And it was possible that, not only would she have no sympathy for Neesha, but she could well know Mr. Nelson and Todd, and would be more than willing to earn a bonus by turning Neesha in.

So Neesha had run, taking the bag with the clothes that Ben had given her.

She was hungry when she finally got back to the mall—it had been a while since that McFlurry, and she'd refused Ben's offer of a snack. Still, she went to the bathroom first, to change her shirt in one of the stalls.

There were five different tops in the bag Ben had given her. They were in a variety of colors and prints, each more beautiful than the last. She picked the blue—the plainest one—since her goal was merely to be clean and not draw attention to herself. Besides, she would probably forevermore associate fancy clothes with the vast myriad of clients who'd passed through her tiny room, with its pink-trimmed furniture and collection of dolls and picture books that were locked behind glass.

Right up until the end, she'd refused to dress herself unless it was part of the services rendered—part of the show. This meant that every time a "visitor" came to call, the stern-faced women with their rough hands and pinching fingers would enter Neesha's room without knocking, and dress her in whatever outfit was required. Only rarely was it the kind of shiny, flashy, sexy items—thongs and bra tops—that she'd found in Eden's drawer. Instead she often wore a gymnast's leotard—that was a big favorite—or a schoolgirl's uniform, or a pink shapeless baby-doll dress with ankle socks and shiny black shoes.

The women had learned to wait to dress her and do her hair until the client was in the building. And even then, one of them would sit with her until the door opened.

But that was over now.

There were elastic hair fasteners at the bottom of the bag—large enough to hold her heavy mass of hair up in a ponytail or even a bun. Neesha unfastened her braid and combed her long hair out with her fingers, wishing yet one more time that she had a pair of scissors so she could cut it all off.

She'd tried using a plastic knife from the food court.

It hadn't worked.

She put her old shirt into the bag and exited the stall, giving herself only the briefest glance in the mirror. Yes, her new shirt covered her. Yes, she'd scooped all of her hair up off her neck and twisted it into that severe-looking bun. It made her look only slightly older, and she found herself longing for a hat and sunglasses.

Because Mr. Nelson and Todd were still out there, looking for her.

And Neesha knew that neither would rest until they found her.

CHAPTER
SIX

Markie-Mark Jenkins wanted to visit Dan Gillman one last
time before he and Izzy went wheels up and headed back
to San Diego.

And because Izzy didn't want to get into the gnarly details of why
he didn't want to go with, he found himself walking through the halls
of the one place where he least wanted to be this morning—the one
place he could actually come face-to-face again with Cynthia, since
she worked here.

Still, he walked quickly and kept his head down and made it without mishap into the relative safety of Gillman's room.

Dan was stuck here in the hospital for at least another few days—
maybe less if he could convince the doctors that he wasn't going to
overexert himself. The nursing staff was also monitoring the fishboy for
signs of infection, still calling him a "medical miracle," because he'd
survived quite a few touch-and-go days in the ICU after having first
been brought in

But apparently Dan hadn't gotten that particular memo, because
he was looking remarkably average as he slept with his mouth open, his
hair going every which way, and his face smashed against a pillow that
bore a dark spot of his allegedly miraculous drool.

He'd kicked off part of his blanket, and sure enough, there was the
leg in question—the one that everyone had dourly expected would

need amputation. But Dan's little piggy toes looked pink and healthy, and Izzy felt a hot rush of gladness that he usually didn't associate with anything having to do with his arch-nemesis.

As Izzy and Jenk came farther into the room, Jennilyn LeMay, Danny's first-rate, top-notch, high-class, too-good-for-him girlfriend stood up from where she was sitting in an uncomfortable-looking chair next to the fishboy's bed, and put her finger to her lips.

"He's been sleeping so badly at night," she told them almost inaudibly. "He didn't want to nap, but...When he finally does fall asleep, I just don't have the heart to wake him."

Danny wasn't the only one sleeping badly. Jenn looked exhausted, and had clearly given up all attempts at looking professional, which was actually an improvement, in Izzy's book. She was one of those women whose coif surrendered to a bad hair day with the slightest change in the weather, and who invariably snagged her stockings if she walked or moved. She was the one who'd lose a button on her strait-laced suit jacket thirty seconds before the Big Important Meeting, and she, alone, would get splashed when a car went through a puddle going round a corner. It was her shoulder the baby would throw up on while his diaper leaked on her sleeve, and while riding the subway, she was guaranteed to get jostled and spill her coffee down the front of her blouse.

She also had what Izzy thought of as a milk-maid complexion and physique. She was a tall, strapping, healthy young woman with gorgeous, fresh-looking skin. And she looked far more natural in the jeans, sneakers, and curve-hugging T-shirt she currently had on, with her baby-fine hair pulled back into a ponytail, all makeup scrubbed from her ordinary yet extremely not-unpleasant face.

"You look like you could use a break," Jenkie told her. "We'll sit with Danny for a while, if you want."

Jenn looked uncertain until Izzy added, "We'll stay until you get back. Go on, I can hear the coffee from the mess hall singing your name in three-part harmony. *Jenny, I've got your number, I need to make you mine...*"

She smiled when he sang and dimples appeared, and as Izzy gazed through her glasses and into her eyes—a nondescript light brown until combined with that smile—he felt a flash of understanding as to why Dan was so into her. She *was* pretty damn cute.

"I've never heard *that* song before," she said dryly. "Oh, wait, except for every single day in sixth grade."

As she turned and slipped out from behind the curtained partition, Izzy also made note of the way her generously curvaceous behind filled her jeans. Some people might have thought of her ass as being *too* generous, but the bottom line—pun intended—was that without the business suit and the sensible flat pumps, she *was* a seriously nice-looking woman.

And yet, she was completely against Dan's usual type for a fly-to-Germany-because-you're-in-the-hospital girlfriend. She was quite the standard, however, when it came to a meaningless vacation fling—a no-real-strings opportunity for the movie-star-handsome SEAL to get some.

In fact, Dan himself had concisely described his usual MO to Izzy, a mere few months earlier: *Everyone wants to get laid. That's just a fact of life. But there are ways to do it. Strategies. You don't just automatically follow your dick. You use your head with the brain. You find the chunky girl with the really pretty friends. She's low maintenance and low drama, plus she's wired to believe that you're too good to be true. She expects to be dumped, so when you do it, she lets go immediately.*

Problem was, Jenn had overheard Dan as he'd spouted that elegant monologue to Izzy. She'd reacted as strongly as one might expect.

And she'd been so intent on putting distance between herself and Dan "Yes, I Really Did Just Call the Woman I'm Sleeping with Chunky" Gillman, she'd fallen into the clutches of a very nasty, crazy-ass son-of-a-bitch who sliced and diced woman as part of a lifelong hobby.

Danny had literally helped their team leaders blast through a wall to find her, at which point she'd fallen into his arms. But Izzy had seen the remains of some of the crazy serial killer's victims, and *he* would have fallen, sobbing no less, into Danny's strong arms, too, had he been the one tied up and at the top of the nasty-ass dude's "to-do" list.

Still, the arm-falling-into had been temporary. Several hours after Jenn's release from the hospital, Danny had shown up back at the hotel room the SEALs were sharing, looking a little shell-shocked at the fact that she'd sent him away. She'd apparently also told him that if he truly were serious about her, he should come back to visit her—after his next trip overseas.

She'd wait, she'd told him, but she wouldn't wait forever.

It was a variation on the *if you love someone, set them free* theme, and good thinking on Jenn's part.

It had, however, driven Dan completely crazy.

He'd spent most of their time overseas in the computer tent, sending Jenni e-mail. And apparently whatever he'd sent her had worked. Because here Jenn was, playing the role of the dickweed's girlfriend, sitting patiently by the side of his hospital bed as he snored his days away and kept her up all night in a bad and entirely unromantic way.

Izzy leaned against the bed and shook it.

"What!" Dan said as he jerked awake. Or nearly awake. As SEALs, they'd all learned it was best to snap into high alert before their eyes even opened. But Danny had gotten soft these past few weeks in the hospital. Or maybe it wasn't his fault. Maybe he was still heavily medicated.

Either way, the man was in a serious fog. He wiped the drool from the side of his face with his non-IV-attached arm as he looked around for Jenn and didn't find her.

"She went for coffee," Izzy reported cheerfully as he sat down in the chair she'd recently vacated.

"How are you doing?" Jenk asked Danny, who shook his head.

"Fucking low-grade infection," he complained. "I keep telling them I'm fine, but they're afraid to release me. Guess it's really broken, huh?"

Jenk shook his head as he looked down at the cast on his arm. "Yeah, what a pain in the ass. But they're finally shipping me stateside.

I'm going to desk-it in Commander Koehl's office for a few more weeks." He smiled. "Don't get me wrong, I'm not *really* complaining. The timing's actually pretty good. I'll get to watch Lindsey expand."

"And puke her guts out every morning, noon, and night," Izzy said.

"No, so far she's good," Jenk said.

"Famous last words," Dan said.

They were in agreement. "Yeah. Cut to a close-up of Lindsey as she lunges for the porcelain god," Izzy said, and look at that. He and Dan actually exchanged a *we know something Jenk doesn't know* glance. He resisted the urge to check his cell phone, see if he'd gotten any tweets about hell finally freezing over.

"Hey, there you are."

The voice that interrupted them was definitely female and oddly familiar. They all turned to see a woman coming through the curtain—gorgeous and young, with thick blond hair tumbling down around her shoulders. She was wearing a little black hormone-jangling dress that hugged her trim yet completely female body, topping it off with a pair of strappy high heels and red toenail polish at the south end of a pair of truly exceptional legs.

Despite it being 0940, she looked like a million bucks, dressed and made up for an evening out in one of the town's pricier restaurants.

Izzy was certain that he knew her from *some*where, but he squinted, unable to remember where they'd met, or even when. Damn, she was hot. And, to be honest, if he'd sat down next to *her* at that bar last night, the evening could well have ended with a different outcome.

Of course, she was probably supernice, too. And as long as he was being honest, he needed to admit the fact that, should he have sat down next to her at that bar last night? He would've come up with a dozen solid reasons for not sleeping with *her*, too.

1. She was not Eden.
2. She had never been Eden.
3. She was never going to become Eden . . .

Yeah. He was such a loser. He would have said no to her, too.

Dan and Jenk were also struck dumb and staring—gaping almost—and the woman laughed as she came around to the other side of Dan's bed.

"You have no idea who I am, out of uniform like this, do you?" She was looking at and speaking to Dan, whose messy hair and need for a morning shave now made him look like he belonged on the cover of GQ—now that his eyes were open and his mouth was closed, that is. She held out her hand to him, and the gold bracelet she wore on her slender wrist sparked in the fluorescent light. "Sheila Anderson. I'm glad to see you're still in one piece, sir."

Ah, of course. It was Marine Private S. Anderson, who'd helped Izzy save Dan's life. She'd cleaned up pretty damn nice.

But Danny, in his wooziness, still hadn't put two and two together. He did, however, shake lovely Sheila's lovely hand.

"I'm sorry," he said, no doubt frantically searching through his vast system of mental files of women he'd banged, and coming up—correctly—empty. "Sheila...?"

"Or maybe I should say, I'm glad to see you're still in one piece, Oh Great One. It was touch and go there, for a while."

Dan laughed his relief as dawn broke. "Oh! Right. Yeah. Private, um, Anderson. Out of context, you know? That and, um..." His gaze slid almost involuntarily down to that awesome dress's extra-awesome neckline, and he forced it back to her face. "The hair."

Yeah, right.

But she laughed again. "I usually wear it like..." She tipped her head and exposed a very lovely length of smooth, soft neck as she gathered her golden fairy-princess tresses into a severe ponytail. "Does that help?"

Dan nodded. "Yeah, sorry, I, um—"

"No worries," she said as she let her hair bounce back around her shoulders. "I *am* a little overdressed for a hospital visit. There was a party last night and...I had too much wine and stayed over with a friend who's a nurse. I thought I'd pop in to say hi, as long as I had the chance."

Okay, so the magnificence they were seeing was actually morning-after-Sheila, and yes, on closer examination, Izzy could see that her mascara was slightly smudged. But only slightly. And he knew that Dan and Jenk were thinking the same thing he was. If *this* was what Sheila looked like after an evening of too much wine... It was hard not to imagine what she'd look like during a very private party, one held in bed, sans that dress.

Of course, she chose that exact moment, while Izzy was—despite her not being Eden—imagining her naked, to turn to him and say, "Nice to see you again, too. Zanella, right? I'm glad you're okay."

And oh, shit. Private Anderson had no clue that she was on the verge of revealing a state secret.

Izzy nodded, uncertain of what to say, but she was already on to Jenk.

"How's your wrist?" she asked.

But Jenk didn't get a chance to answer her, because someone else had come to the curtain.

"Excuse me. I'm looking for Dan Gillman."

This time the voice was that of a heavy smoker, his baritone gravelly and rough, with a hint of N'Orleans. He was older and Army— a master sergeant—in BDUs that were faded yet neat and sharply creased, his boots polished to a high gleam.

His dark hair was graying at the temples and his face...

It was like looking into a wormhole and seeing a version of Danny from the future.

If, that is, Danny quit the SEAL teams, joined the U.S. Army, smoked two packs of cigarettes a day, and drank himself into an alcohol-induced stupor every night for twenty-five years.

Beside him in the bed, Dan looked as if his tension level had ratcheted to DEFCON two. Izzy was on a similar edge. This was also *Eden's* father. Which made this guy Izzy's father-in-law.

"You found him," Sheila said brightly, failing to pick up on Dan's discomfort. Her tone, unfortunately, held a *come on in* subtext. "Wow, you've *got* to be his father. Genetics in action..."

Izzy stood up as Dan Gillman the elder came into the little

curtained-off area, as father and son were face-to-face for the first time in God knows how long.

He didn't know all of the details of the Gillman family history—only bits and pieces. Such as Dan senior had left his wife Ivette for good after Dan junior—aged eleven or twelve—had threatened to kill him. Or maybe the threats were the result of Danny finding out that his father was leaving and not coming back. Izzy wasn't sure of the exact chronology.

But he suspected domestic violence of some sort had been involved, and he knew that Danny still hated his father with a passion. It had been a point of contention between Dan and his sister Eden, who'd gone to live with the man when she'd turned eighteen.

The older Gillman now smelled as if he'd stopped at the nearest bar and consumed a serious amount of liquid courage before coming here.

He was playing it upbeat and friendly, though. "Hey, son, how're you feeling?" he asked, but didn't give Danny time to answer. "I spoke to the captain. He's an excellent doctor—a good man. I've known him for years. He says you're going to keep the leg. I was glad to hear that." He turned to Sheila. "And you must be Danny's girlfriend, come all the way from New York. Aren't you a pretty little thing. I swear, this boy has the sweetest tooth when it comes to women. He must've gotten it from his father."

And yes. There was Jenn, back from the mess hall with her coffee in hand, stopped short by the master sergeant's words, just outside of that curtain. Her eyes widened slightly as she looked over at Sheila, as the blonde laughed her musical laugh.

Oh, shit. Izzy stood up, uncertain of what to do.

Sheila was too busy flirting with Dan Gillman the elder, to notice Jenn standing there. Or maybe she was flirting with the younger Gillman, because she sent Danny a loaded little smile, too. "Don't I wish, but... No, I'm not. We're just... good friends. I'm a marine. We were stationed at the same base for a while. I was there when the sniper opened fire and I helped get Dan airlifted out."

Dan was too busy trying to incinerate his father with his eyes to notice either Sheila's suggestive pauses and smiles or Jenn.

"Well, doesn't *that* give a whole new meaning to *send in the Marines*," Dan's father said, but then he sobered. Figuratively. And took the opportunity to take Sheila's lovely hand. "Thank you for saving my son's life."

Sheila turned to Izzy. "It was actually Zanella who did the actual lifesaving, by sharing his blood," she said, spilling that very big secret, even as Danny talked over her.

"Oh, please." He spoke to his father—apparently he couldn't keep it in any longer. "You have some nerve, coming in here and—" But then he turned to Sheila. "What did you say?"

"No, that was Jenk," Izzy corrected her, trying to signal her with his eyes, but she wasn't looking at him.

"Yeah, that was, um, me," Jenk agreed.

Sheila laughed. "I was there. It was totally Zanella." But then she noticed the shock on Dan's face and the now-awkward silence in the room. She finally looked back at Izzy and then over to Jenk. "Was that . . . something I shouldn't have said?"

"It was *you*?" Dan asked Izzy. "What the *hell* . . . ? Did you actually think I would have a problem with that?" He turned and saw Jenn and included her in his disbelief. "What am I, a fucking child?"

"You watch your mouth in front of a lady," his father admonished, his focus still on Sheila.

Dan looked at the man. "You're fucking kidding me, right?"

The elder Dan bristled and even took a menacing step toward his son, and both Izzy and Jenk moved to intercept. Jenn, too, came farther into the room.

"Danny," she said, but Dan didn't hear her.

He was furious, and happy to take it out on his father, pushing himself so that he was sitting up. "Yeah, that's way more familiar, *Dad*. Go on and backhand a man in a hospital bed, that's just your speed. And since I'm not twelve anymore, it's the only way you'll come even *remotely* close to achieving contact." But then he turned to Izzy. "What the hell, Zanella?" he said again. "Did you seriously think I'd have some kind of sixth-grade problem with—"

"I didn't have a vote," Izzy protested. "I was kind of unconscious when the decision was made." But Jenn spoke over him, and he was happy to yield the floor to her.

"Okay," she said loudly. "This is definitely counterproductive. Danny, don't you dare get out of that bed. Your father is leaving." She motioned to Gillman the elder. "Come on, Master Sergeant. If you spoke to the doctor, then you know that what Dan needs right now is rest, not stress."

"I'm sorry, you're right, I didn't mean to..." Dan's father had already begun to retreat, but then he stopped. "I'm sorry, ma'am," he said, stiffly, politely, "but I was hoping to get a chance to meet Dan's girlfriend. I was wondering if you could—"

He cut himself off, no doubt because he'd finally taken the time to focus on Jenn and he saw that she wasn't in uniform.

"Oh," he said. "I'm sorry, I thought you were the nurse. Are you...?" Try as he might, he couldn't keep his incredulity from his voice or his face.

"Oh, good," Danny growled. "Insult my girlfriend."

"I didn't mean—" Dan senior started, even as Jenn quietly said, "Danny, it's all right."

"No, it's *not* all right," Danny said. "What does he think, he can just walk in here and pretend he gives a shit, and then turn around and look at you like that?" He turned to his father. "You met my girlfriend, now go."

"Call your family," Dan senior ground out. "They're worried about you."

"Danny," Jenn was saying, over his father's words, "*please* sit back. They're not going to let you go home if you..."

Izzy didn't hear the rest of her sentence, because he'd already nodded at Jenk, silently asking him to assist in clearing the room, even as he took Master Sergeant Gillman by the arm and led him out into the hallway and over to the elevators.

"I don't think we've officially met," Izzy said even as Gillman muttered, "Jesus, I fucked that up. What is wrong with me?"

"Besides twenty-five years of being an alcoholic?" Izzy asked. "Or...now I'm thinking you probably meant that as more of a rhetorical question, so I'll just stick to what I know." He held out his hand. "I'm Irving Zanella, petty officer first class, U.S. Navy SEALs. I'm a teammate of Dan's. I'm also your daughter Eden's husband. Dad."

"*You're* the asshole who knocked her up?"

"No," Izzy said, taking several hasty steps back, because it sure looked as if Dan-the-senior was going to follow the time-honored Gillman tradition of punching Izzy's face before getting the whole story. "I'm the guy who married her when she needed help, because some *other* guy knocked her up. Which makes me more of a loser than an asshole. At least according to, um, *my* definition..."

His father-in-law was looking at him like he was shit on a stick, so Izzy took a deep breath and asked the question he'd vowed he wouldn't ask ever again. "Have you heard from her lately? Eden? Is she doing okay?"

Dan was silent as Jenkins escorted Private S. Anderson and her little black dress out of his part of this hospital room, as Jenn pulled the curtain all the way over to the wall, giving them at least the illusion of privacy.

"For the record," she said as she sat in the chair down by the end of his bed instead of the one within arm's reach, which made his heart sink, "it was Jay Lopez's idea—to tell you that the blood was Jenk's."

"Lopez," Dan repeated.

"He was sure you were going to lose your leg, Danny, and he thought if you had any chance at all, it would be hindered, not helped, by the idea that you'd received such a huge transfusion from Izzy. Who, by the way, was the only one whose faith in you never wavered." She paused. "Besides me."

"It's sobering," he said quietly. "To see myself through that lens. I mean, it's crazy to think that Lopez was right, but... Lopez was probably right. Fuckin' Zanella. He makes me..." He laughed his self-disgust. "And then I go and double down on the crazy by being unable to keep from turning back into a twelve-year-old when my father comes to visit." He shook his head, wishing he could rewind and take a do-over, ashamed not just because she'd witnessed his childish behavior, but also because he hadn't pushed aside the stupidity and focused on what was important—not allowing his freaking girlfriend to get emotionally stomped by his asshole father. Forget about Sheila, and what Jenn must've thought by seeing her there, dressed up like that. "I'm so sorry, Jenni."

She gazed back at him, and he knew she absolutely hadn't forgotten about Sheila—who was she, why had she come to visit him? The questions were in her eyes. But she didn't ask, and Dan knew she wouldn't. She was too much of a class act. She would just bury her doubts, but they'd always be back there, eating away at her. He knew that, too.

So he broached the topic. Just flat out. "Private S. Anderson," he said. "I didn't get a chance to properly introduce you, but frankly, I didn't even know her name was Sheila until today. I met her pulling civilians out of a bus, after the car bomb exploded." He gave her the full story, including the fact that Private Anderson had been a little flirty when they'd first met, including the fact that he hadn't quite known how to respond, and that, yes, he'd been flattered. He told her that the flirting had stopped, though, when Anderson—he purposely called her by her last name—had been up to her elbows in his blood, applying pressure to his wound as Izzy went to get aid.

Jenn sat and listened and nodded. "Thank God she was there." And then she said, "I ran into your doctor while I was getting coffee. Your latest blood test came back clear."

That was great news. Almost as good as the fact that Jenn apparently considered Sheila a nonproblem, not worthy of further discussion.

"They're willing to think about sending you home," Jenn continued, "as long as you stick to the no-exertion rule and don't overdo it." She smiled ruefully. "I was, like, *You* do *know he's a SEAL*...? The captain actually laughed—I think we may have finally bonded."

Jenn's opinion of the doctor's humorless bedside manner was pretty low, but he spent most of his days in surgery, performing amputations on soldiers and servicemen and -women who hadn't been as lucky as Dan.

Lucky—to have a teammate like Zanella. Jesus, Dan still couldn't wrap his brain around that.

"But he agreed that it would be a good idea to release you, *if* you had somewhere to stay," Jenn went on with a caveat, "with someone who made sure you got the rest you need...?" She cleared her throat. "It occurred to me that, well, Mark Jenkins and his wife have a spare room. I know she's pregnant—Lindsey. But she's still working, and since Mark's got a cast on, that first week he's home might...Well, I thought it would be worth asking them if you could..."

"Oh," Dan said, then cleared his throat, too. "I thought, I don't know, I guess I just assumed we'd...go back to New York? Together?"

And yes, he was definitely feeling much, much better, because the hard-on that he'd awakened to find after his nap was back with a vengeance at the mere *idea* of being alone with Jenn in a place that had solid walls and a door that locked. It had been a long time, but he still knew exactly, precisely what it felt like to be inside of her. And he desperately wanted some of that. ASAP.

"I didn't want to assume," she said quietly.

Seriously?

"May I come stay with you in New York?" he asked. "Please say yes, and then go *run* and get your buddy Captain Chan to release me tonight."

Jenn's smile was a little sad. She didn't speak, didn't move. She just looked at him.

But she'd come all the way from New York City to sit beside his bed, and Danny knew that he'd won whatever battle they'd been fighting over their relationship. Hell, he'd won the freaking war. He'd scored the telling victory over two weeks ago when he'd opened his eyes to see her standing there. She loved him, too. She could no longer deny it.

And Jesus, he liked winning, despite the fact that the responsibility scared the shit out of him.

He held out his hand for her now, and she came over and took it.

"I need you, Jenn," he admitted, even though it was harder than hell for him to put voice to those words. Fighting the rush of emotions that threatened to clog his throat, he asked her again, "May I stay with you in New York for a while?"

This time she nodded. "Of course."

Eden was in Las Vegas, which was the last place on earth Izzy would've thought to look for her.

As he input the cell number and address that her father gave him directly into his phone, he was aware of Jenkins hovering at his elbow, the shorter SEAL's trepidation nearly palpable.

"It's probably better if you don't tell her you gave this to me," Izzy told the senior Gillman as he double-checked his entry for *Zanella, Eden*, with the info that the man had scribbled on a piece of cocktail napkin, no doubt when his daughter had called him.

"Just pass it along to Dan and tell him to call her," the older Dan said as he got into an elevator going down to the lobby. To the lobby and then out into the parking lot, into his car and off the base, over to town, to the nearest bar...Did any of them really have any serious doubt about his destination? "And I'll have done far more than I promised her I'd do."

The elevator doors closed behind him and Izzy waited a few seconds before pressing the down button himself.

"Zanella," Jenk said. They'd been friends a long time—ever since Izzy saved his life. Gee, maybe Jenkins and Gillman should start a club. Lopez could join, too, along with Tony V., after that incident in Thailand. "I'm not going to tell you what to do."

"Good," Izzy said. "Don't."

"But I do think you need to slow down. Take a deep breath—"

"How is that not telling me what to do?" Izzy asked.

"Just stop and think," Jenk said as the elevator door opened again with a *ding*. "At least figure out what you're going to say before you get there."

"I'll do that," Izzy said. "On the plane." He handed the scrap of paper to Jenk and got into the elevator. "Give that to Dan. Make sure he calls to tell Eden he's all right."

"Iz," Jenk said plaintively as the doors slid closed.

Izzy stopped them with his hand and they sprang open again. "I just want to see her," he told his friend. "You know, talk to her? In person? I know she's done with me and I'm . . . I'm done with her, too."

"You're not acting like it, bro," Jenk said.

"I know," Izzy said. "But I'm just going to keep saying that to myself and . . . maybe by the time I get there, it'll be true, and I can, I don't know, have some kind of closure."

The elevator starting ringing—he'd held the door open for too long.

"You want me to come with you?" Jenk asked, even though he must've said forty times in the past five hours just how psyched he was to get back home to see his adorable pregnant wife. "Let me come with you."

"Thanks," Izzy said as he let the doors close. "But no."

"Call if you need me," was the last thing he heard before the elevator took him down.

LAS VEGAS
TUESDAY, MAY 5, 2009

Eden's cell phone finally rang in the early hours of the morning, long after Ben had fallen asleep in her bedroom, exhausted by the medically and emotionally taxing day.

It wasn't her father, but it was someone else, calling from Germany. She recognized the country code. She closed her eyes and said a brief prayer before flipping it open.

"Hello?"

"Eden. It's Dan."

It was her brother's voice. It was her brother calling. "Oh, dear Lord," she said. "Oh, thank you, *thank* you for calling me. Thank God you're all right." But then she realized that just because he was able to dial a phone, that didn't mean he wasn't horribly maimed. "There was this letter saying that you were wounded, and Ben and I were so scared and... *Are* you all right?"

"Yeah, I'm fine," he told her. "I'm getting out of the hospital tomorrow morning and... Sorry if I frightened you. Is Ivette there?"

Like Eden and Ben, Danny, too, called their mother by her first name.

"I'm not... I don't live with her," Eden told him. "In fact, she and Greg don't even know I'm back in town. I came because Ben..." And the relief that filled her over the news that Dan was okay triggered some kind of release, and it all came out of her, in one giant rush, even as she lowered her voice to keep from waking Ben. "Oh, Danny, he said he kicked Greg's ass yesterday, but you should see the bruises he got. He was trying to hide them, but he changed his shirt and... That man is a monster and a freak, and Ben says he's not going back, and I'm not going to make him, how could I? Especially when they keep saying they're going to send him to one of those reparative therapy camps? They have him scheduled to go to this awful place in June, but what if Greg sends him someplace earlier after this? I'm trying to earn enough money to hire a lawyer so I can get custody of him, but I'm afraid if I break the law it's going to make things worse—" She broke off, realizing that this was the last thing he needed. He was still in the *hospital,* and she was dumping all of this on him like a little whining girl. "I'm sorry. It's just... This is harder than I thought."

There was silence on the other end of the phone.

"But I'm handling it," Eden said, forcing back her tears. She would not cry. She *would* not cry.

There was more silence, but then Dan sighed. "Shit," he said.

"I'm sorry," Eden said again. She took a deep breath. "The truth is, I *could* use a little help—well, okay, a lot of help—but before you say no, I'm not asking you to come all the way out here to save us. That's not what this is about. In fact, I'll come to you so we can talk. Ben and I'll take the bus to San Diego—"

"I'm not going to San Diego," he told her. "After I'm released I'm going to New York City for at least a week."

It was Eden's turn to be silent.

"How come Ben didn't e-mail me?" Dan asked, and it was kind of nice, because he was asking the question in a regular voice, as if they were having a normal conversation between a brother and a sister. It wasn't some kind of dysfunctional shouting match, the way it usually was when they spoke.

"He did. A few weeks ago," she answered him, in the same conversational tone. "We figured you were, you know. Out there. Busy." She forced a laugh. "Which apparently you were. Getting yourself injured. I *am* sorry about that..."

More silence. And then he said, "I didn't know it was that bad with Ben. I knew it was getting to that point, but I didn't think...I thought I'd have more time."

"Me, too," Eden said. "But...I can't let him go back there. To have to live in that house with Greg? Really, Danny. And I've been reading about those ex-gay camps..."

"Yeah," Dan said. "I know. I have, too."

And hope sparked. So Eden groveled. "I would never ask you this if it was just about me," she said quietly. "I hope you know that. I know I've used up all your patience and...Financially, I've...Pushed you too far. I know that. And I'm okay. I'm working. I have a job. I'm doing better than okay. I'm making enough to support Ben, too—and to pay you back everything that I've ever borrowed from you, but...You know that Ivette will never let Ben live with me. Not unless"—she closed her eyes and just said it—"you said you lived with us, too. In San Diego. Of course."

Danny was their mother's pride and joy. Captain Perfect. The offspring who could do no wrong. Of course, it didn't hurt that he still sent a huge chunk of his pay home every month.

He was silent again on the end of the line, all the way across both the continent and the Atlantic Ocean, where it was much later in the day than it was here.

But whatever time it was in Germany, Eden could hear him breathing.

"Look," he finally said. "I'm going to have to call you back. I'll call you soon, okay?"

"Yeah," Eden said, then quickly added, "Dan, wait..." before he could hang up.

"I'm still here."

"Thank you," she told her brother. "Even for just *thinking* about doing this for us. Thank you so much."

"Yeah," he said, his voice gruff before he hung up.

LANDSTUHL, GERMANY
TUESDAY, MAY 5, 2009

"Shit," Dan said again after hanging up the phone.

"Trouble?" Jenn asked, and he nodded, glancing up only briefly to meet her eyes, before looking down again at the cell phone he held in his hands.

Something was cooking in that big brain of his—something that was making the muscles jump in the side of his jaw and his elegant lips set in a tight line.

"Is Ben okay?" she asked, and this time when Danny looked up at her, there was a flash of what seemed to be annoyance or even anger in his eyes.

Which was, in part, what made his next words so surprising.

"Marry me," he said.

Jenn laughed, but then stopped, because it was clear that he wasn't making some kind of crazy joke. He was serious.

Her breath caught and both her throat and chest were suddenly tight as tears stung her eyes—but not in a good way. Not in an *Oh my God, I can't believe this, I'm so happy I could cry* way.

"Danny," she said quietly. "That's not the solution."

"But it is," he told her, and he actually meant it. His conviction was impressive. "Of all the places in the world where Ben could live, where he would thrive and be happy, New York City's got to be in the top three. And yeah, I know it wouldn't be the easiest thing. Instantly having a teenage kid to deal with. I know it's asking a lot. Plus, it's expensive to live there, I get that—"

"Whoa," Jenn said. "Wait. What? You want Ben to live with *me*, in New York City...?"

His brown eyes were dead serious. "With us," he corrected her.

"Except you'd be stationed in..." Where were the SEALs stationed on the East Coast? Virginia, wasn't it? "Little Creek?"

Danny was shaking his head. "No—hell, no! Wow, I'd never ask you to... Jenni, I'm talking about leaving the teams. It's coming up on that time again, but I just won't re-up."

She was stunned. "Oh, my God."

"You really thought... Jesus, I wouldn't ask you to do that, any more than I'd ask you to move to San Diego. You work in New York. You have a life there."

"What about *your* life?" she asked.

He looked away from her so that she wouldn't be able to see that he was lying. "I'm ready for a change."

Jenn just sat there, gazing at him, until he looked up.

"I knew this was coming," he insisted. "I've been thinking about it for a while. Even before I met you." He winced. "And I didn't mean it the way it sounded—like I was thinking of the best way to handle this, so I was looking for someone to marry, to help me take care of Ben. Believe me, if I was looking for easy solutions, I'd've found someone who lived in San Diego."

"I think you're wonderful," she told him, "to want to do this for Ben, but there's got to be another way. What about your sister?" Not Eden, the other one. The older one. What was her name? "Sandy."

"She's a nightmare," Dan told her. "I can't count on her for anything."

"Your older brothers...?" He told her, in one of his many e-mails, that Ivette was his father's second wife, that he'd had two sons from a previous marriage—John and Christopher. Dan had spent the occasional weekend with them when he was growing up—they'd taught him to hunt and fish. But they'd also dropped off the map when his father and Ivette divorced. He hadn't seen either of them in years. "Maybe this would be a good time to get back in touch."

But Dan shook his head. "They hated us. They blamed Ivette for wrecking their family. I didn't get it when I was a kid, but now...? I do. And since Ben's not even related to them..."

"Okay. Eden, then. It sounded like Eden had some kind of a plan."

"Yeah," Dan said. "She wants us to get an apartment together in San Diego—her, Ben, and me." He shook his head. "I couldn't live with her. I couldn't."

"But you could stay in the Navy, if you did that," Jenn pointed out. She leaned forward. "Ben's what? Fifteen?"

Dan nodded.

"It's only three years until he's eighteen, and then your life's your own again," she told him. "Three years isn't that long a time—especially considering you'll be away for a large portion of it."

"So...Is that a *no* to marrying me?"

Jenn smiled at him through that tightness that just wouldn't leave her chest. "It's a *no* to being a part of your not-particularly-well-thought-out-but-very-gallant sacrifice. I mean, even if you had to leave the Navy, you and Ben could come to New York. You don't have to marry me to do that."

"I guess I was thinking, you know, if there's a custody fight . . . ?"

"From everything you told me, your mother adores you," Jenn said. "She's going to let Ben live with you. It's hard to believe she won't."

"She does what Greg tells her to," Dan said. "He might start a custody battle as a way to hit me up for more money."

Jenn stood up. "I'm going to call Maria." Her boss and best friend, a New York State assemblywoman, was also a lawyer. "See what she thinks."

She started to dig in her purse for her cell phone, when Dan reached out and caught her by the belt loop on her jeans. He pulled her in and down so that she was sitting on the edge of his bed.

"I didn't mean to come on too strong," he told her. "I just thought—"

"That you didn't have options," Jenn finished for him. "But you do. We'll talk to Maria."

But she could see both doubt and trepidation in Danny's eyes, even as he tried to smile. "I could do three years," he said. "For Ben's sake. Provided you promise to spend every vacation with me—and invited me to crash at your place in New York anytime Eden drives me crazy. And provided you're right and I don't have to be married to get custody."

She kissed him. "I'll do better than that," she said. "If I'm wrong about the custody thing, and it comes down to it? I'll marry you. Because I could also do three years. And I could do it in San Diego, too."

"I'd never ask you to do that," he said again.

"I know," Jenn told him, pushing his hair back from his face. "But that doesn't mean I can't offer." She kissed him again, then reached for her phone. "Let me call Maria. Because I also need to tell her that I'm taking that extra week off." Maria had told her to take as long as she needed, and Jenn definitely needed.

Because she and Dan were going to Vegas.

LAS VEGAS
TUESDAY, MAY 5, 2009

Neesha veered sharply left, into a clothing store where music played much too loudly, whether it was morning or evening. She went all the way to the rear of the store before she dared to glance back, out at the food court and...

The two men leaning against the wall hadn't moved. They weren't looking over here. Their body language hadn't changed at all.

One was keeping an eye on the tables, the other was looking down at his cell phone.

They were standing in the very spot—more dimly lit than the rest of the mall—next to the barbecue counter, where she usually stopped and pretended to fix her shoe because from that vantage point, she could quickly scan the entire food court and make sure she saw no familiar faces—of Mr. Nelson or Todd or another of his goons—in the crowd.

She moved closer to the store's entrance, wishing she had the confidence to pretend she was shopping—to grab some of the shiny hangers that held pretty, brightly colored clothing, and carry them around to the front of the store as she checked every single rack.

But she was terrified of being accused of stealing—shoplifting, it was called. And even though the store was filled with girls who were even younger than she was, they each had a mother with them, and the clerks didn't look at them askance.

Still, the two men who were searching for someone—that much was clear—didn't so much as glance in her direction, so she shifted closer, hoping for a better look at their faces.

Not that she knew each and every one of Mr. Nelson's guards, but she did know quite a few.

Neesha moved behind a rack of dresses just to the left of the entrance and peeked out.

No, she didn't think she knew them. They were both tall and

broad—both with faces that were called white, even though they weren't really. The one with the cell phone was bald, with a beard that decorated only part of his chin.

The other man wore a hat covering his hair despite the day's heat, and sunglasses hiding his eyes despite the fact that the sun was long gone. It was hard to see his face, but he had a tattoo that came up out of his shirt collar, on his neck and even up onto part of his cheek.

She'd seen a lot of tattoos, and would have remembered seeing that one before.

Maybe they *weren't* looking for her.

Still, she stayed where she was, watching them, even though her stomach rumbled with hunger, even though one of the suspicious clerks positioned herself nearby and folded shirts with barely con-cealed hostility.

And then it happened. The man with the sunglasses nudged the bald man with his elbow, and gestured across the food court with his chin.

The bald man pocketed his phone and led the way toward . . .

Ben.

At first glance, the boy looked a lot like him—tall and thin with dark hair and a pale face, black shirt, and jeans.

But it wasn't Ben. This boy walked awkwardly, clumsily. Ben flowed when he moved. He had a grace to him that reminded Neesha of one of the dancers she'd watched on TV.

This boy also was part of a pack. He was with four other boys, al-though they all backed away when they realized the bald man and the sunglasses-wearer were heading directly toward him.

"You," the bald man said as he pointed at the boy who looked like Ben, his voice carrying, even across the still-crowded food court. "Don't move. Las Vegas police. We have some questions we want to ask you."

Police? Could they really be police? Neesha watched, and sure enough, they both flashed what could have been badges, like the cops did on *NYPD Blue*.

She couldn't hear any of the questions, all she could see was the boy's fear as the bald man took him by the arm and pulled him ever farther from his friends, but closer to her. He kept shaking his head. No. Over and over again. Rapidly. Vehemently. No.

And then both men looked up, and Neesha saw, too—it was the security guard who'd approached her and Ben while he was being hassled by that teen pack, outside of the coffee shop. He was coming toward them now, and she could hear his words as he spoke. He had that kind of voice. Higher-pitched and easy to hear over the din of other conversations.

"That's not him."

The bald man let go of the boy, said something Neesha couldn't hear, and the boy ran off.

"Don't run in the mall," the man in the guard uniform called after him, but the boy ignored him. In fact all five boys disappeared very quickly, heading for the main entrance. He laughed. "I guess you scared him."

And now the bald man and the sunglasses man shook hands with the guard—as if they were introducing themselves. As if they hadn't met before this.

In fact, Neesha heard the guard say, "Nice to meet you, Nathan. Jake."

And the bald man—Jake—drew something from his jacket pocket. It was a piece of paper that he opened like a birthday card. He showed whatever was inside of it to the guard, who was nodding. Yes.

And his voice again carried to Neesha.

"That's definitely the girl I saw here yesterday."

CHAPTER
SEVEN
Las Vegas
Wednesday, 6 May 2009

C losure.

Maybe seeing Eden again *would* give him closure.

Izzy clung to that thought as he maneuvered his piece-of-shit rental car into the steady stream of traffic heading away from the airport and toward the glittering city of pipe dreams and false promises.

There were three kinds of people who made the pilgrimage to Vegas: desperate souls searching for salvation and an easy fix to their financial woes, and desperate souls hell-bent on escaping their humdrum little lives and an easy fix to their financial woes.

Izzy had always taken the third approach, coming to the city with a limited amount of cash in his pocket, ready and willing and expecting to lose it all in exchange for some serious entertainment and a short respite from his responsibilities. He usually ended up bringing home more than he'd left with, even after staying in a nice hotel, eating some truly exceptional meals, and drinking copious amounts of beer. And he'd also usually always gotten laid in the process, sharing his happy-fun-time with some equally carefree young lady who'd been brainwashed into believing that hedonistic and incredibly inspired ad campaign — *What happens in Vegas, stays in Vegas.*

Except the last time Izzy was here, he'd gotten married.

And maybe the slogan was true, because the relationship didn't last long outside of the city limits. And here he was, not even a year later, back again, because his wife—soon-to-be-ex-wife—had come home.

She hadn't returned to her literal home, as in the structure where her mother and evil stepfather still resided, and Izzy was grateful for that. If he had discovered from Eden's father that she'd moved back into the house where he'd once found her locked in the bathroom by her stepfather Greg, with no food, trapped there for hours...

Izzy would've been driving a whole lot faster right now. That was for sure.

As it was, he took his time, because he still hadn't figured out what he wanted to say to Eden when he saw her again. And Jenkins was right. He shouldn't wing it. He should go in at least with the talking points highlighted in his mind.

1. Why did you leave like that, without saying good-bye? Do you have even the slightest clue what it felt like to walk into that apartment and find you gone? Erased from my life, vanished without a trace. And okay, I'll cut you miles of slack on this one, because Pinkie'd died and you couldn't have been thinking clearly in the days and weeks that followed.

2. But why did you refuse to see me in Germany, month after month after motherfrakking month? Didn't I deserve at least a *little* respect and the common courtesy of the words *I need more time alone* coming directly from your mouth, instead of your friend Anya's? At some point, the grieving process has to allow for at least occasional moments of rational thought over knee-jerk urges. And okay, I've never lost a baby, but I lost a good friend and I still miss him. I always will. His death changed me, irrevocably. But *time heals all wounds* is the cliché that it is because it's true. And the pain changes into something that's not so unbearable—a little at first, and then more and more, and yet you still made Anya send me away, and I don't know why.

3. Did you ever think, even once, that maybe Pinkie's dying

might've hurt me, too? That I might've needed some help and comfort in dealing with the loss? That maybe we could have helped each other, held on to one another, gotten through it together...? And maybe the answer to this one is no, you didn't think about me at all, because you never gave a shit about me. I was just some schmuck you took advantage of—a loser who gave you and your unborn child food and shelter and health care. And as soon as you didn't need those things, you couldn't get away from me fast enough, could you?

4. But if you hate me so much, or if there's something about me that repulses you so completely, then why the *hell* did you try so hard to get with me during those weeks we were together? Because that is some seriously twisted shit, sweetheart. I made it clear that I wanted to keep sex separate from our matrimonial deal. I told you over and over that my help was not contingent on anyone going down on anyone else. But you worked it, over-time, to make our relationship be all about how badly we both wanted my dick inside of you, until it finally happened. And I just can't wrap my brain or my ego around the idea that you didn't honestly want it as much as I did.

5. Maybe I just want you to look me in the eye and tell me to my face that it was all a fucking lie. That there wasn't a single real, honest moment between us...

Izzy's cell phone had GPS, and he used it now to navigate his way to the apartment building where Eden was living. He drove around the block and then pulled to a stop slightly down the street so he could sit and look and not be noticed.

The building was pretty nice. It was a two-story complex with the apartment doors opening into a center courtyard with a lush garden. There were two entrances into the place—one from a parking lot that was off to one side, and the other from this street. There were probably sixty or seventy apartments or condos altogether.

Eden was in 214—up on that second floor.

Izzy scanned the second-floor windows that faced the street. All but one had blinds that were tightly closed. The one that was open had flowers—bright red—sitting on the sill. But really, 214 could have been around the other side, overlooking the parking lot.

It was stupid to sit here speculating whether that apartment was where Eden was living, when he could figure it out quickly enough by going into the courtyard and looking up at the layout of the second floor.

So he got out of the car, locking the doors behind him. And he approached the entrance to the courtyard on foot.

The early-morning sun was hot on the back of his neck—the day was looking to be a scorcher. Not a big surprise since the city was in the middle of the flipping desert.

There weren't many other people out. A dark-haired girl sitting on a bus-stop bench, across the street. An old lady walking an equally ancient dog. A man in a suit in a hurry, talking on a cell phone.

This part of town wasn't terrible, but it wasn't particularly great, either. Still, the building seemed much nicer than what he'd expected her to be able to afford and—Shit!

It was Eden. She was less than ten yards away from him, coming out of the complex's entrance, dressed in jeans and a T-shirt, sneakers on her feet, hair up in a ponytail, with a big, slouchy bag over her shoulder. She was moving fast, and she picked up her pace as she saw that a bus was coming, heading downtown along the busy street.

Izzy quickly turned away to hide his face, but it wouldn't have mattered if he hadn't, because she was so totally focused on booking it to the bus stop on the corner.

He stood there, dumbstruck at the sight of her. She was solid and real and not just the figment of his overheated imagination, the focus of his dreams—both fantasy and nightmares. She looked healthy and trim—back to her pre-pregnancy weight—and dressed the way she was, she looked like a college student, rushing off to class.

It was only when the bus pulled away from the curb with a noisy squeal of air brakes that the spell was broken.

And Izzy ran for his car, determined to follow and find out where, exactly, Eden was in such a hurry to go this early in the morning.

Neesha watched from across the street as the very tall man with the shaggy hair, angular features, and very broad shoulders jumped into a tiny car and peeled out, following the bus.

Following Ben's sister Eden.

He wasn't one of the two men who'd been searching for her at the food court last night, but that didn't mean he didn't work for Mr. Nelson or Todd. The way he'd moved when Eden had come out of her apartment building had been pure subterfuge. He hadn't wanted Eden to see him, to know he was there, and so she hadn't.

Neesha sat on the bench, afraid to move, afraid that someone else was watching, even now.

She'd come here this morning to warn Ben—to tell him not to go back to the mall, to make sure he didn't get hurt.

But now she didn't dare climb the stairs to the second floor and knock on his door—or even use the key that he'd pulled out from beneath a potted plant in the courtyard downstairs. She didn't dare to do anything—except dig out the last of the money Ben had given her and board the bus when it finally arrived, and ride it into the city, where she could lose herself in the crowds.

Wishing she were brave enough—and ashamed that she wasn't.

And knowing with a growing sense of dread that she wouldn't be safe until she got well out of town—and that she wouldn't get out of town without a whole lot of cash.

Izzy pulled over to the curb in a loading zone, just down the street from D'Amato's, where Eden had gone in the back door. It was, as the signage proclaimed, a GENTLEMAN'S CLUB where LIVE HOT GIRLS danced, i.e. stripped, 24/7!

It shouldn't have surprised him. And on one level, it didn't. There weren't many jobs anywhere for someone with Eden's lack of education to earn more than minimum wage. And there was no way she could have afforded an apartment in that relatively uncrappy part of town on even eighty hours a week of minimum wage.

At least not without her fucking some guy so he'd help pay the bills.

And okay, that was harsh, but true. Although the fact that she was working here probably meant that she *hadn't* hooked up with anyone new—and yeah. That was just wishful thinking on his part.

Eden Gillman was not the kind of woman who went for very long without a man in her life, and Izzy well knew it. Maybe being reminded of that would help him find closure—his seeing the low-life scum that she let into her bed instead of him. Or maybe he didn't need to see the guy. Maybe he just needed to know his name.

Izzy took a deep breath and then he took another, even as his mind continued to race.

Maybe she was a waitress here, because the signs also boasted GOOD FOOD, but no. A woman as beautiful as Eden didn't work carrying trays in a place like this.

He knew he should drive away—just put the pedal to the metal of this rental car—all the way back to San Diego, where he could start the ball rolling on getting that divorce.

But he pulled the car into the club's valet-only VIP parking lot instead, and tossed the attendant his keys, because he was hungry and he wanted breakfast and the freaking place allegedly had good food, so why the hell not?

Probably because he was feeling distinctly out-of-body as he walked around to the street-side entrance of the strip club. He'd found, from past experiences, that that was never a good sign. Still, his feet took him toward D'Amato's heavy wooden door.

The location was a seedy one. Yes, the sidewalks were clean, having recently been hosed down—a luxury not every establishment paid for, here in the land of scarce water. And the club was near some of the bigger conference hotels and no doubt had some relatively upscale patrons. And sure enough, there was a sign by the door advertising a convention breakfast special—two eggs over easy, arranged like a pair of breasts atop a mound—their word—of corned-beef hash Mexicali. Served with Erma's Cloud Nine potatoes and choice of toast and juice and a bottomless cup of coffee. All for $7.99; $12.99 if you wanted a bottomless mimosa or Bloody Mary.

What a fucking awesome deal.

Plus, any charges that showed up on your credit card would no doubt read *D'Amato's*, instead of, oh, say, *the Pussycat Lounge*. Just in case either the boss or the wife objected to breakfast meetings held in strip clubs.

But the area was peppered with "massage parlors." And Izzy had absolutely no doubt that—should he request the service—for a slightly larger tip, the valet would set him up with a hooker to hoover him, right there in his car, in the parking lot.

Izzy opened the door and went inside, nodding to the gargantuan bouncer who stood near the entrance. Guy was former Marine Recon—he'd had his unit's patch tattooed onto his tree trunk of an arm. Either that, or his boyfriend was the marine and was currently active duty, over in A-stan. Probably not, but the modern world was full of surprises and not all of them were unpleasant ones.

Just some of them.

Izzy paused for a moment to let his eyes adjust to the sudden severe drop in light and to get his bearings.

The place was set up like almost every other strip joint around the world. There was table seating in front of a small center stage, which in this place was the lowest point in the club. There were also runways, like spokes on a wheel, leading out into the main floor, with up-close-if-not-quite-personal seating around them for those who were there not to partake of the "good food" but only to drink and ogle girls who pole-danced for their supper.

Four different tiers, each higher than the last, created a stadium-seating effect. And it was clear that proximity to the stage was a pricier experience than sitting up in the cheap seats, even though the higher level gave patrons a clear shot of the poles and various other dancing surfaces. But down front, the tables were large and bore white cloths. As the altitude rose, the tables grew significantly smaller and were topped with plastic. Here in the back, they were positioned much closer together, too.

A bar was along the rear wall, up on this highest level. And because this was Nevada, there was also the obligatory row of slot machines, and even a blackjack table off to one side.

And oh, look. There was a handicapped ramp so that physically challenged patrons could get their wheelchairs from the upper levels down to the main floor. How very PC.

Of course, making sure there were clear and easy-to-access aisles to that main floor was of paramount importance to the dancers. They earned tips from the myriad of patrons who wanted to see their naked bodies from a closer vantage point, and experience the thrill of slipping a dollar bill against that unattainable smooth skin. There were three generous aisles in the place, the rug-covered surfaces worn bare by the constant traffic.

It was cool and windowless and smelled half like a frat-house base-ment and half like a damn good diner—the "good food" advertisement seemed to be true. Which meant that the "Live Hot Girls" sign was probably correct as well, even though there were currently no girls, hot or other, anywhere to be found.

In fact the girl who was coming toward him now, wearing a wait-ress apron over a stained white blouse and carrying a tray filled with plates of eggs and pancakes and a pot of coffee, hadn't been a girl for forty years. She was definitely hot, though. Izzy could see beads of sweat standing out on her forehead.

"Sit wherever you want," she honked at him in her three-pack-a-day voice. "Don't worry, the dancers will be out soon. They're having a staff meeting."

A *staff* meeting? Seriously?

He sat all the way in the back, in the shadows, as his stomach churned with anticipation and dread. His hunger was long gone—if it had ever actually existed. Up at this altitude the breakfast menu was printed onto the place mat that was on the table, which was pretty smart since Izzy wasn't keen on touching a menu that any of the club's other cheap-seats patrons had handled. And that was saying something because his gross-out factor was usually quite high.

The waitress approached. "What'll it be, hon?"

"The special, please," he said, because he knew he had to eat something. "Orange juice, whole-wheat toast—dry. Coffee, black and ASAP. And just out of curiosity, do the dancers often have staff meetings?"

"Only when there's a new girl, causing trouble," she told him darkly, taking a mug from another table, setting it in front of him and filling it with coffee from that pot on her tray.

"Trouble?" he repeated, making it a question.

"Really just learning the ropes," she said. "Some of the older girls get jealous, particularly when the new girl is as pretty as Jenny is."

"The new girl's name is *Jenny?*" Izzy asked.

"Jennilyn LeMay is her stage name," she said, and he almost fell out of his chair. The woman snorted. "God only knows her real name."

God and Izzy. Because there was no way on earth that a stripper with Dan's girlfriend's name coincidentally worked at the same club with Dan's sister. It was a move that was pure Eden, because in truth? Although Izzy would never say this to Dan—even he wasn't *that* stupid—Jennilyn LeMay was one kick-ass stripper name. And Eden clearly never imagined that anyone—especially her brother—would ever find out where she earned her weekly paycheck. So why not use his gf's awesome name as an alias?

It would have been funny except Izzy seemed to have left his sense of humor in the rental car.

"Thank you," he made the effort to tell the waitress, but she was already beelining it toward the kitchen, to put his order in.

Leaving him to sit there, clutching his coffee mug, waiting with his heart in his throat for his wife to come out on that stage and take off her clothes.

He didn't want to think about what this was that he was feeling, this turmoil of adrenaline-laced emotion.

And then he didn't have to think because the music started—the heavy funk beat of "Brickhouse"—nice choice. And there they came—out onto the stage and runways.

He found Eden immediately. She was over to the left, but in the front, next to a blond Amazon, and she deserved to be there—of course, he'd always thought she was the most beautiful woman on the planet.

She was wearing outrageously high fuck-me heels that sparkled in the stage lights, and a tight skirt that could've been part of a bathing suit, it was so small. It hugged her hips, leaving her stomach and midriff bare, exposing a sculptured mix of muscles and soft female curves and a tattoo that peeked out from the skirt's top, that no doubt covered the scar from the C-section that had saved her life all those months ago. The bottom edge of the skirt barely covered the panties she wore beneath it, and as she turned around, moving in vaguely unison steps with the other dancers as she circled one of the poles, he saw that the skirt intentionally didn't cover her world-class derriere. And yeah, as if to illustrate, she bent over with her long, shapely legs spread wide in another choreographed bump-and-grind move, and it was more than clear that the piece of clothing—if you could call it that—she wore beneath that skirt was a thong.

Her full breasts were covered by a halter top that fastened in the back and around her neck, tied in big loops that would be easy to undo, when the time came.

Her dark hair was loose around her shoulders and it gleamed and bounced as she moved her head, as Izzy shifted in his seat to see past the waitress who'd returned with his breakfast.

It was then that the entire group of dancers simultaneously lost the bulk of their clothing.

It was an amazing effect—the lights changed and the music got louder—and Eden instantly shed both the skirt and that top. It happened so fast, if he'd blinked or been distracted by the appearance of his corned-beef hash and eggs, he would've missed it.

She would've just appeared to be suddenly, dazzlingly nearly naked as she wrapped one long leg around that pole and moved to the music as the early-morning crowd woke up and roared their approval.

But because Izzy was watching her closely, he saw how it had happened. The skirt unfastened at her hips, the top opened between her breasts and slipped down her arms. She tossed both costume pieces to one of the waitresses on the floor as the entire group of women broke choreography and went into doing their own thing.

Eden's thing was all about the men who clustered around her runway. She gave them eye contact and plenty of smiles as she ran her hands across her own perfect body—touching where she damn well knew that every man in that room wanted to touch. Her neck, her shoulders, her arms. Her breasts, her stomach, and lower, and then down the smooth insides of her thighs... She watched them, smiling the entire time. But her smile didn't look at all calculating or manipulative. It was somehow inclusive—part very bad girl, absolutely, but also part sweet young thing—eager to please.

And the crowd ate it up.

Izzy exhaled hard as he watched her work, his food growing cold in front of him. She'd always been good at turning the sex up to an eleven whenever anyone male was around. He'd thought it was dangerous, the way she did that, her total *you know you want me* attitude—but she was now clearly making good money from it.

It was also clear that there were regulars who'd come specifically to see her. She spoke to them as she danced, bending close to let them slip dollar bills between the strap of her thong and what Izzy knew firsthand to be the smooth softness of her skin. They held the bills out before they reached for her, and he knew they were showing her their denomination. It was clear she didn't accept anything lower than a five or maybe even a ten. Or shit. A twenty. Why not, right?

He stood up, his breakfast untouched, and pulled a ten from his wallet and dropped it on the table to pay for his meal.

Izzy didn't have all that much cash left—maybe a hundred twenty dollars, tops—but he took the rest of it out and headed toward the lower floor of the club.

It was stupid. He knew he should just walk away, walk out the door. But he'd come this far. And he finally knew what he wanted to say— what it was that he wanted to ask her.

So he worked his way through the crowd to the edge of the runway where she was defying gravity around that pole. Up close, her skin was even more beautiful, her breasts full and tightly peaked from the relentless air-conditioning. Or maybe the way she was dancing was turning her on.

It sure as shit was working for him. Or it would be working, if he weren't close to overwhelmed by a wave of sadness that swept through him.

Was this closure?

God, he hoped so.

Up close, Izzy saw a whole lot more of that tattoo she'd chosen— a swirl of hearts and roses in an intricate design—to cover the scar left when Pinkie's already deceased little body had been plucked from her, in an effort to keep her from dying, too.

And as he looked up from that scar, past the enticing swell of her breasts and into that face that he hadn't seen in months—except in his dreams...

Eden glanced down and saw him, too.

Her eyes widened, and she froze. She just stopped dancing as a myriad of emotions flickered across her face. Shock. Disbelief. Horror. She drew her arms up as if to cover her naked breasts, which was actually kind of funny.

Or would have been, in a different dimension.

"Are you okay?" Izzy asked as he held out the remaining cash he had on him. Somehow the idea of slipping it into her waistband just didn't seem right.

She shook her head, no, and it took him a second to realize that she was doing that in response to the money he was trying to give her, not to his question. "I don't want that," she said, then answered him. "I am. I'm okay."

And there he stood, looking into her eyes as she looked back at him, until she broke first and looked away.

They'd drawn the full attention of every man around her, and some across the room as well. That giant bouncer was pushing his way toward them, no doubt to see if Izzy was causing trouble.

"I really have to..." Eden said.

He set the money down on the runway, near her foot in that fancy shoe. And then, with one last look up at her, into those eyes that haunted his dreams, he said, "I'm glad you're okay, Eed." He forced a smile. "You're pretty freaking great at what you're doing, just... Stay safe."

She nodded, and now there was a different kind of surprised look on her face. It was part confusion, part suspicion, part struggle to comprehend.

"You never did trust me, did you?" Izzy said, then turned and walked away—praying that his still-swelling feeling of sadness and its accompanying urge to weep uncontrollably marked the official end of his healing, and that when he stepped out of the door and into the brilliant sunlight and heat of the Las Vegas morning, he'd finally be free.

Ben headed over to the mall a little before noon, figuring that Neesha would be there.

It was a weekday, and it felt weird not to be in school, but he couldn't risk going—in case Greg showed up, looking for him. Of course, it wasn't as if Ben particularly *needed* a reason to stay away from school.

He'd brought a sandwich with him to the mall—Eden was a taskmaster when it came to not spending unnecessary money. She was the queen of bag lunches, even though she hadn't taken one herself this morning.

Apparently the club she was going to clean today would have

plenty of still-edible leftover food—and there was something definitely not right with the story she'd given him about her second job. She was withholding something. Of course, she'd spoken to Danny last night, and any conversation she had with the brother she referred to as "Captain Perfect" was bound to be fraught with peril and upset.

It was frustrating—the way Dan and Eden couldn't seem to get along anymore. But the Gillman family members weren't known for their ability to talk through disagreements and find common ground despite differences of opinion. And as much as Dan hated their stepfather for his self-righteous insistence that he alone knew God's plan, Dan seemed to hold the very same intolerance for the mistakes Eden had made during her rocky path through adolescence. And most of the time these days, Eden treated Danny with the same disrespect she delivered to Greg—even though Ben knew that she desperately longed for her older brother's approval and love.

The look on her face, when she'd found out Dan had been injured and possibly dead . . . Ben also knew that receiving that news had been devastating for her—and not just because it put a crimp in her plan to rescue Ben.

She'd woken him up to tell him that Danny was all right, that his injury hadn't been too severe. And he knew that she'd cried as she'd hugged him, even though she tried to hide it—the way she always did.

At breakfast, she'd told Ben that Dan would be flying in to Las Vegas sometime in the next few days.

Ben had to keep his whereabouts on the down-low until then.

Shouldn't be too hard to do.

Except he was suddenly aware, as he entered a mall filled with screaming babies in strollers, that he was the only teenager in the place. And it occurred to him that—as much food as there was to "throw away" at this toddler-filled time of day—Neesha might make a point never to come to the mall until after regular school hours.

Last thing she needed was to be picked up for being truant.

It was the last thing *he* needed, too. Ben turned to leave and nearly walked full force into one of the mall guards.

It was the same guy who'd seen him being hassled by Tim and his crew yesterday.

"I'm home-schooled," Ben said, but the guard smirked.

"Like I haven't heard that before," the man said. "Let's see what your parents say."

Ben turned again, intending to bolt, but there were suddenly two very large men behind him, blocking his escape.

"This is the kid," the mall guard told them.

One of the men—his eyes hidden behind mirrored sunglasses—flashed a police badge, and Ben's heart sank. Greg had called the cops, and he was so screwed.

But then the other cop—who looked more like a skinhead assassin from a Quentin Tarantino movie—pulled a cardboard folder out of his leather jacket's inside pocket and opened it up to reveal . . .

Shit, it was a photo of Neesha, crouched next to a dark-colored car. It was slightly blurred and looked like it came from a surveillance camera in some parking lot. But it was definitely her.

"Do you know this girl?" the bald cop asked.

"Not really," Ben said, which wasn't a lie. His heart was pounding, but the truth was, even if they brought him down to the station and waterboarded him, he *couldn't* tell them anything that would hurt Neesha, because he honestly had no idea where she was. "I've seen her around. Talked to her a few times. She hangs out here—a lotta kids do." He added a little surfer-dude het to his voice, laughing a little. "She's, um, kind of cute, you know?"

And oh, crap, he shouldn't have said that, because the body language on the two cops changed. They went from casually inquisitive to fully focused, with Ben as the center of their laser-beam intensity.

"You pay her to have sex with you?" the bald cop asked.

"What?" Ben said, his voice cracking. "Me? No! God. She's just a kid and I'm not . . . No."

"You're not in trouble here, son, okay?" the sunglasses-wearing cop asked, speaking up for the first time. "If she made you an offer you couldn't refuse . . ." He shrugged as if to say, *What are you gonna do . . . ?*

Ben kept on shaking his head. "She didn't."

"I saw her leaving the mall with you," the mall guard said, his tone accusatory. "Yesterday."

Oh God.

"Where'd you go with her?" the skinhead asked.

"We just need to know where she took you," the other cop said. "No one needs to know anything about what you did when you got there. That's not what this is about."

"She didn't take me anywhere," Ben lied. "She helped me get home. I'm diabetic. I was having a low-blood-sugar incident and she helped me get the bus and that was it."

"Where's home?" the bald cop asked.

"Not far," Ben evaded. "Usually, I walk, but I was feeling dizzy. She lent me the money for the fare. But like I said, that was it. I got on the bus, we said good-bye, and I went home."

There was silence as the two cops exchanged a look. The cop in sunglasses sighed. "Okay, son, here's what's going to happen. You're going to tell us your name and your address and we're going to take you home. Because we're pretty sure you're not quite being honest with us and we need to see if your mom or dad recognizes our missing girl, because we think you brought her there with you yesterday."

"I don't have a dad," Ben said, stalling because he knew his only option here was to run. To at least *try* to get away.

"Or," the bald cop said, clamping a ham-sized hand around Ben's upper arm to hold him in place, since he was clearly capable of reading minds, "you continue to act like a stupid little shit and refuse to give us that simple information, at which point we cuff you and toss you in the back of our car and take you down to the station for questioning. Whereupon you'll be required to show us identification, at which point we'll have your name and address, except it'll take us about four hours to cut through the paperwork and get you home, so you'll spend all that time in a holding cell with all the junkie methhead homo perverts, crying for your mommy as they fuck you in the ass. So why don't you just cut the crap?"

"I don't have identification," Ben said defiantly. "I lost my wallet, so good luck with that. Also, I'm not a lawyer, nor do I play one on TV, but I definitely want to see your badges again so I can write down the numbers so I have 'em when I *do* find a lawyer, because that sounded like police intimidation to me, as well as rampant homophobia. As a gay American, I resent that."

"I'm out of here, guys," the mall guard said, scuttling away.

The sunglasses-wearing cop—the good cop—sighed again. "Let's all take a deep breath," he said.

Ben did just that, filling his lungs with air. "Bad touch!" he shouted, pitching his voice as high as he could. "Mommy, the bad man is touching me!"

And every mother's head in that mall whipped around.

The bald cop tried to muscle him out of there, but Ben remembered the self-defense class Eden had brought him to, years ago, at a mall much like this one, down in New Orleans. He went limp as he shouted, "This man is not my father! Help me! This man is *not* my father!"

The cop let go of him, and Ben rolled away, scrambling to his feet. He booked it out of there, skidding on the tile floor as he went around the corner toward the nearest entrance.

The bald cop was chasing him, his feet pounding on the tile as he shouted, "Stop, thief! Someone stop that boy!"

But the shoppers with strollers moved out of his way, and Ben hit the door with both hands, pushing it open. The brilliance and heat of the morning exploded around him as he charged out into a courtyard area with benches for smokers and kids waiting to get picked up by their parents.

There was a pull-off for cars, and Ben headed across it, toward the parking lot, which was crowded here by the mall entrance. He launched himself toward the parked cars, hoping he could lose himself among them.

But there was a police car approaching from his left, along the road that ran parallel to the footprint of the mall. It was moving fast, heading toward him. Ben looked behind him, where—shit—the bald cop was closing in, while the other cop hovered like a goalie, guarding the entrance back into the mall.

He was screwed.

Still, he ran, right through the shrubs and palm trees.

But the police cruiser anticipated his route, and pulled around him, screeching to a halt to block him. "Stop!"

And still, he didn't give up. He went up and over the top of the hood while the uniformed officer scrambled to get out, shouting again, "Stop!"

The police car blocked the bald cop's path, too, but it didn't slow him down much, either.

"Use your Taser!" he was shouting, and Ben glanced back to see them both coming across the hood of the car.

"Freeze!" the uniformed officer shouted.

But Ben didn't stop. He just plunged on across the road and onto a slightly raised area of desert plantings and desiccated mulch, praying that he'd make it to the shelter of the parked cars, before—

Something hit him, square in the back, and the pain it delivered was worse than anything he'd ever felt before, and he screamed. But even worse than the pain was the sensation of losing control of the muscles in his legs as he went down onto the dirt.

If he'd been on the pavement, he would've cracked his head open. As it was, he kind of bounced and then settled. Immobile. Numb, but still oddly humming.

He'd been tased.

"Thanks, Paul," he heard the bald man say to the uniformed officer as they both caught their breath.

"Shoplifter?" the cop named Paul asked.

"Nah," the bald man answered, his voice getting louder as he moved closer to Ben and quickly searched him, his hands going into Ben's pockets. "I'm working a missing-person case. A little girl ran away—the parents are really upset. She was spotted here and this kid knows her and . . . There's mental illness involved. Paranoid delusions.

And that's on top of whatever PTSD the kid carries. She was adopted from some war zone and... It's a real mess. Shit, he's got no ID."

Paul reached down, too, and none too gently cuffed Ben's wrists together before detaching the juice-emitting ends of the Taser from the back of his T-shirt.

Ben still hadn't reclaimed his ability to speak, but he looked up at the cop as indignantly as he could, because, Jesus. Handcuffs?

The police officer called Paul read his expression correctly. "When a police officer says stop, you stop. If you don't, you're breaking the law. I'm taking you in."

Ben managed a sound that conveyed his dismay. It wasn't quite a *no* or a *please*, but it was close.

To his surprise, the bald cop was on his side. "Come on, Paul, the cuffs aren't necessary. There's no need to—"

"I gotta bring him in," Paul said. "You know the rules, Jake. I discharged a weapon. There's procedure and protocol. Besides, aren't you supposed to be in school?"

That last question was aimed at Ben, as the uniformed officer hauled him to feet that didn't work right, and dragged him over to the police car.

"He says he's home-schooled," the bald cop reported, following.

"We'll see," Paul said as he opened up the back door and pushed Ben inside, where he fell over onto the seat, his cheek against the plastic.

He heard the door slam behind him, and the sound of voices as the two men continued to talk. He couldn't make out the words over the roar of the a/c and the squawk of a police radio that cut in and out.

But then the front door opened and he heard and felt it slam as Paul got into the car. He felt the transmission being put into gear and then they were rolling.

They were heading downtown, to the station, where eventually they'd figure out who Ben was and where he lived. They'd also find out that he wasn't home-schooled. He was cutting. As for Neesha, who'd run away from home because she was mentally ill? It didn't matter how long they held him. He couldn't answer their questions, because he didn't know where she was. And when they finally figured that out? They'd bring him back home and deliver him to Greg—who would beat the shit out of him.

Or at least try.

Only, this time, the creep would be ready for Ben to fight back.

This time, Ben was going to get flattened. And there was nothing in the world he could do to keep it from happening.

Unless . . .

He tried his vocal cords again, and this time they worked. "Do I get to make a phone call?" he asked through a throat that felt raw after the way he'd screamed like a girl from the Taser-induced pain.

"Depends," Paul answered him, "if you're under arrest. And that depends if you've got any priors."

"I don't."

"We'll see."

"What happens if I'm *not* under arrest?" Ben asked.

"You call Mommy and Daddy to come pick you up, they bring you home and ground you for two years."

"I live with my sister," Ben said, which wasn't quite a lie.

"Then you get to interrupt *her* busy day, and *she* comes to the station to pick you up and bring you home and ground you for two years."

Okay. Good. That was good.

Or at least as good as it could get with his arms twisted behind his back and his face pressed against a vinyl seat that smelled like sweat and piss.

CHAPTER
EIGHT

Eden's shift was over after the bulk of the afternoon rush, and for once she didn't push to get a chance to dance for another few hours. She just put on her clothes and took a deep breath, bracing herself as she pushed open the door that led out to the club's parking lot.

But there was no one out there besides the valet attendant, who was sitting, bored and steaming, in the shade from a wilting umbrella.

Of course, if she were Izzy, waiting to talk to her, she'd be in her car with the engine running and the air conditioner blasting instead of standing in the hot Nevada sun.

Still, as she shouldered her bag and walked swiftly toward the bus stop, there was no movement from the lot. No tall, obnoxiously attractive Navy SEALs jumping out of their cars and shouting, "Hey, Eden, wait . . ."

And that was definitely relief she was feeling, not disappointment, as her feet took her farther from the club—although she really didn't completely believe it until she hit the bus stop and looked around.

Nope. No Izzy. He hadn't stuck around to talk to her.

She had no idea how he'd found her here—although Danny certainly knew she was back in Las Vegas. Plus she'd given her father her address and phone number when she'd called to ask if he knew if her brother was okay. He'd no doubt given that information to Danny, who used it to call her...

Still, to have Izzy show up like that, at work?

She was mortified.

It was one thing to dance for strangers with their empty, hungry eyes, another entirely to know Izzy was in the house.

Lord, he'd looked good. His face was tan and his dark hair was longer than he usually wore it, but he'd neatly combed it back. He was dressed in a pair of khaki dress pants—and that was crazy weird because Eden couldn't remember ever seeing him in pants even remotely like those. He usually wore cargo shorts and a T-shirt. Or his white dress uniform. He'd worn that, with rows of ribbons on his chest, when they'd gotten married.

But the shirt he had on today had a collar and buttons up the front. He wore the sleeves rolled to his elbows to fight the day's heat.

It was crazy—as if he'd gotten dressed up because he knew he was going to see her but didn't want to go the full-dress-uniform route.

Maybe she no longer rated.

But it didn't make sense—for him to track her down to give her a handful of cash, take her figurative pulse, and then walk away...?

Unless his message had been visual. *Take a good long look at what you threw away, sweetheart...*

He'd certainly taken a good long look at her—which had been so strange. Mostly because, in the past, he'd rarely looked at her without smiling. This morning he'd been grim and unamused. And yeah, he'd faked a smile at one point, but it hadn't touched his eyes.

She'd always loved the way that the warmth of Izzy's smile had echoed in his eyes.

But those days were gone.

Eden shouldn't have cared. She didn't want to care.

Yet still, even though Izzy had left the floor level of the club, she'd been self-conscious all morning long, and had tried to compensate for it—and succeeded, apparently. That success was reflected in her larger-than-usual tips.

Not counting that small pile of cash that Izzy had deposited on the stage. The pile that she'd fully expected to have the opportunity to give back to him after her shift was through.

As she waited for the bus, she dug for her cell phone to turn it back on, and saw she had both a missed call and voice message from the same local Las Vegas phone number.

It wasn't either of her workplaces, and it wasn't her new landlord...

She dialed her voice mail and listened to the message.

Eden. It's Ben. I'm in trouble. I went to the mall to try to find... my friend, and I got picked by the police for not being in school and...

Oh, Lord.

Well, it's more complicated than that; in fact, it's beyond weird, but I'll tell you later. Anyway, look, they ID'd me from my fingerprints—remember when you took me to that SafeKids program, because of my diabetes?

Eden did remember. It was right after they moved to Las Vegas from New Orleans. At twelve, Ben had been, by far, the oldest kid among all of the toddlers at the police station, and he'd been beyond embarrassed. But Eden had insisted. Because he'd participated in a similar program back in New Orleans, they'd been able to find him more quickly, after Katrina.

Well, congratulations, because of that, I'm in the system. And they now have my name and Greg's address, and because I don't have any other priors, they're going to bring me home in some kind of police-department house call of shame, and deliver me into the hands of my loving parents.

"Oh, crap," Eden said aloud.

Yeah, Ben's message said, as if he'd heard her. *I told them that my mother worked until late, but that I also live with my real bitch of a drill sergeant older sister, who's in charge of making me do my homework and making my life miserable. I didn't mention Greg because, Jesus. But I told them that you'd be home in the afternoon—that you usually met my bus, like I'm a freaking kindergartner and they actually bought it. So please, please get over to the house by five o'clock—just sit on the front steps, you know? Like you're waiting for me? Bring ID—they're going to want to see ID. And maybe, just maybe we'll be able to pull this off. And Eden? I'm so sorry...*

The phone system's automated voice clicked on. "To replay this message, press—"

Eden hung up the phone and checked the time. It was 4:45.

The city bus was finally coming, but it was heading in the wrong direction, away from the squalid little house that Ivette still shared with Stupid Greg.

What she needed was a cab, pronto.

She started to run to the nearest hotel where there was a taxi stand, but in the middle of crossing the street, she stopped, realizing what she really needed...

Was Izzy.

Eden looked wildly around, hoping that he was still out there, somewhere, watching her. Just because she didn't see him didn't mean he wasn't there.

If she'd had his cell-phone number, she would have called him, but she didn't have it. Not anymore. She'd thrown it away when his response to her letter had been silence.

But here and now, he didn't appear—like some knight in shining armor.

She was on her own. Which was exactly what she'd wanted, wasn't it?

Eden quit hoping for miracles and hiked her bag farther up on her shoulder and ran.

NEW YORK CITY
WEDNESDAY, 6 MAY 2009

Being in New York again was surreal.

It really hadn't been that long since Dan had last been here—and yet it seemed like forever.

Jenn's studio apartment was exactly the same as it had been last February—tiny. It was cramped with the bed folded up into the couch, and even smaller with it pulled out.

Jenn had clearly left the place in a hurry when she'd gotten the news he'd been injured, and the bed was out and open.

She now set their two bags in the minuscule nook of a kitchen—*that* had been fun, watching her hump his bag up the building's front stairs while he'd stood impotently off to the side and seethed with frustration.

But he wasn't allowed to lift anything heavier than the remote control—a direct quote from the doctor.

"Close your eyes," Jenn had ordered him. "Just don't watch."

But he *had* watched—in particular he'd watched her ass, which looked awesome in the jeans she was wearing.

Except he wasn't allowed to do any strenuous activity—including have sex—for another five to seven days.

Well, which was it? Five or seven? In some ways the point was moot, because as badly as he wanted some, he wasn't getting any tonight. Although Danny was pretty damn sure that five days from now the was-it-five-or-seven question was going to matter pretty intensely.

"We're going to meet Maria for dinner," Jenn told him now, and his surprise must've shown on his face.

He was exhausted. He wasn't normally such a baby, but the flight had been taxing and all he wanted to do was to crawl into Jenn's bed and sleep.

And okay. Not true. What he really wanted was to crawl into Jenn's bed, pull her down beside him, fuck his brains out, and *then* sleep for about fourteen hours straight.

"To talk about the custody thing," Jenn reminded him.

Dan looked up from staring at the bed. "Oh, yeah. Right. Sorry. Great. Thanks for, um, setting that up."

"We're not meeting her until eight," Jenn told him as she came over and peeled his jacket off his shoulders. "You look like you need help here." But then she took his T-shirt and pulled it up and over his head.

"What are we doing?" Dan asked as she efficiently went for the button and then the zipper of his jeans. He knew damn well that she wasn't going to break any of the rules that the doctor had given him on discharge from the hospital. She'd sat in on the session and had actually taken notes. No sex. They'd exchanged an *aw, shit* look when he'd mentioned that.

"*You* are getting naked," Jenn told him with that smile that he loved as she pushed his jeans down his legs, her gentle hands careful of his bandaged wound. "And *I* am going to give you a massage very different from the ones I gave you in the hospital with its curtain walls and zero privacy."

Danny looked at her as she knelt before him, unfastening the laces of his sneakers. "Seriously? You rebel, you." He sat down to help her.

She laughed up at him. "I cleared it with the doctor after reviewing his list of rules. I asked him to clarify and I was right. No sex means no strenuous intercourse. It doesn't mean you can't lie back and think nonstrenuous and relaxing thoughts while experiencing the time-honored tradition of the happy ending."

Dan laughed as together they got him out of his sneakers and socks. "You said that. To the doctor. *Excuse me, Captain Chan, sir, I was wondering if it's okay with you if I give Dan a happy ending...?*"

Jenn laughed, too. "Actually, the term *happy ending* didn't come up. I also stayed away from *hand job* and *blow job* and even *fellatio*. I kept it more scientific and medical and asked was the no-sex rule merely about avoiding strenuous activity, or was there a medical reason you should avoid ejaculation. He smiled and said he had no problem with ejaculation."

"Wow," Dan said, slipping off his briefs. "If I'd've known that, I would've had you do me in the airport bathroom."

She laughed again. "Always the romantic..."

He reached for her, but she moved back, out of his grasp.

"You have to promise to lie still."

"I can do that," he said.

"Absolutely still," she stressed. "Or I stop."

Dan thought about that. "Okay, yeah, that's going to be harder than I thought."

The last time they'd had sex in this very apartment, in this very bed, they'd come close to putting her furniture through the floor. It was one of the things he loved about making love to Jenni. She was passionate and hot-blooded and into being completely physical—and he could be equally ardent, with no fear of hurting her. She was no fragile, tiny thing that could be broken if he didn't watch his every move. Instead he could damn near body-slam her and she would cling to him and moan for more.

And Jesus save him, but just thinking about it was turning his un-comfortable and annoyingly ever-present semi-woodie into a hard-on of epic proportions.

"Maybe it's better if we just... Hmm," she said as he lay back on her bed, as she saw his body in full salute. "*Don't*, I was going to say, but..."

He looked up at her. "I missed you."

He meant it as a whole lot more than just *I missed fucking you*, but it was easier to say in the impossible-to-ignore presence of this particular visual aid, because it was always easier for him to frame any roman-tic relationship around the sex.

And she smiled at his implied joke, but her smile was sad. "Did you?" she asked. But then she shook her head as if it was a stupid ques-tion.

"Very much," he said, but he'd done the damage by bringing up this topic in the context of sex, and he knew she was thinking he still meant it as a joke, like *Check out this awesome measurement device that demonstrates from its massive length, tree-trunk-like thickness, and rock-solid hardness, exactly how long it's been since I've had sex of the non-solo variety...*

He pushed himself up on his elbows. "Jenn—"

She sat beside him on the bed, gently pushing him back down, and then running the decadent softness of her hands down his chest, across his abs, and then even lower...

"Ah, God..."

"Shh," she said. "Lie still."

"I thought it went massage, *then* happy ending."

"Oh, come on, Gillman, haven't you ever had dessert first?"

"I wasn't complaining, LeMay," he said, because he loved the way she laughed when he, too, called her by her last name. "Just wondering if I'd just had the world's shortest massage."

She laughed again. "Sounds to me like you're complaining."

"Nope," he said. "Just trying to figure out how to ask for it again."

"Lie still," she warned. "Or I'll stop..."

It felt unbelievably good, the way she was touching him, and he had to close his eyes and fight the urge to reach for her, too, because Jesus, he didn't want her to stop. He wanted... He needed...

He felt her shift as she took off her glasses and put them on the end table. Then he felt the softness of her mouth as she kissed him, licked him, and he opened his eyes because he wanted to watch. And— shit—he'd inadvertently lifted his hips because he wanted more of what she was doing—more in every capacity.

She pulled back to look at him.

"I'm trying," he said. "I love this—I do, but what I really want is...God, remember when we did it in the kitchen?"

"Kind of hard to forget," she said, still stroking him with her hands as she smiled into his eyes.

"One second we were having a conversation," he said. "And the next..."

"Trust me, I remember."

"I want to do that again," he said as she lowered her head and licked him with the very tip of her tongue. "It was crazy, like I couldn't tell where you ended and I began."

"I was the one with the face pressed up against the toaster," Jenn said, quickly adding, "I'm not complaining. It was actually...really . hot. Not the toaster. The sex."

She was so beautiful—the soft curve of her cheek, the graceful shape of a mouth that seemed always on the verge of quirking into a smile, those incredible far-from-average light brown eyes...

The look she was giving him was admonishing again, which was sexy as hell combined with what she was doing with her mouth— shades of dominatrix. And he could feel his impending release building. All she'd have to keep doing was...oh God, *that*...And he knew he just needed to say the word—she loved open communication of all kinds, but there was more he wanted to say besides *yes, please, yes*...

"No, baby," he told her. "I'm not talking about the sex, although that was crazy, too. I'm talking about looking into your eyes and, I don't know, *knowing* what you were feeling, because I was feeling it, too. And then...just letting it explode like that."

It had scared the shit out of him at the time, and he'd told himself that it was just rocking great sex, when in truth there'd been a connection between them almost right from the start.

Not *right* from the start, because their relationship had begun with his intention to have a short-term fling. It hadn't taken all that much to worm his way into her bed—he was a master when it came to seduction, and, for a wide variety of reasons, she was undeniably up for being seduced.

What he hadn't counted on was liking her so damn much. Liking, and then falling in love...

"I missed you," Dan breathed again, suddenly desperate for her to understand. "Jenni, I missed *you*..."

It was maybe the most romantic moment of his life, because she looked at him again and met his gaze, and he could tell that she believed him—believed him and loved him, and his heart actually lurched in his chest. He was just about to use the dreaded L-word—dreaded because the last time he'd told her he loved her, she'd accused him of overreacting to emotions caused only by her near-death experience.

But instead of saying it—*I love you*—when he opened his mouth he said, "Gahhh..."

Because, Jesus, he was coming, just like that, just *wham*—and he forced himself to remain relaxed, because the last thing he wanted was for Jenn to argue that they couldn't risk doing this again, because he didn't lie still. But she wasn't going to, because he didn't move at all and it was unreal the way his release blasted and roared through him in an overwhelmingly powerful sensation. He didn't fight it, he didn't try to ride it or steer it—he just let it be.

It was. He was.

And when it was over, it wasn't really completely gone. It just changed into something calm and warm and he floated in a lovely place between waking and sleep.

But then he felt Jenn shift, felt the mattress give and then bounce back into place as she flipped a blanket up and over them both, as she stretched out beside him on the bed.

He opened his eyes and turned his head and...

Jenn smiled at him from where she lay, her head on the other pillow. And the feeling of calm intensified, and for the first time since Dan could remember, he felt completely at peace.

"I missed you, too," she whispered, and reached an arm out from beneath that blanket to gently cover his eyes and force them to close—not that she needed to try very hard. "Go to sleep."

WEDNESDAY, MAY 6, 2009
LAS VEGAS

Ben's heart sank as the police car he was riding in approached his house.

Eden was nowhere to be seen. She must not have gotten his message.

Greg's ancient car was in the driveway, however, which meant that *he* was home.

This was going to be butt ugly.

"This one?" the police officer who was driving asked, peering out the windshield at their crappy shithole of a house in this crappy shit-hole of a neighborhood.

"Yeah," Ben said, ashamed at what his two uniformed escorts saw.

Broken glass adorned the dust bowl of the front "yard," shimmer-ing in the afternoon light. The window it had come from was still boarded up with plywood that wasn't weathering well after nearly a year of being exposed to the hot desert sun.

The steps leading up to the front door were cracked and chipped, and the metal decoration on the bottom of the screen had come off on one side and hung at a defeated angle.

The windows that weren't broken displayed sorry-looking, mis-matched, and badly hung curtains, blinds that were broken and bent, or an unsightly mix of both.

The paint was peeling, particularly on the windowsills, and the roof was sagging and discolored, with a badly attached blue plastic tarp that was covering a leak in an ineffective tangle.

And that was just *their* house. The others weren't much better-looking.

Back when it was a new development, in 1969, this little enclave of winding streets and shiny houses had been called Pedergast Gardens. Ben had written a report on it for school after finding one of the origi-nal blueprints for their house up in the crawl-space attic, slipped in be-hind a now-sagging beam.

Thirty-six years later, the shine was long gone and the entire place devoid of anything even remotely gardenlike, as residents used their limited and shrinking funds for food and electricity, instead of paint, new roofs, or water for the landscaping. Some of their neighboring houses had been boarded up and condemned, and some had been decorated with deceptively festive-colored crime-scene tape.

But compared to their post-Katrina housing, it was home, sweet home. Or at least it had been for a very brief time, back when Ben was younger and too dumb to recognize that Greg was an asshat, and that he himself was doomed and already circling the drain.

The police officer parked on the street, out front, as Ben sat in the cage in the back and breathed. Inhale. Exhale. This was going to suck. Maybe he could seek asylum with the police. Confess that he'd failed to mention his evil stepfather, who was going to beat the shit out of him as soon as the cops drove away.

He should, at least, ask what the law was in regard to self-defense. If Greg hit him, he could hit Greg back. He knew that much. But how could he prove it if, after the fact, Greg accused *him* of throwing the first punch?

There were no handles on the inside of the door, so Ben had to wait until the second cop—the stern-faced woman with the cold, unsympathetic eyes—opened it for him, letting him out into the hot, still, afternoon air.

The male officer seemed nicer, more human, but he apparently wasn't even getting out of the car, leaving his partner to complete this assignment.

And really, on the scale of horrible to really horrible, she was better than what he'd expected and dreaded—i.e., being driven home by the detectives who'd questioned him about Neesha in the mall.

But neither the bald nor the sunglasses-wearing cop had showed up at the police station.

And no one else so much as mentioned Neesha, or the fact that she was missing.

Which had been a little weird.

So Ben hadn't brought the subject up, not with anyone.

"You know how when you go to the hospital and the doctor or the nurse takes you aside to make sure you really did just fall off your bike," Ben said to the policewoman, about to launch into a description of life with Greg, when he heard a shout from down the street.

"Hey! Ben!"

It was Eden, coming to his rescue, thank you, *thank you*, baby Jesus.

She was on foot, and soaked with perspiration, her hair bedraggled—looking as if she'd run most of the way over here from wherever it was she'd been working.

"I'm so sorry I was delayed," she called in an odd mix of half shout, half whisper, with her voice pitched slightly higher than usual, and Ben knew she was trying her best to keep Greg from hearing her or recognizing her if he did hear voices from out in the street.

And sure enough, when she came closer, she still spoke quietly in that higher voice. "Are you all right?" she asked him, the very picture of the concerned older sister.

He nodded and she hugged him tightly and said, "Thank the Lord," even as she pinched him in the side. "Thank you, Officer, for bringing him safely home," she added as she released him. "It's been a rough few days. Our older brother, Danny, is a Navy SEAL, serving in Afghanistan. We just found out he'd been injured, but we didn't know how badly, or even if he was still alive. Long story short, he was shot and he nearly died—but he's going to be okay. Still . . . The stress took its toll on all of us, I'm afraid."

The police officer softened—just a bit. She expressed her sympathy and then droned on and on, all about that not *really* being a good excuse for cutting school, about the dangers of running away from a police officer, about the value of this program called Scared Straight— yeah, no irony there—run by a local church, where teenagers were taken to a high-security penitentiary where they had conversations with lifers. It was a good program, particularly for boys his age, blah blah blah.

Ben tuned out, his focus on the house, checking the windows and the door. The longer they stood out here talking, the greater the chances were that Greg would stagger into the kitchen for another gin and lemonade, see them, and come outside.

He would take one look at Eden and start to scream. He'd hated her while she lived here, but he'd hated her even more after she was gone.

Eden showed the cop her ID—a passport that was several years old, with Gillman still listed as her last name and this address as her place of residence. She apologized to the police officer about twenty more times, and Ben himself even threw in a few contrite-sounding *I'm sorries*.

And then they were done.

Except after the police officer climbed back into the cruiser, it hovered there at the side of the road. And Ben saw that she was watching them.

"Oh, Lord," Eden said even as she smiled and waved. "I think she's waiting for us to go inside. Do you have your keys?"

He did, but: "I'm *not* going in there."

"You don't have to," Eden said. "Just unlock the door for me and sit on the steps and pout, like I just told you there'd be no TV after dinner for the next five hundred years."

"*You're* going inside," Ben said.

She nodded. She wasn't kidding. "Someone's got to. Come on. Do it. Unlock the door. Let's get this over with so we can get out of here. Being back like this is giving me a rash."

Ben took his keys from his pocket as he climbed the crap stairs and opened the crap screen door, wincing as it gave an unavoidable screech.

"It's okay," Eden murmured, standing at his shoulder as he put the key in the door and unbolted the lock. "Greg's probably asleep. Besides, together we can definitely kick his ass."

"This wasn't entirely my fault—the thing with the police," Ben had an overpowering urge to explain before she went inside. As if she were going to die or never come back out again. "I went to the mall to find Neesha, and these cops—not the ones who dropped me off but others—detectives, in regular clothes? They were there, looking for her, too. They had a picture of her. One of the mall guards saw me with her. That's why they stopped me."

Eden looked at him, with her hand on the doorknob. "Seriously?"

"It was beyond weird, Eed," he said. "They said she was a runaway—that she was mentally ill, but I don't believe it. Yeah, she told me this crazy story about being sold into kind of a slavery—as a sex slave, I'm pretty sure. And maybe she really does have PTSD or something, but whoever she was living with? If she really was adopted? One of her adoptive parents was doing something wrong. I'm sure of it. Still, after I was at the police station? Nothing. No questions about her, no pictures. The detectives weren't even there. It was all about cutting school and running away from the police."

"Maybe they were satisfied that you didn't know where she was," she suggested, then took a deep breath. "I'm going to be right inside. Open the door again when they're gone, okay?"

Ben nodded and slumped down onto the top step.

And with one more deep inhale, as if she were about to enter a toxic zone and would need to hold her breath the entire time, Eden went into Greg and Ivette's house and closed the door tightly behind her.

CHAPTER
NINE

I t's really not my area of expertise, so I'm going to have you double-check me," Maria said to Dan and Jenn as they sat across from her, with her cluttered desk between them.

They'd decided to meet here, in the assemblywoman's tiny office, instead of having dinner, because Danny was still terribly jet-lagged. Of course, Jenn didn't tell *him* that that was the reason for their change in plans. She blamed it instead on Maria's hectic schedule.

He'd nodded, but he knew. And she also knew that it galled him.

"But if it comes down to a custody battle, in court," Maria told them, "yeah, it's going to send a positive message if you're in a stable, committed relationship."

But of course she was going to say that.

Maria and Jenn had been friends for a long time, and Maria had been an advocate of the impossible, right from the start. She believed, without doubt, that Dan was perfect for Jenn, and was convinced that they would find their happily-ever-after, despite all of their obvious differences.

The main one being that Dan was an incredibly handsome, incredibly buff, incredibly hot Navy SEAL, and Jenn was a too-tall, too-heavy, too-awkward geek who worked as chief of staff for an outspoken liberal and progressive politician—namely, Maria.

"But you don't think that's going to look strange," Jenn said. "Or opportunistic? If, right before a custody battle, we just conveniently get married?"

"Well, it's better if you do it significantly beforehand, of course," Maria said.

"Dan's sister, Eden, is married," Jenn told her friend even as Dan shook his head.

"I'm not getting Zanella involved in this," he said.

Jenn looked at him. Izzy Zanella was already out in Nevada. He'd caught a flight to Las Vegas a full day before she and Dan had left the hospital. If he'd waited, he could've caught a troop transport. Instead, he'd paid for the travel himself.

He'd spent over eight hundred dollars for the flight—just because he wanted to arrive a mere twenty-four hours earlier.

The man was definitely involved, and Danny knew it.

"No more than I have to," he amended his statement.

Jenn turned to Maria. "If it stands to reason that, if Danny and I got married, we'd be in a better position to gain custody of Ben, then doesn't that give Eden and Izzy, who've been married for nearly a year, an even better shot?"

"Except for the fact that they've been separated," Maria pointed out.

"Says who?" Jenn asked. She looked from Maria to Dan. "And I'm not saying that to be a jerk," she added quickly before either could speak. "I mean, *we* all know what happened. But I could describe the very same events by saying that Eden went to live with a friend a few weeks after she and Izzy got married, because he was deployed overseas. Nothing wrong with that. An eighteen-year-old bride has a miscarriage and doesn't want to be alone while her husband is gone? A lot of women would probably go live at home, but Eden's mother was and is emotionally unavailable, so..."

Dan was shaking his head. "I'd rather just get married."

"And I'd rather not," Jenn shot back, and her vehemence surprised him.

Across the desk, Maria was trying to be invisible.

"Wow," Jenn said. "I'm sorry, that came out...far more strongly than I'd intended. I just—" She stopped. Took a deep breath. "I'm absolutely willing to do it. I said I would, and I meant it. But I want it to be the last resort. We're talking about three years of my life—whether it's here or in San Diego. And I'm not saying part of it wouldn't be great. We both know it would. But part of it would be awful—and I'm talking soul-crushingly hard, if you want to know the truth."

"I do," Dan said quietly as he looked up from his perusal of the floor and into her eyes. "I always want you to tell me the truth. Even when...*especially* when it involves soul crushing."

"I'm not saying I don't want to help you with this," Jenn repeated what she'd told him earlier. "I'm here, Dan. I'm going to be here for as long as you need me. But before we go to Plan Z, let's consider A through Y first."

"I'd recommend," Maria said gently, "that you go to Las Vegas tomorrow and talk to Dan's mother, see if you can't convince her to allow Ben to live with you—no custody battle necessary. That's, by far, the best way to go. Parents of teenagers frequently give permission for their kids to live with other family members. It's not that uncommon."

"That was the plan," Jenn said. "But I think we're both a little worried that not only will Ivette be influenced by her husband into saying no, but that they'll put Ben into immediate danger by sending him away to a conversion therapy camp—you know, one of those lockdown prisons where they 'pray away the gay' while depriving him of sleep and food and God knows what else. They'd already made plans to send him to such a place in June, after school got out."

Maria sighed. "How old is he?"

"Fifteen."

She nodded as she reached for her computer mouse, pulling her computer screen closer to her and clicking a file open. "That's a little young for him to go to court to declare himself an emancipated minor, but that could be worth a try," she said as she gazed at her computer. She clicked her mouse again, and her printer whirred to life. "I'm going to give you the contact information for a family law attorney, out in San Francisco. I'm pretty sure she practices in Nevada, too—if not, she'll be able to give you the name of someone who does. She specializes in LGBT issues. She'll know exactly what to do."

She handed the printout to Jenn, who glanced at it. *Linda Thomas...* "Wasn't she...?"

"A friend from college," Maria said. "I'll send her an e-mail, tell her you'll be calling."

"Thanks," Dan said.

"So...Izzy's back with Eden?" Maria asked.

"He went to Las Vegas to see her," Jenn told her friend. "As soon as he heard that's where she was." She turned to Dan. "Have you heard from him? Did he call or..."

Danny shook his head. "Last time I spoke to Eden, she didn't mention him."

"He was crazy about her," Maria said. "He and I talked about her, back in February. A little bit."

"He's a moron," Dan said. "The crazy is all hers. She's freaking nuts, but he doesn't see that because he's staggering through life, blind to truth and reason as he follows his genitalia."

Maria smiled at that. "Most of us stagger through life, blind to what's right in front of our noses. We *all* see only what we want to see. At the risk of overstepping my role here as dispenser of friendly and free legal counsel, I'd suggest that if your mother doesn't immediately send Ben to his room to pack his bags so he can go live with you, you might want to sit down with Eden—and Izzy, if he's willing to help, and I suspect he will be. See if you can't work through your differences and come to some sort of cease-fire, so you can act as a unified team in order to help your brother."

Dan was silent.

"If there *is* a custody battle," Maria continued, "there will be input from social services—a visit from a social worker—and if you're at war with one another, believe me, they'll be aware of that."

As Jenn watched, Dan forced a smile and forced himself to respond. "Please don't get me wrong," he said. "I really do appreciate this information. I'm just having trouble imagining it being even remotely easier with Eden and Zanella in the mix."

"Maybe not for you," Jenn said quietly. "But Maria's thinking of Ben. Danny, look at it from his perspective. He's just done this amazing, courageous thing by coming out. That's hard enough when you have parents who support you. But Ivette and Greg's reaction was to tell him he's broken and needs to be fixed. And maybe it's Greg who's pushing this conversion therapy thing, but Ben's own mother is at the very least acquiescing, and that's got to hurt. A lot.

"So here you come, with this big plan to yank him away from his home—just assuming that he'll be fine with going to live with a brother who's a stranger, who left home, what? Over ten years ago? Which means the last time he's lived with you was when he was in preschool. He doesn't really know you. How does he know you won't be worse than Greg? Talk about scary. And baby, I *know* that you and Eden haven't gotten along very well in recent years, and I know that spending time with her will be—at best—really uncomfortable for you. But as imperfect as she is, she's Ben's sister, too. And having her around could make all the difference in the world for him."

Dan was nodding now. "You're right," he said. "Of course you're right. Jesus, I'm a selfish shit not to have seen that."

"You know how you said love makes people blind?" Jenn told him, taking his hand and interlacing their fingers. "Well, families make us blind and *stupid*. You should see me trying to deal with my brothers. I turn into a complete idiot."

"I doubt that," Dan said. "So, okay. I guess what I should do now is..." He exhaled hard. "Call Eden."

LAS VEGAS
WEDNESDAY, MAY 6, 2009

Eden's cell phone rang, the sound shrill and sharp in the tomblike stillness of this house, where her stepfather was no doubt napping to preserve his strength for another night of prayer—followed by some serious drinking.

Despite her brave words to Ben, she was freaked out and she didn't want to go too far inside. So she was standing there, right by the crappy, warped front door in the crappy little living room, in this crappy little house where she'd spent the hell that had been her high school years.

The tattered sofa was the same one she'd slouched on, watching *Lost* and *Gilmore Girls* and *Buffy* reruns, whenever Greg was too drunk or stoned on the prescription painkillers he took for his back to order her to turn it off.

The coffee table was chipped and stained with rings caused by beverage sweat—marks that hadn't been there when someone from the church had donated it to the Katrina survivors who'd just moved into town, looking for a fresh start. The dishes from Greg's breakfast and lunch were scattered across the top—the man was apparently still incapable of cleaning up after himself. In all the years since he'd married Eden's mother, Eden had never seen him wash a dish or empty an ashtray.

She *had* seen him in a sanctimonious rage, nearly foaming at the mouth as he screamed at her for a long list of sins. Dressing like a whore, acting like a whore, looking like a whore, talking like a whore—the whole whore thing was definitely a personal favorite topic for him. Talking back, or not talking when spoken to—either one could result in punishment. Working too many hours at her after-school job, or not working enough hours—whatever she did, the other was better. Not cooking dinner for her hardworking mother, or making a mess in the kitchen *because* she had cooked dinner for her mother...

There was no way to win with Greg—Eden could only lose.

But the worst was when he preached at her for not going to church as often as he wanted her to, and for not kneeling beside him every night to pray.

The truth of the matter was that the man used his god and his prayer as an excuse to touch her, to get much too close.

None of which her mother noticed as she self-anesthetized.

Which wasn't exactly new for Eden.

She'd had to lock her bedroom door at night against her sister Sandy's husband, Ron, when Sandy and her family had lived with them back in New Orleans. And so she did the same with her latest stepfather, going as far as making a trip to the hardware store and buying and installing a deadbolt because the lock on the regular doorknob was too easy to pop.

She'd also made darn sure she didn't get up to go to the bathroom at night unless she absolutely had to.

Because there wasn't much that was more hideous than opening the bathroom door to find Greg staggering around in the hallway stinking of gin and naked as the day he was born, mumbling about the way she was going to hell, even as he waggled his disgusting dick at her.

Yeah, and *she* was the one who was going to hell for wearing her skirts too short. Right.

The dead last thing she wanted was to see him again—ever—and as her phone rang, Eden grabbed for it, fumbling it out of the pocket of her jeans, to silence it before it awoke the sleeping monster.

Come on, Ben. Give her the signal that the police car was gone . . .

But he didn't and he didn't, and she heard movement from the master bedroom, and then Greg's reedy voice.

"Who's out there? Who's in my house? Benjamin, is that you?"

And Eden opened the door, because maybe she could fool the cops into thinking she was going to drag Ben around to the back of the house for some punishment yardwork.

But as she opened the door, Ben was standing there, opening the screen, and hallelujah, the police car was driving away, turning the corner down at the end of the street.

As she stepped outside, she said, "Run," but Ben was staring up and over her shoulder and the expression on his face was one of such shock, she turned, half expecting Greg to have morphed into a real monster like one of the demons from *Buffy*.

But he hadn't. He was still ugly old Greg—a little uglier and a little older than he'd been the last time she'd seen him, all those long months ago. His T-shirt was stained and his chin was unshaven and his greasy hair was matted and clumped on his head—all of which were horrifying, but a whole lot less so than the fact that he was holding a nasty-looking handgun.

And he was aiming it right at Eden.

"When did you get a gun?" she asked, even as he said, "You! I should've known you were back, stirring up trouble."

She tried to back away, but Greg ordered, "Freeze—the pair of you delinquents!" and Ben was there, next to her, keeping her from retreating farther.

"It's probably not loaded," Eden said to her brother as she looked down the street. Didn't it figure? Now that she could have used a little police backup, the police car was out of sight. "He probably doesn't have any ammunition. Let's just get out of here."

"He does," Ben said as Greg ordered him, "Into the house, young man. *Now.*"

"Even if he does, he's not going to shoot me." Now it was Eden's turn to try to hold Ben back, because he clearly believed that that gun gave Greg the upper hand. "He's not going to shoot anyone. Seriously, Ben, let's just turn around and run!"

"Get into. The house," Greg said to Ben.

"He lives with me now," Eden said.

"Benjamin, I'm counting to three..."

"I would think you'd be happy," Eden said, "to no longer have the responsibility and expense—"

"He *is* my responsibility," Greg said. "And I owe it to him and to God to undo the damage caused from all those years of living with *you.*"

"Yeah, right," Eden scoffed. "Like I made you touch my boobs, every chance you got. Like you weren't going to try to sell my baby to the highest bidder—"

He looked at Ben. "One..."

"Don't you dare go into that house," Eden ordered her brother.

"Two..."

"He's not going to shoot me!"

"I *will*," Greg countered. "A trespasser, breaking into my home—in the company of a stepson who recently attacked me? Oh, I'll shoot and I'll shoot to kill, and it'll be your word, Benjamin, against mine—and my vast array of bruises."

"He's not going to do it," Eden said, holding tightly to Ben's arm.

"Just watch me," Greg said, using both hands to steady the weapon that he had aimed at Eden's chest.

And Ben obviously thought Greg capable of murder because he pulled away from Eden and headed up those stairs, even as he started to cry. "I'm sorry," he said.

"Boo-Boo," Eden said, trying to pull him back, "don't do this!"

But he jerked himself out of her grasp and went past Greg through the door and into the house. And when she tried to follow him, Greg refreshed his grip on that pistol, aiming it now at her face.

"Don't tempt me," he snarled.

And didn't *that* sum up the two awful years that Eden had lived in the same house as this broken wreck of a man. In his eyes, *she'd* tempted *him*. Just by existing, by breathing, by being alive. And he'd relied on his god to lead him from temptation, putting too much faith in the misguided belief that God would do all the work for him. Surely God would have stopped his straying hands if God really wanted to . . .

Eden now froze, because part of her *did* believe he just might pull that trigger, because her mother's fourth husband had never been able to resist temptation before. So she stood there and watched, helpless and filled with anger and frustration, as Greg stepped back into the house and slammed the door in her face.

Izzy had just woken up from a seven-hour nap in the parking lot of a McDonald's and had finally left the outskirts of Las Vegas proper when Dan Gillman called.

"Where are you?" Gillman asked, no *Hey, how's it going?* No nothing. Just *boom*. Demanding question, delivered with typical Gillman

whatever you're doing it can't be as important as what I'm doing attitude.

"Why the hell should I tell *you?*"

If Gillman noticed the hostility and frustration in Izzy's voice, he
didn't comment. Of course he probably didn't notice, because he
didn't see Izzy as anything more than a royal pain in his ass. He didn't
give a shit about what Izzy might or might not be feeling.

"Because if you're in Vegas," Gillman said, "I could really use
some help. I was just on the phone with Eden—the shit's hit the fan
with Ben and Greg. Greg's got a weapon—sounds like some kind of
small-caliber handgun—and he threatened to shoot Eden if Ben
didn't do what he said."

What the fuck . . . ? Izzy turned his steering wheel hard to the right
as he hit the brakes and pulled off the road in a spray of gravel and dust.
And okay. Maybe what Dan was doing *was* more important than what
Izzy was doing.

"I'm close enough to turn around and be back in town in minutes,"
Izzy told the other SEAL as he pulled a youie and reversed his tracks,
pushing the little rental car way up over the speed limit. "In fact, I'm
already on my way. Is she all right?"

"I think so," Dan said, then swore. "I don't know. She was really
upset and I'm not sure exactly what happened. I think Greg pulled the
weapon and made Ben go inside and . . . I don't know what they were
doing over there—she was saying something about the mall and the
police but then her phone went dead. When I called her back I went
right to voice mail. Jenn's still trying to reach her, but we got nothing.
We're still in New York—"

"Where was she when she called you?" Izzy interrupted, driving
even faster, trying not to get bogged down by the most obvious reason
that Eden wasn't answering her phone. There *were* other possibilities
besides her being too dead to pick up.

"Outside of the house," Dan told him. "You know, Ben's and
Ivette's."

Izzy did know. He'd been there before. With Dan. In fact, Dan had tried to kick his ass in the front yard of that very house. Where Eden was right now. Where fucking Greg had a fucking handgun.

"Greg's a fucking idiot," Dan said.

"I know." He was also a drunk. Always great when the deadly weapons were in the hands of the drunken fucking idiots.

"So be careful," Dan warned him. "You remember how to get over there?"

"I do."

"Call me when you arrive," Dan said, still doing his best imitation of the admiral of the fleet, but then added, "Please." Probably only because Jennilyn was standing beside him and had given him a nudge. No doubt about it, the woman brought out the non-asshole-ish side of the fishboy.

"I will," Izzy said. And if Dan could play nice for Jenn's benefit, Izzy could do the same. "Thanks for calling me."

There was a pause; then: "Thank you—for helping like this. I, um, really appreciate it, man."

Izzy hung up his phone, aware that somewhere to the south Satan was ice-skating while flying pigs did loop-de-loops overhead.

CHAPTER
TEN

I t happened unbelievably quickly.

Ben hadn't been locked in his bedroom for more than twenty minutes when the deadbolt clicked and the door opened.

He hadn't expected the police. Eden's various past run-ins with the law made her think of the men and women in blue as adversaries instead of allies. So it wasn't in her nature to call 9-1-1 in an emergency.

And Ben realized as the door opened wider that she *hadn't* called. The two men and a woman who were standing in the hallway definitely weren't police officers.

"How are you, Benjamin?" the older of the two men asked.

Ben stood up from where he'd been sitting on his bed, and backed away. His heart was pounding because he knew what this was, where they were from, and what they were here to do. "Considering I'm on the verge of being kidnapped by the Anti-Gay Squad, I'd say I'm pretty shitty."

"You watch your language, boy!" Greg had cleaned himself up for the occasion. He'd put on a clean shirt and combed his hair. He also held a cell phone in his hands instead of his gun.

And that was how he'd called this terrorist cell. Ben had heard Greg's voice out in the living room, not long after he'd ordered Ben into his room, told him to pack a bag, and thrown the deadbolt behind him.

Ben couldn't imagine that Greg had paid to have their phone turned back on, but apparently he'd invested in a disposable cell phone.

He must've gotten it sometime in the past twenty-four hours, while Ben was gone. He'd been busy, since he'd also removed the deadbolt that Eden had put on the door, back when this was her bedroom. He'd reversed and reinstalled it, so that the latch was now on the outside and the keyhole was on the inside. So that someone could be locked in, instead of out, as Eden had intended.

And Ben didn't have the key. He also couldn't get out the window. They were now both boarded up.

"It's not kidnapping, son," the other man—the one who was in early twenties at most. "You're ill, and your father here wants to help you."

Okay, there were so many things that were wrong about what he'd just said, including that *son*, Ben didn't know where to start. "He's not my father, and it's definitely kidnapping—or didn't he tell you that he locked me in here at gunpoint?"

His words didn't faze any of them. In fact, they all came farther into his room. The woman started going through his dresser and pulling out stacks of his clean socks, underwear, and T-shirts.

"Please don't touch my stuff," Ben said, but she didn't stop.

"He did what he felt he needed to do," the older man told him as the woman found his clean pair of black jeans on the shelf in his closet. "On our website, we encourage parents not to flinch from expressing their love for their children—forcefully if necessary."

"I said don't *touch* my *stuff*!" Ben got louder and even took a step toward the woman, and just like that it was all over.

The two men rushed him and he didn't have time to do more than flail as he tried to fight them off. They were bigger and stronger, and they easily muscled him to the floor before he even drew in enough breath to scream.

Then, Jesus, he was too surprised to scream as the pair of them unfastened his pants and pulled them down, flipping him over to expose his bare ass to the world—and was he the only one here who was picking up on the irony of this? Homoerotic, much, anyone?

But then he realized that the older man had a syringe, and then he did scream as the man gave him a shot, right in the butt.

"What the hell?" Ben said as the older man released him, as the younger one helped him pull his pants back up—and quite possibly copped a feel in the process—before he, too, let Ben go.

As he scrambled to his feet, buttoning his jeans, zipping his fly, it didn't make sense that Eden wasn't there—he expected her to come charging down the hall, at any minute, coming to his rescue.

But then his legs didn't hold him. They felt so leaden and weak. Or maybe the very air was heavy because once he crumpled on the floor he couldn't seem to hold his head up either and his arms didn't work and as he looked up at Greg's friends from the grimy bedroom carpeting he knew he'd lost.

It was worse than being tased.

Whatever was in that syringe made it impossible to stand or even to speak.

And they all smiled at him as he fought the inability to move, as he tried to form two distinct words. *Fuck* and *you*.

"A few months with us," the woman said cheerfully, as if they hadn't just drugged him against his will, as she put his clothes into plastic grocery bags, "and your need to mourn will come to an end. When you feel better about yourself and about the path you're taking in life, you'll wear bright colors again. And *that's* a promise."

I'd do that, Ben wanted to say, *if I could just live with my sister, because I know that she loves me. Do you know where she is . . . ?*

But he didn't get the words out before the woman and the entire room faded to gray.

Fifteen, twenty minutes, tops. That was all it took for Eden to run down to the convenience store on the corner and spend four jillion dollars on a cell-phone charger cord that she wasn't even sure would work.

She ran all the way back to Greg and Ivette's house, struggling to get the plastic package open, intending to go around to the side of the garage, where she knew there was an outdoor power outlet. She and her friend Tiffany used to huddle there on the cracked concrete, in the shade, with the ancient boom box that had been donated by the church—as was nearly everything they owned—plugged in and blasting.

But, now, as she approached the house, she realized that a car was parked out in front. And while it wasn't impossible that, after her cellphone battery had died, her brother had made a few calls and found a friend or teammate in the vicinity, it seemed unlikely that this car belonged to a Navy SEAL. Large and black, it was an older-model sedan, and as she got closer, she saw it was heavy with the Jesus bumperstickers.

It was then, while Eden was still three or four houses away, that a woman came out of the front door, carrying two plastic grocery bags. She was followed by two men who were carrying...

"Ben!" Eden shouted, her lungs burning as she ran even faster. "What did you do to him?"

Her little brother was clearly unconscious, one of his arms hanging down limply, his head lolling back.

And, Lord, Greg was out on the front steps now, pointing toward her and shouting something in his nasal-thin voice, and they all moved faster. The woman opened the rear door, and the two men together pushed and pulled Ben inside, one of them climbing into the back with him. The woman was already in the passenger seat, and the second man climbed in behind the wheel, just as Eden reached the car.

She heard the doors lock as she reached for the handle, and she saw alarm on the woman's face as she looked out the car window and up at Eden.

She was Ivette's age, but she had what Eden and Ben had always thought of as *hairdo hair*. It was cut short, and she'd spent time blowing it dry into a style most often worn by sitcom grandmothers, instead of just pulling it back into a haphazard and messy ponytail, the way Ivette usually did.

She had wide blue eyes and a fleshy face with a lipsticked mouth that made an almost perfect O as Eden used her handbag as a cudgel and swung it.

It didn't break the window. It didn't even crack it. It just thudded ineffectively as the car's engine started with a roar.

Eden moved then, sobbing with her anger, scrambling to put herself in front of the car, to keep them from pulling away.

"That's my brother," she heard herself saying. "Don't you goddamn take my brother! He doesn't want to go with you!"

The man behind the steering wheel could've been cast as the grandpa in the same sitcom with the woman. He had the same kind of too-many-cheeseburgers-and-not-enough-vegetables faces, with big bushy brows over eyes that looked pensive and sad.

The woman was frightened, and the man in the backseat who was leaning over into the front was angry, his mouth contorting as he said something Eden couldn't hear, his eyes dark and burning with hatred as he glared at her. But the man who was driving was neither scared nor angry, so Eden aimed her words at him, imploring him.

"There's nothing wrong with Ben," she said. "Please, don't take him away from me. Please, don't do this..."

But the man put the car into reverse. And putting his arm up along the back of the seat, he turned and looked out of the rear window and backed away down the street.

Eden ran after them, screaming now, cursing them, but he was going too fast, even backward like that, and he quickly pulled away. He swung the rear of the car into one of the neighbors' driveways, jerking to a stop before zooming off with a squeal of tires.

Leaving Eden standing alone, still sobbing and gasping for breath, in the middle of the road, watching until the sedan turned the corner, just as the police car had done earlier.

And when she turned back to look at the house, Greg had already gone inside, the door shut tightly behind him.

With a roar, Eden ran for the house, for the open garage, where a collection of broken rakes and garden tools were in a cobwebby corner.

They'd been there all those years ago, when the Gillman/Fortune family had moved in. Eden and Ben had been the only ones to touch them, that first winter, when they'd planted a flower garden in Deshawndra's honor.

But like Deshawndra, the flowers hadn't lived for long. As soon as spring arrived, they'd wilted and then dried up in the heat.

There was a pickax lying on the concrete floor—Eden had used it in an attempt to break up the rock-hard ground before they'd given up and bought a window box.

She grabbed it now—screw the deadly spiders who lived in this hellhole—and ran with it to the front of the house.

Where she threw her handbag onto the dusty yard after untangling it from her arm, and hefting the heavy pickax up to her waist, she spun with it once, twice...And then she hurled it, like the discuses she'd thrown in gym back in high school, toward the living-room window.

But it was too heavy and it didn't travel far enough. Instead of hitting the window with a crash, it landed in the dirt in front of the house with a thud.

She was going to have to use the direct approach, swinging it up and over her head, closing her eyes against the spray of shattering glass. She ran to pick it up and try again.

As Izzy watched Eden throw a freaking pickax toward the living-room window of the house that Dan Gillman's mother shared with her creepy husband Greg and Dan's brother Ben, all he could think— aside from *Nice form, but you're a little too far back*—was that Greg was in there with a weapon.

So he drove the rental right up onto the lawn, and he opened the car door before he even hit the brakes. He had the engine off and was out and sliding over the sizzling-hot hood a heartbeat after that. In another heartbeat, he'd locked his arms around Eden before she'd picked up the ax again, and he pulled her back, behind the shelter of the car.

She fought him—she was unbelievably angry—and he had to keep her down by lying on top of her in the dust, repeating, "I'm not trying to hurt you, I'm on your side," over and over until it penetrated.

Until she stopped struggling and looked up at him as if she couldn't believe her own eyes. "Izzy?"

He could totally relate. This was off the charts in Unexpected-Land, and he, too, was experiencing some serious what-the-fuck. And not just from the visual of being nose-to-nose, but from the physical sensation of having their legs entangled, of using his hips and stomach and chest to pin her down, her wrists in each one of his hands, pulled up over her head.

Last time he'd had this much contact with her, she'd been round and pregnant. Now she was an intriguing mix of soft breasts and solid muscle—she had to be strong to be able to do that routine he'd seen her do earlier today, on that pole in the strip club.

And even though he was done with her, and he'd said his last good-bye mere hours ago in the club where she was paid to get naked, he could feel his body responding to her, especially when she breathed, "Thank God you're here!"

And now she was struggling to get her hands free for another reason entirely—to throw her arms around his neck and hold him even closer.

Which he let her do.

And yeah, his freaking pitiful body was too stupid to recognize that her thankful and grateful reaction to his presence had everything to do with her little brother's disappearance and nothing to do with her desire to have him drill her, right there, on the rock-hard dust.

He scrambled to sit up, because he knew if he didn't, she wouldn't fail to notice—on account of the fact that her thigh was pressed tightly between his legs.

"Sorry," she said, "sorry," as he disentangled them, and great. She'd definitely noticed, because now she was embarrassed, too. But then she added, "I didn't mean to, you know, *attack* you like that..."

"You didn't," he said. "And I didn't mean to, um..."

He didn't have to finish his sentence, which was a good thing, because he wasn't sure how to end it. *Get a chubby because you're so fucking hot? Reveal myself for the shallow loser that you now know me to be, since even after the piss-poor way you've treated me, I still get a boner whenever I'm within three yards of you and would obviously shag you, if the opportunity arose, at the drop of a hat?*

But he just let his words trail off as she said, "They took Ben," in a voice that quavered. And as she pulled back, she pushed her hair from her face with a shaking hand. And Izzy realized that she was drenched with perspiration, as if she'd just run a marathon. "I couldn't stop them." Her face twisted, like a little kid who was about to cry. "I tried, but I couldn't, and I'm so *stupid*, because I didn't get the license-plate number." She was furious, mostly with herself. But just like the first time they'd met, she was loath to cry in front of him. "I didn't even look to find out the *state*, and I have no idea who they were or where they took him, but Greg knows, the bastard, and I'm going to make him tell me if it's the last thing I do!"

She tried to stand up, apparently determined to return to her attempt to put a hole through that window and climb inside to throw down with Greg—regardless of his weaponry and her lack of same. Izzy grabbed hold of the waistband of her jeans and yanked and she plopped back down in the dust beside him.

"I'm not quite up to speed," he said. "Do you mind slowing down just a little and filling me in on exactly what happened between your phone call with Danny and your Thor, Mighty God of War impression?"

"Did Danny call you?" she asked.

"Yeah," he said. "I wasn't that far out of town, so . . ."

"You were leaving." She didn't ask it as a question. It was a statement that she wanted confirmed.

"I was," he said. "I mean, I got what I came for. You know, a chance to see you. See for myself that you're okay."

She gazed up at him with those eyes that he'd dreamed about, giving him that look that generally meant she was trying her damnedest to read his mind, but in truth didn't have a clue as to what he was thinking.

"I'm working as a stripper," she finally said.

"Yeah," he said. "I did make note of that, the clues being somewhat obvious." He cleared his throat. "So what happened? You were here with Ben, but Greg was locked and loaded...?"

"Greg said he'd shoot me if Ben didn't go into the house," Eden told him. "And Ben believed him and he went inside. I called Danny, and I should've called 9-1-1. I don't know why I didn't, I'm so stupid—"

"Whoa," Izzy said. "You'll have plenty of time later to beat yourself up over any alleged mistakes. Right now I'm looking for the facts."

"Fact: I should have called the police, instead I called Danny, and while I was talking to him, my cell phone battery died. There's something wrong with it. I should've taken it back to the store weeks ago, but I didn't." Eden was brutal when it came to self-recrimination.

"What did you do after the battery died?" Izzy asked.

"I ran to the convenience store," she told him. "The closest one burned down, so I had to go almost all the way to the mall, to the Shell Station. They sell things like power cords and chargers that work in a car? It was insanely expensive, and they wouldn't even let me open it to see if it was going to fit my phone. But I bought it anyway, and ran back. I was gone maybe twenty minutes, but when I got here, there was already a car out front, like Greg had called someone to come get Ben."

"And you think, whoever they are, they're from one of these places where they try to convince kids that they're not really gay?"

Eden nodded, her eyes filling with tears that she fiercely blinked back. "They knocked him out. I don't know if they drugged him or hit him, but they carried him to the car—the two men did. There were two men and a woman. And he was all floppy. He wouldn't've gone with them. Not willingly. God, he could be anywhere by now..."

"But the people who took him," Izzy pointed out, "are probably from somewhere nearby. They got here pretty quickly. Did they say anything to you?"

She shook her head no. "They just put Ben in their car and left. I couldn't stop them."

"And Greg's still inside?" Izzy asked.

She nodded, a murderous light in her eyes. "He knows where Ben is."

"He's also armed and probably drunk. Not a good combination. I mean, armed and an asshole is bad enough."

"I don't care. I want Ben back."

"We'll get him back," Izzy promised her. "Let's just do it without Greg shooting you, okay?"

"I don't care if he shoots me," Eden said, and this time she couldn't fight back and her tears overflowed. "I want Ben back, and I want him safe, and I want it *now*."

This was about more than Ben, who was a smart, resilient kid, and Izzy didn't know what to say, what to do. But he did know what *not* to do—as in help Eden commit the crime of home invasion and risk arrest—assuming they survived Greg's legally allowed self-defense of his property.

Instead, he put his arms around Eden, held her tightly, and just let her cry.

CHAPTER
ELEVEN
NEW YORK CITY
WEDNESDAY, 6 MAY 2009

He got there, Eden's safe," Dan reported to Jenn as he hung up from Izzy's very brief phone call.

"Thank God," she said, glancing up from the laptop where she was writing letters to help a local veterans' homeless shelter find the funding it needed to reopen after a fire. "You okay?"

He shook his head. "I don't know. I guess. I'm just... I'm starting to think it might be better for me to go to Vegas by myself. I mean, you're busy. It's been weeks since you've been home..."

"I can take the time," she told him.

"I hate that I'm pulling you away from things like the shelter. It's important. More important than holding my hand through the relentless and endless bullshit that is my life."

Jenn closed her computer, setting it aside and giving him her full attention. She didn't say anything, she just gazed at him until he shrugged.

"It is," he insisted.

"What do you think is going to happen," she asked, "that I haven't seen before in my own dysfunctional family?"

And Jesus, she'd hit the nail directly on the head, so Dan stopped pretending. "Believe me, my family makes *your* family look like the Brady Bunch."

"You don't know that," Jenn pointed out. "You *can't* know that."

"Yeah, I can. It's going to get ugly," he admitted. "And now that Greg owns a gun...? How do I know, even if I gain possession of his weapon, which I will damn sure do before entering that house—but even then, how do I know he's only got the one? And *that's* just the firearms violence factor—which is a new one for us. Or an old one—I thought it went away when my father moved out. Jenni, I don't want you near that, and yeah, there's more. I'm...embarrassed that you're going to see..." Jesus, this was hard to say. "Me," he managed. "Saying and doing things that...Will make you think less of me."

"That's not going to happen," she said.

"I can't spend any time with them without thinking considerably less of myself," Dan confessed. "When you meet Ivette...You're going to look at her and think, *Shit, Danny left his sister and brother with* this *nightmare?* And I did. I abandoned them. I just walked away."

"You were, what? Seventeen when you left to join the Navy?" Jenn asked. "Give yourself a break. And you might want to look up the definition for *abandon*—I'm pretty sure it doesn't involve sending money home every month or flying to Las Vegas on a moment's notice because your brother and sister need you."

She was absolute in her support of him.

"It feels like it's too little, too late," Dan confessed.

"It's not," she told him.

And when she leaned in to kiss him, he could almost believe her.

LAS VEGAS
WEDNESDAY, MAY 6, 2009

The plan was to wait for Eden's mother to get home.

There was no point in talking to Greg without Ivette on the premises, so the plan was to sit in Izzy's rental car and watch the house until she returned from work.

Wherever that was.

Eden honestly didn't know. But even if she *had* known, she could well have not actually *known*—because Ivette got fired as quickly as she got hired with her still-pretty face and Grand Canyon cleavage.

This way, though, they didn't have to hunt her down. This way, they'd be watching and waiting for her to return.

"What if they don't tell us?" Eden asked as they sat in front of the neighbor's house so as to be not quite so obvious, the motor running to power the air-conditioning. She looked at Izzy. "You know. Where Ben is."

He looked back at her, his dark eyes colorless in the deepening twilight. "Our Plan B is to call Greg's church tomorrow." He put his hand to his ear in the international symbol for talking on a cell phone, and said in voice that sounded a lot like Stewie from *Family Guy*, "Hello, is this the Church of Hatred and Intolerance? Yes, my name is Bob Muncher and I think I've come to the right place for this kind of help. Our son, Dickie, has been singing Elton John songs, in French, in the shower, and *everyone* knows that means he's in there having gay sex with himself, so if you could recommend one of those places where we could send him so that we don't have to face any actual scientific and medical truths about homosexuality..."

Eden had to laugh, but it came out sounding more like a sob. "I want him back tonight. I don't want to have to wait until tomorrow."

"I know," Izzy said quietly as a car slowly drove past them. But it went past Greg and Ivette's house, too, turning the corner at the end of the street. "But, Eed, he'll be okay. He's a pretty tough kid. Wherever he is right now, he knows you're looking for him. He knows you'll find him and get him out of there as soon as you can."

She wasn't so sure about that. Ben knew, firsthand, that she was a screwup when it came to saving the day.

"And he also knows that you've been talking to Dan," Izzy pointed out. "And that the cavalry's on its way." He cleared his throat. "What time are he and Jenn getting in tomorrow?"

"Danny didn't tell me," Eden said. She turned to look at him. "Dick Muncher?"

Izzy smiled back at her. "You just got that now, huh?"

The last rays from the setting sun threw shadows that emphasized the sharp angles of his lean face. He was not a handsome man by most women's definitions, but Eden had always found him heart-stoppingly attractive. He was so . . . alive. His outrageous sense of humor and keen intelligence radiated from him, and sparkled and danced in his eyes.

"Of course, I should talk," he added, looking out at the street, eyes back on their target—the house. "I feel like I'm on a comprehension time delay, too. I'm running everything through the what-the-fuck filter, you know?"

"Yeah," she said. She did know. Being here, with him, like this, was surreal and more than a little awkward—and it was just like him to bring that up. Still, she was enormously grateful for his presence. She took a deep breath. "I can't thank you enough for helping me like this."

"I'm happy to," he said. "This is . . . beyond weird, it's true. But you know me, I'm okay with weird."

"If I were you, I'd hate me. I'd run away from me, screaming."

"I don't," he said, glancing over at her again. "Hate you. I wish things had, um, ended differently between us. There were things I wanted to say."

"I couldn't stay," Eden told him.

"I get that," Izzy said. "I really do understand. Probably more than you think and—Heads up. Is that your mother's car?"

Sure enough, someone in a newer-model SUV was pulling up in front the house. "I seriously doubt it," Eden said. "Unless she's started, like, selling drugs or hooking."

Izzy looked at her.

"I'm kidding," she said. "And no, I don't let anyone do more than look, and screw you for thinking that I would."

"I wasn't—" he started to say as both the driver's and front passenger's doors opened, and two men climbed out into the street. "Okay, maybe I *was* wondering, because, as long as we're talking about this, hooking doesn't seem—to me—to be that big a step away from stripping."

"It is," Eden said. "It's a huge step."

He didn't say anything, but it wasn't because he didn't disagree. He was just focusing again on the two men in the street.

The taller guy was bald, and apparently driving had given him a wedgie, because he took a moment to do some serious adjustments to his balls before following the other guy to the front door. To be fair, though, he clearly didn't know they were sitting here, watching.

"Who are they?" Eden wondered aloud.

"They're not part of the team who kidnapped Ben?"

"No."

"They're both carrying," Izzy said. "Shoulder holsters. You can tell from the way they hold their arms."

Eden couldn't tell, but she believed him. "Maybe they're from Greg's neo-Nazi prayer group."

As they watched, Greg opened the front door a crack, peering out at the two men. There was a conversation in which the wedgie-free bald guy did most of the talking and...

"Okay," Izzy said. "That was definitely meant to look like a police-badge flash, but it seemed kinda short to me—like *Don't look too closely at this ID I picked up from the Halloween Shop, along with my beat-cop costume*... How stupid is Greg, exactly?"

"Exactly?" she asked. "Somewhere between Wile E. Coyote and Homer Simpson."

Izzy laughed. "I'd almost forgotten why I—" He stopped himself, his smile gone, but then finished the sentence. "Loved you." He was careful to make sure she heard that *ed* that made it past tense.

Eden couldn't look at him. And he, too, was now focused on the front steps of the house, where Greg opened the door wider, but didn't invite the two men inside. He turned on the porch light—amazing that it actually had a bulb that worked—and pushed open the screen so that he could take a piece of paper being handed to him. Again, it was the bald guy's mouth that did most of the moving.

Meanwhile, Izzy had fished his cell phone from his pants pocket—he was still wearing those completely-out-of-character khakis, although he'd torn the knee keeping her from her second attempt at putting that pickax through the window—and was snapping photos. Of the men talking to Greg. And of the SUV with its Nevada plates.

"These aren't the men who took Ben," Eden said, making sure he understood.

"I get it, Obi-Wan, but it's kinda suspicious, them showing up like this, right after Ben was taken." He checked to make sure he got the plate number, zooming in on the digital photo, and then snapping his phone shut, when he saw that he had. "I'm just being thorough."

Greg was squinting at whatever was on that paper—some kind of picture—and shaking his head.

"Maybe they really are cops," Eden said. "This whole awful thing started when Ben got stopped by the police, at the mall. He told me that the detectives were looking for a friend of his. This little Asian girl who ran away from home. He said they showed him a picture of her."

Greg handed the paper back, and pulled the screen door shut. But then he opened it again, and took something smaller from the bald guy. It looked like a business card. And this time, after latching the screen, he closed the front door, too.

The two men—maybe cops, maybe not—were moving down the steps, taking a look at the yard, the broken glass from that window Eden had trashed nearly a year ago glittering in the porch light. They didn't miss the pickax, either. It still lay where she had thrown it, beneath the living-room window.

The place looked exactly like what it was. The home of desperate people who not only lived hand to mouth, but made bad decisions about which bills to pay first.

Izzy rolled down his window slightly, turning off the a/c fans so they could—maybe—hear what the two men said to each other as they headed for their SUV. And sure enough, they'd raised their voices to converse over the roof.

"...could offer a reward," the man with the hat was saying. "Doesn't have to be much. Ten thousand dollars."

The bald man was heading for the driver's-side door, which put him into the middle of the road, closest to Izzy's cracked window. "For ten K," he agreed as he opened the door, "he'd get his kid home from that camp and make him suck both our cocks at the same time. And claim he was doing it for Jesus."

The other man laughed and said something as he opened the passenger door, but Eden missed it, because the bald guy had already closed his door and started the engine with a roar.

Which is when Izzy said, "Oh, *shit*."

He grabbed her, wrapping his right arm around her and pulling her close so swiftly, she slammed up against him. He was so solid, she nearly had the wind knocked out of her and she looked up at him in stunned surprise.

"What—" she said, but then she couldn't say more, because just like that, he covered her mouth with his and was kissing her.

It was as sudden as the body-slam embrace, and it was a very high-octane kiss, with exactly zero acceleration to get to that place. On a passion scale from one to ten, it started at around six hundred, just *bam*, with his tongue in her mouth and his hand on her breast, and she gasped her surprise.

But before she could react in any way whatsoever, the headlights of the SUV went on, like spotlights in their faces, and she understood.

They could either be fully lit, in plain sight of the two men in the SUV while they were suspiciously sitting and watching Greg and Ivette's house, or they could be fully lit while they were innocently sitting in Izzy's car, making out.

Pretending to make out.

Problem was, pretending felt an awful lot like the real thing.

Still, she kissed Izzy back, looping her arm around his neck and hitting him with the same level of passion that he was dishing out, running her fingers through the decadent softness of his hair as she tried her best to eat him alive without going so far as to throw her leg across him, to straddle him right there in the front seat of the car.

Even though—God help her—she wanted to.

Pretending. This was only pretending. But Lord, it felt so good—the ardent way he was kissing her—and Eden knew with a flash of certainty that he *wasn't* pretending. He'd always wanted her, and he obviously still did, even though she'd hurt him as badly as she had.

And didn't *that* give her the ultimate power?

Except for the fact that she was powerless when it came to her feelings for this man. Her heart had leaped at the sight of him, when she'd realized he'd come zooming, once again, to her rescue. She'd almost kissed him like this right there, in the dust of the front yard, after he'd pulled her down behind his car.

But she *did* have the power, because it was now clear that—if she *had* kissed him? He would have kissed her back, exactly the way he was kissing her now.

He'd always tried to bury it—his lust for her. He'd tried to hide it or dress it up, disguising it as something loftier—as love. And he'd probably even fooled himself. A lot of men did. *I love you* really only meant *I want to get with you.*

Seeing him again—sitting here and talking to him—was... devastating. It was heartbreaking. It was soul shaking. It had pulled Eden back, hard, into that crazy place of longing and wanting. Longing for something she knew she'd never have. Wanting to believe words she knew couldn't be true. *I love you . . .*

But *I want to get with you . . .*

That she could handle. And as long as she knew what she was doing, as long as she stayed in control . . .

The SUV was pulling past them, heading down the street, and Eden broke free from that kiss, turning her head away as if she'd suddenly become aware of the light, hiding her face against the wide expanse of Izzy's shoulder, as the too-bright headlights slid past their car.

And then there they were, sitting in the dark again, both breathing hard.

"Sorry." Izzy's voice was raspy, his breath hot against the side of her face as he exhaled hard, as he moved his hand from her boob but still continued to hold her in his arms. "I didn't know what else to do."

"No," she whispered as she, too, kept her arms around his neck. "It's okay. If they were cops, I didn't want to have to answer their questions."

"The cops are the good guys," Izzy said, still not releasing her.

"Not always," she said. "But you are. You're always the hero. Coming to my rescue." She lifted her head to look at him, and the look in his eyes was one that she'd remember on her deathbed. It was desire, pure and sweet.

"Eed," he breathed, "I think I might be on the verge of really screwing this up—our new friendship, our impending amicable divorce—"

She didn't let him finish. She just kissed him.

And on a scale from one to ten, it was completely off the charts.

Eden kissed him as if the world were ending.

Izzy saw it coming, and even though he saw it telegraphed in her eyes, in the way her tongue briefly moistened her lips, he still couldn't quite believe it. And he certainly didn't do anything to stop it.

But then, as she kept kissing him, he *could* believe it, because this was Eden, and she wasn't just kissing him, she'd actually thrown her leg across him and straddled him—which was possible only because he'd adjusted the seat as far back as it could go and had reclined it quite a bit, too.

And it was very, very clear that she, too, was hell-bent on screwing up their impending amicable divorce. Or maybe she wasn't. Maybe this was her crazy-ass definition of being amicable.

Either way, it was obvious that they were both extremely willing passengers aboard this particular bad-idea bus. And as she reached between them to verify that that was, indeed, him in all his glory and not the gearshift, he knew that, this time? He wasn't going to be the one to stop them.

He was done with that.

He'd spent nearly his entire premarriage relationship with Eden slowing her down to an absolute stop, and look at where that had gotten him. Decidedly unfucked for all of his gallant efforts, except for their very brief wedding night. Oh yeah, and except for the ultimate fucking she'd given him shortly thereafter, by walking away.

Now, however, hoh *jay*-sus, she was simultaneously reaching into his pants even as she pressed and rubbed herself against him, all the while kissing the shit out of him.

His own hands weren't idle. He'd sent them on an assignment up beneath her T-shirt, to find and unfasten the front clasp of her bra. Her skin was cool and silky, and—mission accomplished—he filled his hands with the unfettered softness of her breasts as she moaned her approval.

She stopped kissing him to pull back slightly, her goal apparent— to unzip and free him from his pants.

His own choices were a) to pull up her shirt so he could kiss and lick the sweet tautness of her nipples into his mouth, or b) to start working to get her out of her jeans. That was going to be quite a task, involving an Olympic-worthy dismount—not to mention the impending awkwardness and self-consciousness that would no doubt come with her being half naked in a fishbowl-like car on a fairly busy suburban street.

True, there was currently no traffic and the streetlamp on the corner had long burned out. The circle of light from Greg and Ivette's porch lamp didn't begin to reach them, but still, Izzy was pretty certain that the odds of him actually getting laid right here, right now, were slim to none.

He did not doubt, however, that he was going to get a very lovely BJ, which was fine by him. Fine, that is, by this new, heart-hardened him.

Still, if he had his druthers, he'd prefer the big bang, and he took the optimistic route and unfastened the top button of her jeans, his fingers against the smooth warmth of her stomach. She was wearing jeans with a button fly, so he kept going—and found she was wearing the same red satin thong that she'd worn while stripping.

That discovery was either off-putting or hot, and he decided to let it be hot. And it did, absolutely, make him even harder as he remembered the way she'd moved when she'd danced. Or maybe he was responding to the unobstructed touch of her impossibly soft hands as she finally untangled him from both his pants and briefs.

And there it came—the dismount he'd been expecting. She pulled away completely, leaving him the use of his own hands to recline his seat a bit more, and to push his pants and briefs a bit more down his thighs, away from any impending spill zone.

But when he realized what she was doing—kicking off her right sneaker and pulling her right leg free from her jeans in the age-old sex-in-the-car tradition of not getting completely undressed—he dug for his wallet and the condom he always carried there in the event that he bumped into Veronica Mars and Lieutenant Starbuck from *BSG*, and they wanted to do him simultaneously.

Or in the event that he bumped into Eden.

He kept that condom there, he had to admit, mostly because of Eden. Although before today, the idea that she'd seriously want to do him had seemed as absurd and impossible as a three-way with outer-space-themed fictional characters, even though one of them was only named after a planet.

But he now took it out of his wallet, dropping the leather bifold that held his ID and credit card onto the floor of the car so he could more quickly cover himself. He focused on the task at hand—penis, latex, rolling it carefully down—so he didn't have to think about the fact that he shouldn't be doing this.

And there, alas, it was: *He shouldn't be doing this.*

Izzy pushed the unhelpful thought away. Latex. Penis. Happy,

happy penis. Not *quite* as happy as it had been under Eden's sure touch, but that was going to change very quickly, very soon.

He shouldn't be doing—

Oh, yeah, asshole? Why the fuck not?

Because you still love her, dim nuts. And maybe—just maybe—she loves you, and this is some kind of a test—

You are such a fucking moron. Test? She doesn't love you. This is just her twisted way of saying thank you. Just shut up and get it while you can. She'll be gone again, soon enough.

And where will that leave you? Freaked out and feeling like the shit that you are, because you know *that she thinks all guys want just one thing from her, and here you are on the verge of proving her right.*

Eden ended Izzy's mental argument with himself by coming back, slipping her completely naked right leg over him.

But no doubt about it, despite how far back he'd reclined his seat, that steering wheel was going to interfere. So even as she came toward him, he lifted her up, and moved them both up and over the parking brake, and quickly reclined that seat as far as it could go.

He reached out and touched her then, sliding his fingers up the entire gorgeously smooth length of her leg. She, in turn, had reached for him again, one arm bracing herself as she balanced there above him, and she stroked him even as she maneuvered him toward her, pushing him just a little bit inside of her, and then a little bit more.

He watched her face, just letting her have complete control. Her eyes were closed, and she'd caught her lower lip between her teeth. But then, God, as she pushed herself down, all the way down, she opened her eyes and looked back at him.

Izzy had no idea what kind of expression he was wearing, but she seemed to think a conversation was in order.

"I was a little afraid it would hurt," she whispered.

"Hurt?" he echoed, aware as hell that he was about as deeply inside of her as he could possibly be. At least in the front seat of a car like this. He wasn't quite sure what to do. Move her off of him?

"But it doesn't," she said before he could do anything. And then, as if to prove it, she began to move on top of him, pulling herself up and almost entirely off him, before sliding slowly back down. "Definitely not."

Yeah, *hurt* wasn't the word he'd use to describe what she was doing, at least not on his end.

"Why were you afraid it would hurt?" he asked, even though he was pretty sure he knew the answer, as he lifted his hips up to meet her in a move that made her moan.

"Why would it?" he asked again, because it was clear she'd forgotten—or was ignoring his question.

"Because it's been so long," Eden told him in a sigh, closing her eyes as he again pushed himself home.

"For me, too," he admitted, even as his heart pounded at the idea that Eden hadn't been with anyone else. Of course, she hadn't exactly said that... Still, it was a nice fantasy—one that he was happy to run with at this moment. "Damn, sweetheart, at the risk of ruining your evening, I think I got three, maybe four more of those left in me. I usually last much longer. In my defense, I think I might be a little distracted by the whole in-the-car thing, too."

She laughed as she lifted herself up and began another long, slow slide back down. "Are you seriously apologizing? In advance? For the most awesome sex I've had this year?" She leaned forward and caught his mouth with hers, kissing him, even as she moaned again at his extra push.

And then she didn't pull back again, at least not the way she'd been doing it for the past few moments. She moved against him, faster, hard, then even harder, as if, even though he was filling her completely, it still wasn't enough.

So he gave her more, pushing himself as deeply as he could inside of her, his hands on the softness of her ass as he anchored her in place and thrust himself up and up and up.

"Oh, yes," she broke their kiss to say. "Yes!"

So Izzy kept doing what he was doing, even though it meant he couldn't stop his own release from ripping through him, and really, there was nothing he could have done to prevent it, but he was hyper-aware that she still hadn't come. But then she did come, God, and as she did, she moaned his name.

And forget best sex of the year, it was the best sex of his life, and he was so fucked, because the voice in his head had been dead right.

He was still in love with her.

Of that he no longer had any doubt.

CHAPTER
TWELVE

Time of day had held no meaning when she was in her cell.

Neesha had slept when she was tired, and had eaten whenever the food arrived. Since the food had been for the clients, too, she would know that a visit was imminent whenever a meal was laid out on her table at some strange hours of the day or night.

Of course, if there was preparation involved—a costume or other instructions regarding her hair or hygiene, one of the women would come in, in advance of the food. They wouldn't knock on the door. They would simply enter, unannounced. If Neesha was sleeping, they would wake her. If she was watching TV, they would take the remote and turn it off.

At first the visits were infrequent—no more than one or two times a week. But as she got older, they increased to the point of one or two each day. And when she complained, the women who prepared her warned her to hush. They told her there were only two options for one such as her, who had started working so young.

One was to transition to work as a young woman, eventually being moved to a house overseas. Her days and nights would no longer be as luxurious as they had been—her visits would increase to a dozen or more a day. Which she would accept, graciously, cheerfully, and thankfully, with no complaints.

Because the other option—whether she remained here or was

moved abroad—was for her to be sold for vast sums to a man who would take her to his home, where she would be at his beck and call until he tired of her. At which point, he would kill her and feed her chopped-up body to his dogs.

And she would never be missed, because she had been smuggled into the country after her mother had died—after she'd been sold to Mr. Nelson to pay her mother's debts. She was illegal. Exploitable. Nonexistent. No one knew she was here, and no one cared.

If she ever escaped—God forbid—and went to the police, she would be arrested on sight.

Neesha knew this was true, because she'd watched news programs as often as she could, as she'd taught herself to speak and understand English. She'd seen the anger Americans held toward illegals. She'd heard the ugliness and hatred in their voices. She'd seen the rancor on their faces, even toward children.

Especially toward children.

She would be deported. Shipped off to a country where, should she let it slip that she was a sex worker, or even just that she'd lived in America and that she'd repeatedly committed the sin of fornication— regardless of the fact that she'd been willing or not—her punishment would be death. She would be stoned to death or burned or even buried alive for disgracing her family.

And she knew *this* was true, because she'd seen footage and pictures, shown to her by the woman who tended her. She also knew that they were meant to frighten her.

And they had done just that.

Time of day had held no meaning when she was in her cell—not the way it did now that she'd made her escape.

Now her mornings were for cleaning up and resting. She'd found a safe haven in the public library, where she'd convinced the librarians that she had accompanied her fictional father on a business trip. She would be here with him, she'd told the friendly women with the kind eyes, until the end of the summer. She always dressed the same, in dark pants and a white shirt, because it was her school uniform and she was working here in the library on an assignment to learn to read English.

She'd wash in the bathroom sinks and drink from the water fountain, and then she would curl up in the corner, in a comfy chair and look at books by a very strange doctor named Seuss.

One of the librarians found her books to read in Indonesian, after Neesha had told her that she was from Jakarta. But she couldn't read those books, either—it had been too long. Still she pretended that she could, and thanked the woman, who then proceeded to show Neesha a computer program that calculated the number of miles from Las Vegas to Jakarta.

And she'd nearly cried when she'd seen how very far away it was—that city where her grandfather still lived—*if* he still lived after all these years. It was on an island that was hardly more than a small dot in the huge vastness of an ocean called the Pacific, and it was then that she knew she would most likely never again see her grandfather or her home.

She entered the library each day with caution, sitting outside, across the street and watching the entrance for about an hour before the doors first opened.

She would stay there, inside in the coolness, until the afternoon, when she went to one of three shopping malls that she'd discovered. There she would find enough food to last her throughout her day.

Nighttime was the most frightening—she feared the dark and all that could hide in the shadows. At first she'd kept moving, stayed alert, even as she tried not to call too much attention to herself—a girl on the street, alone.

Still, there were those who saw her—a group of women, some not that much older than she was—who beckoned and called to her. "Come and join our party!" And "When you get tired of wandering and decide you want to make some real money, come back and find us, here on Paradise Road. But, girlfriend? First find some hotter clothes so you at least look fourteen..."

But Neesha's wandering took her away from the brightly lit main streets, and into neighborhoods that weren't too far away, but where people lived not in big buildings, but in individual houses. And she returned there when darkness fell, and she curled up on patio furniture, with the comforting sounds of TVs bleeding through the walls and windows.

Sometimes she slept.

But she'd neither eaten nor slept since she'd seen the two men looking for her at the mall, since she'd known for sure that Mr. Nelson and Todd were closing in. She'd stayed far from the library, too.

She'd kept moving. All day and into the night.

But now she crouched in the shadows. And she watched the apartment where Ben lived with his sister. There was no sign of anyone else watching. Not the big man who'd been out front yesterday, or the two men she'd seen at the mall.

She was the only one hanging around. Everyone else moved quickly to get inside, away from the relentless heat.

And finally, after many hours, she knew that she had to take a chance. That maybe Ben's sister *could* help her.

At the very least, maybe Ben was home. And this time she would take him up on his offer of a shower and a snack.

Her stomach rumbled as she crept from the shadows and found Ben's key under the potted plant. Dr. Seuss had taught her to read American numbers, and she climbed the stairs to the second floor, and found the door with the two, the one, and the four.

She knocked before trying the key, but no one answered, so she slipped the key into the lock, the way she'd seen Ben do, and the door opened for her, with a click.

It was dark in the apartment, and she slipped inside, moving swiftly through the rooms, and yes, no one was home. She was alone.

Izzy stayed silent as Eden rested her forehead against his shoulder, as they still both struggled to catch their breath, as the passion segment of their insanity ended and the messy cleanup part began.

Something, obviously, needed to be said, and *So, how much do I owe you?* was probably not the way to start the conversation if he wanted to live to see another day. Even though her *I'm afraid this might hurt, it's been so long* comment seemed like something a girl would learn to tell her clients in the very first classroom session of Vegas Hooking 101.

The only thing she'd left out was a breathless *and you're so, so big*.

And yeah, the voices in his head had both been right. He was a fucking moron, he was still in love with her, and he was pissed as hell at himself for being so weak because she definitely wasn't going to learn to trust him if all he did was prove he was no different from all the other guys who only wanted to fuck her.

And at the same time, he knew with an absolute certainty that he'd done the right thing for himself. Because even if he'd kept her at arm's length, professing his undying love, she not only wouldn't believe him, but she wouldn't give a shit. All he'd have was a boner and a missed opportunity to get off, and he'd been there, done that. Because she was *never* going to trust him, and she was, eventually, going to leave again. If things got too difficult—which they probably would in about seventeen seconds—she *would* walk away.

It was her MO and he could count on it.

Besides, the truth was, he *did* want to fuck her. Forever and endlessly. For the next solid year of his life, nonstop, if possible. After which he'd be dead, but his corpse would be smiling.

To his surprise, she spoke first as he reached forward to kick the car's a/c up into a higher gear.

"I missed you," she murmured, her voice muffled because her face was still pressed against his shoulder. But that was definitely what she'd said.

And Izzy didn't quite know what to say, so he went with the naked truth. "Yeah, I missed you, too."

She pulled back then to look at him, and even though night had fully fallen long before she'd pulled off her jeans, there was enough light from the dimly glowing dashboard so that, up close like this, he could see her face, and she could see his.

She wasn't smiling—in fact, she looked as if she were fighting tears. And she said, in a very small voice, "I don't blame you, you know, for giving up on me."

And with that she nodded over at the other seat and added, "Could you . . . ? Do you mind?"

He obeyed automatically, picking them both up and over the parking brake. Somewhere in there, she pulled off of him, neatly sliding into the passenger seat. She grabbed her handbag from where she'd thrown it in the back and dug through it, pulling out a plastic baggie filled with tissues as he attempted to comprehend.

"Wait a minute," he said. "What? I *what?*"

She handed him a small stack of the tissues, which he used to adios the condom, because it was definitely better to have this conversation without his dick hanging out, doing its postsex shrinky-dink imitation.

"I know I shouldn't complain," Eden said as she slid her leg back into both her stripper panties and her jeans, managing to slip her foot into her sneaker with dead accuracy as it emerged from the pants leg. A smooth, solid reminder that this was not her first time at the rodeo. "Since I didn't exactly come back to San Diego to see you, after I left Europe."

She lifted her hips to rebutton herself and adjust her pants around her, then reached up beneath her T-shirt and refastened the front clasp of her bra.

At which point Izzy slapped on the car's interior overhead light with the back of his hand. "You've got to be fucking kidding me."

She recoiled at his vehemence, squinting at him in the sudden brightness even as she straightened her messy hair, pulling it back into a ponytail.

"I flew to Germany every single fucking chance I got," he told her, his voice actually breaking with his disbelief. "*Every* chance."

"Sorry," she said, bristling. "I know you were busy—of course, you were busy and it was a long way to travel. And I don't mean to sound ungrateful, because I know it took me forever to get my act together, but...God, you didn't even write back."

"Write?" he asked. "*Back?*"

"After I sent you that letter," Eden told him. "At Christmas...?" She was looking at him with an added *you asshole* in her eyes, but then she realized his stunned shock was for real. "You didn't get it."

She said it in exact unison with his "I didn't get it." Part of him was completely ready to buy this—the idea that their months-long separation had been due to a simple miscommunication—and was ready to fall into her arms, weeping and proclaiming his undying love.

But part of him was emotionally detached, watching as if from outside of his own recently well-fucked body as she told him exactly— *exactly*—what she knew he'd want to hear.

And that skeptical part of him needed to do a serious cross-examine. "But I came to see you in January. *And* February."

"You came to...?" She was convincingly confused. "You mean...?"

"To Germany," he clarified. "I spoke to Anya."

And now she was shaking her head, and laughing a little. "I left Anya's right after Christmas. I got a job in Bremen. I told you that..." She rolled her eyes. "In the letter you never got."

Izzy was now shaking his head, too. "Anya said you wouldn't see me. She didn't say that you weren't there."

"That doesn't make any sense," Eden insisted. "Because I *wasn't* there."

"Yeah, well, I'm telling you that it happened."

"I'm not saying that it didn't, I'm just saying—"

"I sent you e-mail," Izzy told her, and it was hard to keep his tone from being accusatory, like she was the one with the crazy-ass story that she was making up. Which she probably was.

And she knew what he was thinking. "I'm not lying," she said. "I didn't get any e-mail from you."

"Yeah, well, I sent it," Izzy said. "Practically weekly. *How are you? I'm worried about you. Please call me just so I know you're okay...*"

"To what address?" Eden asked. "I changed servers so often. And after I left Anya's, there were entire months when I didn't have Internet access. I still don't have regular—"

"One was AOL," he said. "Another was gmail. None of it bounced."

She shook her head. "I haven't signed on to those accounts since...I don't know when. The AOL address was...Well, Jerry and Richie both had it, so I adjusted it so that everything that wasn't from Danny or Ben went into my spam folder."

Convenient. Blame it on her ex-boyfriend and his drug-dealing rapist-asshole boss. "I guess you didn't want to hear from me."

"I didn't," she admitted. "Not at first."

"So what'd your letter say?" Izzy asked. "*Merry Christmas. I've sufficiently recovered from Pinkie's death, so come fuck me?*"

She went very still, just sitting there, looking down at her sneaker-clad feet.

"Sorry," Izzy said. "That was...unnecessarily harsh."

"You think I'm lying," she said quietly—her words a statement, not a question.

"Yeah, Eden," he said, just as quietly. "I do. I think you need help again, and I think I'm conveniently here, so you just jumped me."

"Oh God," she started, but he wasn't finished.

"And I don't just think it, I *know* that *you* know that I am still so freaking attracted to you. Even after all the bullshit. Even—what is it?" He looked at the clock glowing dimly on the dash. "Ten minutes after you screw me like there's no tomorrow and damn near blow off the top of my head, I am unable to keep from thinking about a replay. In fact, I'm already planning it. Where: pick a hotel room, any hotel room. All you have to do is ask, and I'll get us a two-grand-a-night suite at Caesars Palace and it'll be worth every freaking penny. How: me on top this time, with your feet up by my ears, with the lights on so I can watch. When: as soon as humanly possible, because holy crap, I'm already turned on again, just thinking about it. Feel free to grab hold of my lie detector to check."

She was silent, looking down at her feet again, pretending to try not to cry. Or maybe she was really trying not to cry. Either way, it didn't matter.

"So, that's what I want," Izzy told her. "Completely bullshit free. You need my help with this thing with Ben? You got it. Truth is, I would've helped you without the sex, because I'm a sucker that way. But you played that card, sweetheart, so . . . Game on."

Eden refused to cry, even though her heart was breaking. It was stupid. *She* was stupid, but when he'd kissed her so hungrily, she'd actually hoped . . .

"What do you want me to say to you?" she asked Izzy quietly.

She'd hoped that they could pick up where they'd left off, that she could convince him that she'd never lied to him and that she could be trusted.

"The truth would be nice." His face, his eyes, were hard as he looked at her in the dim dashboard light.

But Eden knew that he didn't want the real truth. He wanted her to confirm the fictional version of his own private reality, a reality that he was convinced had happened.

"I never wrote you a letter and I ignored the e-mail you sent," she said. "Is that what you want me to say?" Her voice shook despite her best efforts to keep it steady. "Well, screw you, because I'm *not* going to lie. I wrote you a letter, because it felt like the things I had to say shouldn't come in an e-mail or a text message, and because I was too scared to call you. And I *didn't* get your e-mail, and I *didn't* know you came to see me in January or February—Anya never told me. And I *do* need your help with Ben, but that's *not* why I did . . . what I just did. I did it because we're still technically married, and I promised you that I wouldn't have sex with anyone else, so I haven't. And it hasn't been a big deal, because I haven't even wanted to. But seeing you again was . . . It made me feel so, I don't know, alive, okay? And then you kissed me, and even though I knew it wasn't real, it couldn't be real, I just . . . I wanted to, okay? I did it because I really, *really* wanted to. And because I thought you did, too."

The tears that she'd been holding back escaped, and she wiped at them furiously with the heels of her hands, refusing to dissolve into a puddle of pain in front of this infuriating man.

"I thought it would be good," she whispered. "And yes, I did it so that you'd stick around, but not because I need your help. I did it because you're not the only one who wanted to do it again before it even freaking started!"

She didn't see him move.

One moment she was sitting there, beside him in the darkness, and the next he'd pulled her into his arms.

Only this time there were no car headlights on them.

Still, he kissed her, hard, and she not only let him, but she kissed him, equally hard, back, even as her heart broke.

Ben woke up with absolutely no idea where he was, aware first and foremost that both of his hands were cuffed up and over his head by pieces of stiff plastic that secured him to the metal frame of a narrow bed.

The mattress was plain and not covered by sheets or blankets—just stained blue-and-white ticking—and none too comfortable.

The room itself was small and windowless, with a single door down at one end, and another cot at the other end, where sure enough, another boy lay, also locked to the frame.

But he was cuffed by his ankles, probably because both of his wrists were bandaged. He was also awake and watching Ben in the dim light from a single overhead bulb.

"Welcome to hell, cutie pie," he said. His hair was buzz-cut short, and he was dressed in gray. Gray baggy T-shirt, gray sweatpants. He pointed up toward the corner of the walls and ceiling, to the left of the door. "Security camera. But it's visual only. No audio. We can speak freely. So, are you here for me, or am I here for you?"

His words didn't make sense. Of course Ben's brain was still foggy. He remembered Eden. And Greg, with a gun. And—shit—the two men and the woman, that shot of something in his butt... "Where are we?"

"I told you," the other boy said. He was skinny, with bony elbows and a lean, narrow face and big eyes. "It's hell. Other than that? I'm not really certain. I think maybe we're in New Mexico. Or Arizona. Possibly Las Vegas. The interior courtyard is definitely arid. All I can say for sure is, *Toto, we're not in Connecticut anymore.*"

"How long have I been here?" Ben asked.

"I don't know," the boy said. "You were here when they brought me in, after my latest pedicure and stone massage. That was a joke. You had your last pedi, *son*, maybe for the rest of your life. You meet Weird Don yet? He's like, barely twenty-two, and he calls us younguns *son*. You know, I think I'm probably a visual aid, to help welcome you to the program. Like a Doobe and a Don'tbe, and I'm the Don'tbe. I'm guessing the black nail polish you're wearing is a clue that you probably didn't volunteer for this twelve-week torturefest. Nor did I. And see, I'm their latest problem child. Week twenty-two, and I still insist that if God wanted me to be heterosexual, he wouldn't have made me fall in love with my boyfriend, Clark. But, WWJD—what would Jesus do? Clearly, He, too, would agree that starving me to death while depriving me of sleep is oodles better than acknowledging that just *maybe* I'm never going to deny my true, God-given sexual orientation."

"Why don't you just say what they want to hear?" Ben asked. "I mean, just to get *out* of here..."

"They make you chant things," the boy said. "Over and over again. Like *These urges I feel aren't natural.* And *My feelings are bad and wrong, and if I don't stop them, then I am working hand in hand with the devil...* Oh, here's a good one. *My parents are ashamed of me, but I will work to make them proud.* I don't need to chant that—the first part—forty thousand times, day in and day out, to know that it's true. I say, *My parents are ashamed of me, but not half as much as I'm ashamed of them.* Maybe you can do it, new boy. Maybe you can re- peat their lies, and get out of here undamaged. But they keep you hun- gry, and they don't let you sleep, and they freeze you in tubs of ice, and heat you in saunas until your brain feels cooked, and then the things they make you tell yourself start sounding like they might be true and . . . Don't bother trying to kill yourself. It doesn't work."

He held up his bandaged arms so Ben could see them better. "Not that I actually wanted to die. In fact, I have real incentive to live. Two words: Clark Volborg loves me, too. Okay, that was more than two words, but you get the picture. I thought slitting my wrists would get me into a real hospital with real doctors with real degrees who would actually help me escape. But my parents signed off on a form that . . . See, I'm a high flight risk, so they opted—completely—for in- house care. God help me if I get appendicitis. God help me . . ."

"What's your name?" Ben asked softly.

"My old name or my new one?"

"You have a new name?" Ben asked.

"You will, too," the boy told him. "They'll give you one, or maybe use your middle name. My middle name was Devereaux, which, let's face it, was just too gay. So they call me Chip, which is pretty stupid. Like Chip isn't totally gay, too. Although, look at me. You could call me Motherfucker Tittylover, and because that was *my* name? It would be *totally* gay."

"What's your real name?" Ben asked.

"Peter Sinclair, the fucking third, of the Greenwich Sinclairs. But don't bother, we'll both get demerits if you use it. I see you got the dou- ble cuff. That'll change to a single after they give you the full list of don'ts. As in don't whack off unless you're in the special whack-off stall in the bathroom—it's plastered with pictures of naked women. All those breasts, it's disconcerting, and you've got to keep your eyes open, and yes, there's a camera. They'll be watching. Particularly Weird

Don. He's probably monitoring our camera right now—you are *so* his type." He laughed. "Look at you, you believe me. Well, you *should* believe me about Weird Don. But the whack-off stall? This is an abstinence-only program, *son*, and abstinence means abstinence. You so much as scratch your balls and you'll be walking around with your hands cuffed behind your back, faster than you can sing a chorus of 'It's Raining Men.'   •

"Of course, rumor has it that the abstinence rule is dropped during the last week, right before graduation. They give you Viagra and they bring in these girls and—You have a boyfriend?"

Ben shook his head. "No."

"So maybe it'll be okay with you," Peter said. "To hook up with some twenty-dollar whore for a five-minute session, just to get the hell out of here. The drugs'll make it happen, and you can lie back, close your eyes, and think of England. But me, I made a promise to Clark. I made a *vow*..."

He started to cry, a soft, keening sound that he tried to hide, that sent chills down Ben's back.

"I'm getting out of here," Ben said. "Soon. My sister, she's going to come get me."

The quiet weeping turned to forced laughter. "Dream on, new boy. Because unless she's got an AK-47, she won't get past the front door. If she can even find the front door..."

"She'll find me," Ben whispered. "I know she will."

But as Peter Sinclair the fucking third finally fell silent, as his breathing turned from ragged to slow and steady, Ben had his doubts.

The call came around 0115, as Eden dozed beside him in the front seat of the rental car.

At around 2100, Izzy had driven them over to the main road to get coffee and sandwiches, to gas up the car, and take a bathroom break—but in truth to find an ATM, and a drugstore to buy more condoms, since they'd used the only one he'd had. When they'd returned, Eden's mother still wasn't home.

And as eager as he was to break open the entire box of condoms and give his loving wife the replay that she claimed she wanted, it was obvious that she was struggling to keep her eyes open after a hard day of dancing naked for the teeming masses.

Still, she'd fought it, until he'd convinced her to go to sleep by promising her he'd wake her in a few hours to take a shift watching the house. Which, of course, he didn't do. She wasn't the only liar in the car.

As Izzy's cell rang in the darkness, Eden awoke, taking a sharp breath in as she realized where she was and who she was with and remembering—no doubt—what she'd recently done with him.

"It's Dan," Izzy told her as she pushed her hair back from her face. He answered the call. "Yo," he said, "Gillman. I'm here with your sister. I've got you on speaker."

"Great." Danny sounded exhausted and as if there was nothing about this situation that was even remotely great. Still, Izzy gave him points for trying. "Jenn and I are in a cab, on the way to JFK. Our flight gets into Las Vegas a little before 0900."

"You want me to pick you up?" Izzy asked.

Dan sighed. "Yeah," he said. "Thank you. That would be terrific. World Airlines, flight 576. Although . . . I assume you've got a rental? Not your truck?"

"It's a rental," Izzy told him. "Considering I came straight from Germany, getting my truck would've been—"

"Does it seat five?" Dan asked. "Comfortably? I mean, enough to make the road-trip back to San Diego?"

"Hmm," Izzy said as turned around to look at the backseat, even as Eden said, "Yes. We can absolutely make it work. Ben's really skinny. You *are* talking about the four of us and Ben. Please say yes."

"Yeah," Danny said. "I just spoke to Ivette."

"Oh, thank God!" Eden clasped her hands and brought them up

to her mouth, like someone who'd just been told by an expert from the *Antiques Roadshow* that Great-Grandpa's collection of outhouse seats was worth fifty thousand dollars.

"She's been working as a home health aide," Dan continued as tears filled Eden's eyes, "and her current client, well, he's dying. He thinks she's his dead wife, and he wants her there, so... She's been pulling a lot of around-the-clock shifts. Who knew she had that in her? Anyway, I got her to agree that Ben would be better off with me, living down in San Diego. So..."

The tears overflowed. "Thank you. Oh, Danny, thank you."

"I, uh, didn't mention you."

Eden nodded as she fiercely wiped her eyes, as she sniffed and wiped her nose with the back of her hand. "That's probably best."

She didn't let it show in her voice, but Izzy didn't miss the regret and disappointment that flashed across her face as she struggled to rein in her emotions. In a family filled with massive fuck-ups, she was perceived to be the black sheep and always would be. Although Ben, being gay, had to be running a close second these days. Dan, however, was the golden boy and clearly had retained that elevated status with their mother.

That had to be hard as hell not to resent, but she didn't. She was obviously beyond grateful that Danny had appeared and used his shining superpowers to help her set their little brother free.

And Izzy couldn't help himself. He reached for her, gently smoothing her hair back from her face, tucking a stray strand behind her ear, as Danny's voice continued from the tiny speaker of his phone.

"But I am going to count on you, Eden," her brother told her, tightly, stiffly, almost formally, as she turned and looked at Izzy—an expression that he couldn't read on her impossibly pretty face. "To be there. To take care of him when I'm not around. To keep him out of trouble. To keep yourself out of trouble, too."

And okay, that was a pretty dickish thing to say. Izzy made a face, but Eden turned away, pulling free from Izzy's hand as she nodded, even though Dan couldn't possibly see her.

"I know," she said. "I will."

"Maybe you'll do for Ben what you couldn't do for yourself," Dan said, which was a *really* dickish thing to say.

But Izzy held his tongue as Eden said, "Danny, I promise—"

He brushed it off. "We'll talk more when I get there. Is your place big enough for us to stay with you while we're in town?"

"There's a pullout couch, in the living room," she said, glancing over at Izzy again, almost apologetically this time. "I don't know how comfortable it is, but... You can have the bedroom."

"That's not necessary," Dan said. "And it's only for one night. We'll leave for San Diego in the morning, but I'm looking to save money, so... A three-bedroom apartment won't be cheap."

Three-bedroom? Wait a minute. Was Dan expecting Eden to live with him and Ben, too? Somehow Izzy had imagined Dan sharing a place with his brother, and Eden having her own separate apartment.

Or—yeah—moving back in with him.

Holy shit, sometime between *Oh, yes* and *Oh, YES*, Izzy had apparently gotten a little ahead of himself.

"I've got some savings," Eden was telling her brother, clearly on board with the whole three-bedroom apartment plan, which left Izzy absolutely out in the cold and crying bitter tears into his pillow as he remained decidedly alone and unlaid. Unless she was actually thinking they could all live together like some really dysfunctional version of *Full House*. "Plus, I'm working full-time. I'll help pay the bills. And if we need to, Ben and I can share a room."

And... Izzy was back to weeping and unlaid. Okay, then. She definitely wasn't factoring him into any of her plans. Good to know.

"We'll talk when I get there," Dan said again.

"What about Ben?" Eden asked. "Where is he? Can we go pick him up?"

"He's at a place called Crossroads, right there in Las Vegas. I've already spoken to them. Ivette made arrangements for Ben to be released to me, so... We'll go there directly from the airport. Look, we're here, I gotta go. We'll see you in a few."

"Thank you," Eden said again, but Dan had already cut the connection.

Izzy pocketed his phone. And then there they sat, in the darkness.

"Thank God," she murmured again, and he knew she was, once again, fighting tears.

"You know," Izzy finally said, "sometimes it's okay to let loose. Sometimes the news is just too freaking miraculous."

She laughed, but it came out sounding more like a sob. "It *is* miraculous, isn't it? I almost can't believe it could be this easy."

"Every now and then," Izzy told her, "the good guys catch a break." He put the car into gear and eased away from the curb. "No point sitting here anymore. Shall we . . . get that room at Caesars Palace?"

She snorted her disgust. "I'm *not* going to make you spend that kind of money when I have a perfectly good apartment."

Izzy cleared his throat. "One that you haven't exactly invited me to."

"We're still married," she reminded him. "Which makes half of everything I own yours. Not that I own the apartment . . ."

"Does that include half of your stripper money?" he asked, not just because he was an asshole, but because he was currently a jealous asshole. He was here to save the day in return for a whole lot of steaming-hot sex, only the day had been saved very nicely without him.

Eden looked at him sharply. It *was* the deal they'd made, back before they'd taken their vows. She'd even signed a prenup. Half of everything that was hers was his, and none of what was his would ever belong to her.

He'd had no intention of ever upholding the agreement. He'd only drafted and signed the damn thing because she was adamant about not taking advantage of him. She'd insisted upon it, because the truth was that she only married him for his health care and for the chance to give her baby his name.

Not that either of them had ever expected her to come into any great sums of cash.

But now, as she sat in the car beside him, she squared her shoulders and nodded. "Of course."

It was clear his days were numbered. Still, if he were going to take whatever he could get for as long as he could get it, he'd have to work to be a whole lot less peevish.

"Yeah," he said, "no, sweetheart, see, I was kidding. It was just a bad joke."

"We had a deal," Eden told him quietly.

"I'm not going to take your money," he said. "That's not what I want, okay?" He looked over at her as he pulled out onto the main road, and she was watching him. "You know what I want."

She nodded. And then she reached over and put her hand on his package, grabbing hold of him right through his pants.

"I know because I want it, too," she said, her voice even huskier than usual. "How about you drive this thing a little faster?"

Neesha woke up with a jolt as the apartment door slammed shut, and her heart pounded as she realized that she was no longer alone.

She'd left the light on in the kitchen—the dim one over the stove. It was enough for her to see that it was Ben's sister Eden who'd come home, and she wasn't alone. She was with the big man that Neesha had seen out on the sidewalk. He'd found her and . . . He'd bought her apparently, because he was kissing her and touching her as if he owned her.

Eden was pulling off her clothes as if she couldn't wait for it to be over with—Neesha knew what that was like. She slipped off the couch and huddled behind its arm, near the wall, praying that she wouldn't have to witness Eden's shame.

But the man started to laugh. "Hey," he said. "Sweetheart. Slow down. I'm not going anywhere. Let's do this right. You got a bed in here, somewhere? Because as tempting as it might be to knock your pictures off the walls and/or get a rug burn on my ass—"

Eden laughed, too. "See, now, I'm just appreciating the lack of a gearshift and parking brake." Her voice was husky and she didn't sound at all unhappy or afraid. "My bedroom's over here..."

"Wait, wait," the man said. "I'm stuck. These stupid shoes, there's a knot in the lace and...Shit, *shit!*"

There was a thump, as if he'd fallen. But he wasn't angry, and he didn't lash out at Eden. He was laughing, and she was laughing, too.

"Let me help," she said.

"Ho-kay," the man said on an exhale. "I'm not sure that can be defined as *helping* per se..."

"It helps me," she said. "It's been on my wish list since last July."

"Wish list," he said. "Isn't that supposed to be things you want *me* to do to *you?*"

"It doesn't have to be," she said. "I mean, it's my wish list, right? I can put whatever I want on there."

"You could," he agreed. "Baking cookies in giant chicken suits could be right up there at number six."

"Six?" she said, laughing. "That's at least five, if not four. But only if we're in the same suit and the cookies are chocolate chip."

"Mmm," he said. "Number seventeen: doing the macarena at the White House."

"In the Oval Office," she added. "Out on the front lawn, it's only 117." She whooped in surprise, but then laughed. "Are you really gonna..."

"Carrying you to bed like this is on *my* wish list," he said, his voice getting softer as he moved down the hallway.

"It *is* undeniably hot," she said. And the door closed behind them and their voices were muffled.

Neesha sat there, afraid to move, afraid to be discovered. But then their laughter faded, and she knew neither one would be coming out anytime soon.

So she grabbed her bag and the key she'd taken from beneath the potted plant, and she silently crept across the living room and toward the door, stepping over the clothing they'd discarded.

But then Neesha stopped, because there, on the floor next to a pair of almost frighteningly large shoes, was a wallet.

And even though she knew she shouldn't, even though she knew it was wrong, she bent down and opened it. And there, inside, was a stack of money. It was crisp and beautiful and there was so much of it—ten whole bills, most of them bearing a giant two and a zero.

Praying that she would be forgiven, she took one of them, slipping it into her pocket before she silently went out the door.

CHAPTER
THIRTEEN

D an's sister was beautiful.

The color of her eyes and hair were almost startlingly identical to Dan's, and they had the same basic shade of perfect, smooth skin, although it was clear to Jenn that, at least in the recent past, Eden had spent far less time outside, in the sun.

She'd met them at the luggage carousel, even though neither Dan nor Jenn had checked any bags. She was waiting for them as they got off the elevator, her eyes widening as she saw Dan sitting in the wheelchair that Jenn had insisted he use.

It was telling—the fact that he'd agreed to the ride from the gate. He was feeling much worse than he'd let on during the flight, and she was glad she'd talked him out of making the equally long drive to San Diego tonight.

Of course maybe Eden's wide eyes were all about Jenn, who was looking frumpier and more rumpled than ever after waking up at holy-shit-o'clock to fly most of the way across the country.

"Danny, thank you so much for coming!" Eden had rushed to greet her brother, clearly uncertain as how best to bend and hug him, so she didn't—an awkward moment made even more awkward by the airline attendant nearly pushing Dan's chair into her.

Dan hadn't helped much, his focus on getting out of there. "Is Zanella...?"

"He's with the car. He's circling," Eden told him, leaping back out of the way to keep the wheelchair from running over her feet in her open-toed sandals. She'd clearly gone to some length with her appearance, dressed as she was in a pretty flower-patterned sundress, her long hair twisted up into an artfully messy chignon, her makeup carefully understated. "He didn't want to park and make you walk all that way."

And with that, Dan was whisked away toward the pickup area, leaving Jenn to juggle both of their carry-on bags and to introduce herself.

"God damn it, slow down," she heard Dan say to the chair-pusher. "Jenni, are you—"

"It's okay," she called after him. "I'm okay, we're right behind you, Danny. I'm Jenn LeMay," she told Eden, who took the handle of one of their bags from her as they both scrambled to follow. "Thanks."

"I'm Eden. Thank you so much for coming." Eden was clearly embarrassed by Dan's apparent rudeness. And yes, there was definitely a little bit of amazement on her face, too, as she took in Jenn's stringy hair and tired eyes behind her glasses.

"He's in a lot of pain," Jenn told her, sotto voce. "Since he left the hospital, he won't take the painkiller that the doctor prescribed and…"

Eden forced a smile. "Thanks for, you know, but…he hates me. I know he hates me. It's okay, I'm used to it by now."

"He doesn't hate you," Jenn started.

But Eden interrupted. "I'm surprised he let them give him any painkillers at all. Even in the hospital. He's always been freaked out. You know. Terrified he'll be instantly addicted. Considering our family, it's understandable." She shrugged. "So who knows? Maybe he's not just being bitchy because he hurts, maybe he's also going through withdrawal. Good luck to all of us with that."

At first Jenn resisted the urge to stop short, mostly because Dan and his wheelchair were so far in front of them. But then she did stop, because that distance-created privacy was a good thing. She put a hand on Eden's perfect arm, and stopped the younger girl as well.

And she was a girl. She was only nineteen, even though she looked much older.

"I'm sorry, I shouldn't've made excuses for his behavior," Jenn told her. "But, see, I know how hard this is for him, and I love him...So, I'm inclined to cut him a little slack. But, you're right, he *was* being bitchy and I've heard his end of several phone calls to you, and I just want you to know that I've been slapping him upside the head. A lot lately. More than usual. For being less than polite to you, in case I didn't make that clear."

Eden was just standing there, looking at her, almost perfectly expressionless.

"I guess what I'm trying to say is that, well, I hope you'll be patient with him, at least until his injury heals. I'm going to try my best to help out, at least over the next week and...I don't know if he's mentioned this to you yet, but he seemed to think it might a good idea for you—both of you—to go to an Al-Anon meeting or two—"

"I don't drink," Eden said. "Not since..." She shook her head.

"Well, no, Al-Anon's not...It's like Alcoholics Anonymous, but it's designed for the families of alcoholics. There's a great program for adult children of alcoholics—I'm one, too, and...Well, it really helped my brothers—some of my brothers—and me deal with some pretty intense issues from our childhood. It was good, because now that we're adults, we can have these completely different relationships—healthier relationships—than we did when we were kids, back when we had no control over what was going on around us, you know?"

Eden was looking at her as if she were speaking Greek, but then she nodded very slightly and said, "And Danny...wants to do this? This program? With *me*."

"Yes, he does," Jenn told her. "But it's kind of obvious that it's hard for him, when he's with you, not to slip back into your childhood relationship. So...it might be difficult for him to communicate that to you, until...Well, it's kind of a catch-22, you know?"

"Who are you?" Eden asked, laughing to try to hide the tears that sprang into her beautiful eyes. "His girlfriend or his therapist?"

"Like I said. I've been in your shoes. Younger sister...? Older brothers behaving like total dickheads...?"

Eden's smile and laughter became more genuine.

"I never had a sister," Jenn told Danny's as she pulled the girl in for a hug. At first Eden resisted, her body stiff as if she'd never been hugged by a friend before. "I'm looking forward to getting to know you better. And? When Dan does act like a total dickhead? We are going to join forces and let him know it. Is that a deal?"

Eden hugged her back then, almost fiercely, as she laughed. "Jennilyn LeMay, it's definitely a deal."

"Come on," Jenn said. "Let's go find Ben and bring him home."

Peter Sinclair the third was gone from the cell when Ben woke up.

Whatever drug they'd given him in that injection must've still been in his system, because he'd heard nothing—and it was hard to imagine that other boy being taken away without raising some kind of fuss.

His arms were stiff from sleeping with them up and over his head, and his bladder was uncomfortably full. He was feeling the first signs of low blood sugar—shaky and sweaty and considerably nauseous. He was also experiencing his trademark irritability—normally a telltale signal that he needed some sugar, fast. When he wasn't being held prisoner, that is.

In his current situation, feeling irritable was a given.

He looked around the cell, at the drab walls, floor, and ceiling, at the bare lightbulb hanging overhead, at the other cot, where . . . Yeah, Peter Sinclair had definitely pissed himself at some point in the night. The smell of urine was unmistakable and nauseating.

And definitely the drug had still been in Ben's system last night when he'd talked to the other boy, because at the time, he'd felt oddly calm.

Now, however, his heart was pounding at the idea that he was locked up and tied down—a prisoner here, for God knows how long. He remembered telling Peter that Eden would find him and get him out.

Today, he had no such misconceptions. He was a prisoner here, and he would remain a prisoner here — and there was little he could do about it.

It was hard, as he was lying there, not to think about Neesha, about the god-awful story she'd told him, about what had happened to her after her mother had died. Maybe it was something that she'd made up. Just something she'd told him to impress him or to make him sympathize. Or maybe, like the cop had said, it was a product of her delusional mind.

But somehow Ben doubted that.

And he couldn't imagine the strength that she'd needed, that she'd had, to live as a prisoner for so many years — without hope of release.

"Hey!" he shouted into the silence, his voice rusty from sleep. "Hey! Gay diabetic in here. One is a disease, the other is not. One can be successfully managed through diet and insulin injections. The other is unchangeable and fuck you sideways for thinking otherwise, you sons of bitches—"

The door opened. "Is that any way to talk?"

It was the man Peter had nicknamed Weird Don.

"I'm a diabetic," Ben said. "That means I need to check my blood sugar levels regularly throughout the day so I don't fall into a coma and die."

"You have to get pretty sick for that to happen," Don said, coming into the cell and closing the door behind him with a solid-sounding click. "A lot of boys come in here with ailments. Asthma. Eczema. Acne. It all clears right up when they learn to reject their unnatural yearnings."

"Yeah, that sounds like bullshit to me," Ben said. "I wonder why. Oh, probably because it *is* bullshit."

Don came farther into the room, but he didn't unfasten Ben's hands. Instead, he moved next to the cot and stood there. And Jesus, weird didn't begin to describe the way he was looking down at Ben. "It's not," he said.

"Aren't you supposed to untie me?" Ben asked, yanking at the plastic bindings and making the metal frame of the cot rattle. He glanced over at the camera, oddly glad it was there. "I need to go to whatever passes for the medical facility in this hellhole. To get tested and get some insulin—and some food—so I don't throw up on your fucking shoes."

"That kind of language isn't necessary," the man chided.

"Yeah, I think it is," Ben countered, "because you don't seem to understand what I'm saying."

"But I do understand your pain. I went through this program when I was your age," Don said earnestly. "It helped me. God, how I hated myself..."

"I think you still hate yourself," Ben said. "But me? I think I can probably go now, because for the first time in a long time? I'm actually doing okay in the hating myself department. I met this girl a few days ago, and her courage astounded and kind of shamed me. And then I came here, and I met Peter Sinclair the fucking third, and I've never met anyone like him before, and you know what? I'm going to survive whatever you do to me. I'm going to say whatever I have to say, and I'm going to walk out of here, and I'm going to fool you and your asshat friends into thinking I've seen your stupid light, but when I leave, I'm going to be as gay as the day I walked in here—as gay as the day I was born. And after I leave, I'm going to be on a mission. I'm going to find my own Clark Volborg and we are going to live happily ever after, and in about ten years I'll think back on this, and I'll think of you with pity, because I'll know that you're still here, and that you still hate yourself—when all you had to do was listen to Peter, too, and understand that you're not alone and there's nothing—*nothing*—wrong with you."

It was possible Weird Don had heard none of that, because he said, "You know, you don't have to leave. You can sign papers and stay."

"Fuck you," Ben said, before he realized what Don had just told him—*you don't have to leave.*

And sure enough, as Don left the little room, someone else came inside and cut him free.

It was the woman who'd bagged up his clothes. She held those bags now, as if she'd been standing there with them, in the hallway, all night long. "This way," she said as he rubbed his wrists and rolled his shoulders, as he tested his very shaky legs.

"I need a bathroom," he said. "And some insulin—not necessarily in that order."

"You'll have to wait until you leave this facility," she said tightly as she led the way down the hall, her heels clopping loudly against the industrial tile. "And you can tell your parents that your tuition is *not* refundable."

With that, she pushed open a door and gestured for him to go through it, and holy God, it was the doorway to some kind of lobby, and Danny was standing there, looking like shit, but his eyes lit up when he saw him, and he said, "Ben!"

And Ben's knees crumpled and he hit the floor. And—great—he was pretty sure he pissed himself as his brother's worried face wavered and faded and the world went black.

"I hate this," Eden said as she and Izzy waited in the car in the Crossroads parking lot. "I want to be in there. I want to know what's happening."

She was practically vibrating with nervous energy, and Izzy knew that she was scared to death that something was going to go wrong, and that Danny and Jenn were going to come back out of that building without Ben in tow.

He knew exactly how to distract her—if only they weren't sitting in the car in the broad daylight.

Or maybe what he really wanted to do was distract himself, and the best way to do that, other than the very obvious, was to mentally replay—moment by moment—the outrageously great shagging he'd given her after they'd gone into her bedroom last night and closed the door behind them.

Or he could deconstruct the incredibly groovy good-morning greeting she'd given him after he'd gotten up to take a shower. She'd followed him, slipping past the shower curtain, stepping into the tub with him, wrapping her legs around him as he'd pinned her to the tile wall, beneath the rushing water.

But like all good things, their shower eventually came to an end, and he'd dried himself off with one of her clean-smelling towels as he'd wandered into her living room.

He'd realized immediately that he hadn't given the tiny room so much as a single glance last night. The curtains were tightly closed, and he peeked behind them to see—sure enough—a slightly sagging bouquet of bright red roses—the bouquet he'd seen from down on the street.

The card was still with them, and he reached and flipped it open. *To Jenny,* it read. *Congratulations and welcome. Love, the girls at the club.*

Much better than a card reading, *Thanks for last night. Love, Enrique, your most ardent admirer.*

Izzy let the curtain close again and turned back to Eden's living room. It was furnished with sad and sorry pieces that looked as if they'd been retired—and none too soon—from a frat house. She'd valiantly covered the easy chair and sofa with sheets and blankets to conceal their years of wear. There was a bookshelf and an end table, both of which held a collection of smiling Buddha statues, no doubt belonging to the person from whom Eden had sublet the place.

As he stood there, letting the hardworking air-conditioning circulate around his extremely happy genitalia, he'd found himself thinking of Nurse Cynthia's matching furniture.

Which Eden would probably have loved.

And the crazy thing was? If that had been Eden's apartment, with Eden cooking him dinner in that too-perfect kitchen, Izzy would've loved it, too.

As it stood, Eden kept her own place as neatly tidy. The Buddhas were all dust-free—although the clothes he and Eden had shed upon arrival last night were still strewn in the tiny entryway that was open to the living room.

He collected it all—and his wallet, too—rolling up the pants he'd bought for the occasion and trading them for a T-shirt, shorts, and sandals that he'd brought in his seabag. He tossed Eden's—including her stripper thong—in a laundry basket that was just outside the bathroom door, blocking what was probably a linen closet.

He stashed his bag just inside of Eden's bedroom, wondering—briefly—what Dan was going to say when he found out that Izzy and his sister had reconnected. As in Izzy's tab A had again gone, repeatedly, into Eden's slot B.

But they'd blow up that bridge when they came to it. And what Dan thought about Izzy and Eden rehooking up was hugely secondary to what *Eden* thought about it.

Izzy knew where he himself stood. For him, the pros far outweighed the cons. And while he acknowledged that he might not feel the same in a few days—or hours—when she decided enough was enough and shut him down. But right now? He had both feet planted absolutely in the *fuck me again* column.

And Eden seemed to be in agreement.

Although, they really hadn't done much talking last night—aside from that wish-list discussion, which was part of the foreplay, and really couldn't be taken all that seriously. Like he was really supposed to believe that giving him head was on *her* wish list? It was part of the hyperbole that came with passion-talk. Not that Eden wasn't good at it.

He just couldn't take it too seriously.

After Eden emerged from her bedroom in a sundress that he immediately wanted to take off of her, they'd set to work cleaning up the apartment for his majesty King Danny's arrival. And then it was time to go. Eden had remained pensively quiet during their ride to the airport, so Izzy'd focused on both his coffee and navigating the unfamiliar streets.

It was fine with him—the no-serious-talking. But he'd realized at the airport, after Dan and Jenn had climbed into the backseat of his rental car, that there were things that needed to be said—important things—without Eden's two brothers listening in.

To his surprise, she started the conversation. "She's really nice," she said. "Jenn."

"Jennilyn LeMay," Izzy said, and Eden met his gaze.

"Yeah," she said. "Um..."

"I won't tell," Izzy said, referring to Eden's having borrowed Jenn's name for her career at D'Amato's. He didn't need to spell it out. He knew Eden knew exactly to what he was referring.

"Thanks." She looked out the window again at the cracked tarmac, at the sign in the window of the auto-parts store across the street. FLOOR MAT SPECIAL! FREE FUZZY DICE WITH PURCHASE!

"Do you get, like, a weekly paycheck?" Izzy asked, and she glanced at him again. "If you want, when you give notice, you can ask them to send your last check care of my apartment in San Diego. I'll make sure you get it."

"Oh," she said. "Thanks. But no. They don't pay me—I pay them. To work there. They get a percentage of my tips, so..."

"Really?"

"Yeah," she said. "It's like I'm renting a spot on their stage."

"Wow," Izzy said. "Okay. So, good. You can just give them notice with a phone call and..." Hmm. She wasn't meeting his gaze. "You *are* going to quit working there. Or...?" He let his voice trail off and up.

"Of course," she said, and it was so obviously a lie that he laughed his disbelief.

"It's a little far for a commute," he pointed out. "Five hours? Each way? At least?"

Eden looked at him and apparently decided to cut the bullshit. "It's not like I can get a job dancing in San Diego," she said. "Someone would see me."

"Yeah, I thought that was the idea. A lot of people see you. Kinda hard *not* to see you, sweetheart, when you take off your clothes on a stage, in a spotlight, moving the way you do..."

"I meant someone from the SEAL team," she said. "And they'd tell Danny."

"And you want to earn a living doing something that you don't want your brother to know about because...?"

She reached into her shoulder bag and pulled out a wad of cash that was nearly the size of a softball. "Tens and higher," she said. "These are my tips from one day of work."

Holy shit. "*Let me entertain you,*" Izzy sang. "They ever hire guys? Maybe you and I could be a team. *And now, from San Diego, put your hands together for... Irving and Eden!*"

Eden laughed at that. "You won't even take off your shirt when we make love."

And okay. She was going to refer to last night's mad fucking as *making love.* It was good to know what to call it.

And it was true, Izzy was inclined to leave his shirt on both for pickup games of basketball and for banging fair maidens. He had some pretty nasty scars on his chest as the result of a near-death experience with a terrorist who'd pulled the trigger of an AK-47 that was aimed in Izzy's direction.

He'd kept his shirt on last night, even though Eden had seen his myriad of scars before. He wasn't sure why he'd bothered—it certainly hadn't seemed to disturb her in the past, nor had she so much as blinked this morning in the shower.

Well, she'd blinked plenty. And gasped a whole lot more.

But not because of his scars.

"Yeah, well," Izzy said now. "The whole guy-thong thing is so overdone. So Chippendale's. I thought with the T-shirt on, yet freeballing it, I could bring something a little different to the table. Maybe leave my socks on, too, for the complete dork effect. And then, you know, do some windmills with my man-parts since my sexy-dancing chops leave a lot to be desired...?"

She was giggling. "Ooh, something new for my wish list."

"I think we're onto something really big here," Izzy said, grinning back at her. "Not quite a full monty because the shirt and socks are still on. Although let's face it, if you're on that stage, too, I could be singing and dancing like Justin Bieber and it wouldn't matter, because no one would be looking at me." He pitched his voice into a boy soprano falsetto. "*I need somebody to love...*"

"Ooh, I love that song."

"And why am I not surprised."

Her smile faded as she held his gaze and said, "It's been incredible. Yesterday and last night and...? I really did miss you, you know."

This was a harder lie for him to swallow than the one about quitting work at the club, but it wouldn't do him any good to do anything but take it as she'd clearly meant it.

As proof that he'd distracted her sufficiently.

As a sparkly little memento from right now.

Right now Eden could imagine that she'd missed him for all those months that she'd intentionally stayed far, far away. It was possible that she even believed her softly spoken words. It was probable that in this moment, she truly liked him. She liked talking to him, but better yet and lucky for him, she liked fucking him. Oh, wait, no—making love. She liked *making love* to him.

And she'd continue to like it and him just fine until doing so was no longer convenient.

"Seriously though?" she said, and he waited to see what she was going to say, because he had no idea what was coming next. "I *was* thinking I could stay on the schedule. At D'Amato's. Just for a couple days each week. Consecutive days, because of the drive. For the next few months at least. See, I paid rent on the apartment through the end of July. It was the only way I could get it—to pay the full summer up front. I've been studying to get my driver's license, and I was saving to get a car and...I was thinking I could drive up to Vegas, like, Thursday morning and be back in San Diego early Saturday morning. You know, after working a double Friday shift, too."

"Well," Izzy said. "That's, um..."

"I'd earn more in those two days of dancing than I could make in two full weeks of work at some stupid McDonald's," she said.

"So why not work in L.A.?" he asked her. "If you really want to continue to dance." He used her word for it. "It's a much shorter drive. I bet D'Amato's has some kind of sister establishment in the greater Los Angeles area."

She was surprised. "Wow, I never thought of that. That's . . . A really great idea." She looked at him. "You'd . . . be okay with that?"

"It's far from my place to tell you what you should or shouldn't do," he pointed out. "Although, hot tip? Unless you really, really love doing it? You should find a different job."

"I love the money," Eden said bluntly. "And I don't hate the work as much as I hated getting paid slave wages to douse myself in french-fry grease and cheerfully suggest supersizing orders for people who needed to take a deep breath and order a salad instead—while every male worker in the place grabbed my ass five times a day. Not Rodney. He was my friend. But I had more hands on me working there, in a single shift, than I've had in the entire time I've worked at D'Amato's."

"Really?" Izzy asked, and she nodded. "Wow, that's . . . a problem. I was going to say that, you know, there are other options besides fast food and stripping, but very few come with a bouncer to protect you."

"*Are* there other options?" she asked. "Because I haven't found them. I cleaned houses for a while—until one of the clients came home early and offered to give me ten bucks extra to blow him. Don't worry, I got out of there fast," she added quickly as she saw him start to react. "I was safe, but I'm the one who got fired because *he* said he caught me stealing and that I tried to get out of it by propositioning *him*. And, of course, they believed him instead of me. Which is the story of my life.

"I'm good at being a nanny," she continued, "and even though it's hard work for a lot of reasons, most of the time, women won't hire me. I *did* find work with a single mom in Europe, after I left Anya's, and Stacy—that was her name—she also paid my airfare back to the States. But the job ended when they returned to Chicago, because her mom lived with them, so . . . Ben thought I should try to target gay couples, you know, because there's no threat in either direction? I've looked, but I haven't found anyone who doesn't want full-time, live-in, twenty-four/seven care. Which won't work if I'm going to be living with Ben.

But even if I *could* get a job as a nanny? Which hurts worse? Taking off my clothes while a bunch of losers leer at me, or taking care of someone else's baby after burying my own?"

She looked intently out the window, which usually meant she was fighting the urge to cry.

"I'm sorry," Izzy murmured, which was such a flipping stupid thing to say. Still, he *was* sorry. Incredibly, completely sorry. And not just for her loss, but for his, too.

Eden nodded, clearing her throat. "Right now I think I like stripping more."

"Maybe if you got a college degree—"

"Oh, please." She cut him off, turning to face him. "Like that's going to make a difference? Besides, what's the big? Doesn't *everybody* hate their job?"

"I don't."

She rolled her eyes. "Okay. Everyone who's *not* a Navy SEAL."

Izzy smiled at that. "Maybe, although I suspect not. You know, my oldest brother, Martin, was married to a stripper. Best wife he ever had, and he's had a few. Of course, I was fifteen when he married her, so my judgment was...colored. She used to work her routine in the playroom—with her clothes on. Well, most of the time, anyway. There *were* a few times that..." He cleared his throat. "That's a pretty impressionable age, and, um, Mandee? She was *freaking* hot. Almost as hot as you were up there. Almost. But my point is? She loved it. Stripping. *Loved* it. She and my aunt Carol used to argue about it endlessly. Carol was insistent that working as a stripper is bad for society. The objectification of women, yada yada." He stopped himself. "And I don't mean to belittle that, because it's very real. It's a problem. You're selling sex, and you're selling yourself and all women everywhere short—by making sure an entire subset of men never learns to see you or your feminist sisters as anything more than hot bodies. See, I was listening when Carol talked—almost as carefully as I watched when Mandee rehearsed. But Mandee always argued that that Neanderthal subset—the *let's meet for drinks at the strip club* crowd—isn't likely to ever see *any*

woman as more than a nice pair of tits, so who's to criticize her for making money off of their lame-ass ignorance?

"And really, how different is what a stripper does from all of the ac-
tresses in the movies who get naked for love scenes? And yes, one's
telling a story, I get that. Carol would point that out. But, Mandee
would argue, and I absolutely agree, that there's not a single tastefully
shot art film on this planet that hasn't had the scene with the famous
naked actress used as a visual aid while some huge number of miscre-
ants jacked off to it. Shit, I'm sure there's been jacking off done to
scenes from movies where everyone's got their clothes on. Does that
mean we should ban all movies? Or put all women, everywhere, in
burkas? *That's* definitely not the answer. I *know* we can all agree on
that."

Eden was looking at him as if she were having trouble understanding what he was saying.

So he explained. "My point," he said, "is that if you said to me,
*Izzy, I just love the power that I feel when I take my clothes off up on that
stage, I love it more than words can express*, well, then I'd say that since
you love doing it, and if you're working in a place where you're not
being pressured to do more than dance, if you're careful of your safety
when you approach and leave the club..." He shrugged. "You should
go for it. But if you come home from work feeling the need to scour
your entire body with bleach? You might want to set a limit. Plan for an
end date. Do this for a year or two or even ten, learn how to invest those
wads of money that you earn, and then retire and never do it again."

Eden was nodding, but he could tell from the way she was looking
back at the Crossroads front door again that it was time for a change of
subject.

But first he had to say, "Whatever you end up doing, just keep me
in the loop, okay?"

She met his gaze. "And if I do...you won't tell Danny. Or Ben?"

"I said I wouldn't, didn't I?"

She seemed to believe him, and she nodded. "Thank you."

"So I was thinking you might want to give some thought to Danny being here," Izzy said, "and staying in your apartment, and whether you want him to find out that we, uh, reconnected, or whether you'd prefer we, you know, keep our distance from each other when he's around...?"

"Oh," she said. "Oh. Um..."

Dan was fond of telling Izzy that Eden was certifiably crazy, and maybe she was, because he could tell from her face that she actually thought Izzy had just said what he'd said because he *wanted* to put some physical distance between them. Like last night's fucking-great lovemaking hadn't made him beyond hot for more.

"No, no, nuh, no," he said quickly. "Look at me. Sweetheart. Tonight? You and me? We're getting it on. Even if we have to leave the apartment and, I don't know, go pretend to run an errand so you can jump my bones again in the car. We're gonna find some alone time. Trust me, it's my top priority."

She still looked so uncertain, so he brought it down to the very basics of nonverbal communication and he pulled her toward him and kissed her. It was a *fuck me* kiss, hard and hungry, and he could tell from the way she kissed him back that his message had been successfully received.

And what happened next was completely his fault. He'd loved that sundress she was wearing from the moment she'd put it on that morning, and even though his hand seemingly found its way up under her skirt on its own initiative, the brilliant idea to do so was all his. Although, true, she quickly convinced him the idea wasn't just brilliant but in fact sheer genius by shifting and slightly opening her legs for him to explore even further. So as he kissed her, he kept his hand traveling north against the mind-blowing smoothness of her thigh, on the verge of reaching paradise and...

"Oh, for the love of Christ!"

It was Danny, of course, standing outside the car and knocking impatiently on the window—*bang bang bang.*

They sprang apart, but it was even more awkward than it might've been because Izzy's dive watch got snagged on the seam of her skirt.

And so much for Izzy telling Eden, *I just wanted to remind you that Dan never really liked it when we were together, and since you're the one who's going to have to live with him for the next three years, you might want to withhold the fact that we're banging like bunnies every chance we get. Just on the off chance that it might piss him off.*

"Ben could use some help," Dan said, in that same beleaguered tone, as Eden lowered her window, even as Izzy struggled to get his watch free. "And I thought you might want to know, but obviously I was wrong."

Crap, it was stuck and it was definitely easier to simply unfasten the band and let it remain swallowed up by Eden's dress, than to continue seeming to paw at her the way he was doing.

"What's going on?" Eden asked. "Where is he?"

"He's still inside," Dan said tightly, tersely. "Jenn's with him, because I can't fricking get down on the ground. And I'll be useless in the ambulance, plus I have no idea what his current deal is with the diabetes, so if you're done messing around with Zanella here, you might want to get your ass in there and—"

Eden was already out of the car. She'd started running for the building back when Dan had said *ambulance.*

Izzy turned off the engine and got out, too, trying to be surreptitious about the fact that he needed to adjust his shorts.

Danny, of course, didn't miss a thing.

"What the hell is wrong with you, Zanella?" he asked, but it was clearly a rhetorical question. He didn't wait for an answer as he limped back toward the building.

Which was when the ambulance arrived—holy shit—sirens wailing.

And Izzy took after Eden, passing Danny at a run.

Ben was going to be all right, but the doctor wanted to keep him in the hospital a little bit longer for observation.

Dan looked up as Jenn sat down next to him in the hospital waiting room. "You sure we shouldn't ask for a double room—get you a bed, too?" She wasn't completely kidding. He could see her concern for him in her eyes.

"I'm tired," he admitted, "but I'm okay."

"That could have been bad," she said quietly. "They claim—the administrators at that place—that they had no clue Ben was diabetic. None, whatsoever. Apparently, their standard operating procedure is to lock up their new campers—that's what they call them. Campers. But they lock them up at night. Not just in a cell. Ben just told Eden that he was handcuffed to a bed, with his hands up over his head. All night long."

Dan wasn't surprised. He'd done research on the types of "therapy" used in places like Crossroads.

Jenn was as livid as he'd ever seen her. "I think we should call Linda Thomas," she told him. "That lawyer Maria recommended? I know you're not big on litigation, but...Ben could have died. And with a lawsuit of this magnitude? It's like that case against the KKK. We could force the place to shut down, just to pay damages. Ben could use the money for college tuition...It's not all bad, you know—taking the legal route. And if it's Greg and your mother who were ultimately responsible...? That would give you leverage, if you ever needed it."

But he *didn't* need it. "I just want this to be over for Ben," Dan said. "I don't want to drag it out. I want..." He exhaled his despair. It sounded like a laugh, but it wasn't. There was nothing funny about this. Not at all. "I want one of your massages, and a ten-hour nap," he told her. And this time, when he met her eyes and laughed, it felt more real.

Jenn smiled back at him, her hand warm atop his thigh. "I think we could arrange that," she said. "I've already asked Izzy to drive us back to Eden's. She's going to stay with Ben until he's released, which means when he goes out to pick them up, we'll have some privacy."

Her eyes were so beautiful behind the smudgy lenses of her glasses. Dan leaned forward and kissed her because he couldn't sit here and not kiss her when she was looking at him like that—as if she knew exactly what he was thinking and feeling. But she didn't know all of it, though. Not the stuff that was making him feel so damn defeated.

"Jenni," he said as he took her hand and looked down at her long, elegant fingers. They were almost as long as his, but his hands were far broader and still dwarfed hers.

She leaned in and kissed him again, which was nice, but it was over too soon.

"I got a problem," he admitted. He knew he just had to say it, but it was so goddamned hard.

She saw that he was struggling to find the words, but she didn't do anything more than lace their fingers together and patiently wait for him to get to it. Which he did after inhaling and exhaling hard a few times.

"I didn't count on this," Dan tried to explain. "I didn't factor this in when I did the math. This." He gestured to the hospital around them. "The medical care. The hospital stays." Ben had been in this ER before. A lot. The doctors and nurses all knew him by name, which was great, but also terrifying. Thankfully, they'd had a letter on record, granting parental permission for Ben to receive the treatment he needed, should he be brought in. Which was an additional complication Dan hadn't considered. He was not only going to have to go pick up Ben's school and medical records tomorrow, but he was also going to have to schedule a time to connect with Ivette and get her to sign a whole stack of similar letters for him to take to San Diego.

"His doctor actually told me he's doing really well for a kid with his type of diabetes," he continued, telling Jenn. "Apparently, doing really well means he's only in and out of the hospital a couple of times a year." He shook his head. "I don't know where I'm going to get the money for that. And since he's not my kid—"

"Dan—"

But he wasn't done. "The reason my mother agreed to let me have him," he told her, "is because I promised I'd keep sending her money." He closed his eyes. "I bought Ben from her, Jenni, for a monthly sum. That I now have to deliver. And that, plus the rent on an apartment in

San Diego, plus medical bills of an undetermined amount...? I'm never going to see you. I'm not going to be able to come to New York to visit. I won't be able to swing it."

"So, I'll visit you," Jenni said.

"It's not fair to ask you to do that," he countered.

"You're not asking," she pointed out. "I'm volunteering."

What could he say to that? He just shook his head. No.

"So if that doesn't work for you, are you... breaking up with me?" she asked quietly.

"No! Jesus! God!" He put his arms around her. "I don't know what I'm doing," he admitted. "I just...God, when Ben didn't open his eyes..."

When Ben had fallen in that lobby, when his legs had just—*boom*—given out from beneath him...That had been bad. But when Dan had realized that his brother had lost control of at least some of his bodily functions...He'd nearly killed the sanctimoniously smug woman behind the front desk.

His wounded right leg had kept him from getting down on the floor next to Ben, but that was okay, because Jenn was there.

And there it was. The bottom line. Whatever happened was going to be okay, because Jenn was there.

Except she wasn't going to be there. Not for very much longer. She was leaving in a week.

And Danny desperately didn't want her to go.

Break up with him? Hell, he wanted her to move in and never leave his side again.

But if she didn't want to marry him, she sure as hell wouldn't move to San Diego to live with him and his dysfunctional family. Which, God help him, appeared to include Irving Zanella.

Whose dive watch Dan had in his pocket. He'd picked it up after it had finally disengaged itself from where it had been caught, up Eden's dress.

Jesus Christ.

"He's okay," Jenn reassured him, talking about Ben.

"I know," Dan said. "I'm just..." He shook his head. "Tired." Yeah, maybe this would all seem less overwhelming when he wasn't exhausted.

Jenn gently pulled her hand free and stood up. "I'll see if I can find Izzy. Then we'll go in and say good-bye to Ben, okay? I'll be right back." She kissed the top of his head.

He was busy watching her walk away, and he didn't see Izzy approach—not until the SEAL sat down next to him and said, "Bro, we need to talk."

Dan briefly closed his eyes. "Yeah, let's not do this right now, Zanella," he said on an exhale. "Jenn went to look for you and—"

"I thought sooner would be better than later," Izzy said.

"Yeah, well, not for me."

"Or for me," Izzy agreed, in that same almost-somber tone. In fact he was sitting there minus his usual devil-may-care, fuck-all-y'all attitude. And the expression on his face was believably contrite. "But for Ben and Eden and Jenn...? Let's just get this over with."

"*Over* with?" Dan said, sitting up straighter. "*Over with* is you driving us to San Diego and then getting the *fuck* out of my life."

"I think I'm probably more in Eden's life," Izzy pointed out mildly. "But okay. Have at me. I'm an idiot. I'm a fool, a moron, an asshat, a dipshit. You hate me, you've always hated me, I annoy you, and now I *really* annoy you because I'm sleeping with your sister again. Come on, Danny. Let me have it. Don't hold back."

"Jesus," Dan said, "you're such a *douchebag*. What were you, with her for ten whole minutes yesterday before you got back into her pants?"

"I prefer the term *reconciled*," the other SEAL said. "Before we reconciled. And it was more like a couple of hours, but yeah, I agree. It happened pretty quickly. You're not the only one who's surprised."

"But I'm *not* surprised," Dan told him. "I'm not even close to surprised. What the hell is wrong with you? You're like the stupidest kid in the world. You touch the hot stove, burn yourself, but then turn right around and touch it again."

"Hey, Izzy, there you are," Jenn said, looking from Dan to Izzy and back again. "Everything okay here?"

"Yeah," Izzy said as Dan flatly said, "No."

"What if, yeah, okay, you get burned," Izzy said to Dan, as if he didn't care that Jenn joined their conversation, which she did by sitting down on Dan's other side, and taking his hand in silent support, gently squeezing it. "But you also get—"

"*Don't* say what I think you're going to say," Dan warned him.

"I'm speaking figuratively here," Izzy said. "Okay? What if you touch the figurative stove, and even though you figuratively get burned, you also figuratively get a million dollars. Chances are, you're going to go back to the stove."

"For a million dollars," Dan argued. "Yeah. But we're not talking about a million dollars."

"At the risk of potentially offending you," Izzy said. "By moving from figurative to actual, I can state that I would, absolutely, trade a million dollars to be with Eden."

"*Be* with Eden," Dan repeated, unable to keep his heat from his voice. "Let's cut the crap and just say what we mean. You're talking about—"

Izzy protested. "But you said I shouldn't say—"

"—having sex with my sister," Dan finished. "Which is worth—to you—a million dollars. You *are* fricking stupid."

"It's not just the sex," Izzy insisted.

"You could buy a much nicer girl," Dan shot back, "for a million dollars. Or maybe you're as white trash as she is, and you like the whole *I'm a slut* vibe Eden brings to the table."

He knew, the moment the words left his mouth, that it was the wrong thing to say. He also knew that it was only because Jenn was sitting next to him, holding his hand, that Izzy didn't haul him to his feet and kick his ass. Injury be damned.

"*That* wasn't helpful," Jenn murmured, and Dan couldn't bring himself to look over at her.

Izzy now sat leaning forward slightly, with his forearms on his thighs and his hands clasped together in front of him. He appeared to be relaxed, but Dan could see the muscle jumping in the side of his jaw. His knuckles were also close to white.

Dan knew he should apologize, but the words caught in his throat because he didn't want to. He was that mad. At Izzy and Eden. At the entire universe. At every human being on the planet except for Jennilyn and Ben.

"Will you, um, excuse us for a second, Jenn?" Izzy turned slightly toward Jennilyn, looking past Dan, but not quite meeting Jenn's eyes, either. At least as far as Dan could tell. He seemed to be looking at a spot on the wall across the room. "I have to say something to Dan that he'd prefer you don't hear."

"I don't keep secrets from my girlfriend," Dan said.

But Jenn was already rising to her feet. "I'll go see how Eden and Ben are doing." She gave his hand one last squeeze. "Please, no bloodshed."

Izzy waited until she walked away, until she rounded the corner. And even then, when he spoke, he kept his voice low. "I have opinions and predictions about your relationship, too, you know. Plenty of them, in fact. And I happen to think that you're using Jenn and that you're a shit. And I happen to know that if she hadn't come to Germany the way that she did, you'd've hooked up—in a heartbeat—with Sheila Anderson."

"No," Dan protested. "I wouldn't have." But even as he said the words, he knew that it certainly would have been his pattern in the past.

"Yeah, you would've," Izzy argued. "Because that's what *you* do, asshole. You sleep with whoever makes googly eyes at you—as long as they're convenient and as long as there's an end date in sight. Me, I have a weakness for your sister. And yes, I continue to want her— wherever and whenever possible. Am I using her, simply because I know for a fact that she doesn't love me? Maybe I am. And maybe that makes me a shit, too. But I think it just makes me a fool and all those other things that you didn't disagree that I wasn't. But as much of a fool and a dipshit that I am? I am *not* deluded. I know Eden's not going to stay with me for very long. I know what's coming, and my life will go on. But until then? I'm on board this train, this incredibly fabulous train, whether you like it or not.

"So. You think I'm a shit, and I *know* you're a shit," Izzy continued. "But here's how we're going to get along for these next few days or months or yes, years, if I'm that freaking lucky. You watch your mouth when you talk about your sister. You show some respect. And I won't kill you. That sound fair to you? Because it sounds really, *really* fair to me."

Izzy stood up, clearly not intending to wait for Danny's response.

Which was probably good because Danny was stuck on that one most horrifying word that Izzy had said.

Years.

Holy Christ, if everything went *just* right, he was going to share an apartment with Ben and Eden and freaking Izzy Zanella for *years*.

CHAPTER
FOURTEEN

The nearest big city was Los Angeles.

Neesha had gone to the library, to look at a map, but the librarian had waved to her and said, "There was a man here yesterday, and I think he was looking for you," so she made up an excuse — *Oh, I forgot my phone* — and hurried away.

She went instead to a bookstore and wandered until she found some maps in a rack. And she knew the writing that said Las Vegas — she could recognize that and she found it, and found the next-nearest big dot. She'd stopped a friendly-looking woman with a baby in a stroller and asked for help. English was her second language, could she please pronounce this city's name for her?

Los Angeles.

She'd gone from there to the bus depot and with her heart pounding, watching all the time for Mr. Nelson or Todd or their men, she stood in line. She'd been here before, hoping that she could sneak onto a bus and leave the city. But she'd seen the security. She saw how it worked. People would come to this counter, hand over their little plastic cards or bills similar to the one she'd taken from Ben's sister's client. They were given a piece of paper that they would then show to the driver as they boarded their bus.

At last it was her turn and she moved to the counter. She was separated from the woman who sat back there by a thick window of plastic, although there was a narrow hole at the bottom.

"Destination," the woman said, her voice sounding strange and metallic. Neesha didn't know what that meant and she froze.

The woman sighed and rolled her eyes. "Where are you going?" she said, still in that metallic voice, but much more slowly, each word carefully pronounced.

That Neesha knew. "Los Angeles."

"One way or round-trip?"

Again, Neesha had no clue. She shook her head.

"Child, *where* is your mother?" the woman said.

Another question she could answer. "She's dead."

"Oh, Lordy," the woman said. "Okay, all right. Are you coming back to Las Vegas or are you planning to stay in L.A.?"

L.A.—she'd heard of L.A. on the television. Was that the same as Los Angeles? She hoped so.

"I'm not coming back," Neesha said.

"One way, then," the woman told her. "Cash or credit?"

Cash was another word for the money Neesha had taken, so she took the bill from her pocket now, and slid it through the slot beneath the plastic window.

"What's this?" the woman said, as if she didn't recognize it.

"Cash," Neesha said.

"Oh, honey, this is just a *fraction* of what you need for a ticket to L.A."

Neesha didn't know *fraction* and she stared at the woman in confusion.

"One way to L.A. is fifty-five dollars," the woman told her, pushing the bill back out that slot. "You're thirty-five dollars short."

"I'm sorry."

"I am, too. Child, if you need help—"

Neesha shook her head as she took the money she'd stolen, jammed it back into her pocket, and hurried away.

She was running out of both options and time.

. . .

Ben was asleep when Izzy came back to the hospital.

Eden went out into the hall so their conversation wouldn't wake him.

"He's doing well," she reported. "The nurse went to see about getting him discharged so we can bring him home. We have to sign some special paper, some kind of disclaimer or something, because they'd prefer to keep him overnight, but his insurance won't cover it, and since Danny's getting a little nutty about all the money, I thought... Besides, he's good. Ben. He says he feels much better and he really wants to leave, and since he's been dealing with the diabetes for years...I trust him to have a good read on his own body."

"Good," Izzy said. "That's good. If you trust him, I trust him, too."

She was staring up at him—she knew it, and she forced herself to blink, to smile. "Good," she repeated, too—a little inanely.

Izzy did that to her. It was weird. When he was with her, as he'd been nonstop since yesterday, she got slightly more used to his presence. But after he'd been gone, even just for the few hours during which he'd driven Dan and Jenn back to her apartment?

Seeing him again gave her a real jolt.

It wasn't that he was the most handsome man she'd ever encountered, because he wasn't. He had a lot of uneven edges and sharp angles to his face—a certain cragginess. That was the best word for it, and even that wasn't quite right.

There was an honesty to him—a tactlessness, at times—and it was reflected in the expressions that he wore. His face was constantly in motion, and when he did become still, it was almost startling. And when he smiled...?

He was beyond beautiful.

Eden had spent some time last night, just watching him smiling in his sleep.

But his face wasn't the only thing that gave her a jolt upon seeing him again.

He was tall—taller than most men—and powerfully built, with upper arms that were probably wider in circumference than Ben's thighs, which okay, wasn't really saying that much because Ben was such a twig, but still. When Izzy wore a T-shirt like the one he was wearing now, it really emphasized how muscular he was. And the shorts...He always wore the style that went all the way down to his knees and had plenty of pockets of all kinds that he kept filled with Lord knows what, yet the cut still managed to showcase the rather ridiculously nice butt that Eden knew was beneath. Although seriously? A man who looked the way Izzy did when he was naked should've been required to never wear clothes. His legs were long and tan, his calves covered with sun-bleached hair. He was wearing sandals—the kind with a tread on the bottom, that he could run in— and even his feet looked big and strong.

But it was Izzy's eyes that Eden found herself transfixed by—as lovely as the rest of him was to look at, even while unclad. It was his eyes—and the life and humor and heat she found within them—that amplified his smile and took her breath away.

"What," he said now as he gazed back at her, and she realized that she was staring again. He wiped his mouth with his hand. "Do I have pizza on me? I have to confess that I stopped to get a slice. I got one for you, but I kind of ate it, too." He made a face. "Sorry. I'm an ass. Say the word, and I'll go back—"

"No, that's okay," she said. "I'm not really hungry and...I'm going to make Ben dinner when we get home, so..."

"Two slices is just an appetizer," he said. "I'm completely up for dinner, too."

"Or maybe we should stop somewhere," Eden said, "so we don't bother Danny and Jenn. Did you get them set up okay?"

"Done and done," Izzy told her. "I put them in your bedroom and I didn't have to wrestle Dan to the death to do it. Oh, and I found the clean sheets where you said they were, no problem. I also got the pull-out bed made up for us—well, sort of. The mattress is pretty crappy and the metal frame wasn't...Whatever. It's fine. Long story short,

Jenn helped me put the mattress directly on the living-room floor. We also got the air mattress inflated for Ben. Jenn put sheets on it, too—it's all ready to go."

"Thank you so much," she said.

"Danny's still hurting pretty badly. Plus, he's running on empty after all the travel," Izzy told her, "which is frustrating the shit out of him. By the time I left, he was already in bed. I was glad Jenn was there, to babysit him."

Eden glanced at Izzy's watch, which she was wearing on her wrist. Even at the tightest setting of the strap, it was still loose and she had to turn it to see the time.

It was barely 6:30, which meant it was barely 9:30 eastern time. Which was *very* wimpy for Dan, who often went for days without more than a nap, even with jet lag.

"Oh, good," Izzy said as he saw his watch. "You have it. I was wondering where..."

"Dan picked it up," Eden said as she unfastened it and handed it back to him. "He, um, gave it to me with a disapproving glare before he and Jenn left."

Izzy met her eyes. "Awkward," he said in a singsongy voice, which made her laugh, despite her embarrassment. "Although, to be fair, sweetheart, we *are* married. He's the one who's carrying on outside the bonds of holy matrimony. A million-to-one odds says that fireworks *and* rainbows are exploding over your apartment complex right about..." He glanced at his watch. "*Now*. That Jennilyn LeMay is no idiot. She negotiated their alone time like a pro—and not because she and Dan wanted the privacy to sing Michael Jackson's greatest hits."

Eden laughed and let the struggles and problems of the day fall away from her. And yet, at the same time, she suddenly, desperately wanted to cry. Izzy was being Izzy, but he still wasn't quite the same Izzy that he'd been last summer, when he'd married her. Now there was an edge to him, as if he didn't give a crap about anything but getting with her again. And again. And *again*.

Although, really, what did she expect?

"Plus, think about it," Izzy continued. "Do you really think Danny-Danny-bo-banny could snag a woman as classy as Jenn, based purely on his witty charm and sunny personality?" He answered his own question. "Not a chance. Girlfriend's hooked up with him to get some of that first-class Gillman boo-tay."

Jenn wasn't the only one.

And he echoed Eden's very thought by leaning close and lowering his voice. "I, too, am fond of fireworks and rainbows. I'm thinking we can have that dinner, bring Ben home, get him set up with some popcorn in front of the TV, and then? After it's nice and dark? Find a reason to run that errand, maybe go in search of a twenty-four-hour pharmacy. Fill a fictional prescription or pick up some of that shampoo that you just ran out of that you absolutely must have . . . ?"

"Not fictional," Eden said, loving the feel of his body next to hers. He was so solid, she just wanted to lean against him and lose herself in his arms. "The prescription. Ben needs to get more glucagon. He used some recently and . . . Kids with diabetes use it when they have a sudden severe low—low blood sugar. It's kind of like the opposite of insulin. He's supposed to have two doses on hand at all times, and we *should* get that refilled, so . . ."

"Two is one and one is none," Izzy murmured. "It's a Navy SEAL philosophy."

"A Navy SEAL and a gay, diabetic kid," she said. "Who knew you'd have so much in common."

"You know, one of the guys in our team is," Izzy said. "Gay. Not diabetic. You can't be a SEAL if you're diabetic. But you can if you're gay."

"Seriously?" Eden asked.

He nodded. "Don't ask, don't tell—so I'm not going to tell you his name, but . . . Yeah."

"And . . . Danny knows?"

Izzy nodded again, his eyes on her mouth, like he was thinking about kissing her.

Eden moistened her lips—she couldn't help herself. But she

wasn't ready for this conversation to be over, so she leaned back a little. Just a little. "Do you think that's why he's so okay about Ben? Because he knows this other guy who's...?"

"I do," Izzy said.

"I was a little worried," she confessed, "that Danny was going to side with Greg, and then I'd have to fight them both. If I could've, I would've just taken Ben and disappeared. But you can't go off the grid with a kid who needs insulin shots."

"I'm really glad you didn't," Izzy said, using one finger to push her hair behind her ear. It was the slightest of touches and yet it sent a clear message that was echoed in the heat in his eyes.

Ben's glucagon prescription wasn't the only thing that was going to be filled tonight. The anticipation was almost unbearable.

"Fireworks and rainbows," Eden said, wanting him to laugh, "and marching bands. Personally, I like it when there's a marching band."

And he did laugh at that, his smile softening his face, but in no way eliminating the heat in his eyes. If anything, his eyes grew hotter.

He shifted even closer so that their thighs touched, so that her breasts brushed his chest, and God, she wanted to run out to the drugstore right then and there. "I can deliver a marching band," he promised her. "And...? A tiny car filled with clowns."

Now she was the one who was laughing. "I think that's probably more scary than romantic. I mean, in the cosmic scheme of things."

"Hmm," he said. "So you think marching bands are romantic. Interesting."

"Romantic's the wrong word," she said. "Maybe... passionate. Marching bands are like fireworks—passionate and... Well, not at all subtle."

"Passionate and not at all subtle can be delivered at a moment's notice," he murmured, pulling her face up to finally give her that kiss.

And oh, Lord, he was, absolutely, delivering passionate and not at all subtle, and it was impossible not to melt against him, to all but beg him to devour her, her hands in his hair, her body tight against him.

"And why am I not surprised, missy," a reedy and all too familiar voice interrupted, "to find you behaving wantonly in a public corridor."

Eden pulled away even as Izzy let her go and there he was.

Greg.

Her mother's latest husband—Eden was loath to call him her stepfather—was coming down the hall with the nurse who'd gone to get Ben's discharge papers.

His face was pinched from the effort of walking farther than from the couch to the kitchen, and his limp was pronounced. Which could well have been an act, because in the years that Eden had lived with him, he'd frequently played the pity card while out in public.

But there was a big difference between making people feel sorry and making them feel repulsed—and he was definitely in danger of the second. And not just to Eden.

He'd combed his greasy hair for the occasion, but he'd missed a spot that was still tangled. His fly was thankfully zipped, but his pants were less than clean, with a big stain on his left thigh and a slight tear in the knee. He was wearing a navy-blue windbreaker that seemed oddly out of place in the evening heat. Eden knew it was to cover his shirt—he'd probably spilled something on it, on the drive over. He kept the jacket in his car for that very purpose.

"It's Mrs. Zanella now, not *missy*." Izzy didn't hesitate. He stepped protectively in front of Eden. "And you're not welcome here."

"I'm the boy's father," Greg said.

"No, you're not." Eden said it in near-perfect unison with Izzy.

"Yes, actually," Greg said. "I am. I adopted him after your mother and I were married. When we found out she was no longer able to have another child, which was disappointing, but...It was clearly God's will."

Dear Lord, wouldn't *that* have been awful? A toddler living in *that* house. Eden didn't want even to think about it.

"God moves in mysterious ways," Greg continued sanctimoniously. "He made Benjamin my son for a reason. He wants me in his life."

"Your wife—Ben's mother," Izzy said far more quietly and evenly than Eden would have managed, "gave him permission to live with his brother, Dan, in San Diego."

"But not with her," Greg said with a dismissive glance at Eden.

"Eden is Ben's sister," Izzy said, and there was hard steel hiding beneath his still fairly easygoing tone as he put his arm around her, his hand warm at her waist. "She's also my wife. You should keep that in mind, in case you're thinking about insulting her."

Izzy smiled at Greg, and even though it touched his eyes, it was different from his usual grin. And Eden remembered him smiling like that last July, while they were in serious danger, under siege from an army of men who'd kidnapped her and wanted to kill them both. She didn't remember much about that night because she'd gone into premature labor and had lost a lot of blood. Most of it was a blur of pain and fear.

But she did remember Izzy and his promises. *Everything's going to be all right…*

And she remembered his smile.

The nurse who was with Greg shifted—obviously uncertain and wondering if she should hand the discharge papers to Greg or to Eden.

Eden took the decision—and the papers—out of the woman's hands. "Ben's coming with us. We're going to take him to Danny, who isn't here right now only because he was recently injured in Afghanistan—surviving a near-death incident, much to your disappointment, I'm sure." She felt Izzy caution her, his hand tightening on her arm.

"I don't care if you're going to take him to live in the White House, or with the man in the moon," Greg shot back, letting his voice get louder. "He's *my* son, and I will not just give him away! Not until he's cured of his illness."

"Cured…?" Eden started.

"Okay," Izzy said, stepping between them again. "Hold on…"

But her argument with Greg had woken Ben, who called for her from his hospital room. "Eden...?" His voice broke with his anxiety and he sounded like the frightened child he'd once been.

"I'm right here, Boo-Boo," Eden reassured him, rushing toward his room. "I'm not going anywhere."

But Greg spoke over her. "Get dressed and gather up your things, boy," he ordered as he followed her into Ben's room. "I'm taking you home."

Ben was horrified when he realized that he was right—he *had* heard his stepfather's voice. He was sitting up in bed, his blanket clutched to his skinny chest as he looked from Eden to Greg to Izzy and the nurse, who had followed them in.

Eden gave him her best Izzy smile and reassured him. "I'm not letting him take you anywhere." She spun to stop Greg, getting right in his face even though his breath was awful. "Over my dead body."

"That's easy enough to arrange," Greg said.

And Izzy took him down.

One minute she and Greg were standing there, nose-to-nose, and the next, Izzy had pushed her back, out of the way. She bumped into Ben's bed with the backs of her legs as Izzy and Greg hit the floor. And she realized that Greg had reached into the pocket of his windbreaker, where, for all they knew, he could well have been packing his handgun.

Then Greg was howling, with his face against the tile, Izzy's big knee jammed into the middle of his back, his right arm twisted up behind him as the SEAL searched him for a weapon.

And came up empty-handed.

The nurse had already dashed away, no doubt to call for security, as Greg continued to scream, "You broke my arm! You broke my arm!"

Izzy looked up at Eden, absolutely no apology in his eyes. "I wasn't willing to wait and see if he was carrying," he said. "I'd do it again, in a heartbeat, but...The shit's about to hit the fan." He aimed his next words to Greg. "It's not broken, asshole. Believe me, if it was broken, you'd know it." He then included Ben in what he was saying, raising his voice so they could hear him over Greg's noise. "You both need to keep a clear head, stay cool, okay? Whoever's coming might get rough with me, but that's okay."

"It is *not*—" Eden started.

Izzy cut her off. "Sweetheart. It's okay. I'm a kind of large guy and that's going to scare the guards, so they're going to get loud when they see me. But they're not going to hurt me, I don't bruise easily, and it *is* going to be okay. Nod your head—it's okay. Ben, you too. Come on, help me out here."

Eden nodded jerkily, and she turned to see Ben nod, too.

"Excellent. Eden, call your brother and Jenn," Izzy continued. "We could use them down here—understatement. And Ben? Look at me, bro. This *is* going to be okay. Seriously. No one's going to make you go home with numbnuts here." He looked down at Greg. "Last chance, asshole. If I let you up, will you walk away? Let Ben go to San Diego with—"

Whatever Greg said as he continued to sob, it clearly wasn't what Izzy'd hoped to hear, because he shook his head with regret. "Okay then," Izzy said as he looked back at Ben. "You've got the power, kid. You listening to me?"

Ben nodded again.

"The nurse is going to come back in here," Izzy told Ben, "and you need to pull her aside and say this: *Ask me if I feel safe with Greg.* And when she does, you answer her honestly—you got that?"

But Ben didn't get a chance to respond, because time was up.

And sure enough, two security guards came into the room, and when they saw Izzy, with Greg still pinned beneath him, they got loud, just as he'd said they would.

Izzy was calm and he just kept talking in that even, unruffled voice, now to the guards. "My name is Irving Zanella, I'm an active-duty Navy SEAL, just back from Afghanistan, and I am on your side. This is my father-in-law, who threatened my wife and her brother with a loaded handgun just yesterday. When he reached into his pocket as he was threatening my wife here today? I wasn't going to wait to see if he was stupid enough to carry concealed in a hospital. Turns out he's not. His arm is *not* broken, regardless of what he's saying..."

Despite all the shouting and noise, in the middle of all of the chaos, Izzy looked over at Eden and smiled.

And she was pretty certain that, before the guards led both men out of Ben's room, she heard Izzy humming a bar or two of the song that went *Three cheers for the red, white, and blue*—a tune that was most frequently performed by marching bands.

The police officer was hot. He was young, and he had dark hair that he wore longer than Ben would have expected from an officer who used that much starch in his uniform. But maybe his hair just grew really quickly and he hadn't had time to get it cut.

He had a baby face that made him look a little bit like he'd dressed up as a cop for Halloween, and he sighed as Ben finished telling his story for a second time.

"Lemme see your arms again," he said, and Ben obediently held out his hands, palms up.

His wrists were bruised and sore, the skin red and scraped from being cuffed to the cot by the plastic restraints all night. His shoulders were sore, too. But there wasn't any visible proof of that.

The nurse—her name was Betsy—who hadn't left his side since he'd asked her for protection from his stepfather, made an anguished noise low in her throat. "I can't believe I didn't see that when you were admitted," she said.

"I was trying to hide it," Ben told her. "I was embarrassed. Besides, I thought it was over. I thought I was safe."

It was a magic word, *safe*. He was thankful Izzy had told him to use it.

But maybe he'd used it too often, because the cop—Officer Kellen was *his* name—tilted his head, and said, "Your father's insisting that your brother-in-law, Irving Zanella—coached you as to what to say to us."

Ben shook his head, no. "Izzy told me how to ask for help," he said. "And he told me to be honest. That's all."

"This is a big deal, son," Kellen said. "So if you're *not* being honest—"

"I am," Ben said. "And while I really appreciate the kindness you've shown me, would you mind, very much, not calling me *son*? I have a problem with people who really aren't that much older than me trying to be paternal. Or maybe you're playing the folksy card—trust me, it's not working. And as long as I'm being bitchy here about what we call each other? Greg Fortune is *not* my father. He says he legally adopted me? If he did, I didn't have a say in it."

Kellen sighed again as he flipped through the pages of notes he'd taken with his ridiculous stub of a pencil. "And you think if you went home with him...?"

"I have no doubt, whatsoever," Ben said, holding the police officer's steady gaze, "that he would send me back to Crossroads—and that I'll spend tonight cuffed to a bed, too."

Kellen glanced at the nurse. "I gotta be honest. This is a new one, for me. The father—Greg—is saying the same thing. But he claims it's no different from a military school, that yeah, they're strict..."

And so much for Ben's hopes that he'd lucked out and gotten a police officer who'd actually marched in the Pride Parade. But the nurse leaped to his defense.

"This boy ended up in the hospital," she said sharply, "because this man who claims to be his father neglected to mention that his alleged son was diabetic before sending him to that awful place!"

"He's contrite about that," Kellen said. "He said it was an oversight. A simple miscommunication. They've now been informed—it won't happen again. Parents are allowed to make mistakes." He looked at Ben, and sighed again.

It was over. He'd lost.

And now Ben was going to throw up. Or faint. Or both. He pushed his chair back from the table and put his head down between his knees and breathed as he tried not to shake.

He could feel the nurse's hand on his back, but she couldn't help him. It was up to Officer Kellen to decide whether or not he should get the Department of Child Protective Services involved or send Ben back home.

So Ben pushed himself up as far as he could, his elbows on his knees, because Jesus, he could still keel over any second, so he wanted to keep his center of gravity low. And he looked at the man and he begged.

"Please," he said, with his heart in his throat. "I'm not a bad person. I know I got picked up for truancy yesterday, but that was because my stepfather hit me, and I was staying with my sister, and I was afraid he'd find me if I went to school. The detectives scared me, and I ran. I shouldn't've—I know that. But it hasn't happened before, and it won't happen again. My grades are okay, I keep my head down, and I don't get into trouble. The only thing I'm guilty of is being gay. Being honest about it. And that's not going to change by being tied up, or starved or sleep-deprived. That's what they do there—at Crossroads. There's another boy in there. He was in my cell for a few hours last night—he was tied up, too. His name is Peter Sinclair—write that down, too, okay? Sinclair. He's been there for months, against his will. He was tied up by his feet because his wrists were bandaged—he told me he tried to kill himself so he'd get sent to the hospital, but they didn't let him go. They're withholding food from him and they're keeping him from sleeping, too—they moved him out of the cell before I woke up. What they're doing *isn't* being strict—it's fucked up." He glanced at the nurse. "Excuse me. But it is. And it's abuse. And you know what? Even if you could squint your eyes and pretend that it's an appropriate punishment for kids who are bad, that it's not that different from what they do at those schools that are called military schools, but have nothing to do with the military and everything to do with discarded kids whose parents can't handle them? Even if you believe *that,* then you need to ask yourself if I really deserve to be punished for doing nothing worse than simply being me."

Officer Kellen was clenching his teeth, the muscle jumping in the side of his face as he tapped his pencil stub against the name—Peter Sinclair—that he'd just written on a fresh page of his notepad.

"*Please*," Ben said again. "Go over there and talk to Peter before you let Greg send me back. And maybe? If you have even half of a heart, you'll get him, and every other kid who doesn't want to be there out of there, too."

"Okay," Jenn said as she closed her phone and came back inside, into the hospital lobby, where Dan was waiting with his sister and Izzy. Dan was sitting with his head back against the wall, his legs stretched out in front of him, arms crossed. His eyes had been closed, but he opened them now. She knew he was running on empty. He'd fallen asleep midsentence, just a few hours earlier, after she'd given him his re-quested "massage." "Here's what Linda told me."

"Who's Linda?" Izzy asked. Apparently the police officer who'd made the scene after the SEAL had had his altercation with Dan's step-father had decided that Izzy's rough treatment of Greg had been war-ranted. It probably helped that Greg was as Looney Tunes crazy as he looked, and that he truly believed he had the right to use threat of death from a loaded weapon to discipline a teenager. Last Jenn had heard, Ben's stepfather had been talking to the police officer—Kellen was the young cop's name—and earnestly insisting that everything he'd done was completely okay. It was tough love. And yes, he was, absolutely, intending to send Ben back to Crossroads, as soon as possible...

"Linda's the lawyer that Maria recommended." Eden filled him in as Jenn stuck her cell phone into the back pocket of her jeans and sat down next to Danny. "Maria Bonavita—the assemblywoman that Jenn works for? She's—"

"I know Maria," Izzy cut her off.

Eden looked at him.

"What?" he said. "I know her. That's all. We've met. I slept on her living-room floor when crazy people wanted to kill her. With Lopez.

He was there. And Tiny Tony V. Danny, too. We told ghost stories, and why am I telling you this?"

"Why *are* you telling me this?" she asked.

Izzy shrugged and turned back to Jenn, who'd flipped her legal pad back to the first page of notes she'd taken during her phone call. "So. Linda the lawyer," he said. "What did she say?"

"That the Department of Child Protective Services will do everything they possibly can to keep a child with his parents—"

"Even if the parents don't want him?" Eden asked. "I mean, they *don't* want *him*. Not really."

Izzy reached over and took her hand.

"It's going to be an uphill climb," Jenn said. "Our best shot is to present a united front. We're talking about moving Ben out of state, which is even more questionable from CPS's standpoint. Linda thought the best possible way to get that kind of custody is to have Eden and Izzy apply, because they've been married for almost a year now. There's stability there—sort of. I mean . . . um . . ."

God, this was awkward. She hadn't thought before she'd spoken. And the way Dan had described it, Izzy had come to Vegas to talk to Eden about getting a divorce. But they acted more like newlyweds, which, of course, Danny believed was just Eden being Eden and messing with Izzy's mind, but Jenn wasn't as sure. She saw the way Dan's sister looked at Izzy, and the way he looked back at her. There was something there.

"That option's certainly on the table," Izzy said quietly. "For Ben's sake, I'd certainly be open to, um, staying together at least a little bit longer."

Danny cleared his throat, and shot Jenn a look that had shades of *I'm having an aneurism* in it.

She kept her own expression carefully neutral. "Okay," she said. "That's good. Linda also thought it would go over well if the plan was for, um, the four of you to share an apartment."

"Is that . . . really necessary?" Eden asked.

"It is. Linda also thinks your best shot," Jenn answered, "is to put pressure on your mother. She told Dan that it was okay if Ben went to live with him. We need to be sure she knows that Greg is making the noise he's making, and see if she can't talk him down. We also need to check to find out if he really did adopt Ben. I'll be looking into that tomorrow."

"I've called Ivette's cell phone four times," Danny reported, checking his cell phone. "And left four messages."

"Getting in touch with her is a priority," Jenn said. "Because what we really want is to settle this outside of CPS. As soon as they decide that Ben really is in danger from Greg—and that initial process takes about three days—they'll launch a full investigation and hold a hearing. But once that happens? There's no going back. A guardian *ad litem* is appointed, and Ben is put into foster care. If that happens, Linda's going to find out if we can petition the guardian to let Ben live with you until the hearing, or if we have to actually apply to be foster parents and go through the whole interview process. She's going to call me back about that."

"So it's possible that—if CPS gets involved," Eden clarified, "Ben will go into foster care, even though we're sitting right here, waving our arms, begging to take him in?"

"That's right," Jenn told her.

"This hearing," Izzy asked. "It basically all comes down to a judge who decides...Who Ben should live with?"

"Nope," Jenn said. "It's all about Greg and Ivette. The judge decides whether or not Ben will be safe if he continues to live with them. The guardian has a lot to say about that. Of course, you'd all get to speak at the hearing—Ben, too. And we can bring in experts—and there're a lot of them—who agree that being gay isn't something that can be changed by a place like Crossroads. But ultimately, it's up to the judge. If he decides that it's in Ben's best interest to go home to Ivette and Greg, Ben goes home."

"And then to Crossroads," Eden said darkly.

"If the judge decides not," Jenn said, "then Ben becomes a ward of the state of Nevada. And it's only *then* that Izzy and Eden can apply for custody."

"What if the judge—or the guardian," Dan asked, "is homophobic?"

"That could be a problem," Jenn admitted. "I actually anticipated your asking that, and asked Linda to look into the possibility of Ben declaring himself an emancipated minor." She looked at Eden. "That's kind of like him divorcing his parents."

"I know," she said. She forced a smile. "But thank you for . . . Thank you."

They were all silent then, as Jenn flipped through her notes, checking to see if there was anything she could add to what she'd already told them.

Dan cleared his throat again. "How long does it all take?" he asked. "If CPS decides there needs to be a full investigation? How long until the hearing?"

"It happens pretty quickly," Jenn told him. "We'll have about thirty days."

"Thirty days is quick?" Dan asked, laughing his disbelief. "God damn." He was really shaken. "I'm going to have to get leave, but it's probably going to be without pay and—"

"I have some money saved," Eden said.

"I do, too," Izzy told Dan.

"Still, I'll need to find someplace to stay." Dan was in heavy worst-case-scenario mode.

"You can stay with me," Eden said. "I've already paid rent on my apartment through the end of the summer. It's not like that'll be an additional expense."

"But *five* of us?" Dan asked. "In a one-bedroom apartment?" He looked at Jenn and there was such despair in his eyes. "Four, really, because you're leaving in a week."

"You know that I can stay longer," she told him, and he nodded. But she knew he'd never ask her to make that sacrifice.

"We can make this work," Izzy said.

Dan laughed. "Said the asshole who thinks everything's fine as long as he's screwing my sister. Newsflash, Zanella. She's just not that hard to get."

"Danny," Jenn said, purposely keeping her voice mild. "I think maybe *you're* the asshole."

Izzy, meanwhile, had clenched both his fists and then opened his big hands wide, in a mock Bob Fosse jazz-hands move. "Not hitting you."

Eden just looked miserable.

"Sorry," Dan muttered to her.

"Maybe," Jenn started, but Dan cut her off.

"Maybe we should just kill Greg," he said.

"It's probably better not to joke about that," Jenn said.

"Who's joking?"

"Really, Danny. I know you're upset, but that's just not—"

"Sorry," he said again, and he reached for her hand. His eyes were filled with regret and shame and pure desperation. "I *am* sorry." He pushed himself to his feet. "May I speak to you privately, please?"

"Of course." Jenn followed him away from Izzy and Eden, over to the sensor-triggered doors that slid open, exposing them to a wave of ovenlike heat.

Dan went into it and moved far enough away so the doors would slide closed again. "I was hoping Linda would force my hand," he told her.

Jenn shook her head. She didn't understand.

He clarified. "I was hoping she'd say that we should, you know, get married. That *that* would be our best shot at getting Ben."

He was looking at her with those eyes, with that face, and Jenn knew that hitting him was not the proper response to what he'd just said. *Force his* . . . Fabulous. She nodded instead. "But she didn't say that."

"Marry me anyway," he said.

"Wow," she said. "Way to be romantic, Gillman, and really pick the moment."

He looked around them, as if suddenly aware that they were standing outside of a hospital in Las Vegas, Nevada. "I was thinking about it earlier," he admitted, "but that wasn't the most romantic moment, either." His smile was sheepish, and she knew exactly to which earlier moment he was referring.

"Instead you decided to wait," Jenn said, "to see if Linda's advice would *force your hand.*"

Danny winced. "Yeah, I heard that when it came out of my mouth, and I knew it was wrong. I'm sorry—"

"Was it?" she said. "Wrong? It seems kind of accurate to me."

"It scares me," he said. "How much I need you."

Need, not want . . .

"You're going to get through this," she told him. "And if you start trying to *think* before you speak, and if you stop yourself before you say something that's completely asshole-ish? You're actually going to have a real relationship with your sister when everything's said and done. Maybe Izzy, too—"

"Yeah, I doubt that."

"Definitely Izzy, too," she said. "For someone so smart, you can be a real dumbass. This thing with Ben is an opportunity. Embrace it."

"I'm trying to," he said. "I'm trying. To. With you."

Jenn nodded, looking out over the parking lot, because looking into his eyes was just too hard. "If you want me to stay through to the hearing, Dan, for God's sake, just ask me to stay."

"I thought that's what I was doing," he said.

"I can't stay forever," she told him, because God, she didn't want him that way. She didn't want to be convenient, or needed during times that were hard. She wanted him to love her—and to not be scared by what he felt—and her temper flared. "I can't. But I'll stay to the hearing, if you just freaking *ask* me."

But she'd injured his pride. "Maybe I don't want you to stay if you're not going to marry me," he said, clearly choosing to embrace his unpleasant inner child.

Jenn just looked at him.

"Yeah, okay," he said. "That's a lie." Now it was his turn to scan the parking lot, and as he did so, he sighed. And he closed his eyes briefly before he turned back to her. "Please, Jenn, will you stay?"

She could see from his eyes that she'd hurt him, but that made two of them, didn't it? She nodded as she took out her cell phone. "I'll call Maria and let her know that I'll be . . . seriously delayed."

"Thank you," he said. "I'll be inside, trying not to be an asshole."

"Danny," she said.

He stopped and turned back. "That came out kind of asshole-ish," he acknowledged, "but I was being serious. I'd like to have a sister again. Zanella, though, I could really do without."

"Maybe he'll grow on you," Jenn suggested. "I kind of like him."

"You like everyone," he pointed out.

"I don't like Greg," she said. "He's a douchebag."

Dan laughed at that. "I bet you hardly ever said douchebag before you met me. I think that might be my word."

She thought about that. "I think you're right," she agreed. "My brothers were fond of dickhead and a-hole. Like taking the double-S out makes it family-friendly. A-hole. It actually sounds worse, doesn't it?"

He laughed— "Yeah"—but then his smile faded and he got serious again. "I love you," he said. "I don't tell you that enough. I should've mentioned it, right before the whole, you know, *marry me.*"

Typical Navy SEAL behavior—refusing to give up, hoping to change her mind. Even though what he'd actually said was *marry me anyway.* Kind of the way his *I love you* actually translated to *I love you enough to try to make this work.*

Jenn held up her phone because Maria's line was ringing. "I gotta . . ." she said, and she turned away to leave a voice mail as Dan finally did give up and head inside.

• • •

"So here's the deal." Officer Kellen sat down on the hard waiting-room seats, across from Izzy and Eden. Danny-Danny-bo-banny was coming in from his private conference with the impossibly patient Jennilyn, and he hustled over to hear what the police officer had to say. "There's no way I'm letting the kid go home with the stepfather."

"Oh, thank God," Eden said in a rush of air as she released the breath that she must've been holding. "Thank you so much."

"But I'm kind of stuck," he said, "because if I send Ben home with you, and this Crossroads place turns out to be considered by law to be a private school, then, yeah, Ben's parents have the right to send him there, and we're all screwed. Including me. Child services can't get involved every time some kid doesn't like the education choices his or her parents make."

"This is different," Eden said.

"Yeah," Kellen said ruefully. "It's a political issue, the gay thing."

"It's a civil rights issue," Dan corrected him.

"That local and state politicians are going to jump all over," Kellen said as he looked from Eden to Izzy to Dan and then up at Jenn, who'd come back inside. "And that church the stepfather belongs to—they can get loud and ugly. You really want Ben in the middle of that?"

"I don't see that we have a choice," Dan said.

"Maybe you do," Kellen said. "Still no luck reaching the boy's mother, right?"

"She hasn't called back," Dan said, checking his phone again.

"So let's buy some time," Kellen said. "The hospital wants to keep Ben overnight, for observation. So let's keep him here tonight."

"His insurance won't cover—" Danny started.

Eden cut him off. "It's a good idea and I have money. I'll pay for it."

He looked at her. "It's hundreds of dollars."

"It gives us time for you to find Ivette," Eden countered.

"Who always does what Greg says," he pointed out, "which brings us right back here, except now we're out hundreds of dollars."

"Overnight means Ben'll be released in the morning," Izzy argued. "Into *our* custody, because I'm willing to bet that Greg won't be getting up before noon."

It was a good point, but Danny wasn't buying it. "You know who wins in this scenario?" He was pissed. "Officer Kellen wins."

"Danny," Eden said as Jenn provided a descant, "That's not true."

But it *was* true, and Kellen knew it and was embarrassed. "I have a two-month-old daughter," he said quietly. "If I lose my job . . ."

"We appreciate all you've done," Jenn said, her hands on Dan's shoulders as she stood behind him.

"I just think you stand a better shot," Kellen said, "keeping this out of the system." He stood up. "I'll go tell the stepfather that Ben's staying overnight." He forced a smile. "Maybe he'll do us all a favor and get violent. If I have to arrest him, that's going to reflect poorly if you do need to get CPS involved."

Eden stood up, too. "Can we see Ben now?"

Kellen nodded. "Go on in."

CHAPTER
FIFTEEN

The mall closed in fifteen minutes.

Eden scanned the empty food court, looking for the girl named Neesha whom she'd met in her own living room.

"She's tiny," she told Izzy now. "Chinese-gymnast tiny, except she's not Chinese, she's . . . I don't know really. Asian, but not completely. Kind of like . . . if animé came to life. Huge brown eyes, straight black hair. When I saw her she was wearing these dorky black pants and a white blouse, like she was playing dress-up secretary."

"Okay," Izzy said evenly, even though she knew what he was thinking. This was supposed to be a pretend errand. They were supposed to be parked along some dark deserted street right this minute, blowing each other's mind.

But back in the hospital, she'd promised Ben she'd look for the girl. He hadn't wanted to stay there overnight because of his concern for his new friend. "I need to warn her about the cops at the mall—if those men even *were* cops," Ben had told Eden.

And although he didn't say it—and she didn't, either—Eden knew her little brother was thinking about Deshawndra, his best friend back in New Orleans. About the way they hadn't stopped and hammered on her grandmother's door after they'd left their home, with Katrina's winds rising. About the way they'd just let Deshawndra stay behind— and die.

In talking—just very briefly, when the nurses had been out of the room—they'd discovered that the police detectives who'd stopped Ben in the mall certainly seemed to be the same two men who'd come to the house and talked to Greg while Eden and Izzy had watched. And combined with the fact that the so-called detectives *hadn't* shown up at the police station after Ben had been Tasered, and that all of the questions about Neesha had vanished once Ben was in the uniformed officers' custody...

It was weird enough for Eden actually to *want* to go out looking for the girl.

Besides, she'd promised Ben.

So here they were. At the mall, minutes before closing.

"Apparently she eats other people's trash," she told Izzy, and he picked up a french fry from a tray that had been abandoned on a table and ate it. "Oh, yuck."

"I've eaten way worse," he said. "Out in the world. Bugs, for example."

"Well, okay," Eden said, laughing—because it was hard not to laugh when Izzy was grinning at her like that. "In the bugs-versus-cold-french-fries contest, the cold fries win. But still, yuck." She headed for the restrooms. "I'm going to check the ladies' room."

"Hey, you want an ice cream?" Izzy called after her, taking out his wallet and ordering himself a cone from the half-asleep girl behind the Häagen-Dazs counter. "Can you make it half raspberry, half vanilla?" He glanced back at Eden. "Sweetheart...?"

"No, I'm good, thanks," Eden called back.

"Huh, that's weird," Izzy said as he frowned and flipped through his wallet, before finally taking out a bill and handing it to the girl in exchange for his cone. As Eden turned the corner, she heard him ask, "Have you happened to see a small Asian girl, around twelve years old? Well, she looks twelve, but she's more like sixteen. She hangs out here and..."

The hallway to the bathroom was brightly lit and tiled and endlessly long, as if the department of health decided this was their best shot at having the people of Las Vegas get some desperately needed exercise. There was a water fountain cut into the wall, but it wore an "Out of Order" sign—no big surprise there. Half of the stores in this mall had gone out of business, their windows boarded up with big "Coming Soon" signs. But that's all they said; COMING SOON, and then a big empty nothing.

The women's-room door had the standard silhouette of a lady in a dress, along with some graffiti. Apparently Naomi was a ho and Hector had a tiny wiener and Eden was willing to bet that neither of those things was quite true.

She was just about to push open the door and look inside, when the men's-room door opened. And who should come out, but one of the two men who'd questioned Greg while Eden and Izzy sat watching from the street.

It was the bald man with the mangina, and from up close, Eden could see that his baldness wasn't completely by choice. He had the equivalent of a five o'clock shadow, but only on part of his head—on the sides and the back. He was older than she'd thought as she'd watched him from the car, with skin like her father's—her real father's—that was toughened from the sun.

He was also with a woman—a girl, really—who wore makeup as if she were trying to win a contest for the largest number of gallons used in one single application. She was putting on lipstick as she followed him out of the men's room, as if she'd just smeared the half tube she'd previously worn all over the skinhead's dick, and yes, the *back off, bitch* hate-filled glare she gave to Eden was definitely reminiscent of high-school-age territorial behavior.

Except the man she was with was so un-high-school, it was almost funny. He was old enough to be the girl's father, and really, it was not fair for Eden to judge her for that. She herself had once been the queen of terrible choices when it came to choosing whose dick to suck—and Danny clearly thought she still was—but Lord, so much of what and whom she'd done had been out of anger and hurt, and from just wanting, desperately, to feel as if she mattered, somehow, to someone.

Except, by doing what she'd done, she'd become exactly what she'd feared she was: a worthless empty shell with a willing mouth and open legs.

But here and now, the man was looking at Eden with eyes that were pale gray and flat—and narrowing slightly because, yes, she was standing there, staring back at him. She'd also exhaled an involuntary little "oh" upon recognizing him, which she quickly covered by pulling out her cell phone—pretending its vibration had startled her—and pushing open the ladies'-room door.

"Naomi, are you in here?" she called as she leaned down and scanned for feet, but the room was definitely empty, "because Mama's calling me again, and..."

She let the door close and opened her phone and put it to her ear.

And if this man was a cop, then the world was also flat, Elvis lived in Ohio, and Eden herself was next in line to be the pope. Whoever he was, though, he seemed satisfied that she wasn't a threat. But as she said, "I'm here, Mama, I'm here," he took the time to give her one last appraising look that succeeded in completely undressing her.

It was a nearly palpable look, meant to intimidate, but she'd learned not to respond. She'd learned that *she* had the power, and she could shut him down and shut him out quickly and effortlessly.

The day she'd been hired at D'Amato's, she'd gotten a crash course in men, from Nicola Chick, aka Chestee von Schnaps of the basketball boobs. Nic had taught Eden to recognize and identify the different types of men who came into the club to watch the women strip. They all wanted eye contact with the strippers, but some men would pay more for a *fuck you* look in response, instead of a *come hither* smile. But certain men—such as this one—seethed with such danger and misogynistic hatred that Eden—on Nic's sage advice—would have done neither.

If this man had looked at her like that in the club? Eden would have gone blank. Zero expression, nobody home—so that any rudeness and impropriety would bounce off, avoiding any potential escalation. She'd mark him, though—be aware of where he was sitting, and be alert as to if and when he moved. And she'd avoid eye contact after that, and would be sure to point him out—discreetly—to the bouncers as well as the other women, after she left the stage. And she'd take a taxi home after her shift.

Yes, Nic had been full of good advice, all of which Eden had heeded.

She'd also told Eden to save the acting for the stage. Men could be total boneheads (Nic had used a different, more colorful word), so it was best for a beautiful woman to wear a safely neutral expression when the room wasn't filled with bouncers to protect her.

Right here and now, though, she wasn't Eden the stripper and she wasn't Eden the civilian, either. She was Naomi's beleaguered sister, who was browbeaten by their mother. She most certainly hadn't attended Nic's impromptu stripper school, so Eden let herself cower and turn away from the skinhead—but not so far that she couldn't monitor him in her peripheral vision.

Her reaction again apparently satisfied him, because he followed BJ-Girl down the hall to the food court—to where Izzy was no doubt asking everyone he saw if they'd seen Neesha. Who Ben had been convinced was in some kind of danger, which was why Eden and Izzy had come to the mall.

Was it a coincidence that this man was here? Was he looking for Neesha, too, as Ben believed? Eden didn't want to take that gamble. Plus, Izzy had said earlier that the man was armed. And she saw it now—a bulge under his left arm, beneath a jacket that he definitely didn't need in this heat, except to conceal the fact that he was carrying a weapon.

Besides, she'd hung around with plenty of losers who pretended to be tough guys, and some of them actually were. And she knew enough to be willing to put big money—in fact *all* of her savings—on her gut, which told her that this man was beyond dangerous.

"She's not in there, Mama." Eden continued her charade, pretending to talk on her phone as she began walking swiftly, following the two of them. "I will. I will. I *will*." She exhaled hard. "I *am* running, Mama.

I'll be *right* there." She snapped her phone shut and with a murmured, "Excuse me, I'm *so* sorry," she pushed her way past the skinhead and the girl.

And sure enough Izzy was talking to the men who worked the stir-fry counter. He was laughing at something one of them said as he kept scanning the food court, eating his ice-cream cone.

Eden's heart actually leaped when she saw him. He was so big and strong and true, and when he saw her coming toward him, his sudden smile of pleasure made him look impossibly handsome, and that, combined with the simmering heat in his eyes...

She knew in that instant, as if she'd been struck by a bolt of lightning, that this situation with Ben was one of the best things that ever happened to her, because it had brought this man roaring back into her life. And she knew that even though Izzy was here, he didn't trust her completely—why would he? And she *also* knew he was trying to make their time together be all about the sex—why wouldn't he? She couldn't blame him for that. Besides, she was glad for it, because she knew it made him want to stay. And if she could just keep doing that— make him want to stay...

Maybe he'd never leave.

But there was no time to jump into his arms and kiss him senseless. Skinhead wasn't far behind her, and whether he was a police detective or not, he was dangerous. And the last thing she wanted was an altercation with a dangerous man in a nearly empty mall, or even worse, a deserted parking lot. So she ran toward Izzy, widening her eyes at him, hoping he'd understand and play along. "Come on, Billy Bob, we gotta run. Mama's got her panties in a twist!"

He laughed his delight as she grabbed his hand and pulled him toward the entrance where they'd parked. He was clearly happy to be part of whatever game she was playing, even when his ice cream fell off his cone and hit the floor with a splat.

"Hang on there, Irma Lou, I gotta clean up this mess," he said as he refused to be pulled farther, as he dutifully stopped to clean up the spill.

"Izzy, come on, just leave it, we've got to hurry," Eden whispered as she looked back toward the food court to see the skinhead talking to the Häagen-Dazs counter girl, who turned. And pointed.

Directly at Eden and Izzy. As if she were saying, *Yes, that's the man who was asking me questions about the same little Asian girl that you've been looking for...*

Skinhead turned, too, which was when Izzy spotted him, as he tossed the wad of ice-cream-covered napkins, cone and all, into a nearby trash container. "Whoa, isn't that...?"

"Yes," Eden said, as Skinhead shouted, *Hey!* "Run!"

Someone was in the apartment.

Dan caught Jenn's arm and hauled her back behind him as he put his finger to his lips.

"Light's on," he told her soundlessly, and her eyes widened. They'd left the place dark after throwing on their clothes and hurrying back to the hospital after Eden's latest distress call, but now there was a faint glow coming from the bedroom window.

Damn, he was tired, he was sore, and he didn't want to do this right now. But what he wanted even less was for Jenn to look at him the way she was currently looking at him, like he was some kind of invalid.

"It's probably nothing," he breathed as he pushed her even farther back from the door. "The landlord or the super or whoever the hell runs this place probably dropped off a package. Or maybe came in to fix that freaking annoying dripping faucet in the kitchen sink."

He'd been planning to do that himself, first thing in the morning, because holy Christ.

Jenn wasn't convinced as she dug through her handbag, frowning slightly. "Still, you always tell me that the right thing to do is to call the police." She pulled out her cell phone, flipping it open.

Danny stopped her before she dialed 9-1-1, because he seriously doubted that whoever they were going to encounter on the other side of that door was engaged in any felonious activities. What were the odds of Eden actually having anything that anyone would want to steal?

"Seriously," he said, "if I really thought someone dangerous was in there? I'd make you go downstairs."

"Make?" Jenn repeated, eyebrows rising.

"*Ask* you to go downstairs," he amended to appease her, even though his *asking* wouldn't have borne any kind of question mark. It would have been delivered as a command.

He could tell from the look Jenn gave him that she knew that, too.

Still. Potential landlord visit aside, it was probably one of Eden's ex-boyfriends who'd turned on that light. Or maybe it was a current boyfriend who was going to be disappointed when Dan showed him firmly to the door and took away his booty-call key. And in the cosmic scheme of things, it was probably better that this happened now, while Zanella wasn't here to make it uglier than it had to be.

And come to think of it? It was significantly better that it happened now, instead of whoever-he-was creeping in, in the middle of the night, and crawling into bed with Dan and Jenn. No doubt about it, if *that* had happened, someone would have gotten hurt, and it wouldn't have been Dan or Jenn.

Even with his injury, Dan would have kicked some serious ass.

"Just be ready in case I'm wrong," he told Jenn now.

She was not happy about that. But she knew him well enough to not tell him—unnecessarily—to be careful. He damn well knew his limitations, although they would go completely out the window should he in fact be wrong and the threat be real.

It was one thing to have to go back to the hospital to get his leg repaired for breaking the rules about strenuous sex, but another entirely to do it after taking out an attacker who'd put his woman at risk.

Still, Jenn was watching him carefully—and he didn't want her to accuse him of being reckless, so he stepped to the side of the door, and pushed it open with one hand, with a bang, then dipped his head into the doorway, lower than where a head should be, for a quick look-see.

There was no immediate threat—no gunmen standing in a horseshoe, waiting to cut him into pieces with their room brooms. In fact, there was nothing that he could see that looked out of the ordinary besides those lights being on, so he gave Jenni one last *stay back* look and moved inside, keeping close to the wall.

And there was their intruder—a girl—kneeling on the mattress that Jenn and Zanella had put out on the living-room floor, as if she'd fallen asleep waiting for them to come home. The expression on her face was one of sheer terror, and Dan immediately held his hands palms out and down in a nonthreatening position. "Jenni, I could use you in here..."

Jenn entered the open doorway far less theatrically, but her very female presence didn't reduce the panic in the girl's eyes by as much as Dan had hoped it would.

"Whoa," Jenn said. "Little girl. Very little girl. Hello. Are you...You must be Ben's friend." She glanced at Dan. "We should call Izzy and Eden, let them know we found her." She smiled at the girl. "Ben was really worried about you."

The girl looked toward the door that Dan was still holding open with his foot, and said through frozen lips, "Is Ben...?"

"He's not here, but he's okay," Jenn said in that easy way she had of making everyone immediately comfortable. It didn't work on this kid, though. The girl was now looking at the door as if considering making a run for it. "He's spending the night in the hospital. He got a little sick."

"His diabetes?" the girl asked, her anxiety level getting even higher, which Dan would not have believed possible if he hadn't seen it with his own eyes.

"Yeah, but he's really all right," Jenn said. "He's really only staying over at the hospital because there was a problem with his stepfather. I'm Jenn, by the way, and this is Danny, Ben's brother."

The girl's eyes flickered over to him only briefly as Jenn continued, "We're staying here, with Eden and Ben for a while. He didn't say much about you—only that he was worried and he wanted Eden to try to find you. Are you a friend of his from school?"

She took her time answering, as if she had to think about it. But she finally shook her head, no. She offered no other information.

Which didn't daunt Jenn. "I'm sorry, Ben told me, but it's been one of those nights, and . . . What's your name?" she asked.

But the girl stood up. "I should go." She picked up a plastic shopping bag.

And because she looked as if she were going to simply dash out the door that Dan was still holding open, he shifted slightly, so that he was directly in front of it.

She stopped short and looked at him as if he were the horrible villain in some melodrama, about to tie her to the railroad tracks while he twirled his mustache. He knew he was tired and he tended to look like shit when he was tired, but come on.

"Are you sure you don't want to stick around?" Jenn asked. She had her phone out and was dialing it—no doubt calling Eden. "I'm not sure exactly what Ben wanted to tell you, but it was important to him— important enough for Eden to go out looking for you."

"I have to go." The girl shook her head, absolute in her desire to leave.

"I went right to voice mail," Jenn told Danny. "Do you have Izzy's number?"

He dug for his cell phone, even as he told the girl, "I need the key. That Ben gave you? With so many of us living here—for a while, anyway—it's better not to have people who aren't, um, family, coming in and out." He smiled to soften his words, but she didn't look reassured.

But she had the key in her pocket and she found it and held it out for him, even as he dialed Izzy's number. "Ben didn't give it to me," she admitted. "I saw where he hid it and . . . I'm sorry, I shouldn't have come in."

"How about you knock next time or leave a note on the door," Dan said as he took the key from her. His fingers touched hers and she actually flinched, pulling swiftly back as if she'd been burned. "Whoa. Thanks. Um. Ben *should* be here tomorrow. And I know he'd love to see you. So come back then, okay?"

Izzy didn't pick up, either. *Yo, his* recorded voice said in Dan's ear, *I'm busy. Leave a message. I'll call you back.*

Busy. Right. No doubt he was *busy*—with Dan's sister in some dark parking lot.

"Thank you," the girl said, and Dan was about to step aside to let her go when Jenn spoke up.

"Honey, wait, I think you dropped this," she said, holding out a twenty-dollar bill that she'd picked up off the bed.

The girl burst into tears, and Dan looked over at Jenn, who was definitely as surprised as he was.

"No," the girl sobbed. "I didn't drop it, I left it there. Because I took it. I stole it. From Eden's... visitor. I shouldn't have and I'm sorry."

"Eden's *visitor?*" Jenn didn't understand, either.

"Her client," the girl said fiercely, scrubbing at her face to try to stop her tears. "And I ate her food and used her soap, too, but I can pay her back. I *will* pay her back. There's work down on Paradise Road. I just needed to borrow some of her shiny clothes. She has so much, I didn't think she'd mind. I just wanted to look like the others, because I *won't* dress up like a schoolgirl because I *don't* want to have sex with the freaks!"

"Okay," Dan said. "Whoa. *What?*" He looked at Jenn again, but her jaw had dropped, too.

"Just tell her I'll pay her back," the girl insisted, "and that I'm sorry."

She moved toward the door, even though Dan was still solidly blocking her exit as Jenn again said, "Wait."

But she didn't wait.

She came right up to Dan, and the look in her eyes and on her face was something he'd never seen before and hoped he'd never see again. It was such an awful mix of little-girl sorrow and soulless calculation and bitter, angry defeat. She looked him up and down in such a disconcerting way, like a piece of meat.

"If you want me to stay, you have to pay," she said as she reached out and grabbed hold of Dan, right through his pants.

"Holy shit!" He was so surprised and horrified that as he jerked himself out of her reach he also moved away from the open door. And she immediately and swiftly slipped out of the apartment, closing that door behind her.

By the time he scrambled back, opened the damn thing, and looked out into the courtyard, she was long gone. And there was no way that he was going to chase *that* girl anywhere where there weren't several dozen third-party witnesses.

"Did you see what she just did?" he asked Jennilyn, his voice going up a full octave in his disbelief. "She grabbed my junk. Shit, what is she? Eleven years old? I think I need to *shower*. Jesus, could there be any bigger soft-on in the history of the world? I may never get it up again."

Jenn shot him a look as she went into the bedroom, no doubt to see if anything was missing from their bags. "I think, in time, you'll manage," she said.

"Okay," he said, following her. "Yeah, but only after I scour myself with bleach."

"That *was* pretty awful," she agreed as she ... pulled open the drawers of the dresser? "But kids can be ... When I was that age? I was pretty strange."

"Yank-a-stranger's-crank strange?" Dan asked. "I don't think so. Jenni, that girl was serious. She wasn't joking. That look she gave me ... You didn't see it, but holy Christ. That is one *very* fucked-up kid."

"Hmm," Jenn said, because the bottom two drawers contained sequined bathing-suit tops and, Jesus Christ, what looked like G-strings in a rainbow of colors. "Eden does have a lot of ... rather shiny clothes, doesn't she?" She looked up at him, her eyes concerned behind her glasses. "Where does your sister work, Danny? She said she has some money, and that this place is paid for until the end of the summer, but ... How exactly did she manage that?"

*   *   *

Izzy clicked the rental car unlocked as he and Eden ran toward it, across the otherwise empty mall parking lot. He was on E&E autopilot—escape and evade—and he ran right up and over the hood to get to the driver's side, as Eden scrambled in through the passenger door.

"Go, go!" she said as he flung himself in, even as he put the key in the ignition. The bald cop was still in hot pursuit and gaining fast.

The car started with a roar and Izzy jammed it into reverse out of force of habit—the rental had Arizona plates, which were only on the back instead of back and front and were therefore out of their pursuer's line of sight. The entire lot around them was clear, so he just slammed his foot on the gas and went sailing backward at an accelerating speed, the car transmission whining.

When he was far enough away for their pursuer not to see the plate and thus be able to identify them, he hit the brakes hard and put the car into drive.

It was only then that his brain clicked into manual, and he said, "Why are we running from this guy? Why don't we talk to him? Maybe he can give us some answers."

"There's something off about him," Eden told him. "Something...bad. Izzy, go! Just trust me, please, *drive!*"

So he went, peeling out of that lot like his ass was on fire as Eden breathed, "Thank you."

Izzy glanced in the rearview, at the shadowy figure of the man who'd finally stopped running, back there in the empty lot. And it was only because he looked right at that moment that he saw it—a muzzle flash.

"Holy shit," he said, "he's shooting at us."

"What?" Eden turned to look instead of ducking for cover, so he reached over and pulled her head down, practically onto his lap as he gunned it. "Oh, my God!"

He heard a thud as a bullet hit the back of the car, which was a double what-the-fuck. What kind of weapon was the cop carrying, anyway? A standard service revolver wouldn't have that kind of range.

There was another muzzle flash and another and the mirror shattered on his side of the car, and Eden clutched at him, her voice tight with fear. "You have to put your head down, too! Izzy! Get down! Get *down!*"

"I'm kinda driving here," he said even as he tried to slouch lower to appease her without putting them in jeopardy from a traffic accident. "It's okay, sweetheart, we're okay, we're out of range now. We gotta be." He hoped.

Eden loosened her choke hold on him and started to sit up, but he held her firmly in place. "But let's not tempt fate," he said as he pulled onto the loop road around the mall, tires squealing as he made the turn without slowing down.

They probably *were* good now, because even though the weapon the cop was using had a bigger-than-normal range, it probably didn't have smart bullets that could track a vehicle around a curve or find them while they were behind a line of scrub brush.

And okay, revision time. Dude was probably *not* a cop if he was unloading his weapon, willy-nilly, in a public parking lot, without calling out a warning.

Izzy followed the signs to the exit, still traveling at high speeds—for all he knew their trigger-happy friend's buddy was in his SUV, ready to give chase. As he left the mall, he spotted a ramp heading onto the highway and he took it, hauling ass and merging into the still-heavy traffic that was heading away from town. The key was blending in— with all of the other cars that had recently had their left-side mirror shot to shit.

Okay, that was something he was going to have to fix, as soon as possible. A gaping hole in the place of a driver's-side mirror was far more common than a mangled mirror with a bullet hole. The good news was that it would be easy enough for him to make that change— from mangled to missing—as soon as they stopped.

But it wasn't until after he'd put a few miles onto the car's odometer that he started to breathe easier. He realized then that Eden was a little too quiet—and that she was shaking. And yeah, she wasn't the only one. That entire incident had freaked him out. Big-time. It was one thing to get fired on when he was with his very capable and highly trained SEAL team. But it felt very, *very* different when he was unarmed and alone with Eden.

Who could have been killed.

"You okay?" he asked her as he took an exit off the highway. "Because I am *jangling* from that adrenaline rush." There was a traffic light that was red and a few cars waiting for it to change at the end of the ramp, and he purposely stayed back quite a bit from the last car in the line. He wanted the extra space to maneuver, should he need to. "You can sit up now, if you want."

She did just that as she swept her hair back from a face that was much too pale, and she looked at him with eyes that were brimming with unshed tears. "Are *you* okay?" she asked.

And she didn't wait for him to answer, she just launched herself at him and kissed the holy bejesus out of him.

Which was not unpleasant. Not even close. And Izzy knew without a doubt that all he had to do was find a deserted little street or the dark corner of a grocery-store parking lot, and she was going to rock his world. Which was exactly what he needed right about now—a little *thank God we're alive* sex to calm his ass down.

Still, he had to keep one eye on the rearview, just to verify that they still weren't being followed as the light turned from red to a brilliant and glorious green. And then, hallelujah, they were moving again, and driving while he was being kissed was harder than it looked in the movies, but compared to having Eden get shot at, it was a walk in the park.

All of the cars took a left at the end of the ramp, so Izzy defied convention and went right. And...would you look at that. They were in corporate headquarters land.

They were completely surrounded by office buildings with impeccably landscaped grounds and acres of neatly paved parking lots—

nearly all of them empty and dark at this time of night. It was, without a doubt, a sign from God—a giant thumbs-up from the Big Guy—to have some happy-fun.

Izzy killed the headlights before he pulled into the least well-lit lot that he could find. He made his way to the darkest corner, where he jammed the car into park and gave his full attention to kissing the holy bejesus out of Eden, too.

She wasn't shy about what she wanted. She didn't try to be coy or cute. She just put her seat back as far as it could go and then lifted herself up so he could clamber over the parking brake and assume the position to deliver. She was a multitasker, so she helped him unfasten his shorts at the same time, which freed him up to find one of the condoms he'd pocketed before leaving her apartment early this morning.

She must've ditched her panties somewhere along the way, and dear sweet Jesus, he now loved her sundress even more than he did before, because all she had to do was straddle him and...

"Oh, yeah," he said on an exhale as she took him, hard and deep, as she moaned his name, which was, as it always was, a total turn-on. Except yes, that *was* still the condom that was clenched in his hand instead of covering his penis, where it was far more useful in terms of its efficacy.

But Eden wasn't thinking about anything but right now as she moved atop him. She was caught up in the moment, and Izzy knew he had to be the one to call the time-out, except damn, it felt undeniably fantastic to be alive. And without the rubber between them, he was feeling alive to the mega-nth, and it probably felt the same way to her—but shit, that was selfish-asshole thinking. *Let's take a risk and not use a condom because it'll feel so much better for you, sweetheart...*

He couldn't get her pregnant. Except he *could*, quite easily—just by doing what they were doing. Even if he gritted his teeth and kept himself from coming while she climaxed, it could happen. Sperm escaped. Pretty damn regularly. So he gritted his teeth for an entirely different reason and lifted her off of him, saying, "Hang on, sweetheart, let me, I gotta..."

"Oh, shoot..."

Reality penetrated her desire-filled fog as he quickly covered himself, even as he tried to make a joke, "No actually, shoot is what I *shouldn't* do until this thing is on."

But Eden either didn't hear him or didn't find him funny because she said, "I didn't...I wasn't trying..." She was afraid he thought that she'd jumped him, condom-free, on purpose.

"Shh," he said. "It's okay."

But she was still distressed, so he kissed her, which always seemed to bring it down to the bottom line for her. He also used the opportunity to slide the barely-there straps of her dress down her arms, which caused the triangles of fabric that covered her breasts to fall a tantalizing bit. And when she took it further and pushed the straps completely off her arms, it had the effect of a cloth cover being pulled from a masterpiece. Ta-da.

And Izzy knew he must've made some kind of noise of appreciation at the marvelousness of the beautiful, deliciously full breasts that were directly in his face, because she laughed softly, and then moaned as he kissed and licked and tasted and touched.

And she shifted then, reaching between them, and just like that, he was back inside of her, but not with the near-frantic, mindless urgency with which they'd started, but with something even better. Full awareness of what they were doing. Together. To each other.

Which wasn't to say he didn't miss the mind-blowing sensation of going without a rubber. Because he did. How could he not?

Eden was thinking along the same lines, because she spoke, her voice breathless in the stillness. "If I went on the pill, we wouldn't have to use condoms."

He lifted his head from his worship of her breasts just long enough to say, "True."

But if she went on the pill, it would take a month to get up to speed, so did that mean she was intending to stick around for at least that long? God, he hoped so.

"I'd like that," she breathed. "Oh, Lord, that feels so good..."

"This?" he asked as he used his lips and tongue to suckle her, gently at first and then harder.

Her moan may have been a yes, and it was emphasized by her pushing him more deeply inside of her, and jay-sus, he felt his eyes damn near roll back in his head, too, as she gasped, "Oh God, it's *too* good, but I still want more..."

And he knew what she meant, because he did, too. And that *more* was damn near impossible to deliver, here in the confines of this little car. For what he wanted, he needed a bed. And a lot of mirrors. And maybe a sex chair that hung from the ceiling by ropes. And then about fifty years of privacy to give Eden all the *more* she wanted, whenever she wanted it.

She was on the same page. "I want to do this on a bed," she told him. "I want to do what we did last night, all night long. I don't care if Danny and Jenn are in the bedroom. We can be quiet. You can be quiet, right? Because I can be quiet. I can..."

She kind of blew the point she was making by coming with a not at all quiet "Oh, Lord! Oh, yes! *Yessss*..."

Izzy couldn't help but laugh, and it was one of those extremely in-the-moment moments where he, with full cognizance, made note of the fact that yes indeedy, he *was* giving Eden an Orgasm with a capital O, and that she was clutching his T-shirt with both hands as he got to look up at her beautiful face and her gorgeous, tightly peaked breasts, as she continued to stroke his pole with her most intimate parts not merely because doing so made her feel so good, but because she wanted to send him into orbit, too.

And it seemed impossible that he could enjoy this more than he already was, but since he was *right* there, eyes open both figuratively and literally, he saw her open her eyes, too, and he saw her smile at the fact that he was laughing. She looked into his eyes and whispered his name like he meant something special to her. And he knew that, at least for the next few heartbeats...?

He absolutely did.

• • •

When Neesha saw how it worked, she faltered.

Girls would linger on the street, and men would pull up in their cars. The girls would get in. The cars would drive away.

On the bright side, being in a car limited the amount of violence that any potential client could deliver to her. It also limited the type of sex she could deliver in return, unless, of course, the client drove the car to a deserted part of town.

And wasn't *that* a terrifying thought.

Although the thought of merely getting into a car with someone was a terrifying one, too. It gave the client the ultimate power, since they could use that car to take her not merely to a deserted part of town, but also back to Mr. Nelson or Todd.

So Neesha hung back, ducking into a hamburger joint to use the bathroom and check to make sure the scanty, sequined top she'd taken from Eden's drawer covered her, heart pounding, already ashamed of herself for choosing to do that which she'd vowed she'd never again do.

But her choices were limited, and she'd latched onto the idea that she'd be safe—safer—in Los Angeles, with a burning determination to get there.

Or die trying.

"Customers only," the man behind the counter said sharply, and sure enough, when Neesha looked up, she saw he was talking to her as he handed a bag of food to a tired-looking blonde in high heels and a very short skirt.

She didn't know what he meant.

"The bathroom," he said, with plenty of attitude, "is for customers only. You want to use it, you buy a burger or fries. Otherwise, get your whore-ass outta here."

Neesha turned to leave, but the blond woman spoke. "She's with me," she said in a raspy heavy-smoker's voice that had the same kind of drawl that Neesha had heard when she'd watched *Dallas*. "Give me another cheeseburger, Richard, and supersize the fries. Honey, come on over here. You're new in town, aren't you? You working with anyone yet?"

Neesha nodded yes, then shook her head no.

"Looks like my latest girl blew me off," the woman said. "Probably too stoned to lift her head offa the bathroom floor. But I got a gig lined up. A private party not far from here, and I sure could use some help. I'll give you...Hmm. Twenty-five for the night, plus a five-dollar bonus for each gentleman you take into the back room."

"You taken up highway robbery now, too, Clarice?" the counter man said.

"Hush, you." The woman didn't even look back at him as she held out the bag with the food to Neesha. "I'll have you back here in two hours, hon, tops. With cash in your pocket."

Neesha looked from her to the counter man, who was shaking his head.

"What's a private party?" she asked Clarice, who smiled.

"Why don't you come on over here," the woman said, clicking over to a table in those heels, "and sit down. Have a bite to eat and I'll tell you exactly where we're going and how it all shakes down."

CHAPTER
SIXTEEN

Izzy came, hard and fast.

Without making a sound.

Which was a whole lot more difficult than he'd thought, but *definitely* doable.

Eden kissed him then, still laughing, because—as she nearly always was—she was on his wavelength, and she knew exactly what he was thinking. Yes, they would definitely be doing this again, later.

Her kiss was impossibly sweet and almost unbearably tender—the kind of kiss two soulmates share at the end of a movie about them finding each other again after ten years apart. It was the kind of kiss that would happen right before the credits rolled and the happy-ever-after was solidly in hand.

And as Eden pulled back to look at him in the dim light from the rental car's dashboard, he saw tears in her beautiful eyes and he found himself—rather suddenly, as if he'd fallen out of his bunk onto the hard, cold, metal deck in the middle of a deep REM sleep—pulled out of what should have been the afterglow of a truly magnificent moment.

His body was still humming from his recent release. She was still warm and soft around him, and her breasts were still tantalizingly bare.

She was so fucking beautiful. But Cynthia was beautiful, and Maria was beautiful, and Tracy had been beautiful, and Renee had been, too. Izzy had bumped into beautiful often enough in his life to know that mere beauty wasn't enough. It was the brain clicking away in Eden's gorgeous head that had brought him running back for more.

And when Danny's credo popped into his mind—*Is the fucking you're getting worth the fucking you're getting?*—Izzy's current answer was an immediate *Hoo-yah, yeah.*

But that didn't make it hurt any less when she whispered, "You know, I never stopped loving you."

And he knew how to play the game. He knew that was his cue to embrace the lie and to kiss her back with that same Hollywood tenderness while he murmured, "Ah, baby, you know, I still really love you, too."

But he was tired of it—of her revisionist history. And even though he knew that in this moment she believed it was true, it goddamn wasn't. If she'd really never stopped loving him—if she'd ever really loved him in the first place—she would've let that love give her strength and comfort when Pinkie died instead of running her ass away and hiding from him all those goddamned months.

So he hesitated and some of what he was thinking must've flickered in his eyes, because she got very still and asked, "Do you believe me?"

Of course I do. Izzy knew he should say it. It was his ticket to getting his rocks off again later tonight—which he already wanted to do, pretty freaking desperately.

But he was also filled with an overwhelming urge to be honest and just say no.

And in the end, he didn't have to say anything, because she said it for him, as she pulled herself off of him, as there was nothing for him to do but lift himself over the parking brake and back into the driver's seat.

"Of course you don't believe me," she said quietly as she pulled up the front of her dress and got her straps back into place. "I don't blame you, I really don't. And it's okay. It is. I always do this—too much, too soon. It's just... what I do. I get scared and..."

She shook her head and didn't finish her sentence, and yet it was the most honest thing she'd said. She got scared. No shit, Sherlock. And when she was scared, she tried—any way that she could—to make her future less of an unknown and as secure as possible. And if she had to do that by making herself indispensible via copious amounts of sex...?

So be it.

"I'm going to be honest with you here," Izzy said, just as quietly as he set to work cleaning himself up. The condom went in a plastic grocery bag because tossing it onto the pavement of the parking lot wasn't merely nasty for poor Ferd Quertmansonton, who was going to be late for work tomorrow morning, and therefore he'd get stuck parking here in the distant reaches of the lot. Which meant he would be even later because he'd have to make the hike to the office building through the blistering heat, so he'd hurry and wouldn't look where he was stepping as he got out of his car, which meant he'd skid on the used condom, which wouldn't just gross him out, but would give him an excuse for his tardiness as he'd stop to make a call to security, who clearly wasn't patrolling the lot as often as they should at night, the negligent bastards. And *that*—the potentially stepped-up security—would be *très* nasty for Izzy, who had already marked this location as a place to return for some desperately needed privacy, should the five-people-living-in-a-tiny-one-bedroom-apartment thing become temporarily permanent. Of course, *that* was also dependent upon *Eden* still wanting to continue getting jiggy after they had this conversation, in which he *was* going to be honest.

"But I want to start out with us both in the same place, okay?" Izzy continued. "So you have to be honest, too. Here it comes, ready?"

Eden wasn't looking at him, and it was possible that she shook her head no.

He said it anyway. "The sex? Me and you? Is freaking unbelievable. I mean, I'm talking fan-fucking-tastic."

She smiled at that, but she still didn't look at him. She was giving her full attention to turning her panties—white, but not at all virginal—right side out.

"Do you agree?" he pushed her, as he tucked himself in and zipped his shorts back up. "A simple yes or no will suffice."

"Yes," Eden conceded.

"Good," Izzy said. "It's now an established fact that we both think the sex is great. Let's put another indisputable fact into our little world. Because I think we can probably also agree that you didn't marry me because you loved me."

"What if I did?" she said suddenly, turning to face him. "You don't know what I was feeling."

Eden could be pretty freaking convincing when she wanted to, but...

"Ah, come on," Izzy said. "You still barely know me. I'm just some teammate of your brother's that you collided with once, when you were having a really shitty night."

And then, six months later, she'd made the mistake of implying that the not-*entirely*-shitty night she'd spent at Izzy's place had resulted in her being six months pregnant. And instead of denying that it was impossible, that the baby couldn't be his because they hadn't had the kind of sex where essential baby-making body parts had connected, Izzy had gone with Dan, to see Eden, who was back with her mother and stepfather in Vegas. And he'd been so charmed by and enamored with her all over again that he'd offered to marry her—to give her health care for her pregnancy and delivery, *and* to give her someplace to live besides that crappy house with her fucking lunatic stepfather— the same fucking lunatic stepfather who was now breaking their balls about Ben.

It *hadn't* been about sex—Izzy and Eden's legal arrangement—or so he'd claimed. But they both knew that it *had* been about sex at least on *some* level, because Izzy'd been as hot for her then as he was now. Except back then, he'd kept his distance as much as he could, because he'd been stupid enough to believe that he was courting her. He'd stupidly believed that if he took his time and tamed her, like some wild animal, she would come to trust him, and maybe even love him, too.

"After that, we had what, one date?" Izzy reminded her now. "And then yeah, okay, I helped save your life, except I didn't get there soon enough, did I? I didn't get there in enough time to save Pinkie."

And there it was, lying right there in the car between them. The real reason Eden had left. Even though the doctors had all agreed that her baby wouldn't have survived to full term, regardless of whether she'd been kidnapped and manhandled by crazy people.

She hadn't believed them.

Except now she was not only shaking her head, she was reaching for his hands. "Izzy, please, you can't believe that—it's *not* true. There was nothing you could have done." Her voice shook and her eyes filled with tears. "There was nothing anyone could have done. Pinkie was already dead. Believe me, as soon as I was out of the hospital, I tried to find out what caused it, was it something that I did or didn't do, something I ate? God, I was sure it was, but I did all this research and . . . No. It wasn't your fault, and it wasn't my fault. It *wasn't*. It's a miracle, you know, the way that an egg and sperm can grow into a perfect human being, and it makes sense that it doesn't always happen right, not a hundred percent of the time. Some babies don't get made properly— there are all these scientific words for what happens to them, but the bottom line is that they can't live on their own, and they die. Most of them die in the first three months of a pregnancy, but some of them are stronger than they maybe should be, so they live a little bit longer with something really wrong with them, the way Pinkie did."

Eden believed what she was saying—and not just for right now, either. Her conviction rang in her every word. And Izzy was glad for that—that she didn't blame herself for something she couldn't have prevented.

"But if you didn't blame me," he said, and goddamnit, he had to wipe his eyes because he, too, had tears in them, and his voice shook, too, because talking and thinking about Pinkie always broke his heart, "why did you leave?"

He'd shipped out, overseas on assignment with Team Sixteen, on the same day Eden had been released from the hospital. He'd come back several weeks later to find her gone, his apartment cold and empty.

"Because you didn't believe me," she said, her voice very small in the darkness. "I knew you thought I lied about who Pinkie's father was."

And Izzy couldn't deny that.

She'd told him it was Richie, her ex-boyfriend Jerry's low-life, drug-running boss, who'd gotten her pregnant—and not with her permission, either. She'd pissed Richie off when she'd tried to convince Jerry to get a real job, because working for Richie was likely to get him arrested. Richie'd warned Eden to back off, but when she persisted, he'd sent Jerry out of town, then wormed his way into her apartment, gave her roofies, and videoed himself having sex with her. Which, when Jerry saw that video, transformed him from boyfriend to ex.

Ironically, the asshole had stayed tight with Richie, who claimed he'd made the recording only to show his buddy Jerry proof that Eden was regularly stepping out on him.

Izzy'd seen the video, and it was pretty damn obvious that Eden had been under the influence of some kind of chemical substance at the time it had been recorded.

"I was upset," he said. "And I was *wrong*. As soon as I was thinking clearly? I knew what must've happened. Richie wasn't alone with you when he made that tape. He couldn't have been."

And it was obvious—after Izzy'd had some time to think about it—that at least one other person had been there, with Richie, working the camera. And whoever that person was? *He* was Pinkie's biological father.

Because Richie had been African-American, and Pinkie's father had been white.

Which meant that Eden hadn't merely been raped that night. She'd been the victim of a gang bang.

"Goddamnit," Izzy said now. "Thinking about it makes me sick."

"I don't remember any of it," she reminded him quietly.

Which was one of the reasons she'd been so open to the idea of bringing Pinkie into the world, and having him be part of her life. His had been a seemingly immaculate conception.

"You know that Jerry's in jail," Eden said now.

"I hadn't heard that," he said.

"And Richie was killed, along with most of his crew," she said. "Some kind of meth lab explosion. At least that's the story I heard."

Izzy looked back at her steadily because there was an unasked question in her eyes. "I didn't have anything to do with it. You asked me to stay away from him."

Eden nodded. "The sex video's also off the Internet," she said.

"*That* I did," he admitted. "With the help of a friend who's a lawyer."

"Maria?" she asked, with the most amazing amount of casualness.

Izzy had to laugh at that. "No," he said. "I would *never* have asked her to . . . See, Jenn's boss is also a New York State assemblywoman. I think she wants to be the president someday, and she wouldn't have wanted to get anywhere near a video like that. No, I, um, got some help from a guy named Martell Griffin, who works for Troubleshooters Incorporated. You don't know him, he's from their Florida office."

She nodded. "Thank you for doing that. And . . . Please thank Martell when you get the chance."

Izzy nodded, too, and they sat for a moment in silence. And then he figured what the hell, so he kept going, said more. "You know, sometimes when you say . . . the things you say? Like before? That you never stopped loving me? It makes me feel like crap, like you're trying to, I don't know, play me or"—she looked up and over at him at that, her eyes practically flashing in the darkness—"or maybe just manipulate me into . . . doing I don't know what, because I already told you I'd stay. And can I give you a hot tip, sweetheart?" He didn't wait for her to respond, he just said it. "All you have to do is look me in the eye and say, *Izzy, I'm glad that you're sticking around. I appreciate that very much.* And if there's something else that you need from me? Something I'm not giving you? Damn it, just freaking ask already. Don't make me have to guess. And don't..." *Take money from my wallet without asking.* He didn't finish the sentence because bringing that up right now would be dangerous.

"Don't what?" Eden asked, but he just shook his head.

If he said, *Hey, about that twenty-dollar bill you took from my wallet at some point last night...?*

And she said, *What twenty-dollar bill?*

And he said, *The one that was in my wallet after I went to the ATM and then bought that box of condoms, but* wasn't *in my wallet when I bought that ice cream at the mall, even though I had my wallet with me at all times, except when I was sleeping last night, when you and I were alone in your apartment...?*

And if she said, *I didn't take your money,* then he'd have to say, *There you go, fucking lying to me again* or *I must be mistaken,* even though he absolutely, positively knew that he wasn't.

He also absolutely, positively had no idea *why* she should have taken a twenty from him when she was carrying around that freaking huge-large roll of tips from work, but he'd lived long enough to know that some people got off on stealing other people's shit. And just as she didn't really know him all that well, he really didn't know Eden, either.

The solution wasn't to get in her face about it, but instead to be more careful about safeguarding his cash. And he should probably include his heart along with his wallet, because as often as she said things like *I never stopped loving you,* he had to stay focused and remember that he *hadn't* tamed her. And he never would. She was wild and, like the lyrics to that old Joni Mitchell song, *wild things run fast.*

Eden was going to leave again.

It didn't matter what she said. He had to keep believing that her leaving was a given—another simple fact like the sex was great, and she hadn't married him because she loved him—or his flipping heart was going to get trashed.

"Don't what?" she asked again. "Because if there's something you need from me, then you have to say it, too. Don't make *me* guess, either."

"I don't want you to lie to me," he said, going for a cryptic explanation. "I'd rather we just not talk about certain things."

"Kind of the way *you* don't want to talk about Maria?" she asked. "So you don't have to lie to me?"

Izzy looked at her. "Are you actually jealous?"

She was. He could see it in her eyes, hear it in the way she said Maria's name. She didn't answer for a long time, and to her credit, when she finally did respond, she didn't lie. She simply said, "I shouldn't be."

"Damn straight," he said, because he, too, was unwilling to reveal the truth—that there was nothing for Eden to be jealous about, that he'd gone without sex for all those months, that he'd passed up some extremely golden opportunities to get laid, including with Maria, because he, in fact, *had* never stopped loving Eden. And yeah, he'd sooner cut his own heart from his chest and throw it on the floor for her to step on than tell her that. Let her think he and Maria Bonavita had screwed each other neon blue for all those days he'd been in New York City. Maybe it would make Eden stay with him a little bit longer.

"I'm not trying to play you," she said quietly. "And I'm *very* glad that you said that you'd stay to help with Ben. I do appreciate that. Very much. I just... The sex is really great, I agree, and... I appreciate that, too."

And okay. He was sitting here, getting thanked for having sex with the most desirable woman he'd ever known. And yeah, somehow during this little conversation, they'd switched from using her label— making love—to his. Having sex.

And that was probably better, too.

"I think," Eden continued, "that I have this, I don't know, estrogen-based thing inside of my head that creates... confusion. When I... have sex, like we have? Really *great* sex?"

And okay again, he really loved that she was saying that, with a huge emphasis on the *great*. His bullshit meter was silent, which meant either she was being honest, *or* that he was willing to be manipulated as long as she waxed poetic about how awesome it was when he banged her.

But she wasn't done. She said, "I feel these, I don't know, really huge, overwhelming feelings and . . . It feels a lot like love, but maybe it's just . . . Maybe what I really should have said before was . . . that I never stopped *wanting* you."

Oh, ding.

And maybe, in the cosmic scheme of things, that should have been just as difficult to believe as *I never stopped loving you*. But Izzy was happy to take this particular ride through MakeBelieveLand aboard the Eden-Wants-Him bus. And who knows? Maybe she *was* telling the truth.

Whatever the case, he could respond to her statement by being completely honest in return. So he did. "Same here," he said. "And I'll raise you one. I don't think I'll ever stop wanting you."

She smiled at that, but it was a touch sadly. "That *I* don't believe."

"It's a fact," Izzy told her, "that I'm happy to have to keep proving to you."

Now her smile was more genuine. "Well, good," she said, but then her expression went back to serious as she added, "You know, I also left, the way I did after Pinkie died? Because I couldn't breathe. Everything just hurt too much. I had to go somewhere, where you weren't, and I'm so sorry if I hurt you, but I just . . . I don't know. I guess I had to learn to just . . . *be*."

He had nothing to say in response to that.

"You don't have to believe me," she whispered. "But I hope that you do."

"I believe you," Izzy conceded. "I know how hard it was for me, to lose Pinkie and . . . Still, I'm not going to say it's okay, because it's not. You *did* hurt me. Pretty fucking badly. But I do accept your apology."

"I'm glad," she said quietly.

And when she looked at him like that, with the sorrow and regret in her eyes mixed together with something that looked a whole lot like hope, he had to look away. Because if he gazed back at her, it was too easy to pretend that this could be something that it wasn't.

She *was* going to leave him. She *was*. It was just a matter of when.

But right now she was here, although it was definitely time to head all the way back to the real world, where Dan and Jenn were waiting for them, back in Eden's crowded apartment.

Izzy powered down the window, reached out, and pulled what remained of the dangling mirror off the car. There were sharp pieces of glass still attached, so instead of tossing it into the backseat, he popped the trunk and got out of the car and stashed it back there.

As he climbed back in, Eden was now looking at him as if he were crazy, so he explained. "The broken mirror makes us easier to spot," he said as he put the window back up. "Having it be missing altogether, well, we're a little less easy to identify this way."

"Do you think that...whoever he was, he's still looking for us?" she asked.

"I think?" he said as he put the car into gear and headed out of the lot. "That first thing in the morning—I'm talking 0600—we need to head on back to the hospital to give your little brother a double dose of our very best what-the-fuck faces."

"There's definitely something," Eden agreed, "that Ben didn't tell me. Something that this girl told him."

"We'll get him to talk," Izzy promised her, turning his headlights on as he pulled out onto the road. "But first, we'll bring him home."

"Greg's gonna—"

"Greg's not going to be at the hospital," he reassured her. "Not that early in the morning."

"He might be," she worried. "For some reason this is important to him. And if Danny doesn't reach Ivette..."

"Greg's not going to be there," Izzy said. "I know this because I sent him a little present earlier this evening. A little let's-be-friends gift from his relatively new stepson-in-law, with an implied apology for twisting his wrist."

Eden was incredulous. "You want to be *friends* with *Greg?*"

"Hell, no," he told her. "I just wanted him to get shitfaced drunk tonight so that he'd be guaranteed absent in the morning, when Ben is released. My present was a case of liquor from Ye Olde Wine Shoppe, where their motto is No *party too large or small—we deliver to your door.*"

Eden was laughing, but at the same time she ferociously wiped her eyes with the heels of her hands. "That's unbelievably brilliant," she said, her husky voice even thicker with emotion. "Thank *God* you're here."

Neesha puked.

Behind the huge garbage bin, out behind the steakhouse where the private party had been held.

A private party with an even more private back room.

Neesha and the blond-haired woman named Clarice had been kept busy for the full two hours.

Most of the men in the party had just wanted her to dance for them or sit on their laps while they touched her or slipped dollar bills into her sequined bra and panties. But she'd gone into the back room five separate and thankfully very short times.

All of the men paid Clarice upfront, and Neesha'd performed their requests in a daze as she realized how wealthy she would have been had she not been working all those years as a slave.

And even though most of the money the men had paid went to Clarice as her "commission for finding the gig," Neesha now had five ten-dollar bills in her pocket. Fifty dollars. It was more money than she'd ever had in her entire life.

And with one more night like this one, she'd have the cash she needed to pay back Ben's sister for the food and the clothes, and to pay for that ticket for the bus to L.A.

One more night, and she'd never have to do this, not ever again.

"You okay, there, hon?" Clarice said as she lit a cigarette and exhaled a long, large cloud of smoke.

Neesha nodded as she wiped her mouth.

"I gotta go. The babysitter's gonna start calling me. I don't want to piss her off." Clarice took one last drag on her cigarette, then tossed it onto the pitted pavement, grinding it out with her pointy-toed high heel. "You need a ride back...?"

Neesha shook her head. No.

"We good for tomorrow?" Clarice asked.

Neesha nodded again.

"I'll meet you at the same place," she said. "At the Micky D's." She smiled but it didn't soften the hardness of her once-pretty face. "Those good old boys sure do like you Asian gals. You are going to make us both rich." She paused. "You got a place to stay tonight, hon?"

Neesha nodded again because she didn't trust Clarice entirely, and didn't want to get into her car with her again. It had been hard enough, driving over here with her, earlier.

"Six o'clock, then," Clarice said as she clicked and clopped her way over to her car and beeped open the lock. "I know it's early, and I used to think it was better to start later, to let those boys get good and drunk, but this is Las Vegas. They're drinking hard at noon. Wait too long, and the older gents can't get it up."

"I'll need more," Neesha said, and Clarice turned to look at her in surprise. "Tomorrow night. I want half."

"Well, aren't you the greedy little bitch," the older woman said, her musical laughter softening the harshness of her words. "I'll give you forty."

Neesha didn't understand that. Clarice has already given her more than forty dollars, that couldn't be what she meant. She shook her head and kept it simple. "Half of what they pay you."

"Hmm, I don't know, hon..."

Neesha turned to leave, even though her heart was pounding. Finding Clarice had been a lucky break. Not having to get into the client's car and risk being recognized by someone who would drive her back to Todd or Mr. Nelson...? It was worth a lot to Neesha. Still...

She didn't take more than a few steps before Clarice said, "Well, all right. I guess giving you half is fair enough. But I will expect you to chip in now and then to help pay for gas."

But there wasn't going to be a *then*. There would only be tomorrow night.

"Do we have a deal?" Clarice asked.

Neesha nodded.

"See you tomorrow at six," Clarice said, and got into her car.

She started it with a roar and pulled out of the lot, leaving Neesha alone in the shadows.

One more night of hell, and she'd finally be free.

Jenn woke up to the sound of raised voices from the living room.

"What the hell is *this*?"

"Oh, my God, did you actually go through my *things*?"

Danny and Eden.

"Is this really how you get your money?" Dan asked his sister as Jenn scrambled to get out there. "By wearing this shit and *selling* yourself?"

The lights were blazing and Eden and Izzy were still in the little entryway, as if they'd just come back home from searching for Ben's friend.

Even though the mall had to have closed several hours ago.

Dan was standing there, too, just inside the living room, at the edge of the air mattress Jenn had helped Izzy set up, back when they'd thought they'd be bringing Ben home with them tonight. Dan had taken some of the be-sequined costumes—if they could even be called costumes, they were so insubstantial—from the drawer in the bedroom. They lay glittering, on the floor, where he must've thrown them at Eden's feet.

Oh, Danny. "I thought we decided we'd do this in the morning," Jenn said, "when everyone wasn't so tired...?"

But Dan didn't even look at her—his full attention and his outrage were focused on his sister.

"I'm willing to do whatever I have to do," Eden shot back at him as she bent down and picked up her things, her movements jerky with her anger. "To help Ben."

"Oh, you do this for *Ben*," Dan said. "I'm sure he'd be *so* proud."

"It's not like it's illegal," Eden pointed out, which was something Jenn and Dan had talked about extensively before they'd decided to go to bed and leave this discussion for the less murky light of day. Or rather, *she'd* decided that. And apparently she hadn't noticed when Danny hadn't agreed.

Earlier, Jenn had surfed the web, using the wireless from a nearby coffee shop to research Nevada's laws that legalized prostitution. It was pretty mind-blowing.

She wasn't sure whether it was a good or bad thing—the fact that the sex trade in this state was regulated, and that there were rules that, at least on the surface, seemed to protect the women who rented out their bodies.

It also seemed pretty obvious to her that prostitution was going to exist, regardless of whether or not it was technically legal. The sale of sex flourished all around the world, even in countries where it was punishable by death—to the woman, that is. Men tended to get off with a much lighter penalty.

But in a society like the one here in Nevada, where prostitution was acknowledged and regulated—at least in some of the state's counties—there were assurances that the women who did the work, who were normally exploited, would actually be paid a living wage.

Maybe.

Danny had seen the entire subject in a more definite black-and-white. He believed—absolutely—that it was wrong to pay or be paid for sex.

But the bottom line was that, in parts of Nevada, it *wasn't* illegal for a woman to sell her body. Just as Eden had pointed out.

"But it *should* be," Dan said now.

Izzy, meanwhile, was shaking his head as he stooped to help Eden. "It *is* pretty uncool, bro, to go through her things like that. Considering you're a guest here...?"

"Why don't you just stay the fuck out of this, *bro*?"

Izzy straightened up to his full height and got in Dan's face. "Why don't you just dial it down, *asshole*? It's just *not* that big of a deal."

"It's a *huge* deal!" Dan was incredulous, and on that point, Jenn had to agree. "I can't believe you actually *knew* about this, Zanella. And you didn't fricking *tell* me? What the hell is wrong with you?"

He shoved Izzy, who bumped into Eden, nearly knocking her over. "Hey!"

"Danny," Jenn said, stepping forward.

He didn't look at her, he just looked—briefly—toward her. "This doesn't concern you, either," he said tightly—ouch—before turning back to Izzy, who'd moved right back to where he was before Dan had shoved him.

"It's none of *your* business," Izzy told Dan, with an edge to his voice that Jenn had never heard before. Not to that degree. And it scared her. Both of these men were trained to kill with their hands, and she did *not* want this fight to become physical. "What your sister does, the choices that she makes. It has *nothing* to do with you. It never has."

"Except she's my sister," Dan shot back. "And she's doing... what she's doing, and everyone knows that she's Eden fucking Gillman."

"I use a stage name," Eden said defensively, but then glanced over at Jenn and gave her the strangest, almost apologetic look. "Sort of."

Stage name was a weird thing to call it. Jenn would have expected her to use the word *alias*. Except maybe Eden saw the whole thing as a performance, which it was, Jenn supposed, on a very basic, very disturbing level.

"I can't believe you're okay with this," Dan lit into Izzy again. "Jesus, I expected you to have a meltdown when you found out. But no, you're such a *twisted* son of a bitch, you probably *like* that she's getting paid for—"

"I realize that this doesn't *concern me*," Jenn said loudly over him, "but I honestly believe this entire conversation will be *far* more productive if we have it in the morning."

Izzy's voice got even harder as he got into Dan's face. "What I like or don't like doesn't play into it, because I don't own your sister."

"Obviously not." Dan turned back to Eden. "What the hell are you going to say if we have to have an interview with Child Services? They're going to ask you where you work. Do you just think they're going to be like, *Great, let's just put the kid in the custody of the whore.*"

"Don't call her that," Izzy warned.

"I have a second job," Eden said. "At a coffee shop."

"Am I even here?" Jenn asked. "Or am I invisible?"

"Of course you do," Dan told his sister, speaking over Jenn. "Because there are two things that you've always been good at. Lying and being a whore." He looked at Izzy. "Hard not to call her that, when that's what she is. Starting back when you were, what? Fourteen. With John fucking Franklin. Giving it up for a beer, in the back of his car."

And, oh, dear God, he couldn't have issued a more formal and direct invitation to be punched if he'd handed Izzy an engraved card saying *Daniel Gillman the third requests the honor of your fist in his face.*

The only thing that stopped Izzy was the fact that Jenn moved quickly and stepped in front of Dan. Apparently, she wasn't invisible after all. At least not to Izzy, whose face now matched the scary edge to his voice. She wasn't so sure that Dan could see her, though.

He was already egging Izzy on. "You want a piece of me, douchebag," Dan said. "I'm *right* here. Come and get me."

"Don't do this," Jenn said. "Please. Both of you just step back and take a deep breath."

"Jenni, stay *out* of this," Dan ordered her.

Eden, meanwhile, had recoiled as surely as if Dan had slapped her. But she immediately fought back. "So nice of you to just take John's word for what happened—without even *asking* me! Of course, right, I was thirsty, and I figured why not trade my virginity for a beer. That's exactly what *every* teenage girl dreams about!"

"I didn't need to ask," Dan shot back. "It was Sandy, all over again!" Sandy, their older sister, had become addicted to both alcohol and drugs at an insanely early age.

"No," Eden shouted back, "it wasn't! Because I'm *not* Sandy!"

"Yeah," Dan said, his voice breaking with his frustration and anger, "you're *worse*!"

Both Jenn and Izzy moved at that exact moment, both of them speaking simultaneously—Jenn saying, "Danny, stop it!" while Izzy went with, "Gillman, just shut the fuck up!"

And it was then that it happened. And it happened so quickly, but despite that, Jenn knew *exactly* what went down. It was an accident. Completely. It was as much her fault as his. She turned toward Danny, whipping her head around to add, "*right* now," just as he reached to physically pick her up and move her out from between himself and Izzy. He was going for her shoulders with both of his hands, but because she turned the way she did, his left hand connected, hard, with her face.

It sounded as if he'd slapped her, and God, the force of the contact actually made her ears ring and her teeth rattle, and shoot, she must've cut the inside of her lip because now she even tasted blood.

She staggered and stepped to steady herself, but the edge of the air mattress was right there against her ankle, and she tripped and went down. The mattress broke her fall, but they'd filled it a little too full, so she bounced and rolled off the other side onto the carpeted floor with a very loud thump.

Dan scrambled to help her, and she should have paid more attention to the look of absolute horror that was on his face, but her temper flared, because *this* was what happened when people had discussions about volatile topics when they were overtired, and he *had* agreed to wait until the morning but apparently he'd lied just to get her to shut up about it already, so she smacked at his hands as she pushed herself out of his reach saying, "Get away from me! Don't touch me! You've done enough, Dan, just...*don't*!"

Izzy and Eden were frozen there, shocked, but it was Eden who moved first, roughly pushing her brother out of the way as she came to help Jenn sit up.

Dan didn't resist, he just let himself get shoved off the mattress and onto the floor with an equally loud thud.

Eden had tears in those eyes that were the same rich shade of brown as Danny's, and as she looked at Jenn's face, she caught her lower lip between her teeth. "Izzy, we could use some ice. There are dish towels in the drawer, second one down, left of the fridge..."

But Dan pushed himself to his feet. "I'll get it," he said in a voice that was so tight that Jenn barely recognized it. He swiftly went into the kitchen.

With him gone, Eden didn't waste any time. "Has this happened before?" she asked Jenn almost silently, her words nearly hidden by the crunching sound of Dan grabbing some ice from the freezer.

"God, no," Jenn said. Did she *honestly* think...? "Eden, really, it wasn't...I got in his way."

"Yeah, like *that's* a new one." Eden didn't look convinced as Dan came back in with ice wrapped in a white-and-blue dish towel. He looked as if he were either going to cry or be sick. Or maybe both, simultaneously.

"It was an accident," Jenn told her, told Dan, too, even as he spoke over her. "Jenni, I'm *so* sorry. I'm—"

"It all just comes sailing back around, doesn't it?" Eden interrupted him as she took the ice from him and showed Jenn where to hold it against her cheekbone. "You try to break the cycle, but it's harder than it looks, because we learn these terrible things when we're children, and then, somehow, here we are, and it's okay to hit your girlfriend as long as you cry convincingly enough when you say you're sorry afterward."

"Oh, my God," Dan said. "Jesus, no, that's not what happened. Jenni, Christ, I didn't—"

"I don't think you're allowed to talk right now," Eden cut him off.

"It *was* an accident," Jenn said again, but Dan had already turned away, his hand over his eyes, because he actually had started to cry.

"It starts that way," Eden told her grimly. "Daddy would cry and apologize, and maybe it *was* an accident at first. Maybe it started because he wasn't careful. He moved too fast. He got too angry. His hand slipped. At first."

"Yeah, well, this is *not* going to happen again." Dan was adamant.

"He'd say that, too," Eden said.

"How could you possibly remember that?" Dan asked. "You were a baby when he left."

"Sandy told me," she informed him. "Back when she was still talking to me. And I *do* remember some of it. All these mysterious uncles who'd come over to pick Ivette up to go out for dinner while Daddy was overseas? It's amazing that Ben's the only one of us who doesn't share the same father. And Daddy would come back and he'd find out, because she really didn't give a shit, because it all started because *he* didn't keep *his* pants zipped. He slept with her best friend. *He* told me that. While I was living with him, in Germany, last year. It was right after they got married, when Ivette was pregnant with Sandy. And she was too young and stupid to know that was it. Game over. He wasn't going to change. He wanted to own her without giving up his own freedom. And she said she still loved him, so she stayed, but I really just think she didn't have anywhere else to go. And even if she *did* love him? She also hated him, so hello Uncle Mike and Uncle Steve and Uncle George. And then Daddy'd come home and get drunk and call her names. Bitch and slut and whore. And *that's* like hitting, too, you know, Dan." Her voice shook. "That's abuse. And you didn't break *that* cycle, at least not with me, so if I were you, I'd be thinking long and hard about the fact that it's highly probable that you didn't break the other one, either."

Jenn couldn't stay silent any longer. "I disagree. What happened here *was* an accident"—she pushed herself up so that she was standing—"that absolutely came about because Dan was being an idiot. But he's not a girlfriend-beating idiot. I know him." She dropped the towel with the ice and put her arms around Dan, but it was like holding a statue or hugging a tree. He didn't respond at all, as if he were afraid to touch her in return.

"Danny, I know you," she told him. "I know you would never intentionally hit me. And you know this, too. You're *not* your father. You'll *never* be your father..."

He broke away from her, bolting for the bathroom.

And when Jenn started after him, Izzy, who'd been uncharacteristically silent all this time, stopped her. "Let me," he said.

"It was an accident," Jenn said again.

Izzy looked from her to Eden and back as he nodded. "I know that," he said. "But I think he's going to have a little trouble believing it from you."

CHAPTER
SEVENTEEN

J enni, God, I'm so sorry," Danny said as Izzy closed the bathroom
door behind him.

The other SEAL was on his knees, eyes tightly closed, bowing
to the porcelain god, having just sacrificed his dinner into its murky
shallows. Izzy helped them both out by reaching forward and flushing
the monster.

"She knows that," Izzy told this man who, despite trying as hard as
he had, had never managed to become his friend.

Dan didn't open his eyes. "Leave me the fuck alone."

"Yeah, well, small apartment, single bathroom," Izzy pointed out.
"I kind of need to go. Don't move—I'll just piss past your head."

Danny did more than open his eyes at that—he actually hit the
pause button on his current state of sheer misery as he turned to look
at Izzy in disgust and disbelief.

Izzy smiled back at him as he hoisted himself up to sit on the
counter of the sink. There wasn't much counter, so he was half in, half
out of the sink itself. Still it was the proper visual aid to reassure Dan
that he was only kidding about that piss-past-your-head thing.

"I'm on Team Jenn for this one," Izzy told Dan. "You're not your
father, Gillman. Never have been, never will be."

Dan didn't want to hear that—and he tried to slip back into his post-vomit, beat-himself-up state. "Seriously, Zanella, I don't need your bullshit right now."

So Izzy reached over with his foot and gave the man a not very gentle push, making him lose his balance and bump his shoulder into the wall near the toilet-paper holder.

"Hey!"

"Fuck you for the way you treat your sister," Izzy told him. "You're an asshole and a total dick, and if you weren't so pathetic with your *I'm so tired* and your *I'm so jet-lagged* and your *Poor me, I almost lost my leg and now I have an ouchy boo-boo*, and *Don't let me tear open the stitches because I still might bleed out and die*, I'd kick your ass down to the street and pound you black and blue."

And okay. Maybe that was too much, because now Dan was getting angry back at him and was about to issue a challenge for Izzy to just fucking try it.

So Izzy pushed himself off the sink and did exactly what he'd threatened. He unfastened his pants and took a leak right there in the empty bowl.

And instead of standing up, Dan pushed himself even farther back into the corner, against the wall, to stay out of the splash zone. "Jesus!"

"There are times," Izzy said, raising his voice a little to be heard over the pleasantly tinkling waterfall, "when I fucking hate the things you say and do. But I *do* know that you would rather die than hurt Jennilyn. I know how much you love her—hell, I probably know that better than she does. And I also know, as flipping crazy as you drive me most of the time? You would never intentionally hit your woman. What happened was an accident. And I believe what you said—that it will *never* happen again." He shook himself off, zipped up, flushed the toilet, and went to the sink to wash his hands. "In fact, I'd bet my life on it."

Dan was silent, just sitting there, staring down at the floor as Izzy dried his hands on one of Eden's mismatched towels. Given her tendency to be thrifty, she'd probably picked them up at some second-

hand store. If she was still around by Hanukkah or Christmas or whatever she celebrated—Festivus?—he was going to buy her a really nice,
really thick and fluffy matching set. And sheets that were criminally
soft, and shit, maybe a whole new apartment's worth of furniture.

"You're an asshole, Gillman," Izzy repeated now, "but you're an intelligent asshole, and deep down you're a good guy with a heart of fucking gold. So if you're really worried about it—maybe about what Eden
said about the name-calling, which is definitely uncool, bro—then you
should go in. You know, for counseling. It can't hurt. That Al-Anon
stuff, too, you know, for adult children of alcoholics? It's a good idea. I
read a lot about it back when..."

Back when Eden had first left, and Izzy had been certain it would
only be a matter of time before she'd return. He'd wanted to be ready
to help her, however he could.

"I read about it," Izzy finished.

But Danny knew exactly what he hadn't said. "You're the one who
needs counseling. What you're doing? With Eden? It's fucked up."

Izzy nodded. "Yeah, I know."

"I couldn't do it," Dan said, shaking his head. "Even just the
thought of Jenn with other men...I mean, I don't own her, either,
but...I just don't know how that could be even remotely okay."

"Well, she's not *with* them," Izzy pointed out. "I have to admit that
the look-but-don't-touch rule plays heavily into it. You know, the
making-it-bearable."

And now Dan was looking at him as if he'd just spoken in Man-
darin Chinese. "Look but don't..." he repeated.

It was as if a cartoon lightbulb was switched on glaringly bright
over Izzy's head, at the exact same moment that a second one lit up
over Dan's noggin.

"Holy shit, bro," Izzy said, "did you actually think—"

"Jesus," Dan spoke at the same time, "I thought Eden was, you
know, hooking, but—"

"Your sister's an exotic dancer," Izzy told him, getting the facts out
there as quickly and efficiently as he could. "A stripper. On a stage. In

a club called D'Amato's. No one touches her. The bouncers are solid, the rules are absolute. I've been there. There's no back room, although the parking lot is sketchy. But inside? What you see is absolutely all that you get."

"Jesus," Dan said again. "I thought..."

Danny actually thought his sister was a prostitute—and holy crap, no wonder he'd been so amazed at the idea that Izzy was down with that.

For two men who were both smart enough to become Navy SEALs, they were pretty freaking stupid to have failed to notice that, for the entire past discussion, they'd been talking about two different things.

Like Izzy, Dan was now sitting there, rerunning everything that had been said since Eden and Izzy had come through the apartment door.

Danny had called his sister a whore because he'd actually thought she was. A whore. Professionally. Because it was legal to turn tricks in parts of Nevada. And in other parts, like Las Vegas's Clark County? The cops tended to look the other way.

Not that any of that made it okay. At least not for Eden, and Jesus, not for Izzy, either.

Out in the living room, Eden and Jenn had no doubt had a similar revelation, because there came a quiet knock on the bathroom door, then Jenn's voice: "Dan? Danny? I'm sorry to bother you, but we were wrong. Eden's a *stripper*. But even that's kind of secondary to the fact that while she and Izzy were at the mall asking about Neesha, someone shot at them. With a gun."

Izzy reached over and opened the door as Danny looked up at him, in disbelief. "Jesus Christ, Zanella," he said, "what the *hell*...?"

"Neesha," Eden called quietly as Izzy followed her through the door that accessed the stairs leading down to the basement, where the building's laundry room was located, along with about a dozen storage spaces with garagelike metal doors that slid up and down and were secured with padlocks.

She didn't like coming down here in the daytime—at night it was even spookier. But having Izzy with her was a real game changer.

"It's me, Eden," she called. "Ben's sister?"

But there was no answer, no sound of movement, and when she looked inside, the laundry room was empty.

Eden watched as Izzy went down the row of storage spaces, checking that each lock was secure—in between glances back at her. No doubt to make sure she wasn't about to crumble.

It had been a day and evening filled with more than its share of unpleasant and frustrating surprises, that was for sure.

"I can't believe Neesha was here," Eden said, now, because she just knew Izzy was about to start talking about Danny's incredible disrespect, and she didn't want to go there. Not now.

"Yeah," Izzy agreed as he came back down the hall toward her. "It's a pretty cruel irony."

Apparently, while she and Izzy and Danny and Jenn were at the hospital, Neesha had used the key Ben kept hidden outside of the apartment to come in, take a shower, eat a meal, and commit petty larceny by stealing several items from Eden's stripper clothes drawers.

Not that Eden wouldn't have lent her what she needed, should Neesha have just asked. After all, she had an excess.

On her second day of work, she'd inherited an entire costume trunk from a woman who was exactly her size, who was leaving D'Amato's to have a baby. She wasn't planning on coming back and had given it to Eden in a pay-it-forward way. So Eden had ended up with far more stripper clothes than she'd ever need—two dresser drawers full—which Neesha had apparently found while snooping through Eden's things last time she was here with Ben.

"While you were in the bathroom with Danny," Eden told Izzy now, "Jenn said that Neesha came over to snag one of my stripper outfits. She said that's at least partly why she and Danny thought what they thought, because Neesha said something to them about borrowing some clothes that didn't make her look like a little girl, because she didn't want to have to have sex with the freaks."

"Really?" Izzy asked.

Eden nodded as they went back up the stairs. "Why do guys find that hot?" she asked. "The little-girl thing?"

"I don't know," he said, "because I don't."

She glanced back at him. "So, like, if I dressed up in, you know, a Catholic schoolgirl uniform, you wouldn't like that?"

"Hmm," he said. "That's kind of a touchy question, considering a lot of people think you're kind of permanently wearing a schoolgirl uniform, because you're too young for me. People including your brother."

"He's an idiot."

"He certainly is opinionated," Izzy said evenly. "And some of his opinions *are* idiotic. But the math is the math. I'm eleven years older than you."

"Ten and a half," she countered. "And it's not a problem for me. Your being so elderly."

He smiled at that, as she'd hoped he would. "Good to know. And as long as we're being honest here, your being nubile has never been a problem for me. And if you really got into the whole wearing-a-school-uniform thing, I'd muscle through. Although I'd prefer you waiting to don it until you're fifty and I'm sixty-one."

"So you *do* think it's hot."

Izzy laughed. "Sweetheart, if you wore a giant Hefty trash bag and asked me to wear bubble wrap around my head while we got it on, I'd find *that* molten-lava hot. You want to role-play and pretend we're historical figures—I'll be George, you be Martha? I'm there. I'm still reeling from the missed opportunity at the mall. I was totally ready to be Billy Bob to your Irma Lou."

"I think Billy Bob was Irma Lou's brother," she told him, dancing out of his grasp.

"Oh, that's so wrong," he said, stopping there on the stairs.

"Yeah," Eden said, turning to look down at him. She rarely saw him from this vantage point, and it was nice. He was extremely attractive from every angle, and the amusement in his eyes made her smile back at him, even though the information she was about to give him was nothing to smile about. "About as wrong as Neesha, who looks like she's around twelve telling Danny that she'd stay only if he paid—and then giving him a crotch grab."

"Whoa, did Jenn tell you that?" Izzy'd started up the stairs, toward her, but that stopped him short again. He laughed his disbelief as she nodded. "It's been one hell of a night for Danbo, too, huh? Did his head explode?"

"Probably." Eden smiled again despite her deep and growing concern for the girl. "Am I a bad person if I admit that I really wish I'd been there to see that?"

"It's okay," he said. "I'm a bad person, too."

"Jenn said it really freaked him out."

"Yeah, I bet." He laughed again.

Getting grabbed like that had been Dan's big surprise of the night—that and accidentally clobbering Jenn.

Of course, *that* had been Jenn's big surprise. Getting knocked on her butt by her supposedly perfect boyfriend.

While Eden had been horrified, she hadn't exactly been surprised when it had happened. And yes, Izzy'd since convinced her that Dan wasn't the domestic violence train wreck Eden had instantly imagined, just waiting to explode off the tracks. Still, she knew for a fact that her brother had to learn to slow down and be more careful. Because even though accidentally decking your girlfriend wasn't even half as awful as intentionally punching her in the face, it was still a *very* bad thing. And although Dan wasn't quite as tall and as broad as Izzy, he was still a big and very solid man.

Eden knew, because she'd gotten in Dan's way and been knocked over by him a time or two in the past few years. Never intentionally— that was true. But that didn't make it hurt any less.

As far as the evening's other surprises went, Greg showing up at the hospital fell under the category of bad, while Dan's continuing inability to reach Ivette was no surprise at all.

Getting shot at while at the mall—a big surprise for everyone, including Dan and Jenn when they'd found out.

After the complete story had been told, Eden had overheard Izzy and Dan talking about being better prepared—as in making sure the next time someone fired on them, if there was a next time, their only option wasn't to duck and cover. She hadn't pushed it, but she knew that they were cooking up a plan to get armed.

And then, of course, there was Eden's surprise at finding out that her brother and his new girlfriend believed she earned her living on her back. It had been devastating, realizing just how little Danny thought of her.

Of course, he'd made it clear, after emerging from his bathroom conference with Izzy, that he didn't think very highly of her choice to become a stripper, either. Yeah, she wasn't selling her body for cash, but to him, it was damn close. Eden may not have been a whore, but in his eyes—it was so obvious—she was a whore-lite.

But it was possible that that was how he'd see her, even if she'd announced she was ridding herself of her worldly possessions, entering a nunnery, and devoting her life to try to out-Mother-Teresa Mother Teresa.

"You okay?" Izzy asked her now as they emerged into the courtyard. Eden was looking around to see if Neesha was there, and she realized she'd gotten too quiet.

She glanced over to find Izzy watching her with that look in his eyes that made her believe he already knew what she was thinking. Still, she nodded. Chin up. "Yeah."

"Rough day," he said, unwilling to just let it all go.

Eden nodded. "But Ben's safe at the hospital," she said. And that was the most important thing. "Right?"

Izzy smiled his reassurance. "He's very safe," he said. "The nursing staff's on high alert. Even if our skinhead shooter finds out Ben's there,

he's not going to get anywhere near him. Not in the pediatrics ward."
He paused. "But if you want, after we finish searching for Neesha, I
could go back over there. You know. Just sit with him."

"You'd do that?" she asked, even though he was standing right
there, completely bullcrap free and totally sincere in his offer.

He smiled and tried to shrug it off. "It's not a big deal."

But her heart was in her throat, and all of the stress and emotion of
the past few days was pressing against her eyes, making them flood with
tears that she had to work furiously to blink away, because Izzy was
with her. She wasn't in this alone—for at least as long as she could
keep his interest up.

He'd told her, back in the car, that he'd keep on wanting her, forever. But she'd learned the hard way that forever was a myth.

"Is it okay if I come, too?" she asked him, in a voice that didn't
quite sound like her own.

Izzy continued to look at her with those eyes that could see
through her. "You really going to let your brother chase you out of your
own home?"

"It's not my home," she said. "It's just a ... temporary place to ...
sleep."

Eden had to turn away, because the way he seemed to be able to
see inside of her head was just too disturbing. What if he realized she'd
meant what she said in the car, that she really never had stopped loving him?

But he didn't want to hear that, didn't want to know. He didn't
want anything from her besides really great sex.

Which was more than she'd hoped for, but at times like this, when
she was tired and feeling emotionally battered? It seemed heartbreak-
ingly inadequate.

The courtyard was empty—Neesha wasn't waiting for them there.
No one was out there—at this time of night, the building's residents
didn't linger. Besides, it was still unnaturally hot. In the desert it was supposed to cool off at night, but tonight the air felt like an eye-melting blast
from an oven, which was particularly disconcerting in the darkness.

Still, Eden started to make a quick circuit of the place, heading out toward the street so they could walk completely around the building. The streets were mostly empty, too. The few cars that went past moved purposefully down the road—people heading home after a night of work.

"You know, he doesn't know you," Izzy said after they'd walked for a bit in silence. "Danny. So you shouldn't let his disapproval—"

"You don't know me, either," Eden cut him off. He'd said those very words to her just a short hour ago, back in the rental car, in that parking lot. "Can we just move on to a different topic? I mean, if you want, I can tell you how this one ends. You say, *yeah, well, I know you better than Dan does*, and I remind you that *you* thought I might've been hooking, too. And then we fall into an awkward silence, because you can't deny it, so then we both feel like crap. Or at least I do."

"When did you last have one?" he asked, apparently choosing to forgo the awkward silence and feelings of crap and move back to their previous conversation. "A home that wasn't just a place to sleep?"

Eden had to think about it, because the first thing that popped into her head was a crystal-clear memory of cleaning his apartment, in San Diego, right before she'd left. The space was all Izzy's and yet... She'd never felt out of place there. In an odd way, she'd belonged. But, again, she knew he didn't want to hear that. He'd think she was manipulating or playing him or just flat-out lying. So she tried to remember and came up with...

"New Orleans," she said. "It was... rocky at times, but Dan was already in the Navy. We moved into a new house—new for us, I mean—and it was small but nice. There was a garden and... Ivette was with Charlie—he was this great big black man with this big laugh and I think she actually might've really loved him.

"Sandy was just out of rehab, and when she first married Ron—she met him at AA—things were pretty good. Ron owned the store—sporting goods—and we all worked there. Even Ben and me, after school and on weekends. It was the closest thing to normal we ever had."

They'd almost felt like a family.

But Ron was an addict, too, and he'd relapsed first, then Sandy, not long after the store suffered smoke damage, after another shop in the same building had a fire. Ron's insurance wouldn't cover the ruined merchandise, and things quickly went to hell in a handbasket. Sandy and Ron lost their house in the resulting fallout, and moved in with them, kids and all, as they both struggled to reclaim their sobriety and get their business back on its feet.

Then Charlie had had a heart attack and died, out on the driveway. It was right around that same time that Eden had been so sorely deceived by John Franklin, with whom she'd lost her virginity. Danny had come home for the funeral and had heard John's bragging about what had gone down in the back of his car—and ever since then her brother had treated Eden like she was some foul-smelling dog crap that had attached itself to the bottom of his shoe.

And yet all of that had been child's play compared to Katrina.

Izzy was thinking the same thing. "Then Katrina happened," he said, "and the shit hit the fan."

Another topic she didn't want to discuss.

Except Izzy couched it in terms of Ben. "I didn't mean to eavesdrop," he said, "but I heard you talking to Ben and . . . I just, um . . . I get it, you know? Why we're still out here looking for Neesha."

"He still feels awful about not saving Deshawndra," Eden told him, because she could talk about that part of it. "I do, too. She was this funny little black girl whose family had lived in Orleans Parish forever, and she and Ben were always trying to get me to play some stupid game with them, but I usually didn't and I should have, because when I did, I always had fun. She lived with her grandmother, and they both died up in their attic. And Lord, when I say it like that, it sounds almost peaceful, but it wasn't, it couldn't have been. They made it up there so they wouldn't drown because the water was up to the roofline, but then they were trapped. It had to be two hundred degrees up there in the days after the storm—it was a hundred in the shade. The autopsy wasn't clear whether they cooked to death or died of thirst—either way it was painful and awful and I know Ben's spent a lot of time thinking about it, because I have, too. And Deshawndra's mother—she was serving in Iraq. Can you imagine coming home to that?"

"I can't," he said.

"Deshawndra was smart and she was tough," Eden said. "She wouldn't take anyone's crap. Never. Not even mine. And she could *sing*. She and Ben had this plan to go try out for *American Idol* as soon as she turned sixteen, and now—"

She broke off and focused on walking, on looking down the street for Neesha. But nothing moved on the sidewalks. There was no sound but the shush of the tires on the road as another car went past.

Izzy was silent, just waiting for her to continue.

So she did. "Her grandmother was a retired music teacher, and still gave clarinet and piano lessons to the neighborhood kids, including Ben. I swear, he lived in that house. After he found out they both died, he just, I don't know. He shut down. We moved to Houston first—not by choice, but more because we ended up there. That was where Ivette met Greg—they were both in physical therapy. She broke her arm and he'd been in a car accident, and suddenly she found God—along with Greg's big insurance settlement—and then they were married. Except, just like that, the money was gone—I still don't know how they blew it—and the honeymoon was over, but we were moving to Las Vegas. And Ben kept everything locked up inside, partly because Greg is such a dick. Neesha's the first friend he's made in all those years. I think maybe he feels like . . . if he can help *her*, he can maybe forgive himself for not insisting Deshawndra and her grandmother get into our car when we left."

"He was eleven," Izzy pointed out. "Most eleven—or fifteen-year-olds, for that matter—don't have a say in who does or doesn't get into the car they're riding in."

"But he was driving," Eden told him. "He was, then I took over, and . . . I should have stopped to get them. But I couldn't. I . . ." She shook her head. She really didn't want to talk about this anymore. She didn't want to *think* about it.

"*You* were driving," he repeated.

"It was Ron's car—my brother-in-law's."

She and Izzy had made a complete circuit of the block and were back on the main road, where a bench sat at the deserted bus stop. She pointed to it. "Mind if we just sit for a few minutes?" she asked. "I want to give Neesha a chance to come out of hiding. You know, maybe if she's nearby and she sees us...?"

"That's a smart idea," Izzy said as he sat down beside her. "So how come the two of you were driving? As if I don't know?"

"Ron was high. Can we not talk about Katrina?"

"Well, yeah," he said. "I just...I know what it's like to lose a friend and..."

"Frank O'Leary." She named the SEAL who'd died in the same terrorist attack that had left those grim-looking scars on Izzy's chest.

He looked surprised.

"You told me about him," she reminded him.

"I know," he said. "I just didn't expect you to remember his name."

"Why wouldn't I?" she asked.

Izzy was looking at her with an expression on his face that she absolutely couldn't read. But then he kind of laughed. "Because we talked about him, I don't know, *once*, a long time ago?"

Eden glanced behind her, hoping that Neesha would appear. But she didn't. Lord, she was tired, and she didn't want to sit here, talking about things that made her want to burst into tears and throw herself into Izzy's arms, and say things he didn't want to hear. So she brought them safely back to sex—where they were both in agreement. "I remember all of our conversations. Including one you'd probably prefer I forget."

Izzy definitely laughed at that, and she knew *he* knew that she was talking about a conversation they'd had on their wedding night, after she'd gone down on him for the first time, where she'd referred to his man-parts as "Mr. Big."

No, Izzy had said, pulling sharply back to look at her. *Nuh-uh. No way are you naming my dick.*

Too late, she'd teased him.

No it's not.

You can call him whatever you want, she'd said, *and I'll—*

Great, he'd interrupted her. *I'm going to get a little boring here and call it "my penis." Not Mr. Penis, not mister anything. No him, no, thank you. With the understanding that I do appreciate the ego-stroking behind the whole big thing. I mean, you're the mastermind behind* Pinkie, *so it could've gone in an entirely different direction. But here's the deal, Mrs. Zanella, I have an absolute no-name policy for body parts.*

As far as nicknames went, that *Mrs. Zanella* had made them both freeze with the eye-opening reality of what they'd just done at the little Happy Ending Wedding Chapel. They were legally married. For richer or poorer, for better or worse.

Ten long months later, even after spending all that time apart, Eden was still Mrs. Zanella—at least in the eyes of the law.

And despite the fact that she'd all but promised never to utter those words again, he was still Mr. Big.

"I know what you're thinking, smart-ass," Izzy said. "So stop it."

Eden had to laugh, even as she leaned slightly forward to check if that really was a shadow that moved across the street, or just her tired eyes playing tricks on her. Come on, Neesha... "Okay, Amazing Kreskin. If you're so good at reading my mind, what am I thinking *now?*"

"You're still thinking about Katrina," he said, "because you're still hoping Neesha will show up, and thinking about her makes you think about everything Ben lost because the levees broke, even though you hate thinking about it. Eed, I have to confess that I've been thinking about it, too—for a long time. Ever since I knew that you were there and lived through it. I always wondered what *you'd* lost, and now I know a little bit more. I know you lost your home."

Eden just shook her head. She'd lost so much more than that. She'd lost everything. She'd lost her*self,* for too many long, dark years.

"I know you don't want to talk about it right now," Izzy said. "But if you ever do...?"

She made herself nod, okay, but she wouldn't say anything. Not now, not ever. Because Izzy really didn't want to know. He thought he did, but if he ever found out...?

He wouldn't believe her. Her own *mother* hadn't.

And there it was. It wasn't so much that *he* didn't want to know, but that *Eden* didn't want to face his disbelief.

Their silence stretched on as she focused on a passing car, watching its taillights moving down the street, hoping that when it disappeared, Neesha would come out from wherever she'd been hiding.

But the car turned a distant corner and nothing moved in the shadowy stillness of the night.

And Izzy let Katrina go. He went back to their earlier conversation, pre-Mr. Big.

"You know, I'm kind of like you," he said. "A nomad. We moved a lot when I was a kid, and because I was the youngest, I rarely got my own room. They just kind of stuck me on the couch, wherever we lived. I was a post-vasectomy surprise—I ever tell you that?"

Eden shook her head.

"Obviously, the procedure didn't work." He smiled. "My brothers were all much older than me, and my parents were pretty much done with raising kids when I came along. I'm not complaining—it was an interesting way to grow up. Always sitting with the adults, never really treated like a child. At least not by my parents. My brothers could be pretty brutal, because I was always tagging along. School was optional—depending on whether or not my brother Martin was home. He was my Obi-Wan Kenobi, if you know what I mean."

"*Help me, Obi-Wan Kenobi,*" she said. "*You're my only hope.*"

"Exactly," Izzy said.

"How many brothers did you have?"

"Four," he told her. "Martin was the oldest—he was fifteen when I was born; then there's Nick, who's a year younger than M., then the twins, the Double D—Dougie and Don. They were two years younger than Nick, twelve years older than me. I was like the weirdest only-child ever, because they all left home and went to college or whatever, and then came back and lived with us at one point or another, sometimes with their wives or girlfriends and/or children in tow. But by then I was, I don't know, nine? Ten? And suddenly I was kicked out of my room again, and there were infants in the house. Which got old really fast for my parents, but not for me. It was a good excuse to not go to school. *I'm babysitting.*"

"So you...just didn't go?" Eden asked.

"Pretty much," Izzy said. "But it was okay, because I was reading and doing math on a college level when I was seven, so school was really just a place to handle the boredom by getting into massive amounts of trouble. It was probably better for everyone when I didn't show up. Although I prolly could've used the socialization skills — assuming I was capable of learning them. Which I'm not sure I was. Anyway, my point, when I started telling you all this, is because we moved so often — I'm talking at least once if not twice every year. My parents' passion was to buy old houses — really old antiques — and fix them up and sell them, so it was chaos on all levels, living in a construction zone, always going — or not going — to a new school...So, it's hard for me to think of any one place as home. I mean, right now I'm still living in that same apartment, but when I'm there? It doesn't feel like anything special. It's like it's just a giant box that holds my shit. It's where I sleep when I'm in San Diego."

"I liked your apartment," she said.

"But it's not home," Izzy told her. "I know all these people who are so wrapped up in having things, you know? And they buy a house and they get what they think is perfect furniture and...Jenk — you know Mark Jenkins? He and his wife, Lindsey, are having a baby, and he's all about moving out of their condo into a house with a yard. The kid's not going to be hitting a swing set for another few years — she's only a few months pregnant..." He shook his head. "But the truth is, home's an illusion. We try to create this place that's supposed to make us feel happy or safe, when in truth it's the people who are around us that matter. Where we are has nothing to do with it."

"I'm safe right now," Eden said. "When I'm with you, I feel very safe. Can I say that? Am I allowed?"

Izzy smiled at her then as he took her hand, interlacing their fingers. "Yeah," he said. "I'll accept that as a fact. As a Navy SEAL, I tend to make people feel either very secure or extremely insecure."

"I'm in the first subset," she told him.

"Glad to hear it," he said. "For the record? I'm personally feeling pretty happy right at this moment, so . . . Home, sweet home on a bus-stop bench, you know?"

And sitting there with Izzy, in the heat of the Las Vegas night, Eden *did* know. But she didn't dare tell him so.

Jenn still had a reddish mark on her face where Dan had hit her, and the sight of it made him sick.

"You weren't kidding when you said this was going to be hard for you," she said, after Eden and Izzy went out to look for Neesha.

"I won't blame you," he said, "if you decide that you . . . should go."

She was standing there, with her hair still rumpled from bed, wearing her pajamas, looking at him as if she were truly considering catching the next flight back to New York.

But then she asked, "Which would be harder? Doing what you're doing here, with Eden and Ben, or learning how to walk and live your life with only one leg?"

Her question caught him completely by surprise, but the answer was obvious. "It definitely would've been harder to lose my leg," he admitted. "Because this would've still been happening, only without me here to help. Yeah, right, I'm really helping. But still, I'd've been going crazy, plus dealing with losing . . . Jesus, *everything*."

"Not everything," Jenn said quietly. "You know, I came to Germany partly because everyone was saying the doctors were going to have to amputate, and I didn't want you to have to go through that alone. I wanted to be there. For you. To help you, if I could. And I know I probably wouldn't have—"

"Yeah," Dan said. "It would've helped. It *did* help. Having you there." To his complete horror, he started to cry again. "Jenni, Christ, I'm so sorry. I'm—"

"Shhh," she said, moving into his arms and just holding him. She was so soft and warm and she smelled so good—like everything he'd ever wanted. Like happiness and laughter and the incredible peacefulness he felt, just lying with her in his arms. "It's okay."

"No, it's not. What if Eden's right?"

"She's not." Jenn was absolute. "She doesn't know you. Not the way I do."

"I'm going to go in." Dan told her what Zanella had suggested. "For counseling. Because, Jesus, that scared me . . ."

He felt her laugh. "Well, hey, you know me. I'm never going to try to talk anyone out of a little counseling—touchy-feely liberal that I am. But . . . Don't go for me, Danny, go for *you*. Go, because what you're doing here, with your family, is hard. And because everyone needs a little help when things are hard."

Danny nodded and wiped his eyes as he made himself let her go. "God, you haven't even met my mother and . . . Jenn, I really think you should go back to New York."

"Back to that again, huh?" she said. "I guess I didn't make my point. Danny, listen to what I'm saying: I was ready to hold your hand as you talked to your doctors about being fitted for a prosthetic leg. I was ready to help learn to care for your stump until it healed. I was *ready* for all of it, as hard as it was going to be. And I was ready for you to try to chase me away."

And great, now she was crying, and it was getting him going again.

"And I wasn't going to let you do it. I wasn't going to be chased," she said. "And this? Yeah, it's hard. But it's not *half* as hard as that. So why would I leave, when I know that you need me?"

Dan kissed her. "I do," he said. "God, baby, I need you."

And she kissed him back, and for that moment, with Jenn in his arms, he could almost believe that she was right and that everything was going to be okay.

At least until the next anvil dropped on their heads.

CHAPTER
EIGHTEEN

B en got dressed.

Quietly, even though the other bed in the hospital room wasn't occupied—probably because, even though the people here were nice, they didn't want him to get any of his gay on another patient.

Like it might be contagious.

The night nurse—Sherry—had just been in to check both his blood pressure and his blood sugar levels, and he was fine. She'd tiptoed away, and he'd led her to believe that he hadn't even fully woken up when she'd pricked his finger.

Even though he'd been lying here, waiting for her to do her thing.

Now he moved toward the door, peeking through it and down the hall toward the nurses' station. There was a woman sitting there—her blond hair was gleaming in the overhead light as she focused all of her attention on the desk in front of her.

The hallway was otherwise empty.

He'd have to crawl past her, silently on his hands and knees, because there was only one way in or out of this ward. It was good that it was set up this way—it kept him safe from any unauthorized visits from Greg or Ivette.

But right now it wasn't the unauthorized visits he was afraid of.

No, it was the impending *authorized* visit tomorrow morning that scared the crap out of him. Because what if he did everything he could do, and he still lost the fight? What if he and Danny and Eden called CPS and requested their help, and they turned around and decided that, no, Crossroads *was* a school, and his parents had the right to send him to whatever school they wanted.

He couldn't go back there. He'd end up like poor Peter Sinclair.

So he crept out of his room and into the hallway while the nurse's head was still down. And he got onto his hands and knees and crawled.

It was a piece of cake—to sneak past her like that. He'd spent years perfecting his technique, moving silently, invisibly, as he avoided Greg and his mother. He'd entered and exited his house through his bedroom window so often, it felt almost strange walking in through a door.

This wasn't even half as hard as that, because he knew if he got caught, the nurse wouldn't hit him.

But he couldn't get caught, so he held his breath as he moved past the desk and headed toward the elevators—toward the freedom that was just around the corner.

Danny's cell phone rang in the darkness, and Jenn sat up as he rolled over and grabbed it.

"It's Zanella," he said. He punched TALK and spoke into the phone. "What's wrong now?" And apparently something *was* wrong, because he almost immediately added, "Shit!"

Jenn switched on the lamp on the bedside table as Dan swung his legs out of bed and pushed himself painfully to his feet. "Hang on, I'll look."

But Jenn was capable of moving much more quickly, and she beat him over to the bedroom door. "Look for what?" she asked, even as she did a quick scan of the living room. It was empty.

"Eden and Izzy went to the hospital to check on Ben, and he's gone," Dan said tightly as he followed her out.

"Oh, my God," she said, turning on the kitchen light. The bathroom was empty, too. "He's not here."

"Eden's ready to go to war with Greg," Dan reported, "but the nursing staff are swearing up and down and sideways that he didn't come back to the hospital. They're checking security tape right now. Izzy thinks Ben might've self-released—snuck out." He took the various locks off the apartment door and opened it, looking out into the courtyard. "He's definitely not here," he told Izzy.

"But if he did leave the hospital," Jenn pointed out, "under his own steam, wouldn't he come here? It's hard to believe he wouldn't. He's going to need insulin, and it's here, in the fridge. Does Eden know if he has a key? Was the one Neesha used an extra, or...?"

Danny asked, via Izzy, and came back with, "Eden says there were only two keys to the apartment. The second was hidden down in the courtyard."

Dan had that key right now. Jenn followed him back into the bedroom, where he searched the pockets of the pants he'd been wearing yesterday as she quickly got dressed and unplugged her cell phone from its charger. When he found the key, she took it from him. "I'll put this back downstairs," she said. "In case Ben comes and looks for it while we're out looking for him."

"We should start by renting another car," Dan was already telling Izzy as he nodded at Jenn. "But I agree completely. When we go to Greg's, we go together. Tell Eden that's nonnegotiable. Now that we know he's got a weapon, we have to make sure he doesn't have it in his possession when we—Yeah, yeah, I'm with you." He paused. "No, she still hasn't called me back. Trust me, I would've called you right away if Ivette had been in touch."

Jenn left the door open a crack as she went outside and down the stairs to the courtyard.

The air was hot and still and the night seemed to settle around her like a too-warm blanket. Nothing blew, nothing shifted, nothing moved.

It wasn't the first ceramic pot beneath which Eden and Ben had hidden their spare key, and it wasn't the second one, either. It was the one all the way over in the corner, in the shadows. Jenn headed swiftly toward it, well aware that Danny was going to be impatient. As tired as they both were, he was going to want to be ready to head out, to go looking for Ben as soon as Izzy and Eden came back from the hospital.

She had to dash back upstairs and wash her face and find a pony-tail holder and maybe her baseball cap. She should go through Eden's kitchen cabinets and refrigerator, too, looking for something for Danny to eat. To properly heal, he needed plenty of both rest and pro-tein, and right now he was getting neither.

She also wanted to search the cabinets to see if Eden had one of those padded cooler bags, so they could bring some of Ben's insulin in the car. From what she understood, strenuous physical activity—like hiking home from the hospital in this heat—would screw up Ben's usual schedule when it came to his insulin levels. And as for the added stress?

Kids with diabetes did best, Jenn had read, when their lives were free from intense stress of any kind.

She lifted the pot and slipped the key beneath and turned to go back to the elevators when—dear God!—there was someone, a man, standing right there in the shadows, blocking her path.

She jumped back and squeaked and had her cell phone open and about to dial for help with one hand, the other drawn back, about to swing and defend herself when the man said, "Jenn?" and she realized it wasn't a man, it was Ben.

It was *Ben*, and instead of dialing 9-1-1, she quickly dialed Eden's cell number, because Izzy was probably still on with Dan. "Thank God," she told him. "We were just about to launch a citywide hunt for you, starting by kicking down Greg's front door. Do you have *any* idea how worried we were about you . . . ?"

On the other end of the phone, Eden picked up. "Jenn?"

"We found him," Jenn told her as she reclaimed the key and pulled Ben with her into the better lit part of the courtyard. "Or rather he found us. Ben's here, he's safe."

"Oh, thank you, *thank* you," Eden breathed.

Ben, meanwhile, had crumbled. And even though he was nearly as tall as Danny, he was still just a kid. Because unlike his older brother and sister, who'd no doubt spent years learning to keep their emotions safely out of sight, he didn't even try to fight it—he just let go and started to cry.

"I'll call you back," Jenn said to Eden, and hung up her phone.

"I'm so sorry," Ben told Jenn as he looked at her, his thin face pinched, his blue eyes intense despite being flooded by tears. "I just couldn't go back to Crossroads. I'd rather *die.*"

"No, honey," Jenn said, wrapping her arms around him, her heart in her throat. "Don't say that, Ben. You don't mean it."

"But I do," he said, with a quiet certainty that frightened her. "I should've just let Greg shoot me when he was waving that gun around..."

"You did the right thing," she told him, holding him even tighter. "When a crazy man has a gun, you do what he says. Believe me, I've been there, too—I know what it's like, and it's not easy. But you take it one minute at a time, one breath at a time, because it's going to end. Everything bad always, eventually ends. But not if you die. If you die, it's over."

He pulled back to look at her, to wipe his nose on his sleeve. "But maybe it's better—for everyone if—"

Oh God. "How could it be better?" she asked him sharply, because damn it, he was really scaring her.

"Easier," he said. "I meant easier."

"Not for Dan," she told him, absolutely. "And not for me, having to stand at his side as we *bury* you? You honestly think that's *easier?*"

He'd flinched at her insistence at making sure he understood what he was saying. Suicide *wasn't* a painless oblivion. There *was* an afterward—as family and friends tried to pick up the shattered pieces of their lives.

"I'm just...I'm never going to change," he told her in a voice that was so quiet she almost didn't hear him. "I'm never going to be the son that my mother wants."

"Well then, fuck her!" Jenn said, and he looked up in shock at the violence of her words. "She's been a shitty mother anyway. Not just to you, but to Danny and Eden, too. Probably Sandy as well, but I've never met her, so . . . But you know, I used to think it was weird, the way you all call her Ivette, but I get it now, I do. She's not your mother, Ben. You know who your real mother is? Eden is. And Danny is, too. So if it comes down to some crap Ivette tells you versus the truth from Eden and Dan, what are you doing listening to Ivette?"

Ben just shook his head.

"Who are you going to believe?" Jenn asked him again. "Are you going to believe Ivette—who's just echoing what stupid, ignorant Greg says—or are you going to believe Danny and Eden and Izzy and me? And the *billions* of other people in the world who also know—beyond the shadow of a doubt—that there's absolutely *nothing* wrong with you, that you are exactly as you were meant to be, and that a world without you in it would be a much sadder, darker place."

He was silent for several long moments. But then he said, "I just don't get why she doesn't love me."

"She's broken," Jenn told him quietly. "Some people are just . . . broken. It's definitely not you, kid. Because I just met you, and I already love you." She held out her hand to him. "So come on. Let's go inside and let your brother know that you're safe. We've got to figure out what to do next. The staff at the hospital are probably freaking out."

"Let's just go to San Diego," Ben said as he took her hand and walked with her toward the elevators. "Ivette and Greg'll eventually forget I was ever there. Kind of the way they did after Eden left. Ivette actually got in touch with her by e-mail and told her not to come back."

"Well, that's one way to do it," Jenn told him. "I'm not sure it's the right way, but that's one of the things we're going to figure out. But this I promise you: we're not letting you go back to live with that awful man, and we're not letting you go back to Crossroads."

Ben nodded, but she could tell that he still didn't completely believe her.

CHAPTER
NINETEEN

I t was close to noon before they made it back to the apartment.
Ben had really screwed the pooch by sneaking out of the pediatrics ward.

The nurses who'd discovered he was missing last night had called the police, thinking it was Greg who'd somehow snatched him. They'd sent a squad car over to the house, where they'd found Ben's stepfather in the middle of a honking nasty bender, thanks to Izzy's creative gifting. The man had been halfway through his second bottle of scotch and had answered the door buck naked. The abusive comments he'd made to the female police officer had resulted in his fugly ass being dragged to the station, where he'd spent the rest of the night in the drunk tank.

And normally, Izzy and Eden both would've celebrated Greg's impending court date, but in this case? With Greg the only so-called adult at home, with Ivette still off the map, and Ben gone walkabout from the hospital? It had sent the alarm lights over at Child Protective Services into a real tizzy of a red alert.

And that dreaded three-day preliminary investigation had been opened.

The caseworker—a nice but harried man named Larry—had told Izzy that if Ivette didn't turn up in these next few days, he would be required to launch a *full* inquiry, which would take thirty very long days.

And probably result in Ben being placed in foster care for the duration. Only after that could Izzy and Eden and Dan petition for custody of the kid—and they might not get it, on account of their wanting to live out of state, in San Diego.

Because of that, they'd quickly devised a new plan. It was the same as their old plan, but now they had a limited amount of time to make it happen: find Ivette and get her to convince Greg—who *was* Ben's adoptive father, as it turned out—to join her in giving permission for Ben to move to San Diego to live with Danny, Eden, and Izzy. And then go before the state social workers and psychologists and put on the show of a lifetime and convince them that there was no need for that further investigation. Convince them that it would be in Ben's best interest to live in the happy, stress-free, sunshine-and-rainbows home that Dan, Eden, and Izzy would provide for him, in loving three-part harmony, together in California.

Izzy was ready to do it. When push came to shove, he could lie his balls off about how happy he'd be to share an apartment with his dear friend and teammate Danny. It was Dan he was worried about, gagging as he told that massive untruth.

"Don't you have to get back to San Diego soon?" Eden asked him as they went up the stairs to her apartment. Dan and Jenn had gone with Ben to his first round of official interviews at CPS. Izzy and Eden weren't needed until the family session, which had been scheduled for tomorrow afternoon.

"I'm good at least until the end of next week," he reassured her. "I already spoke to the senior chief."

She nodded. She looked exhausted, and this was probably not the time to bring this up, but they were alone, and he had to grab the opportunity.

"Speaking of work," Izzy said as he followed her down the outside corridor to her apartment door. "You should probably call your boss at D'Amato's and tender your resignation. That way, tomorrow? When you're asked about your employment, you won't have to lie."

Eden nodded again as she unlocked the door and he followed her inside. "It's just such good money." She put her handbag down, kicked off her sandals, and flopped onto the mattress on the living-room floor. "Lord, I'm tired."

"I'm not trying to tell you what to do," he started.

"Believe me, you've made that more than clear," she said, eyes closed, her voice muffled by the pillow.

"Well, good then," he said.

She didn't say anything more. She just turned over onto her back and looked up at him. "Why are you still standing there? Aren't you tired, too?"

Izzy sighed because that bed, especially with Eden in it, was looking pretty freaking tempting. "Yeah, but . . . Duty calls."

She sat up. "Seriously?"

He nodded as he found his duffel bag and started emptying it— both his clean and his dirty clothes, onto the shelf next to the VCR. "Agonizingly so. Why don't you nap—I'll be back as soon as I can."

"Whatever you're doing, I can help."

"Yeeeah," he said, drawing the word out. "I'm not so sure about that. Ben gave me his key. I'm going to do a little authorized B&E over at Greg and Ivette's, before Greg comes home from his truly big adventure at the police station."

She knew one of the reasons why. "You're taking possession of his gun."

"Handgun," he corrected her. "Gun is . . . Never mind. Yes. That's one of the things I'm doing, including making sure he's only got the one."

"What else?" she asked, then answered her own question. "Ben's clothes and money—he's got money hidden in his room."

"Yeah," Izzy said. "He told me where, and . . . I'm also in charge of finding the name of the home-health-care agency that Ivette works for. We gotta locate her ASAP. We should be able to get the address where she's working from them, so we can go over there and talk to her."

Eden pushed herself to her feet. "I can definitely help with that."

"Sweetheart, thank you, but I don't want you to have to go back there."

"If no one's there," she pointed out, "it's just a . . . really ugly place. If home has everything to do with people, then hell probably does, too. Right?"

"I'm not completely sure about that," Izzy told her. "There are places I wouldn't want to go back to, even if the people who made them hell were long dead and gone."

"But if you're going to be there, too," Eden told him as she unzipped her dress and let it pool at her feet, where she stepped out of it in his own private strip show, "I can go anywhere. I just want to put on sneakers, in case we have to run."

"Sneakers," Izzy repeated, unable not to laugh. "I assume you're going to put on more than sneakers. Which is not to say the look wouldn't work for me . . ."

She was heading into the bedroom, where she kept her clothes, but now she stopped and gazed back at him. Dressed as she was in only those barely-there white panties, she was impossibly beautiful.

Maybe stopping to take a quick nap—fifteen, twenty minutes tops—wasn't such a bad idea.

Eden smiled, because, as always, she knew what he was thinking.

"I honestly don't know how long I've got before Greg gets home," he told her, hefting the empty bag. "So really, I should go now, and I should go alone."

"I'm not afraid of him."

"I know you're not," he said. "But if I'm in there, and he *does* come home? I can get out and he won't even know I've been there. If you're with me, it's not going to be as easy."

"I could wait by the front door," she said. "Be your lookout."

"Eden, please get dressed," he said. "You're killing me."

"Is that a yes?" she asked him, crossing first one arm and then the other over her breasts, which really didn't help all that much, in the giant cosmic scheme of things. She persisted. "Is it?"

Izzy sighed again. "Wouldn't you rather take a nap? I'd rather take a nap."

But she shook her head, no. "I just like it better when I'm with you," she said quietly. "I like being with you. So, no. Unless you're going to take a nap, too..."

And okay. She had him with that.

"Get dressed," he said, bending down to pick up her sundress and toss it to her, so she could hang it in her closet. "But if Greg comes home while we're there? You don't mix it up with him, do you understand? Even if he pisses the shit out of you."

She smiled at that as she nodded, and he felt compelled to add, "Eden, I'm serious, here. If we're over there, and he comes home, you go out the back door and you get into the car and you lock the doors. And you turn the radio up loud and you stick your fingers in your ears so you can't hear his crap. Whatever he says and does, we don't touch him."

She understood. She nodded again, very seriously. "Thank you."

"Please get dressed," he said again, and she left the room to do just that.

The house was silent and smelled of stale cigarette smoke and garbage.

Greg's dishes were still out on the coffee table, exactly where they'd been the last time Eden was in here, just a few short days ago.

Her stepfather had added to the mess—an empty bottle of liquor was on the table, along with mustard-smeared take-out wrappers from McDonald's.

Izzy had come in first, and now he motioned for her to be quiet and wait by the front door. His eyes were dark with his concern—she wasn't trying to keep the repugnancy she was feeling from her face—and he leaned in close to ask her, "You want to wait in the car?"

"I'm okay," she told him. It was hard to hold his gaze. He scared her a little bit when he got like this—all hard intensity, no lurking amusement.

"I'm trusting you here, to be honest with me," he told her.

"It's harder than I thought," she admitted. "I want him to come home so I can take another swing at him with that pickax, for sending Ben to that place."

Izzy smiled then at that—briefly, fiercely—before the intensity was back. "But you won't, though, right?"

"I won't," she promised.

"Hold this, I'll be right back."

Izzy had brought his empty bag inside with them, and he handed it to her now before he swiftly and silently went through the house, checking all of the rooms to make sure that Ivette hadn't returned.

But Eden knew that if her mother was home, the cigarette smell wouldn't be stale. There'd be smoke in the air. Unless, of course, she'd passed out on the couch. Or the bed. Or the floor.

"We're clear." Izzy came back and locked the front door, putting the chain on it. This way, if Greg came home, he wouldn't be able to come right inside. He took his bag back from her. "Our priority is to get his handgun. Ben said Greg kept it in the closet in the master bedroom. What I need you to do while I'm looking for that—if you're up for it—"

"I am."

"—is to search the living room, under the sofa and chair cushions. I want to make sure he doesn't have a second weapon that he keeps hidden. So if he's got a favorite place to sit and watch TV—"

"I'm on it," Eden said.

He was still standing there, watching her as she started taking apart the couch, clearly loath to leave her, so she told him again, "I'm really okay. Go get the gun we know about. I'll feel that much safer when it's in your hands."

He nodded and vanished down the hall.

There was nothing under the sofa cushions aside from some popcorn and petrified Cheez Doodles. The upholstery was sticky and gross, but Eden searched carefully, sticking her hands down into the recesses of the furniture.

Izzy was back pretty quickly, and she could tell that he'd been successful by the way he was holding his bag. It was no longer empty, and sure enough, he set it on the floor with a heavy-sounding thump.

With the two of them working together, the search of the room went that much more quickly.

"Let's put everything back the way we found it," Izzy said. "No need to tip him off that we were here."

"Was there anything that led you to believe there's a second gun?" she asked him, looking up from putting the cushions back on the reclining chair. "An empty box, or a different type of ammo or...?"

"No," he said. "We just wanted to be extra careful."

That *we* referred to Izzy and Dan.

"This must've made Danny crazy," Eden said. "I remember him always asking that, first thing, whenever Ivette got a new boyfriend. *Does he own a weapon?* It really freaked him out, the idea of some stranger bringing a gun into the house."

"I bet," Izzy said.

"Do you want me to go into Ben's room and help decide which of his things to take?"

"Maybe you shouldn't go back there," he said.

Eden looked at him. "Why not?"

"There's a deadbolt on the bedroom door."

"In Ben's room?" she asked. "That used to be my room. I installed that lock."

"Not the way it's currently working," Izzy said. "Plus Greg boarded up the other window."

"Seriously?" she said, moving swiftly down the hall to look.

In doing so, she passed the bathroom where Greg had locked her, not quite a year ago—where Izzy had come and rescued her.

She paused at the door of the bedroom that had been hers when they'd first moved in. Ben had moved in with her, sometime later, when Greg had decided he needed the third bedroom for a home office—probably when he realized that Eden really *wasn't* open to the idea of him visiting her in her room at night.

And there it was—the deadbolt she'd installed on her bedroom door. But Greg had removed it and turned it around, so that it could be used to lock someone—Ben—in the room instead of keeping creepy, lecherous old drunks out.

Izzy was right—Greg had also boarded up the second window. She'd broken the first one by throwing a chair through it.

And yet, good, positive things had happened in this very room.

It was in here, sitting on the bed, that Izzy had asked her to marry him. She'd thought at first that he was kidding, but he'd been dead serious.

"Y'okay?" Izzy said, appearing now beside her, solid and tall, and still, as always, concerned for her.

She nodded and flipped on the light and went inside. "Good thing he didn't have a gun when I lived here, too."

"That very thought crossed my mind," Izzy said as he followed her and looked around.

Eden got right to work, making a pile of the few things Ben would want them to take. His CDs. He only had about a dozen, given to him as gifts. He had a few DVDs, too, even though there wasn't a DVD player anywhere in the house.

Izzy put his bag down on the bed and pushed aside the shabby dresser, revealing a spot in the corner where the tired wall-to-wall carpeting had come free from beneath the molding. He lifted it up and pulled out a manila envelope that had a rubber band tightly around it.

It was Ben's stash of money.

"You should just keep that," Eden told Izzy now as she took an extra pair of black jeans and Ben's work boots from the closet. "He told me you gave it to him, while I was . . . away."

"Gave is gave," Izzy said evenly. "I'm not taking it back. Besides, it's pretty impressive that a kid his age didn't just go out and spend it."

"He was keeping it for an emergency," Eden told him as she gave the boots a second look and put them back. They were already too small. "He's a Gillman, even though he doesn't really think he is. We learn from an early age that the sky could fall any minute and you better have a backup plan, because sooner or later, disaster is coming."

T-shirts, socks, underwear—everything they took, they wouldn't have to buy later. At least not until Ben grew out of it all in another few months.

"That's a hard way to live." As Izzy packed it all in his bag, Eden gave the top of Ben's battered desk a quick glance.

He had a small collection of little toys and action figures—things he probably got with his Happy Meals back when he was twelve. She'd had a similar collection—Ariel from *The Little Mermaid,* and Aladdin's monkey, Abu; the Brave Little Toaster and a bendable Gumby and Pokey—all of which had been swept away when the levees broke.

So she took Ben's *Toy Story* figures and his Pokémon cards, his Transformers and several other action figures she didn't recognize, and jammed them into Izzy's bag along with the far more logical socks and briefs.

Izzy noticed—he noticed everything. But he didn't comment.

"That everything?" he asked.

Eden nodded. "What's next?"

"Ivette," Izzy said. "We need to find out where she's working so we can get an address and pay her a visit."

"Kitchen," Eden said. "There might be something stuck to the fridge with a magnet. If not, there's a place on the counter where we always put the mail. I don't know if they still do that now, but . . ."

"Mail as in, maybe there's a paycheck?" Izzy asked.

Eden made the sound of the raspberry. "Greg would've cashed that. They share a bank account. I'm thinking pay stub or envelope left in the rubble—something with the company's return address."

"Show me," Izzy said.

After they'd returned from Ben's interview with the social worker named Larry over at CPS, Jennilyn and Ben sat at the kitchen table, heads together. They were using Jenn's laptop to surf the Internet, searching for three-bedroom apartments in San Diego.

"There are definitely more two-bedrooms than three," Jenni told Dan as he came in to get a glass of water. "Even when I expand the search to include houses. And the prices..." She made a face. "Well, they're great compared to New York City, but..."

"Then maybe we should look for a two-bedroom," Dan said. "I can bunk in with Ben—which won't be that often," he added as his little brother's discomfort levels increased. Jenn had been right—the kid didn't know him very well, and vice versa. Dan didn't have even a fraction of the relationship with Ben that Eden did. And clearly the thought of having to share a room was not a happy one. "The teams've been spending a lot of time overseas and, um..."

And as *those* words left his mouth, Dan realized that they weren't going to inspire any kind of a *yay* response, this time from Jenn, considering the last time he'd gone wheels up he'd nearly died.

Way to work the room, Gillman. Freak *everyone* out.

But Jenn took it in stride. She didn't smile, but she didn't look perturbed. "If it'll mostly be Eden and Ben living there," she said evenly, "then a two-bedroom makes sense. And with Izzy and Eden chipping in..."

"Are they really back together?" Ben asked. He'd already learned to look to Jenn for a bullshit-free answer. "Enough to want to live together? I mean, even just a few days ago, Eden was pretty adamant that it was over."

"Well, you know Eden," Dan started, but Jenn cut him off.

"People sometimes think they know what they want," she told the kid, "and then they find out they're completely wrong. Go figure, you know?"

"I just don't want her to do something she doesn't want to do, for my sake." Ben looked up at Dan. "You, too. I don't want you to have to—"

"I'm actually looking forward to getting to know you better," Danny told him. He tried to make a joke, because the kid was looking so serious. "Although to be honest—I can't lie—I'd rather be sharing a room with Jennilyn."

"I would, you know, sleep on the couch whenever Jenn comes to visit," Ben told Danny, still so painfully somber. It was clear he was trying to be as small a pain in the ass as possible.

"That'd be great, buddy," Dan said, even though his heart sank as he looked over their shoulders and saw the monthly rents of the two-bedroom apartments that were available. Even if he paid half? Along with the money he was going to have to keep sending to his mother... They were going to be eating a lot of pasta and taking a lot of staycations. Good-bye weekend trips to Manhattan, to visit Jenn...

She reached for him, grabbing his hand and squeezing it. "We're going to make this work," she said. "I'll be visiting a lot"—She poked Ben in the ribs and actually made him laugh—"so I'll be taking you up on that sleep-on-the-couch offer."

"Home again, home again, jiggity-jig."

Izzy and Eden were back, and Jenni and Ben both turned to greet them, eager for news.

"Was my money still there?" Ben asked.

"It was, thanks to your continued brilliance in finding hiding places where Greg and Ivette would never look," Eden answered as she crossed to the refrigerator and pulled out an apple from the crisper drawer. "You always were good at that."

Izzy, meanwhile, had set his bag down on the floor, and he met Dan's eyes and nodded curtly, just once. His message was clear—he'd taken Greg's handgun. He also had a shopping bag, and Dan saw that they'd stopped to buy a portable gun safe so they could store the weapon safely, here in the apartment.

It was necessary, but Jesus, it couldn't have been cheap.

Izzy saw Dan looking and said, "It's my contribution."

"That's not necessary," Dan said, but Izzy breezed past, ignoring him as he dropped a rubber-banded envelope in front of Ben.

"What are we looking at here?" Izzy asked. "Whoa, wait, I thought we were going for a three-bedroom?"

"I'm going to share with Dan," Ben said.

"Wow," Izzy said, grabbing the kid around the shoulders, hugging him from behind. "And isn't *that* every fifteen-year-old's dream come true? Not just having a roommate, but having one who's twice your age?"

Ben laughed. He didn't pull back the way he'd done when Dan had tried to hug him. "Believe me, I'd sleep on the kitchen floor, if it meant I didn't have to live in the same house as Greg."

"Hey, so we got everything you wanted," Izzy told him, "except for your porn."

Ben nearly choked in his haste to say, "But I don't have any porn." He looked at Jenn. "I don't have any porn."

"Told you he didn't have any porn," Eden said between bites of her apple. She was grinning and it was clear she and Izzy were teasing the kid.

Izzy straightened back up. "Trust me, he's got plenty of porn," he said. "But he's smart, like me. He keeps it all up here." He tapped Ben's head, then tousled the kid's hair. "How'd the interview with ol' Larry go? You hit it outta the park?"

Ben was laughing now, too, and it was clear, despite the way he was blushing, that he loved the attention and acceptance. "Yeah, it went okay. Particularly since he failed to ask me anything about, you know. Porn."

"I'm sure those questions will come." Izzy grinned back at the kid. "He's just waiting to catch you off guard."

"Porn?" Ben said in a ultra-fake voice, as if he were a terrible actor. "What is this thing, porn, of which you speak . . . ?"

"There you go," Izzy said. "Good boy."

It was also clear, from the way Ben looked at Izzy, that he thought the SEAL was some kind of superhero.

"You have lunch yet?" Eden asked Ben, who shook his head, no. "How about your blood sugar levels? You take 'em?"

"I was just about to," he said.

"Liar, liar, pants on fire," Izzy said as he picked up and looked at the cast-iron Buddha that sat on the kitchen counter next to the stove.

"No," Ben said, laughing. "I really was."

"Do it, please," Eden told him. She was smiling, too, but her words were pure no-nonsense. "Don't wait until you're dizzy, and then go, *wow, how'd that happen?*"

"I know the drill." He stood up, pocketing the packet Izzy had given him. "You, um, looking for some privacy? Trying to get me out of the room?"

Eden seemed surprised. "No, actually, I wasn't."

"Because I was wondering if you found Ivette."

As Dan watched, Eden exchanged a look with Izzy, who rubbed the Buddha's belly before he put it back. "Yes and no," she said.

"Aw, shit," Dan heard himself say, because that didn't sound like good news.

Izzy cut to the chase. "Bottom line, she's AWOL."

Danny swore again.

"As of right now, anyway," Izzy added. "I mean, maybe she's heading home…"

"We found the name of the service she's working for," Eden told them. "A-Plus Home Companions."

"I spoke to Eliza from their main office," Izzy said, "who told me that Ivette was working for a client who was in hospice, who died early yesterday morning."

"I spoke to her…When was it?" Dan turned to Jenn.

"It was late, on the sixth, probably right before he died," Jenn told him. "Maybe she's been dealing with the funeral arrangements—that's why she hasn't called you back?"

But Izzy and Eden both were shaking their heads.

"She was working for the deceased," Izzy said. "His kids apparently hated her. According to Eliza, she was officially off the clock at 0400, yesterday."

"Great," Dan said. "She's on a bender."

"That's what I thought, too," Eden said. "That she absconded with the dead guy's pain meds."

"And because she was in a hurry to avoid the police," Ben chimed in, "she left her cell phone behind."

"Wow," Izzy said, applauding. "If worst-case scenario thinking was a sport, you Gillmans would win the gold."

"Worst case," Ben corrected him, "would have her ditching Greg along the way, for someone even more stupid."

"An ex-con polygamist who'd cook crystal meth in the bathroom," Eden added.

"While selling grenade launchers out of the trunk of his car," Dan contributed, and it was weird. Even though the idea of Ivette being so freaking irresponsible royally pissed him off, he and Eden and Ben were all standing there, smiling at each other ruefully, in a rare moment of harmony.

Maybe because it was either smile or cry. And they'd all lived this nightmare long enough to know that crying wouldn't change anything.

"Even if we don't find her in time," Dan told his sister and brother, "it's going to be okay. One way or the other, we're going to win this thing."

But Ben was clearly worried. "Maybe we could get insulin on the street, and—"

"And your picture will end up on a milk carton," Eden pointed out.

"So I'll dye my hair," he countered. "I'll go surfer blond. I've been wanting to make a change—"

"If you really think that's *all* that would have to change—" Eden started to say.

But Izzy stopped her. "Let's not escalate this yet," he said, aiming his words at Ben, too. "We've still got time to find her."

"Did you get the address," Jenn asked, "where Ivette was working? Maybe we can start there."

"She's in Montana," Izzy told them. "Apparently the old guy knew he was going to kick, and wanted to spend his last few days at his cabin, outside of Missoula."

"Missoula, Montana," Dan repeated. "Fantastic."

"Would it be useful," Jenn suggested, "if one of us flew up there and—"

"No." Dan cut her off a little too sharply, but then reached for her, pulling her up and out of her seat and into his arms. "I'm sorry, baby," he told her, closing his eyes as she hugged him back. "But it would be a waste of time."

"Her air travel was negotiated by the client," Izzy reported. "It's hard to imagine her agreeing to go up there without having a way to get back home."

"But it's not hard to imagine," Dan said, "Ivette cashing in a plane ticket and buying a much cheaper seat on a bus." He looked at Jenn. "Which is why it would be a waste of time. She could be anywhere."

"Including on her way back to Vegas," Izzy pointed out. "If she lost her cell phone—"

"Abandoned it while making her getaway," Ben corrected him.

"Lost or abandoned it," Izzy said. "That explains why she hasn't called you back." He looked around the room from Dan to Jenni to Ben to Eden. "I haven't given up hope. Eden and I left her a message back at the house. We stuck it to the fridge."

"Assuming Greg doesn't come home first, see it, and tear it up," Eden interjected. "Come on, Ben. Get your meter."

As Ben left the little kitchen, Dan saw that Jenn was watching him.

"This *is* going to work," she said quietly, so only he could hear, as she hugged him again.

"I'm going to cry like a baby when you leave," he told her just as softly.

Across the room, Izzy had to be tired—Eden, too. They both were silent, Eden finishing up her apple and Izzy staring almost hypnotically at Eden's ass, which, in the extremely tight shorts she was wearing, left little to the imagination.

Except maybe Izzy was just taking a quick combat nap with his eyes open, because when Eden moved to throw her apple core into the trash, he didn't track her. He just stared into space.

But the SEAL looked up, snapping back to present and alert when Eden quietly asked, "Any luck finding Neesha?"

Dan let Jenn answer. "None," she told them. "I went to that mall, while Dan stayed with Ben down at Child Services, but I didn't see her—or anyone who looked like the man who chased you. Ben would still very much like to find her, though. And oh, while I'm thinking about it! I completely forgot last night...Neesha left you a twenty-dollar bill. She asked us to give it to you, Eden. She said that she took it from you—or maybe, Izzy—I guess, the last time she was here?"

Eden shook her head, refusing the bill that Jenn had pulled from the pocket of her jeans. "I'm not missing any money."

"Twenty bucks?" Izzy asked. "Whoa, that's great. That's actually mine. Wow, yeah. It clears up a...big mystery."

Eden looked at him. "What big mystery?"

"Um," Izzy said. "Well, I *was* missing some money and...Now I know what happened to it." He smiled brightly. "Mystery solved. Yay?"

Eden didn't smile back at him. "You were missing some money," she repeated.

And Danny knew exactly where this was going, and it wasn't going to be pretty. He beat a retreat, pulling Jenn with him toward the living room. She didn't resist—in fact, she hurried him along, and even stopped Ben and pulled him with them, too.

"Show me how that works," Jenni told Ben, pointing to his blood glucose meter.

It was a valiant attempt at giving his sister and Zanella privacy, but it was completely in vain. This apartment was so small, there was no way someone in the living room could help but overhear a conversation going down in the kitchen.

"First you have to wash your hands," Ben told Jenn. "And then you take one of these test strips and put it right here..."

"Great," Dan heard Eden say to Izzy. "My brother only thought I was a prostitute. But you? You thought I was a thief. Thanks *so* much."

"Then you prick your finger on the side, because it hurts less," Ben said. "At least that's what they say. It's all pretty much the same."

"Sweetheart..."

"Don't touch me," Eden said sharply, and Ben looked up, looked at Dan, clearly ready to go to their sister's assistance if he needed to.

"It's okay," Jenn murmured to Ben, even as she met Dan's eyes. "He would never hurt her."

"Why didn't you say something?" Eden asked from the kitchen. *"Hey, Eden, I'm missing some money. Have you seen it?"*

"Because it wasn't that important?" Izzy said, phrasing it as a question, as if hoping it was the right answer.

"Because *you* thought I *stole* it," she countered.

"Can we talk about this later?" Izzy asked, a tad desperately. "We're both really tired and—"

"Neesha didn't take it last night," Eden said. "It had to be, what? The night before? Which means that all this time, you've been willingly—eagerly—sleeping with someone you think would steal money from you."

"It's not that simple," Izzy told her.

"Isn't it?" she asked. "Because from my end? It's extremely simple. In fact, I can simplify it down to three little words: go to hell."

And with that, she marched out of the kitchen, grabbed her handbag, and left the apartment, slamming the door shut behind her.

Zanella, meanwhile, was silent.

They were also silent there in the living room. Ben looked from Dan to Jenni, as if hoping either of them would do something. When they didn't—Izzy and Eden weren't the only ones who were exhausted—Ben stood up.

Jenn tried to stop him. "Honey, we should probably just—"

He shook her off, heading for the kitchen as he asked Izzy, "Aren't you gonna go after her?"

"I don't know what to say," Izzy said quietly. "Because...she's right."

"Well, *I'm sorry* might be a good way to start," Ben pointed out. "*Are* you sorry?"

"More than you can imagine," Izzy admitted.

"Then tell her that," Ben said.

There was silence, then somewhere—from the kitchen?—a cell phone began to blast, its ring tone one of the songs from the *South Park* movie.

"Shit!" Izzy swore.

Ben gave voice to the obvious. "She left her phone home."

"Fan-fucking-tastic," Izzy said as he clomped his way out of the kitchen and over to the door. "Someone call me if she comes back, all right?"

"We will," Ben promised as Izzy left, closing the door far more gently than Eden had.

It was obvious the kid was worried, and Dan tried to smile at him reassuringly. "You know, even if things don't work out between Izzy and Eden," he told his brother, "we're still going to be okay. We'll win custody anyway. We're going to do whatever it takes." He looked at Jenni for support, but she was looking at him slightly quizzically—in fact, her expression was a gentler variation of Ben's *what the hell are you talking about?*

"This isn't about me," Ben told Dan indignantly. "Not at all. This is about Eden and Izzy. She loves him. She always has—and he thought she *stole* from him. That's gotta hurt."

"Well, yeah," Dan said. "That's . . . Yeah. I mean, I'm sure she, you know, loves him in her own way."

"What other way is there?" Ben asked. He wasn't being a smart-ass. He was seriously asking.

"Um," Danny said, and when he glanced at Jenn for help, she was wearing her *yeah, you can be an idiot, but I love you anyway* face. "I don't know."

"You don't know Eden very well, either," his little brother told him, but it wasn't with judgment, it was matter-of-fact, as he came back to sit next to Jenni, who was still holding his meter. He pointed to the display. "This number tells me how I'm doing—if my blood sugar's too high or too low. Either is bad. It's got to be right in the middle."

"And what does this particular number mean?" Jenn asked.

"It means I'm doing great, which also means it's okay if I have some carbs, like pizza for an afternoon snack. Hint, hint."

As Jenn laughed, Dan left them there, talking about Ben's diabetes, knowing that he'd need to take a crash refresher course himself, but far too tired to do it now. Of course, knowing Jenni, she'd be an expert in a matter of hours, and would be able to teach Dan everything he needed to know.

"So you can eat pizza?" he heard her ask his brother as Danny went into the bedroom and lowered himself carefully onto the bed.

He lay there, staring at the ceiling as they talked about carbs and insulin adjustments and their favorite pizza toppings, as Jenni made Ben laugh, as they called for a pizza to be delivered, as they went back into the kitchen because Ben wanted to check something on Facebook, on Jenn's computer, and she was happy to help him.

This was what having a family was supposed to sound like—it was what he'd always imagined it would sound like. And Dan closed his eyes and let their words and laughter wash over him as he relaxed enough to fall fast asleep.

After taking a too-long hike through the mall where he and Eden had been fired upon last night and coming up cold, Izzy finally went downtown. He more than half expected to find Eden at D'Amato's working one of the poles.

It was where *he* would have gone—if he were her, and he wanted to give himself the biggest *fuck you* he could possibly deliver.

Or maybe it wouldn't be a *fuck you*.

She thought her stripping didn't bother him. Because he'd told her as much. Except, at the time that he'd said it? He'd pretty much meant it.

Damn, maybe her truthiness-in-the-heat-of-the-moment-itis was contagious, because this was totally her MO. Say something and mean it at the time, but then feel something completely different when a new day dawned and a new situation arose.

A situation such as Izzy's walking into this place and fearing that he was going to see her up on that stage with a crowd of drooling men around her—all those eyes on her, all those reaching, grasping fingers...

As Izzy went into the club, he stopped just inside the door, letting his eyes adjust to the cool darkness. He looked down at the stage through his eyelashes, as if he were watching a particularly gruesome horror movie, but he didn't see Eden and he didn't see her, and nope, she definitely wasn't there.

Which didn't mean she wasn't in the dressing room, taking a break.

In theory, he wanted to be in agreement that Eden had the prerogative to do what she wanted, to make her own choices, to live her life the way she deemed best. In theory, he could understand the whole seemingly neo-feminist viewpoint that a body was a body, and if people wanted to pay outrageous sums to see her unclad, so be it, and more power to her.

But in practice?

It was a totally different animal.

Either that, or something had changed between today and the night they'd discussed Eden's career as an exotic dancer. Something was different. Some switch had been flipped in Izzy's brain that made the hair stand up on the back of his neck at the mere thought of Eden smiling into other men's eyes, and letting them touch her—just enough to slip their money into her panties, but touch her just the same.

That bill roll she'd showed him only seemed impressive as long as he didn't think about what it meant. Each of those bills came from a hand, which was attached to a man, who'd probably gotten at least a little hard from watching Eden dance.

And no, Izzy didn't like that. At all.

But he hadn't communicated that fact to Eden, so if she *had* come to work, maybe it was just her way of being practical and efficient and earning the most money that she possibly could, while she still could.

Maybe she was going to take his advice so that she wouldn't have to lie to the social worker about where she worked, at tomorrow's meeting. Maybe she'd come here so she could quit—right after she left the stage tonight.

The bouncer with the Marine tattoo was back by the bar, and Izzy nodded to him as he ordered a coffee from the bartender.

"We're out," the man told him, without an apology.

"Seriously?" Izzy asked, because damn, he was tired. A beer was out of the question, and the burst of energy he'd get from a cola would rapidly decay into a sugar crash, leaving him even more fatigued. And to him, diet soda tasted like tea made from metal shards.

"Kitchen's closed tonight."

"Last time I checked," Izzy pointed out, "coffee wasn't food."

"There's a Starbucks three blocks down, across from the McDonald's—for when you're heading home."

That was a solution? "But I want coffee now," Izzy argued, even though he knew it wasn't going to make a cup magically appear.

What did magically appear was the bouncer, who shifted closer.

"All right, how about an iced tea, no sugar, heavy on the lemon," Izzy said wearily, then looked at the bouncer. "Name's Zanella, I'm with SEAL Team Sixteen. I'm going on forty-eight hours without significant sleep. My wife's kid brother was in the hospital and . . . Long story. Bottom line, he's fine, but I'm freaking tired. Anyway, she works here—Jenny—do you know her? Is she on today?"

The big man definitely knew her, and the look he gave Izzy was filled with disbelief. Like, *You really expect me to believe* she's *married to a dirtbag like* you? "I'd have to check," he said. "But I'm not sure why she didn't just tell you. You know. Her schedule?"

"It's been a crazy coupla days," Izzy said.

He nodded. "Navy SEAL, huh?" He gestured to Izzy's hand with his many chins. "Where's your wedding ring?"

"Back in San Diego," Izzy said. "I came here via Germany."

Any American—forget former military—who gave half of a shit about the servicemen and -women who were fighting in Afghanistan and Iraq knew that Germany was one of the places you went when you were wounded.

The bouncer took that in and nodded, but then said, "I don't want any trouble."

"I'm not looking for trouble," Izzy said. "I'm looking for my wife. If you see her before I do, please tell her I'm here. I'll be sitting down in front."

And with that, he took his plastic cup of mostly ice and a little tea and went down the aisle to one of the few empty tables that was directly in front of the stage. It wasn't as close as he would've liked, but it was close enough for her to see him, should she appear.

And if she did appear? Whether her being there was a *fuck you* message or a *whatever*, there was one thing he knew.

He didn't have the right to tell her what to do.

So he'd sit and watch while his stomach churned, and he'd make sure she wasn't harmed or disrespected—at least not more than she already was, simply by climbing onto that stage—and then he'd see her safely home.

"Guy who says he's your husband's out front."

Eden looked up at Big John in surprise, and then turned to peek out from behind the curtains that let Alan, the manager, keep an eye on the floor even while he was up here in his office.

"Center," John told her. "About halfway back."

And sure enough. There was Izzy, dwarfing the little round table he was sitting behind.

He looked exhausted.

And sad.

Far more like the man Eden had first encountered here at D'Amato's just a few short days ago than the troublemaker who'd tried to talk her into having a quickie in the bathroom while they waited for Ben at the hospital.

Izzy had been kidding about the going-into-the-bathroom thing— but his kidding was definitely on the square. Which meant if she'd called his bluff, he would have done it. Without hesitation.

Despite the fact that there wasn't a lock on the bathroom door.

And even though he'd thought, at the time, that she'd stolen money from him.

"I didn't know you were married," John said in his deep-woods Arkansas drawl.

"He's been ... out of the country."

"He was in here a few days ago." John was definitely suspicious, and determined to protect her—even from herself.

"Yeah," she said. "We were separated and I thought we were breaking up, but then we weren't, and ... I think we probably are again. Doomed, you know?"

"You need to slip out the back?" John asked. "I could give you a ride home."

"No," Eden said. "That's all right. I'll just get him and ... He's a good guy, John. Really. He's just ... not the right guy." She corrected herself. "Well, right guy, wrong time. You know what I mean?"

John nodded seriously. "If he hurts you, I'll kill him. You can tell him that. Navy SEAL or not."

Eden forced a smile, even though she felt more like crying. "Give Ricki a hug for me, and tell her I say *hey*."

"I will," John said.

"Thank you," Eden said, "for everything." And she headed out of the office and down the stairs. The dancers weren't supposed to use the door that led directly out onto the club's floor, but she opened it anyway and slipped through.

Izzy didn't see her. Not at first.

But then, even though his back was to her, he somehow sensed that she was there, because he turned. He did a double take — probably because he hadn't expected to see her here while wearing all of her clothes. Or maybe it was because she was coming toward him, not running away.

"I hate you," she said as she sat down next to him. "You suck."

He was definitely tired because he didn't try to hide the emotions that crossed his face. More of that surprise was mixed with a flash of very real gratitude — no doubt because he wasn't going to have to chase her back across Las Vegas.

"I know," he said. "Eden, look, I'm really sorry —"

"The money went missing from . . . where?" she asked, cutting off his apology, as she looked up to watch Darlene dance. She was new, and even though she was delicately pretty, she wasn't very good. She definitely needed a how-to session with Nicola, of the basketball boobs. "From out of your wallet?"

"Yeah," Izzy said. "It went missing from, um . . . Yeah."

"Nice," she said. She didn't want him to see the hurt in her eyes, but she turned to look at him because she needed to ask, "Why would I take your money?"

"I don't know," he said quietly, gazing back at her steadily. "That's why it was a mystery. I couldn't figure it out."

"And it didn't occur to you to ask?"

He looked away from her then, and she knew — exactly — why he hadn't asked. He didn't think she'd tell him the truth.

"Great," she said, unable to look at him as she fought the rush of tears to her eyes. "You didn't ask because you wouldn't've believed me. I don't know why I'm so surprised. I mean, why should you be different than anyone else? You think I'm a liar. *And* a thief. Big fricking deal. I wouldn't believe me, either, if push came to shove. It just . . ."

He reached for her hand. "Eden —"

"It gets old after a while." She jerked her hand out of his grasp, aware that Big John was hovering not too far away, as she caught her breath and steeled herself, forcing herself not to cry.

Which gave Izzy the opportunity to say, "I really am sorry."

"Sorry for thinking I'm a thief and a liar, or sorry that I am one?"

He didn't answer right away, which was telling. "Sorry for every-thing," he finally said. "Starting back the night we met."

"Wow," Eden said. "That's... an awful lot to be sorry about."

Izzy nodded. "Yeah, it is."

"So... What? You'd rather just have never met me?" she asked.

"No," he said. "No." He started to reach for her again, but this time stopped before he connected. "I just would've done everything really differently."

"Like what?"

"Like, I wouldn't have slept with you," he told her. "Not that night, and not the night we got married, either."

Eden looked at him. "Even though that's the one indisputable fact that we both agree on—that we have the world's greatest sex?"

"Is it really?" he asked quietly, his dark eyes so somber. "If I don't trust you, and you don't trust me...?"

"So... you think our not having sex—ever—would have made us trust each other?" she asked, struggling to comprehend.

"I don't know. I'm not sure there's anything I could've done to make you trust me," Izzy told her.

Eden nodded, feeling sick. "So what do we do now?" she asked. If he left, they'd be at a disadvantage at tomorrow's meeting. If he left, they might not get custody of Ben. If he left...

As usual, he knew what she was thinking. "I'm not going any-where." But then he amended it. "Unless you want me to."

"I want Ben to be safe," she told him. She wanted so much more than that, but she knew better than to couch their relationship in terms that dealt with anything other than sex and her little brother.

"Well, good," Izzy said, "because I want that, too."

"Enough to live with me?" she asked. "For an undetermined amount of time—but possibly as long as three years? That's crazy. That's longer than most jail terms."

He sighed at that. "Living with you isn't a hardship," he told her.

"Despite the fact that the sex isn't really all that great?"

"I didn't say that," he said. "I said it's not as great as, I don't know, as maybe it *could* be. And . . . maybe this is a good thing. That this happened. Maybe we could, I don't know, start over."

"Start over," she said, unable to keep her hurt from making her sound surly.

"Yeah," Izzy said. "If we both promise not to lie to each other—"

"I thought I did that," she said. "Last night."

"You didn't say it," he countered.

"Cross my heart and hope to die?" Eden asked. "What are you, twelve?"

"No," he said, clearly frustrated with her, too, but like her, he was hyperaware that Big John was watching them. So he lowered his voice. "I just—"

"How does that work, anyway?" Eden interrupted him. She kept her voice low, too, but she didn't try to hide her upset. "Because if you think I'm a liar, then I could be lying when I promise I won't lie to you. So what's the point?"

"It's just . . . I don't know. A way to start over," he said again. "To start clean."

"Okay, then. I promise I won't lie to you—about anything," Eden told him, sitting back in her chair. "Not even to be nice. Cross my heart and hope to die. So look out if your ass looks fat in those pants, because I'm *not* going to lie about it."

Izzy smiled at that. "I'm not really that worried about—"

"That was a bad example," she said. "A stupid haircut. If you get one, watch out."

"That's a possibility," he said, "having had my share of stupid haircuts. I'll consider myself warned."

"Your turn," she said.

Izzy looked at her and his smile faded. "I promise I won't lie to you anymore, either," he said.

"Have you?" she asked. "Lied to me?"

"Yeah," he admitted.

"About what?"

"About you working here. I don't want you stripping, I don't," he said, then closed his eyes and rubbed his forehead as if he had a headache. "I was pretending that I wanted it to be your choice. *I think you should quit because yada yada,* but if we're going to move forward from here?" He opened his eyes and looked at her, and it was clear that he was dead serious. "No more. Not here, and not in California, either."

Eden gazed back at him.

But he wasn't done. "Not even when I'm away," he said. "*Especially* not when I'm away. I know you think you found yourself a good situation and that you felt safe. Safe enough, anyway, but the truth is, it's dangerous. Besides, you're better than that and... The idea of all those hands on you? I know they're not supposed to touch, but I also know that they do. And I don't want it. I don't want to share."

Eden could tell from his body language that he was expecting her to argue or to come out with some kind of *You're not the boss of me* exclamation. Instead, she nodded. She'd already handwritten her letter of resignation and left it up on Alan's desk. Because this way she *wouldn't* have to lie to the social workers tomorrow. Plus she knew Danny was going to raise a stink if she tried to keep it up. Besides, she didn't like being touched, either. "Okay," she said.

"Really? Just like that?" He was surprised.

"No," she said, a touch snarkishly. "I'm lying."

"No, you're not," he said, "because you promised you wouldn't."

There was something in his eyes, now, that looked a lot like hope.

"You know what sucks?" Eden asked him, "almost as much as you do?" She didn't wait for him to answer. "When I work some stupid minimum-wage job, and the manager puts his hands all over me, and there's nothing I can do about it."

"Yeah, there is something—"

"Something that won't get *you* arrested," she added.

"How about you let me help you find a job?" Izzy asked. "When we get to San Diego."

Eden shrugged. "I'm happy to let you try," she said.

He smiled at that. "There is no try."

"Yeah, well, people generally don't want to hire me," she told him. "Unless they want to get in my pants. Try to get in my pants. And there definitely is a *try*, because they do it. But they don't succeed."

"I'll help you find a job," he said again, "with people who'll respect you."

And there he sat, just looking at Eden, as just a few feet away, up on that stage, Darlene danced. She might as well have been invisible as far as Izzy was concerned.

And Eden opened her mouth and said, "If you get to tell me where I can or can't work, then I get to tell you . . . No more Marias. If you're with me, you're only with *me*. For as long as we're together. Whether it's three days or three years."

"That goes both ways," he said.

"Of course."

"Okay," he said.

"Okay," she said, too.

And she should have felt better. They'd reached an understanding. Like Izzy'd said, they'd started over. They'd set up some guidelines and rules for their relationship. It should have been a good thing.

But all she felt was as if they'd started a giant clock ticking, counting down to the moment Ben would turn eighteen and Izzy would say good-bye.

It wasn't an *if*—he'd made that more than clear. It was a very definite *when*.

And that was on top of the fact that nothing they'd said, not even Izzy's apology, had soothed the hurt that came from knowing he'd believed she'd taken that money right out of his wallet.

Izzy cleared his throat. "About Maria . . ."

Eden briefly closed her eyes. Way to bring her down to another, as of yet unexplored, level of hell. "I really don't want to know."

"Yeah," he said. "You do. She hit on me, but I turned her down."

She looked at him then as her emotions twisted within her. She didn't want to feel so stupidly happy at that news. "And . . . you want some kind of congratulatory medal . . . ?"

He smiled at that. "No, I'm just trying to be forthright. I kind of lied to you about her. You know, by omission."

"Anything else?" she asked. "I mean, as long as we're here in the confessional?"

Izzy laughed, because this place was about as far from churchlike as it could possibly be. But this time, when he reached for her hand, Eden didn't pull away. She just gave up and let him link their fingers together.

"Thanks," he said. "For forgiving me."

"But I haven't yet," she admitted. "I'll get there eventually . . ." Probably the next time they made love—or had sex, as Izzy called it. She felt tears welling again in her eyes, so she took her hand back to brush them away. "Just not tonight. Tonight I'm just going to wallow in hating you."

"Fair enough," he said.

She stood up. "I already quit," she told him. "So let's go make Ben happy and cruise the strip, see if we can't find Neesha."

Izzy looked as if he'd far rather go back to her apartment and sleep for eighteen hours, but he nodded valiantly and even managed a smile. "Just let me stop for coffee, and I'm up for anything."

CHAPTER
TWENTY

She still had a full hour before it was time to meet Clarice, but Neesha headed over to the hamburger place early—being cautious as usual.

She walked from the bus station, where she'd used the bathroom to change into the same halter top that she'd worn the previous night.

She didn't have a jacket, so she'd used one of the shirts Ben had given her to cover the sequins, because she didn't want to draw attention to herself until she arrived at the private party.

It didn't matter that she smelled of perspiration or worse—this was the last time she would ever wear this top. She would return here later and change back into a far less eye-catching shirt, then bring the clothes she'd borrowed back to Ben's sister, along with money to clean or even just replace them.

She'd leave it in a bag outside the apartment door, wishing that she could—as Ben's older brother suggested—write a note. Just to say thank you. And good luck.

But she didn't know how to write in English, and there was a bus that left for L.A. at midnight, and she was determined to be on it, so she wouldn't have time to knock and give them that message face-to-face.

The hamburger place where she'd first met Clarice was now in sight, and Neesha walked toward it with a sense of dread, despite knowing that she'd almost made it past the finish line.

• • •

Izzy needed coffee.

The bartender at D'Amato's had told him there was a Starbucks just a few blocks away, on Paradise Road—which was also where Neesha had told Dan and Jenn that she could find "work."

Eden knew exactly where it was. "It's up on the left," she directed him. "Across from the 'Billions Served' sign . . . ?"

"I got it," he said as he spotted the familiar logo. "Thanks." He glanced at her as he signaled to make the turn into the lot. She'd been quiet ever since leaving D'Amato's, and now she was gazing out the window with no small degree of intensity.

Looking for a Neesha in a haystack.

It wasn't just a case of Eden wanting to be able to tell Ben that they'd spent some time searching. She honestly wanted to find the girl, and Izzy tried to imagine what it had been like, fifteen years old and in charge of getting her little brother and her sister's kids to safety with a category-five hurricane bearing down on them.

She'd driven them out of their low-lying neighborhood in her brother-in-law's car, or so she'd told him. Izzy suspected there was more to the story than she'd revealed.

And now was not the time to ask her about it. Since they'd left the club, she'd answered the few questions he'd asked in monosyllables. *Did you have dinner?* No. *Are you hungry?* No.

He had to wait for a group of businessmen—meetings over and ready to party—who were walking down the sidewalk before he pulled into the parking lot. For this part of town, at this time of late afternoon, both the Starbucks and the fast-food joints nearby were jumping—but mostly with traffic from cars.

The sidewalks were fairly empty. Compared with the teeming crowds out on the strip, this part of the city was a pedestrian ghost town.

"You want anything?" Izzy asked Eden as he put the car into park and double-checked that his wallet was still in his pocket.

She said, "No thanks," as she turned to crane her head and get a look at another group of people coming out of the Mickey D's. But it was a family, trying to get an affordable meal amid all of the vice and sin. They probably didn't even realize that the skinny blonde in the microskirt, who'd walked past them in the parking lot, was a hooker.

Which was probably a good thing, because Dad, with his camera, might've tried to take her picture. As it was, the man took a second and then a third glance as she leaned in the passenger-side window of a pickup truck, to talk to the driver and simultaneously show the world a flash of candy-apple-red panties.

"Lock this door behind me," Izzy ordered Eden, and left the car running, a/c blasting, as he got out. He waited for her to push the lock button, and when it clicked, he moved through the oppressive heat and went inside the Starbucks, where there was, of course, an interminably slow-moving line.

Neesha almost walked right into it.

She hadn't been expecting it—although as soon as she saw it, she didn't know why she hadn't. It suddenly seemed so obvious that Clarice would have certain connections, and would make some inquiries about Neesha.

But there she was—Clarice—talking to one of the men—the bald one—who'd been searching for Neesha over at the mall. He was driving a blue pickup truck. And—God—climbing into the passenger's seat beside him was Todd. It was clear he was there to help identify her—which she knew he could do quite easily.

He'd been one of her regular visitors through the years.

And it was then, upon seeing him, that Neesha made her second big mistake.

She stopped short instead of continuing to walk past, and it telegraphed her surprise, and made her stand out.

Although she was already standing out by being one of the very few people on the sidewalk.

And he saw her—Todd did. She saw him sit up and point directly at her, and she knew she had to run. But this part of town was unfamiliar to her, filled with massage parlors and empty lots with nowhere to hide, and she didn't know where to go.

"Neesha!"

It seemed impossible, but someone was calling her name, and she spun to see Ben's sister Eden, standing outside a car, not far from her, in a coffee-shop parking lot.

And her heart sank, because she was surrounded, because Eden was somehow part of this, too—this plan to capture her and take her back to hell.

They both had vehicles and she was on foot and Neesha knew it was over.

But she did the only thing she could do as Todd got out of the truck and jogged toward the street, and toward her—because God, he had a gun.

She ran.

"Neesha, wait!"

Eden looked frantically back toward the Starbucks, trying to find and signal to Izzy through the heavily tinted window as the little girl bolted down the street.

And oh, dear Lord, she wasn't the only one who'd spotted the girl. A man who'd climbed out of a truck in the McDonald's parking lot was already chasing her, and the truck itself was moving to follow and—

Holy crap, the truck was being driven by the man who'd shot at them at the mall, the man with the shaved head—the man that Eden and Izzy had seen asking questions at Greg's house while they were staked out and waiting for Ivette.

As the bald man moved the truck toward the entrance of the fast-food driveway, Eden looked back at his friend who was following Neesha. She saw the flash of something metallic—a gun that the man was checking to make sure it was loaded—and she knew she couldn't wait for Izzy.

She had to act.

She dove back into the rental car, slamming the door behind her as she scrambled over the parking brake and into the driver's seat. The car was already running, so all she had to do was put it into reverse.

The parking lot and the sidewalk behind her were both clear, so Eden hit the gas.

Izzy stood on his place on line and did his best not to fall to his knees while weeping and shouting, *Venti, venti, venti! For the love of God, all I want is a big-ass cup of coffee*, while up at the counter a man who was actually wearing a sweater ordered some kind of complicated but completely caffeine-free drink—really, what was the point?—and then changed his mind about seven times.

"Oh, my God!" the girl behind the counter said, and Izzy was in total agreement.

Until he realized that she was looking past it's-only-115-degrees-Fahrenheit-tonight-Mommy-where's-my-sweater man and out the window at the parking lot, where a car was leaving plenty of rubber as its tires squealed and—

Damn, that was *his* car.

Eden was behind the wheel, driving like she was insane.

What the fuck . . . ?

As Izzy pushed past the crowd behind him and ran for the door, he caught a flash of her face as she threw the car into drive.

Whatever she was doing, she was aware and determined—not some victim of sudden sleepwalking or in the midst of some kind of weird seizure. She was also alone in the car—unless a carjacker had climbed in and was sitting on the floor so that Izzy couldn't see him.

"Eden!" he shouted as he burst out into the heat of the evening, but she'd already finished backing up and had put the car into drive.

She forsook the traditional route of leaving via the entrance to the parking lot, and instead went for the most direct pathway to the street, which involved plowing over some tired-looking shrubbery and bouncing over the curb, muffler scraping and banging as she went.

The few pedestrians who were on the sidewalk scattered, as did the cars on the street—squealing to a stop or swerving to avoid her—and it was clear she was trying to avoid them all. Most of them.

One man, who was in the midst of jaywalking across the avenue, seemed to be her target, and shit, yeah, she was heading *right* toward him. But when he dove out of the way, scrambling back the way he'd come to take cover behind a parked car, she turned the wheel and hit the brakes, hard.

It didn't stop her from sideswiping the car he was hiding behind, and the sound of metal on metal screamed in the oppressively hot afternoon air as she ground to a stop.

"Eden!" Izzy shouted again, and this time she looked toward him and—Jesus—kind of waved. It was a little *yes, I see you over there, hang on just a sec* acknowledgment as the man she'd nearly flattened scrambled to his feet. Whatever dude was trying to get to was on Izzy's side of the street, but instead of attempting to cross again, he ran toward a truck that was poised and ready to take a left turn out of the McDonald's parking lot.

And suddenly the entire situation clicked into sharp, understandable focus.

Because that truck—a shiny new blue Ford 4x4, no doubt stolen, with a mud-obscured Nevada front plate—was being driven by their old friend from the shopping mall, Baldy McShotMyCar.

Eden wasn't being coerced by the world's shortest carjacker. Nor was she insane.

Although maybe Izzy had to retract that last thought as, while he watched, she stepped on the gas and, with another shrieking metal-kissing-metal sound, separated the rental car from the parked vehicle.

Baldy had been blocked by a car whose driver had screeched to a halt to avoid the rampaging rental car. But now he took Eden's lead and he drove on the sidewalk to get around it and onto the street. He stopped only briefly to let the man Eden had tried to flatten climb in, and it was then that Eden stepped on the gas.

Baldy saw her coming, saw her intention—she was going to ram him in a full demolition-derby move, but another car pulled forward, blocking his escape, and there was nothing he could do but try to back up, gears grinding in his haste.

Izzy was shouting—he heard himself shouting: "Eden, don't, don't, *don't!*"

Because holy shit, the truck dwarfed the rental car. It was like watching Davey and Goliath—except, no, it was like watching all of the guys *before* Davey went up against Goliath; the guys that Goliath had effortlessly crushed. If anyone was going to get hurt here, it was going to be Eden.

But craphell! She didn't hit her brakes, she just hit the truck—*bam!*—and damn it, the air bag should have gone off, but it didn't.

The rental car bounced back, nearly crushing Izzy, who was running toward it. But he danced out of the way, and then he jerked at the door handle, but the fucking thing was locked so he hammered on the window, praying that she was okay.

The truck was only barely dented, but their bags had deployed, which was more than just a pain in their asses, it was a rule changer. They were dead in the water, so to speak, because most new vehicles were designed with a kill switch that kicked in during an accident. It would have to be reset before they could drive away.

And yes, those *were* sirens wailing as police cars approached.

Eden opened the door for him just as Izzy heard what had to be one gunshot and then another—Holy fuck! Baldy and his partner were using bullets to deflate the air bags that were pinning them into their seats.

But this was the same crazy-ass motherfucker who'd unloaded his weapon at them at the mall, so Izzy reached across Eden and unfastened her seat belt, pulling her out and around to the back of the rental car, even as he shouted at her, "Are you out of your freaking mind?!"

As punctuation, the crazy-ass motherfucker took yet another shot at them, this time putting a hole in the windshield right where Eden's head had been, seconds earlier.

And God, if the shooter came out of the truck and around the rental car, they were fucked, because there was nowhere for them to go and Izzy wasn't armed—he'd left Greg's handgun back at the apartment—so he couldn't fire back.

"Get under the car," he ordered Eden, ready to do whatever he had to, to take those motherfuckers down and out with his bare hands, in order to protect her.

She went, immediately, scooting herself along the pavement, as those sirens got louder and louder. But then he stopped her, because, sure enough, the first police car to make the scene was coming from behind them, lights flashing.

Eden saw it, too, and she gasped, "Thank you, Lord, thank you!" and "Are they running away? North?" At Izzy's confused look she clarified, "Are the men with the guns heading north?"

He peeked over the back of the rental, where, sure enough, the bald man and his buddy were nowhere to be seen. They'd deserted the truck and lit out on foot and the only way they could have gone—without Izzy having spotted or been killed by them—was indeed north.

So he nodded, and she must've somehow known he was wondering why the hell it mattered so much to her that they'd gone in that direction, because she told him, "Neesha—they're after her. She was here. I saw her! And she ran south!"

And as Izzy looked at Eden, as he looked into her beautiful eyes, into her face that was as drenched with sweat as his was and now smeared with grime from the dirty street, he realized that she'd put herself in mortal peril. She'd fucking driven fucking *toward* a man that she damn well knew had a fucking weapon, all for the sake of some girl she'd met once.

One time.

Jesus H. Christ, for all they knew Neesha was a criminal, a liar, a thief, a con artist.

And Izzy's head damn near exploded—he was so angry. At Neesha, at Eden, and at himself for being stupid enough to leave the keys in the car.

And his anger mixed badly with the intestine-freezing fear he'd felt over the past few endlessly long minutes as he'd stood there impotently and watched Eden fling herself into danger.

"God damn you," he growled now. "Don't you ever think before you do *any*thing?"

She flinched as surely as if he'd struck her. And that pissed him off even more—the fact that she should look at him like that, as if he'd somehow wounded her, when mere moments ago she was unflinching as she'd gunned the gas, balls to the wall, as if she were freaking bullet-proof and invincible.

She looked as if she were going to say something, but then the police shouted for them both to get down, facedown in the street, hands on their heads—because for all the cops knew *they'd* been the ones who'd fired the shots.

And realization dawned and Izzy could tell from the expression on Eden's face that she *hadn't* thought about the consequences of her actions.

He pushed her down into the perp position, as he assumed it himself, purposely turning his head away from her as he did so. Not only did he not want to hear whatever it was Eden was going to say, but he knew damn well that anything else that came out of his mouth right now was sure to be something he'd regret.

He just closed his eyes and waited for the impending joy of a body search and an ensuing police investigation.

All of which would be endured without coffee.

Although, truth be told? Jangling the way he was with adrenaline and anger, adding caffeine to his system at this point would've been overkill.

CHAPTER
TWENTY-ONE

D anny was silent as Jenn drove the car they'd rented just that afternoon over to the police station to pick up Eden and Izzy.

Well, they'd pick them up, assuming everything went as smoothly as possible and Eden wasn't going to be held for whatever various crimes she'd committed.

"It's really funny how we can't seem to hold on to more than one rental car at a time," Jennilyn said, glancing over at him as she braked for a red light.

"Yeah." Dan looked back at her, his smile wry. "That's the really funny part of all this."

"Sorry," she apologized. "I was just trying to talk about something other than—"

"The fact that we're going to bail my screw-up of a sister out of jail?" he finished for her.

"She's not a screw-up," Jenn told him. "She's actually really brave. I don't know if I would've done what she did. I mean, yes, I would've done it without hesitation to protect you or Ben or my brother's kids...But for someone I barely know? I mean, I would've tried to help, sure, but..."

"What do you call it, though," Danny asked her, "when those so-called courageous actions put someone else in danger? Yeah, Eden saved Neesha from whatever it was those men wanted from her—assuming it really was Neesha that she saw and not some other weird little Asian hooker-girl. But, okay. Let's agree it was her. And great. By getting herself arrested, Eden put Ben back in danger from crazy Greg and Ivette. Do you honestly think anyone at CPS is going to want to let Ben anywhere near Eden now? It *is* called Child *Protective* Services."

Jenn forced a smile, because here it came. The conversation she'd been waiting for ever since Izzy first called from the police station, an hour ago. "Of course not," she told Danny quietly. "But what if Eden truly believed that those men were going to harm Neesha? She knew she's not the only one capable of protecting Ben. She knew that we have a Plan B."

The light turned green and she accelerated through the intersection, aware that he was still watching her. She glanced at him again, and he sighed and said, "Plan B. The plan you hate."

"I don't... hate it," she said. "I just didn't want to do it until we absolutely had to. And with Eden being arrested..." They were pretty dang close to absolutely having to.

He was silent, just watching her.

"Make it nice," Jenn said, trying to be upbeat and positive in the face of this looming disaster. God, this was *not* what she wanted—to do this out of sheer necessity. To leave her job and move all the way across the country to live with this man that she loved, a man who said he loved her, too, but really—mostly—only needed her. She forced another smile. "Do it right, and I'll split the cost of a fancy hotel room with you, so we can have some privacy tonight."

"To do what?" Dan asked. "Let you give me head? Terrific."

She had to laugh. "Oh, wow, and all this time, I thought you liked it."

He laughed, too, exhaling his exasperation. "You know I do—and *like* is an understatement," he told her. "I just want... You know what I want."

And, God, when Dan looked at her like that, she *did* know.

"Three more days," Jenn reminded him. "Unless... Well, if *you* were a doctor and your patient was a Navy SEAL, wouldn't you pad your recommendation for no strenuous lifting or activity by at least three or four days? Knowing that the SEAL was going to cheat?"

He looked at her with such transparent delight, she had to laugh.

"You're going to let me cheat?" he asked, then added, "It's not really cheating. It's more like redefining the rules."

"Fair enough," Jenn said as she pulled into the police-station parking lot. It was crowded despite the time of night—or maybe *because* of the time of night. "Like I said, make it nice, Gillman. And yes, I'll help you redefine the rules tonight."

"I love you," he told her as she found a spot down at the end, and she used the excuse of parking to keep from looking at him, for fear he'd realize just how difficult this was going to be for her.

Dan loved her, yes, but in his own way and . . . Huh. That was funny, that was exactly what he'd said to Ben, about Eden loving Izzy.

"Jenn, really. I've never loved anyone the way I love you. And to think you'd be willing to do this for me is . . ." His voice was thick with emotion and he had to stop and clear his throat. "It's the best gift anyone's ever given me."

And there it was. She didn't *want* the fact that she was helping him gain custody of Ben to be the best gift he'd ever received. She wanted her love for him—plain and simple—to hold that coveted status.

But she was living here, in reality, not in some fairy-tale-flavored alternative universe.

"Well, you're lucky," Jenn said as she put the car in park. "Ben's such a sweet kid. He makes it easy to say yes—to the question that you haven't exactly asked me yet. Not today, anyway." She looked around them at the battered car parked next to them, at the sun-bleached and sagging wooden fence that was in dire need of repair that was in front of them, at the starkly blocklike municipal building she could see in her rearview mirror. "Although this isn't quite the romantic epicenter of Las Vegas. But then again, this isn't exactly about the romance, is it?"

"I don't know," he said, taking her hand. "I think it's pretty perfect.

But I never really needed the soundtrack with the swelling violins, or the glorious sunsets... When it comes to romance, LeMay, all I need is you."

She smiled at that—how could she not? It was both sweet and poetic. And when he leaned in to kiss her so tenderly, it nearly took her breath away.

God, he was good. He'd always been good at getting his way.

He pulled back the merest fraction of an inch to ask her then, his breath warm and sweet: "Jenni, will you marry me?"

He kissed her again before she could answer, and it was clear from the way he deepened that kiss that his thoughts had already wandered to the rule-redefining part of their evening.

But he made himself stop, and he was laughing as he put some distance between them. "It's crazy, but I'm actually nervous that you're not going to, you know, say yes."

He wasn't kidding, so Jenn put him out of his misery and said it. "Yes."

But he didn't kiss her again as she'd expected him to. Instead he just kept smiling into her eyes. "Right now," he whispered, "I am the happiest man on the planet. And taking into consideration that I'm sitting where I'm sitting...? That's saying something."

He just kept smiling at her, so she finally leaned in and kissed him. Maybe if she could just keep kissing him, this wouldn't be so bad, this ache of disappointment that she was feeling, knowing that he was going to marry her because he had no other real choice—at least not a choice he was willing to accept.

But there were things that needed to be done—and discussed.

"So what's it going to be?" she asked, purposely keeping her voice light. "An Elvis impersonator, or—ooh, I know! The Star Wars Chapel. There's got to be one somewhere in Vegas—complete with costumes. We could get married as Wookiees."

Danny laughed, but then his smile faded as he looked at her. "You *are* kidding, right?"

"I don't know," Jenn said. "Make it *Star Trek* and I might not be kidding. To have a ceremony officiated by a Vulcan in a Starfleet uniform?"

But he laughed as he said, "Seriously, baby, let's do this at least semi-right. I heard Zanella telling Lopez—you remember Jay, right?"

Jay Lopez was one of the SEALs who'd come to New York last spring to help protect Maria when she'd received threats from a lunatic. "I do," Jenn said, but then laughed. "Sounds like I'm warming up."

"Works for me," Danny said, and he kissed her again. "Really, Jenni, this is so great. I just...It means a lot to me and...Anyway, Zanella told Lopez that when he and Eden got married, they found this place where they rent wedding gowns, and they'll do your makeup and...He said it was actually pretty nice. And okay, yeah, they used a cartoon version of the bridal march—Bugs Bunny singing 'Here Comes the Bride'—but what do you expect from Zanella and my sister, right?"

"Do they rent tuxes?" Jenn asked. "Because if I'm in a gown..."

Danny nodded but then shook his head. "Yeah, but no, I've got my dress uniform in my bag," he said. "I was thinking that we could swing back home and pick it up. When we get Ben."

"Ben," she said, surprised. "You want Ben to come...?"

"Well, yeah," he said. "And, you know, Eden and..." He rolled his eyes. "Even Zanella. Do you mind? Because if you'd rather it was just me and you—"

"No," Jenn said. "No! That's fine. I'm just...a little surprised."

"They're family," Danny said. "Regardless of everything, they're still..." He shrugged. "They're my family. Maybe we could do something this summer—fly back east—to, you know, celebrate with your family."

Oh God, she hadn't even thought about what she was going to tell her parents and her brothers. *Hi, everybody, I'm in Las Vegas and I'm on the verge of marrying a Navy SEAL that none of you have met. And oh, by the way, we've got an instant teenage ward, whom I'll be taking care of while my new husband goes off to war...* Yeah, probably better to wait and tell her mother *after* the fact. Maria was a different story, though. She could call Maria while Dan was dealing with helping Izzy get his sister released.

"Or, I guess we could wait a few days," he said, because she hadn't responded, "so they could fly out, but—"

"That meeting's tomorrow," Jenn finished for him. "You want to do this tonight."

"I do," he said, "but that doesn't mean we can't—"

"It's decided," Jenn said. "We're doing this tonight." And then she kissed him, because there was nothing more to say, and kissing Danny always helped to ease any and all disappointment and pain.

It helped that the blue truck had been stolen.

And it helped that Eden's description of what went down matched—exactly—the statements from half a dozen witnesses.

And it *really* helped that everyone in a several-block radius agreed that the driver and passenger of the stolen blue truck had definitely had at least one weapon between them, which they'd fired three times.

No one, however, had seen the little Asian girl that Eden claimed to be trying to protect. Or that the man crossing the street toward her had had a weapon that he looked ready to use on the girl.

But the City of Las Vegas took child prostitution *very* seriously, and an investigation had been opened. Unfortunately, that investigation made it impossible for Eden to hide her now-former place of employment. Or her stage name.

And when her brother came into the interview room where she'd been questioned and requestioned over the past few hours, the first thing he said to her was, "Jennilyn LeMay? Honestly?"

Eden braced herself for the storm of crap that was sure to come, but all Dan did was laugh his disbelief as he sat down across from her at the gray metal table. He still moved a little bit slowly and carefully, and she knew his injury was troubling him.

Not that he'd complain.

"You're unbelievably lucky," he told her, "that Jenn thinks it's funny."

"I'm so sorry," Eden said. "It happened so fast. Her name just popped out of my mouth, and—"

"I think it also helps that she's changing her name to Gillman," Danny interrupted her. "We're getting married tonight."

"Oh, Lord," Eden said, closing her eyes. "Danny, I'm so, *so* sorry that I got arrested. Izzy's right. I honestly didn't think beyond—"

"It's actually a good thing," he interrupted her again. "I wanted her to stay, and now she's going to. So, thank you for messing up. There's a first, huh?"

She didn't know whether to take him seriously, and because of that she wasn't sure what to say.

"I know that's not why you did what you did," he continued, "but I'm grateful just the same."

He *was* serious. He was sitting there, looking her in the eye, and thanking her for what she'd done.

God damn you! Don't you ever think before you do anything?

Maybe this was cosmically correct. Izzy was as angry as Dan usually was when she messed up. And here Dan was, cool and calm, and actually *thanking* her.

"Izzy's really mad at me," she told him, fighting back the tears that welled in her eyes.

"You drove a car *toward* a man with a weapon, who'd discharged that weapon at you in the recent past," Dan pointed out. "I'm feeling a little what-the-hell myself."

"The man who was going after Neesha," Eden explained, "had a gun and he was going to kill her. I could tell from the way he was moving—it was like he wasn't even . . . *human* anymore, and I *know* that sounds ridiculous but—"

"It doesn't," he said. "I know what you mean."

"You do?" She gazed at him, and he sat there looking steadily back at her. This was probably the most eye contact they'd had since, well, since that awful year that Charlie had died, when Eden had turned fourteen and stupidly climbed into John Franklin's car.

"Yeah," Dan said. "Killing's not always easy to do. For some people, there's a disconnect. Others...come alive, which can be even scarier to watch." He sighed as he studied her. "You sure it was Neesha? I'm not convinced I could pick her out of a lineup, and I'm good with faces."

"I'm sure," she told him. "I called her name, and she turned."

Dan nodded, and exhaled hard. "Well, okay."

"We need to find her," Eden said. "Whoever those men are? They're serious. She's in trouble."

"You and Zanella can do that tomorrow," Dan said. "Maybe take Ben with you. Tonight I need you to stay with him, because, well, Jenni and I are going to spend the night at a hotel, in the honeymoon suite." He smiled.

Eden smiled, too, because it was so...odd. Her too-serious older brother was having a solid case of the goofies about the fact that Jenn was going to marry him.

So she leaned forward to ask, "You really don't think you could have closed this deal with Jenn, just with a little dinner and moonlight?"

"I tried a few days ago," Dan admitted, "but I kind of screwed it up."

"Wow, I can't imagine that," she said. "The Gillman curse, striking Captain Perfect."

His smile faded. "Jesus, Eden, I really hate when you call me that," he said.

"I really hate that you think I'm a terrible person," she said, and to her absolute horror, she started to cry. She stood up so that she could turn away, her chair screeching as she pushed it back across the linoleum floor.

"I don't think you're a terrible person," Dan said. "I think you've made...some really terrible choices. I think you're great with Ben. And I hope, whatever happens, that you stay close. To him."

"Not you?" she asked.

"Well, I'll be living in the same apartment as Ben," he said, "so..."

"Maybe I'll visit when I get out of jail," she said.

"You're not going to jail," Dan told her. "Izzy's on the phone with a lawyer. The rental-car company's looking like your biggest headache, but Izzy's already up in their grille—literally—about the fact that the car he rented didn't have working air bags. When the dust finally settles, I think the worst you'll have to deal with is a fine and an inability to get a driver's license without taking some kind of punishment class. Driver's ed, you know?"

Eden turned and looked at him. "That's...all? You mean, they really believe me? The police and the detectives and...You?"

"There were a lot of witnesses," he pointed out.

"Ah yes, the witnesses," she repeated. "That's where I've gone wrong, most of my life. My very worst choice was that I didn't make sure, whatever I did, that there were plenty of witnesses."

"Look," Danny said, but then stopped. He looked up at her—he was still sitting at the table—and he sighed and shook his head.

"What," she said, coming to sit back down across from him. "Come on, Dan. Lecture me. We both know that's why you came in here. Because even though I'm apparently not going to be thrown in jail, the entire world now knows that I was working as a stripper and—"

"That's not," he said, still shaking his head. "Why I...Actually, I came in to invite you to my wedding. We're gonna go to the same place where you and Zanella...went. I've seen the picture and...You looked really great..."

Her mouth was hanging open and she closed it. "When did *you* see the picture?" Izzy had worn his dress whites, and she'd worn a rented gown that was designed for brides who were six months pregnant. Her boobs had been humongous and the dress had been so low-cut that it was a costume malfunction waiting to happen, but the picture—a portrait taken as part of the wedding package that Izzy had paid for—*had* come out great.

"You're kidding, right?" Dan said. "I mean, come on. Zanella carried that picture around with him, wherever the team went. He had it laminated. I have this memory of him, on a medical helo, bitching at me for bleeding on the damn thing while he wiped it dry." He paused. "You *do* know what he did for me? The battlefield transfusion...?"

Eden looked at him. "What?" she said. "The *what*?"

"It's called a battlefield transfusion," her brother told her. "I was pinned down by a sniper. I was hit—a bullet nicked my artery." He pointed down at his right leg. "I was dead. I was sure I was going to bleed out, because there was no way they could evac me out of there, not until the sniper was contained, and that just wasn't going to happen soon enough.

"So Zanella gets some medical tubing and some needles, and you know, when I say that, it sounds like he strolled to the local CVS, but this motherfucker had a shitload of ammo and... The sniper motherfucker, not Zanella, although he can be a real motherfucker, too."

Eden nodded. "I get it. What happened?"

"So Zanella leaves the minimal cover that we've got to go get this shit, and then comes back with it and..." Danny shook his head in disbelief. "Apparently—I was out of it by this time—he used himself as my own private blood supply. A needle in his arm, blood going out, and a needle in mine, blood coming in. He gave me so much of his own blood, Eed, he nearly died. He needed a transfusion, too, which is why we both ended up in the hospital in Germany."

"Dear Lord," Eden breathed. "I didn't know. I didn't realize he was in the hospital, too."

"Figures he wouldn't tell you. What a douche."

"How could you call him that?" Eden asked. "He saved your life."

"That doesn't make him less of a douche."

"I think *you're* a douche," she said, laughing her indignation.

"Yeah, well," he said. "You're probably right." But then he got serious. "Some people just don't get along. He pushes my buttons. He always has. He probably always will."

"Have you asked him to stop?" Eden asked her brother. "And not like, *Jesus, Zanella, fuckety-fuck the fucking fuck!* But more like, *Izzy, please, don't do that right now, it's a hot button for me, so I need you to give me some space."*

Danny itched his ear. "I've only done it, you know. The fuckety-fuck way."

"He's really smart," Eden told him. "And he's really, *really* a good guy, Danny. He had a kind of unusual childhood—"

"And *ours* was normal?"

"Good point," she said. "I just think he would really like to be friends with you."

"Well, he's coming to my wedding," Dan told her.

"Best man?" she asked.

Danny made a face. "I... think I'm going to ask Ben to do that."

"That's a great idea," Eden enthused. "Ben will be thrilled—and Izzy will, too." She stopped herself. "Assuming he's over his anger—and capable of being thrilled."

"He'll be over it," Dan told her. "He's got the attention span of a—"

"Don't say it," she warned him. "If he's going to stop jumping on your buttons, you have to give him something in return."

Dan laughed. "Zanella hasn't exactly agreed to anything yet."

"He will," Eden told her brother. "All you have to do is ask."

Ben's sister, Eden, saved her life.

Neesha had absolutely no doubt about that.

Todd had been ready to kill her. He'd told her as much during his visits. *If you try to leave this place, we'll find you. We'll hunt you down and kill you, like the animal you are...*

He was the animal, having sex with a powerless child.

After spotting him, there at the hamburger place where she was supposed to meet Clarice, Neesha had run, despite knowing that it was over, that she was surrounded, with Eden and her car so close by. There was nowhere to go to hide, and no way she could outrun that car, let alone the bullets from Todd's gun.

But she'd run anyway, and when she'd turned to look back, fully expecting to see her death approaching her, she instead saw Eden as she drove her car toward Todd, as if trying to run him down. He'd turned to run—away from Neesha, buying her valuable time.

And Neesha had kept running.

She'd run until she couldn't run anymore. And it was clear, by then, that Todd wasn't going to find her—and that Eden had saved her life.

It had taken Neesha a while to figure out where she was, and then to figure out what she was going to do.

It wasn't a difficult choice. She knew, whether or not Clarice was responsible for bringing Todd to the hamburger place, that she couldn't go back to Paradise Road. She would have to try her luck elsewhere.

Or she could take a risk and go back to Ben and Eden for help.

FRIDAY, MAY 8, 2009
8:12 P.M.

"What do you think of this one?" Jenn held the dress up in front of her as Eden looked up from her perusal of the racks.

Dan's sister frowned. "Too busy and... Too long-sleeved. You've got great arms and beautiful skin. Let's give Danny a heart attack, okay?" She held up a dress that was strapless, with a fitted bodice that had bustier-like stays and a relatively full skirt. "I think you should try on this one."

"Yeah, hello," Jenn said. "Have you looked at me? I'm not particularly well endowed up top."

"But that's why God made Wonderbras," Eden told her with a smile. "There's a lingerie drawer over there." She pointed over to the changing area. "Just pull your size and take the entire drawer into the dressing room with you. I've got the dress."

Eden led the way, and sure enough there was an entire drawer filled with different types of bras in Jenn's simultaneously large and meager size. Large number, small letter, that is.

But Eden was running this show, and she put the gown on a hook in one of the changing rooms, and with the briefest of glances into the bra drawer, she reached in and plucked one out that was both strapless and heavily padded. "What color dress do you want me in?" she asked as she handed it to Jenn.

"Oh," Jenn said. "I really don't know. I guess ... I like ... blue?"

"Blue it is," Eden said. "I'll pick out a couple that'll fit me, and let you choose. Give a shout if you need help getting that on."

She vanished back toward the racks as Jenn went into the changing room and looked at the dress, and then the bra she was holding in her hands. She put it down—there was a chair in there, it was a big open area—and unfastened the robe she'd put on after showering in the spa-like bathroom.

This place was nicer than she'd imagined from its cheesy-sounding, sexual-innuendo name. Of course, a happy ending was what happened at the close of a fairy tale, too. It wasn't just a euphemism for an orgasm.

"You're going to help me with my hair, right?" she called to Eden, her stripper slash fashion consultant slash soon-to-be sister-in-law.

"Of course," Eden called back. "And I'll help with your makeup, too. Although the lady who works here? Izzy calls her Mrs. Fudd, on account of her husband looking like Elmer—we should probably find out her real name—but she's *very* good and—Ooh, look at these! What size shoe are you?"

"Ten," Jenn said as she put on the bra and ... hello! She looked in the mirror, turning to see herself from all sides. Wow, wasn't *that* quite the dramatic effect? Who knew? "I could just go barefoot ..."

"No, no," Eden said. "You okay with a small heel?"

"Define *small*," Jenn answered.

"Two inches?"

"I'd prefer something lower," Jenn said honestly as she took the gown that Eden had picked off the hanger. She slipped it on. "I really like the way Dan is taller than me. Not many men are, and . . ."

"Say no more," Eden said. "We'll go with one inch—just enough to make your legs look like a million dollars." She imitated Dr. Evil when she said those last few words, and Jenn had to laugh. No wonder Izzy was enthralled.

"Except, you know what, Eden? I really don't think anyone's going to see my legs," Jenn pointed out, just at the very moment that she looked in the mirror and realized that there was a huge slit up the front of the dress that completely exposed her left leg, from the very top of her thigh all the way to her foot. "Okay, so I'm wrong about *that*. Wow. I definitely need some help with the zipper."

She pushed open the curtain as she held the dress up to her chest.

Eden was there instantly, pulling up the fastener. "Deep breath," she said. "And don't worry, you won't be holding it in the entire time. There's stretch in this thing. You can exhale . . . now."

"Yikes," Jenn said as she looked at herself in the mirror. The bra gave her cleavage unlike any she'd ever had before, and the shaping of the bodice gave her an hourglass figure, while the skirt hid her too-generous hips and . . .

As large as she was, she *did* have rather nice, very shapely legs. Even *she* had to acknowledge that.

Eden set a pair of shoes in front of her—slip-ons with the tiniest nub of a heel—that were covered with sparkling rhinestones. Jenn wouldn't want to take a hike in them, but they were definitely perfect for this dress.

Still, she wasn't quite sure . . . "Isn't a wedding gown supposed to be demure?" Jenn asked. "I mean, that's the point of wearing virginal white, isn't it?"

"Are you a virgin?" Eden asked, and she didn't wait for Jenn to respond, instead answering for her. "No. Is this Las Vegas? Why, yes, it is. Trust me, this dress is demure for Vegas. I mean, you *could* go with something in red . . ."

Jenn laughed as she turned back to the mirror to look at herself again. "I'm pretty sure Dan wanted me wearing white."

"You look amazing," Eden told her. "And the rental's for the entire night. You can leave in it, you know, go dancing or...whatever. Just bring it back tomorrow before three. Izzy and I didn't get a chance to do that—we went right to San Diego after we got married. But you will. And you should. Danny's gonna want to...Well, wedding night. Right?"

The door opened and Eden turned, ready to pull the curtain closed—in case it was Danny. Which was sort of stupid. Not only were superstitions like that one—the groom shouldn't see the bride's dress before the wedding—ridiculous, they didn't really apply to people who married in order to gain custody of a teenager.

But it wasn't Dan, it was Mrs. Fudd, the woman who helped the strange little man with the faux-British accent who ran the place. The accent was particularly odd because he *did* look quite a bit like Elmer Fudd come to life.

"Finding everything?" Mrs. Fudd asked brightly. She was wearing the most amazing beehive wig, as if they'd caught her on the way to an audition for a B-52s tribute band. Still, she seemed to love her job.

"We're doing great," Eden reported.

"You *are*," the woman enthused as she peeked in at Jenn. "Oh! That's such a beautiful dress, dear. You make quite the striking figure." She turned to Eden. "What about you?"

Eden had put three blue dresses on a separate rack outside a second dressing room, and as the woman looked at them, she said, "Oh, no, dear, those are mother-of-the-bride dresses. You'll want something younger."

She immediately bustled toward the section of the room that held the bridesmaid dresses.

"No, no," Eden called after her. "You don't have to...See, I wanted something with a little jacket, just like these. I'm...a little chilly?"

She was totally lying, and Jennilyn knew exactly why. Eden—who shared Dan's genes and was gleamingly gorgeous—didn't want to risk outshining the bride.

But Eden turned to Jenn to say, "I hope you don't mind. I wanted something that covered me a little bit more. I'm tired of feeling overexposed."

Jenn smiled back at her. "Are you sure you don't want to wear something that'll give *Izzy* a heart attack?"

"Yeah, thanks, but no," Eden said, rolling her eyes. She was trying to be upbeat and light, but Jenn didn't miss the unhappiness in her eyes as her smile became forced. "I don't think that's a good idea. I already almost gave him a real one tonight and...He's still not exactly talking to me."

"You *do* know that you could've been killed," Jenn pointed out.

"A person could be killed just walking down the street." Eden took the dresses she'd picked out into other changing room and pulled the curtain.

"But you weren't exactly walking down the street," Jenn reminded her. "You took a real risk—for someone you barely know."

"Yeah, well," Eden said from behind the curtain, "you should talk—doing what you're doing for Ben."

"I'm doing it for Danny, too," Jenn pointed out.

"And I did what *I* did for Ben," Eden told her. "And for me. And you. For the little girls we once were. And all the other little girls who need help escaping from dangers they didn't ask for, in their crappy lives."

She pulled open the curtain to reveal a dress that, yes, did make her look a little older, with its lace jacket and high-necked top. Still, it fit her nicely.

"I'll wear this one," Eden said, "if it's okay with you."

Jenn nodded. "You look very elegant. I approve."

Mrs. Fudd was on her way back, holding out two different dresses, both of which looked like something Cher would've worn to the Oscars in 1985.

"We've decided on this one, thanks," Jenn cut her off before she could speak. "I think we're ready to move on to hair and makeup."

Mrs. Fudd didn't argue, she just put the dresses onto another rack and graciously led the way. "You both have shoes?" she asked.

"We do," Eden answered as she grabbed her bag, too. "Jenn, pretend you're not listening, okay? Or plug your ears." She turned to Mrs. Fudd. "I'd like to pay for this—all of it—but my brother Danny, he's the groom? I know he'd never let me. So I'm wondering if I can't pay for most of it anyway, and have you charge him for only the very cheapest basic wedding, and I don't know, maybe tell him you're giving him some kind of special military hero upgrade? He's a Navy SEAL and he was just wounded in Afghanistan, and he's trying to get custody of our little brother, so he doesn't have a lot of money to spend, but..."

Mrs. Fudd had stopped, there in the hall that led to the room with the makeup mirrors. She looked from Eden to Jenn and smiled. "Do you want to tell her, dear, or should I?" she asked Jenni.

"I pulled her aside and asked to do essentially the same thing," Jenn confessed to Eden, "while you were in the shower. I know Dan's stressing about money, so..."

Eden laughed. "Great minds think alike."

"They do," Jenn said, hugging the younger woman. "I'm going to love having you as a sister."

Eden hugged her back, hard. "Me, too. And Lord, I'm so sorry for—"

"Shh," Jenn told her, pulling back to look into Eden's eyes. "No worries, no regrets. This is what it is. We're going to make the best of it."

"You're not the only ones who think alike," Mrs. Fudd told them, taking a tissue from her sleeve and dabbing at her eyes. "Both Irving and young Ben came in a few minutes ago, requesting to pay for the ceremony as a wedding gift to the bride and groom. My husband, Alistair, let them do just that—plus he gave them our deepest military discount." She turned to Eden. "I'll let you sort it out with the two of them, so you can be part of the gift giving, too." Then back to Jenn, with a tremulous smile: "But not you—you're the bride. You know, it's a very good omen, dear—when you start your life together surrounded by such wonderful family and friends. Now, come along! Let's do your hair and makeup. We're going to make you both look marvelous!"

FRIDAY, 8 MAY 2009
2030

Izzy had a very definite sense of déjà vu when the music started and the doors at the back of the chapel opened but then immediately shut again.

All the rows of folding chairs, separated by a central aisle with a red carpet runner, were empty—as they had been when he and Eden got married.

But then, unlike now, he'd stood alone at the altar, waiting for her to "process" down the aisle. Back then, they'd invited both Eden's mother and Ben, but Ivette had been securely under Greg's thumb, and neither had showed.

Although if Izzy had known as much about Ben then as he did now, he would have insisted on driving over to the kid's house and helping to arrange a little E&E for him—escaping out his bedroom window, and then evading Greg for the hour that Izzy and Eden had gotten wed.

Of course, that was back before Greg had boarded up both windows.

But right now the kid was standing next to Izzy, between him and Dan, as they all exchanged a look, like, *I thought Eden and Jenn were coming in.*

But then, okay, there it was, the doors opened again, and this time Mrs. Fudd, with her rockin' 1960s hairdo, made sure they stayed open all the way and even stuck little jams into them with her pointy-toed shoes. She nodded and smiled at Mr. Fudd, who was standing in front of them, ready to officiate—if and when the bride ever made it into the room.

But then there they were. Eden and Jennilyn, both holding bouquets of silk flowers. Walking down that aisle together, arm in arm.

Beside him, Ben said, "Whoa," and Danny drew in a deep, sharp breath.

Because, *damn*, Skippy. If Handel's *Water Music* hadn't been playing, Izzy would've been tempted to sing a chorus or two of that old ZZ Top song. *She's got legs, she knows how to use them . . .*

Jennilyn LeMay had transformed into a bona fide, resplendent goddess. She dazzled in that dress, and if Izzy had had any remaining doubt whatsoever as to what Dan saw in her, it was gone.

Not that he was on the verge of hip-checking Danny to the side and trying to marry the woman himself. No, his appreciation was just that—admiration for a beautiful woman, with a capital W-O-M-A-N.

Besides, Eden was walking beside her. And Eden was Eden—she'd look gorgeous in a gunnysack. But in the dress *she* was wearing, with her hair up off her shoulders and her makeup artfully applied, she looked sophisticated and elegant.

Not at all like a crazy person who'd leap into a car and play demolition derby with a pair of truck-stealing, homicidal gunmen.

She looked back at him somberly, as if she, too, didn't quite recognize *him* dressed up the way he was. And the smile she gave him was small and rather sad, as if she knew what he was thinking—that he no longer had any reason to hang around.

Dan and Jenn were going to gain custody of Ben. Izzy had absolutely no doubt about that. One conversation with Jenn, and the social workers were going to start begging her to take them in, too.

Which meant Eden was free to go live her life.

And *that* meant Izzy should probably go and schedule that appointment with that divorce lawyer, the sooner, the better. Because the longer he stuck around, the more likely he was to run into circumstances like this evening, where Eden did whatever the hell she wanted while he was forced to watch with his heart in his throat.

It would be a totally different story, if he could truly make himself not care, if he could just say *whatever* to everything but the freaking great sex.

But he did care. He cared too much.

And unless he got out, ASAP, he was going to get crushed like a bug.

The sound of Danny's uneven breathing brought Izzy out of his private misery and back to the moment: music playing, women still marching down that interminably long aisle.

His lame-ass brother-in-law was having trouble keeping his air going in and out steadily. Danny-Danny-bo-banny sounded like he'd just run a 5K, or as if he'd just taken the stairs up, at a run, fifty flights. He was clearly as nervous as shit and it was entirely possible he was going to fall over. Just, *bam!* Hit the floor. Izzy had experienced a similar loss of blood to his brain when he'd been on the receiving end of a gorgeous processing bride.

Ben was oblivious, just standing between them in his rented tux, grinning his ass off, so Izzy nudged the kid and leaned close to whisper, "Be ready for your brother to faint."

"I heard that," Dan whispered back, his eyes never leaving Jenn. "And I'm fine. I'm not going to fucking *faint.*" But then he exhaled hard—pushing everything from his lungs, in a rush.

And *that* was not a good way to breathe if you didn't want to faint. "Just be ready," Izzy whispered to Ben, who was now wide-eyed.

"Zanella," Dan whispered back, "I would really appreciate it if you would please keep your... thoughts to yourself for the duration of this ceremony. It's kind of important to me."

Well, wasn't *that* a civilized request? "Absolutely, bro," Izzy told him.

"Starting right now," Dan said, adding, "Please."

Two *pleases* from the fishboy, within four-point-five seconds. That had to be some kind of relationship record for them.

Done and done. Izzy didn't say it aloud. He kept it to himself, as requested.

It was then that Eden and Jenn made it up to the altar, where—thank you, baby jeebus—now Jenn could hold on to Dan and keep him from falling on his face.

Before Mr. Fudd began to speak, Izzy took the opportunity to cross over and stand next to Eden.

His wife.

For now.

But probably not much longer.

For richer or poorer, for better or for worse, in sickness and in health, as long as we both shall reside in the same apartment in order to take care of your brother Ben . . .

Yeah, definitely not much longer.

With this ring, I dub thee obsolete.

CHAPTER
TWENTY-TWO

E den went into big-sister mode as soon as they walked into the apartment.

"Test your blood sugar," she commanded Ben as she bustled into the bedroom to change the sheets on her bed.

She and Ben had put on their regular clothes back at the wedding chapel, but Izzy still wore his dress uniform. He stood in the little foyer rather awkwardly, holding his duffel bag—a gleaming white monolith of a man, with rows of ribbons on his chest.

Ben had counted them before the ceremony. He had exactly the same number as Danny.

"I think it's better if I camp out here, with Ben, tonight," Izzy said to Eden, his voice low, as she emerged from the bedroom to get clean sheets from the hall closet.

"Oh," she said. His words had stopped her in her tracks, and she glanced quickly over at Ben, who lowered his head, pretending he was focused on pricking his finger and testing his blood.

"I think it's...best," Izzy said again. "We need to talk and...I'm sorry, but I'm too tired to do it tonight."

Eden turned away from him. "You can have the bedroom," she said. "I'll sleep out here."

"I'm not going to put you out of your own bed."

"It's not my bed," she told him. "It's just the bed where I sleep. So it really doesn't matter."

"If it doesn't matter," Izzy started, "then—"

"For the love of God," Ben interrupted them, "just flip a coin. Or better yet, apologize to each other. Everyone makes mistakes. Get over it, and move on!"

They both turned and stared at him.

"What's your reading?" Eden asked.

Jesus. "I'm okay," Ben said. "Will you just—"

But she'd already turned back to Izzy. "If the mattress on the floor is too uncomfortable—"

"It's fine," he told her.

"But if it's not..."

"I'll tell you," Izzy said, "and we can trade."

"Fine," she said, and went into the bedroom and closed the door.

Izzy took his bag into the bathroom and closed *that* door, leaving Ben alone in the silence. This was even more fun than that awkward car ride home.

The SEAL wasn't in the bathroom for very long. The toilet flushed, the water ran in the sink, and he came out in a T-shirt and boxers, still carrying his bag. He set it on the coffee table that had been pushed aside to make room for both mattresses, and flopped down on the larger one, pulling the sheets and blankets over him. "Get the lights when you're ready to turn in, kid," he mumbled. "No need to rush, I can sleep through a hurricane." But then he opened his eyes and lifted his head. "Stupid thing to say. Sorry about that."

"Whatever," Ben said with a shrug.

"You okay on that smaller mattress?" he asked.

"It's fine," Ben told him, inwardly rolling his eyes. They were all fine. Everything was fine. Except it wasn't. It was very, very un-fine. "Izzy, come on. You've got to go in there and talk to her. I know she's not perfect, but you're not, either. I mean, Jesus..."

But Izzy just shook his head. "I can't do it right now," he said. "I'm still so..." He sighed heavily. "I'm angry—I'm not going to lie to you about that. But I haven't done more than nap in two days, and I need to sleep before...Really, Ben, there're times when talking doesn't help. It only makes it worse, if you can't be careful about what you say and how you say it. And I can't, right now. I know myself well enough to...I'll talk to her in the morning, I promise."

Ben nodded, but he knew the truth.

They weren't talking tonight, because *he* was here. And they wouldn't really talk tomorrow, either, because Ben would still be in the way. They weren't going to talk until they had real privacy, by which point it could well be too late.

Izzy had put his head back down on the pillow and it was possible he was already asleep.

Ben turned off the lights and went into the bathroom to brush his teeth, wishing that he'd never stopped to talk to Neesha in the mall. And yet, at the same time, he was glad that he had. Because without Eden's help tonight, Neesha would have been killed.

Tomorrow? He was going to go out and find her. And he was going to persuade her to come home with him, and sit down with Danny and Izzy and Eden and Jenn. They would know what to do, and they would make sure that she was safe.

And maybe having someone with bigger problems to deal with would help Izzy and Eden realize that life was too short to throw away their relationship.

God, he hoped so...

For the first time in years, Ben had started looking forward to the future. Having Danny and Eden in his life again was a miracle he'd never dreamed possible. And then to add in both Izzy and Jenn...?

Over the past few days, he'd had a glimpse of what life with them would be like.

And after the hell of Crossroads and the purgatory that had been his life with Greg, it was nirvana.

It wouldn't be perfect. He knew that. Money was and would

remain an issue. And it wouldn't be easy, either, when Danny and Izzy went overseas.

But there would be laughter.

And he would be hugged.

Even when he was little, Eden had been the only one who'd ever hugged him. But over the past few days, he'd been hugged by Izzy and Jenn and even Danny, too. That had been weird, and Ben had been surprised and he'd frozen before he could hug his brother back. But he'd hugged Danny tonight, after the wedding and . . .

It was amazing how such a little, seemingly insignificant thing could matter so much. It was amazing how quickly he could move from feeling isolated, desperate, and alone, to feeling surrounded by love and genuine affection.

Ben still didn't quite feel completely safe, but that would change the moment they got into their car and drove away from this city and Greg. And yes, it was a little scary to think about living in San Diego. He'd never been there, not even to visit, and he had no idea what it would be like. School would probably suck, but school was probably going to suck wherever he lived.

It would be bearable, though, knowing he had a place to go—a home—where he could be himself, where he was *loved* for being himself.

Ben looked at himself in the bathroom mirror as he put his toothbrush back in the cup Eden had put out for him. With Dan, Jenni, and Izzy all staying here, all four of the slots had already been filled in the holder that stuck out from the wall.

Except, they weren't. Not anymore.

There was an empty spot.

Which meant that Izzy had already packed his toothbrush.

Whatever talk he was intending to have with Eden in the morning? It was highly likely that it would include the word *good-bye*. That is, if he wasn't lying to Ben, and was, in truth, planning to sneak away before the break of dawn, the way so many of Ivette's countless boyfriends had done.

If Deshawndra were here, she would urge Ben to act. Helping Neesha *could* bring Izzy and Eden together. He could find the girl and kill two birds with one stone.

He could practically hear her voice: *Neesha needs your help. So do those two fools, sleeping in two separate beds tonight. Don't wait for them—you'll be waiting forever.*

But…The men who were after Neesha knew what Ben looked like. They were armed. And dangerous. He couldn't just go to the mall and look for her.

But people see what they expect to see. You made yourself stand out. Now make yourself blend in.

Ben leaned in close to look at his hair in the bathroom mirror. His roots were showing, but to get rid of the black dye job, he'd have to give himself a buzz cut. And he wasn't ready for that.

No, instead he'd go blond. There was a twenty-four-hour drugstore down on the corner. He could sneak out and pick up some Miss Clairol Whatever and be back here in a matter of minutes. He could bleach and color and even cut his hair tonight, and be ready to pop on over to the mall first thing in the morning, stopping at the Salvation Army to trade in his black jeans and T-shirt for a pair of shorts and a shirt in bright colors.

Once he did that?

Without his Goth costume and makeup, his own brother and sister wouldn't recognize him.

Do it.

Ben left the bathroom and went back into the living room, where Izzy was sleeping soundly. He crept past him and lifted the chair cushion under which he'd hidden the stash of money that Izzy and Eden had removed from its hiding place in Greg and Ivette's house. He didn't take the entire envelope—he just grabbed a couple of twenties, because he was uncertain as to how much the hair color kit would cost.

One thing he *did* know? Coloring his hair was going to smell. When he'd dyed his hair black, it had stunk to high heavens.

With a little luck, both Eden and Izzy would sleep through it. If not, he would play dumb. *I couldn't sleep, and I wanted a change...*

Ben pocketed the money and turned off all the lights, and with his clothes and sneakers still on, he climbed beneath the sheets and blankets on the twin-sized air mattress. All he had to do was wait for Eden to emerge from her bedroom to use the bathroom, and mumble good night as if he were already falling asleep...

Then, after she went into her room, he could dash down to the drugstore and be back without either of them ever knowing he'd been gone.

Jenn didn't let Danny carry her over the threshold when they went into the hotel honeymoon suite.

It was more than merely impractical when it came to caring for his recent injury. It was... too much for her to take after the wedding vows and the rings and that incredible kiss he'd given her at Mr. Fudd's command...

You may kiss the bride.

She felt as if she were doing role-playing make-believe with a lover who was far more into the game than she was.

It was doubly strange, because she'd always thought of Danny as someone who had a little trouble living in the moment. He worried a great deal about his family responsibilities, and he always seemed to carry those worries with him.

And yes, she knew he had to be different when out on one of his SEAL team missions. He would have to focus intensely, in order to keep himself and his teammates out of peril. Jenn suspected, at those times, that he compartmentalized and just pushed everything else aside.

Kind of the way he was doing right now.

Tonight, *she* was his full focus, and it was rather disarming.

She'd felt that focus before—on the night that he'd seduced her.

He'd pretended to read her palm and, because of the lines on her hand, accused her of being too pragmatic.

She'd proven him wrong by leaping into bed with him. Or maybe she'd proven him right, because having sex with men she'd just met was not in her usual no-nonsense repertoire.

Of course, Jenn had outdone herself tonight, in terms of nonpragmatic behavior. Or maybe this *was* pragmatic—marrying a man in order to help him save his brother from a terrible, life-threatening situation at home. But it should have been done quickly and quietly—matter-of-factly, minus the trumpet fanfare.

It definitely had felt weird to do it *this* way, all fancy and formal, with the dress and the uniform and the flowers and the pictures and the honeymoon suite.

Still, Dan was so clearly enjoying the entire experience, Jenn didn't have the heart not to smile back at him as he opened the bottle of champagne that had been waiting for them in their suite, chilling in a bucket of ice.

There were roses, too—three giant bouquets—strategically placed around the spacious room.

Everything was lovely—and Danny was, too, dressed as he was all in white, with those colorful rows of ribbons adorning his broad chest.

He poured them both glasses and handed her one and smiled into her eyes as he touched his flute to hers and gave a toast. "To my beautiful wife, Mrs. Jennilyn Gillman."

She'd surprised him at the chapel, when she'd declined to keep her own name. He'd clearly expected her to. He'd also clearly been charmingly pleased that she hadn't, and she didn't have the heart to tell him that it was a strategic move on her part. Although she had no idea if presenting such a unified front would help them gain custody of Ben, she knew it would be useful in the coming months when dealing with his schoolteachers and doctors—with all of whom she expected to have a large amount of contact.

And okay, yeah, maybe she *was* also guilty of being sappy and sentimental, but part of her liked the fantasy elements that accompanied the tradition of a woman taking her man's name. There was a sense of ownership there that went both ways. She was his woman, his wife. And he was her husband, her man.

And she certainly liked the idea of Dan Gillman being *her man*.

"You've been really quiet," he said now as he gazed at her with those chocolate-brown eyes. "Are you okay?"

"I'm a little freaked out," she admitted, taking another sip from her elegant glass.

"I'm not," he said as he set his wineglass on the sideboard, his movement sure and commanding. Maybe it was the uniform, but he seemed bigger, too. Older and supremely confident. Not that he wasn't all those things before, but somehow, tonight, it was amplified. "I *was*, though—a little bit. Right before the ceremony." He smiled. "Zanella actually thought I was going to faint. I mean, I wasn't, but . . . I guess I was looking a little pale. I *do* remember thinking, *Holy shit*."

"I think that's where I am right now," Jenn confessed.

"Mine was a good *holy shit*," he said as he took her glass from her and set it down next to his, turning back to her with a smile.

"Mine's . . . heavy disbelief," she told him. "Mixed with a little fear, you know. Of the unknown."

He laughed as he took her hand and gently pulled her into his arms. She had to tilt her head to look up into his eyes, which was very nice.

"That's kind of funny," he told her, "because for the first time in forever, with you by my side? I feel like I can finally handle anything that the future brings."

His soft words made him romance incarnate, but he took it a giant step further by leaning down, taking his time to look into her eyes before kissing her. It was a replay of the kiss he'd given her in the chapel. Sweet but thorough. Tender but laced with fire. And Jenn felt herself melting as she kissed him back.

And then, in unspoken but mutual agreement, she helped him out of his uniform, even as he helped her out of her dress.

And, God, he was beautiful, with sun-kissed skin covering well-defined muscles. Yes, he was still a little too skinny, a by-product of his recent tour of duty and ensuing hospital stay, but she knew that would change as soon as he was cleared to start working out more strenuously.

It amazed her that he could look at her with the same ardent appreciation, but he did, and it wasn't an act.

Please God, don't let it be an act...

As Jenn fell back with him onto the bed, she pulled herself away from his kisses long enough to remind him, "I'm on top."

"Works for me," he said, kissing her again, even as he rolled himself onto his back.

Which left her straddling him, exactly where they both wanted her to be. He was hard, and she was ready—God, she was more than ready. It had been so long...

But she was also hyperaware of his bandaged leg, and she told him, "Don't you dare let me hurt you."

"You *could* give me a safe word," he suggested, grinning up at her, even as he teased her with his body, sliding himself against her.

"I'm serious," Jenn said, but kind of blew it by laughing, because it was impossible not to laugh when he was smiling at her like that.

"I can tell that you're *very* serious," he countered.

"I'm going to be mad if I have to rush you to the hospital after this. So slow and easy, okay? We've got all the time in the world to attempt to break the bed. Well, not this bed. But *our* bed." God, they were going to have to go shopping for a bed.

Danny's eyes were half closed, and he'd caught his lower lip between his perfect white teeth as he just kept that gentle motion going, sliding himself against her. "Slow and easy also works for me," he told her. "Any other rules I need to know about, Mrs. Gillman, ma'am? Because I'm waiting on your green light..."

Jenni leaned over and kissed him, and he seemed to take that as the *go* he was waiting for, because as he kissed her back, he simultaneously reached between them and shifted his hips and—God!—pushed himself home.

She heard herself moan even as he did the same, and yes, God, yes, it felt so good, but he'd skipped a step.

"Condom," she said, in between kissing him back, even as she moved on top of him, pushing him more deeply inside of her.

"Oh, yeah," he breathed. "God, Jenni, that's so good..."

He was caught up in the moment—she was, too. But she was also the one who could get pregnant, so she forced herself, if not to stop, then at least to reach over toward the box of condoms he'd tossed onto the bedside table.

But Danny knew what she was doing, and instead of helping, of shifting them closer, of pulling himself out and protecting her, he held her in place with one hand and grabbed her wrist with the other, stopping her.

"What if we don't," he breathed as he gazed up at her, and God, he was actually serious.

"I could get pregnant," she told him, but despite her dire warning, she didn't move, didn't pull herself off of him.

"We're married," he said, as if that meant something.

Jenn shook her head. "Danny, I don't—"

"I do," he said. "I meant it when I said I *do*."

She was astonished. "You *want* us to... have a... baby?"

He was nodding yes before she'd finished her question. "Someday. Yeah."

She was staring down at him with her mouth open, but she managed to close it and ask, "Someday like in five years? Because that's really different from someday like in nine very short months."

"It's Las Vegas," Dan said, and at first his words seemed to be a non sequitur. But then he added, "Let's gamble. Let's make tonight special. And if we end up with a souvenir..."

"A *souvenir*...?" Jenn repeated with disbelief.

"That just means it's meant to be. We'll be ready if we need to. Jenni, I love you. Don't you get it? I didn't marry you because it's convenient. I married you because I want to spend the rest of my life with you."

• • •

Dan's very naked wife was looking down at him as if he'd just spoken to her in Hungarian or maybe Vietnamese.

So Dan backpedaled. "It's okay if you don't want to," he told her. "I was just... I don't know, I guess I got a little drunk on the... romance of it all. Our wedding, and then, making love to you after all this time of not being able to...? But I don't want to do anything that makes you uncomfortable. I really don't, and okay, shit, I'm lying. I'm, like, ten seconds from coming because you're so goddamn beautiful, and Christ, this feels so good—"

She leaned down and kissed him, which was close to the opposite of what he'd expected, which was for her to pull herself off of him so she could hand him an apology and a condom.

Instead, she kissed him, and while she kissed him she moved, pushing him even more deeply inside of her, which wasn't just close to it, it *was* the opposite of what he'd expected.

And Danny stopped kissing her long enough to breathe, "Ah, God, baby, are you sure...?" Because although his estimate of ten seconds had been an exaggeration, it hadn't been *that* big of an exaggeration.

And Jenn *wasn't* sure—he knew that, because he knew her—but she didn't say it. She only said, "I've never done this before. Not ever," as she kept that movement going. Languorously slowly, she lifted herself off of him, then pushed him deeply home. Again. And again.

"Me neither," he gasped. He'd never, *ever* wanted to gamble before this—not when it came to sex without birth control. And it sort of made sense, because he'd also never before made love to a woman who was his wife.

"Never?" Jenn asked him. "No temptation?"

"None." Jesus, she was beautiful, and she was *his*, and he pushed himself up to meet her as she lowered herself down. And even though she was a big woman, he was even bigger, and it made her close her eyes and moan and—Christ, yes—grind herself against him, which pushed him still even more deeply inside of her. It was an unbelievable turn-on, especially when she looked down at him with such sheer desire in her beautiful eyes.

"So good..." she breathed as she pulled herself up and then started the whole long, slow slide back down, all over again.

"Jenni," he gasped, it was all he could manage, but she somehow knew that he was trying to tell her that, God, he was going to come, and that the idea of his doing so without a barrier between them was going to blow his mind, because if he *did* get her pregnant, it *was* for-freaking-ever. And he wanted that, more than he'd ever wanted anything or anyone, and Jesus, he wanted to roll her over onto her back and slam himself into her, because he knew that she loved it hard and she loved it ferocious and physical, same way he did, because she was his perfect match in every way and she was *his*. And yeah, slow was nice, he definitely liked slow, too, but it had been *so long* ...

She somehow knew at least *some* of that, and she moved faster and harder, with short, deep strokes that were pretty damn close to exactly what he wanted, especially when he pushed himself up to meet her with enough force to make her gasp.

And Jenni came first, and she came with such abandon, it was beautiful to watch, and he tried to hold on, because he wanted it to last forever.

But he couldn't do it, because she started to laugh—it was *that* good—and when she smiled down at him with such love and trust in her eyes, he knew once again that he'd finally found what he'd spent his entire life searching for. And he felt such a fierce and joyful rush of possession—*mine!*—he let go.

And it was crazy how primal it felt, as if he were claiming her, marking her, and waves of emotion filled him as he felt his release surge inside of her again and again and again, as she gripped him and clung to him and sighed her pleasure.

And then it was over, but it wasn't over, not really. It was just beginning—their wonderful, crazy life together.

And the magnitude of what he'd just done—what *they'd* just

done—settled gently down around him as he held her tightly, as they both caught their breath.

And it didn't freak him out, didn't frighten him, didn't provide even the slightest sliver of doubt.

On the contrary.

He was awed by the strength of his feelings—by her feelings, too, and by the knowledge that she'd already sacrificed so much just to help him, just to be with him, to be part of his life.

She'd given up her job, her home, put her career ambitions on hold...

And Dan knew, right then and there, that she was *not* going to be the only one to make sacrifices for their impromptu little family—or, after tonight, maybe their *not* so impromptu slightly bigger family.

"I love you," he whispered, and he felt her sigh and smile, her face still pressed against his neck.

"I believe you," she said. She lifted her head to look at him and he saw an echo of her words in her gorgeous eyes. "And I love you, too. It feels pretty miraculous, doesn't it? I wish I could go back and hear you say *I do* again. I think I didn't quite believe it at the time."

"I do," he told her, putting all of his conviction into the words.

She smiled and kissed him and whispered, "I do, too."

"Hmm," he said, "does this mean we also get to do a replay of the consummating of our vows?"

Jenni laughed at that, pushing his hair back from his forehead as she gazed down at him. "Are you *trying* to get me pregnant?"

"I might be," he admitted, pulling her down to kiss her again.

She laughed as she kissed him back, because, yes, he was starting to get hard again, and she felt it because he was still inside of her.

"I was thinking," he said quietly, "that it's time for me to leave the teams. Maybe go to work full-time for Tommy Paoletti. For Troubleshooters Incorporated—you know, his personal security team?"

He'd surprised her again. Completely.

"That way I wouldn't be gone all the time," he continued. "And we wouldn't have to wait five years. We could go for it, knowing I'd be around when little Phil or Jill was born."

Jenn laughed. "Phil and Jill Gillman?"

"Kids love it when their names rhyme," he told her, unable to keep a straight face, which gave away the fact that he was kidding. At least about the names he'd chosen for their unborn children.

He pulled her down to kiss her again, even as he shifted his hips, pushing himself more deeply inside of her. Another few minutes, and he was going to be fully ready for round two.

"What do you say, Gillman?" he asked her when he let her up for air.

And she smiled at his use of her new last name. But her smile faded as she got serious. "I think," she said, "that you are an extremely romantic and passionate man. And I also think you should sit with this idea, and see how you feel about it in a few days or weeks. And I also think," she added quickly before he could protest, "that I'll support you, completely, whatever choice you make. But I went into this relationship with my eyes wide open. I know what it means to be married to a Navy SEAL, and I'm prepared for that. So make sure your decisions are for the right reasons, okay?"

Danny nodded. "I really—"

"Shh." She cut him off with a kiss. "We'll have a lot of time to talk about this tomorrow. Right now? I'm pretty sure you can't get me any *more* pregnant than you may well have already gotten me, so...If you're still thinking what I'm thinking, and I'm pretty sure you are"— she moved against him, and smiled—"Yes, I do believe I can read your mind..."

He laughed and kissed her. And he knew without a doubt that meeting and falling for Jennilyn was the best thing that had ever happened to him.

CHAPTER
TWENTY-THREE

Neesha had learned her lesson and was back to erring even further on the side of caution.

She hid in the shadows, in the courtyard of the apartment building where Ben's sister lived, just watching and waiting in the still of the night, while nothing moved.

In all of the hours that she'd been there, she'd watched plenty of people come and go. All had been in a hurry. But then the foot traffic slowed and lights went off all over the compound.

To her dismay, she'd fallen asleep at some point, and she jerked awake, her heart pounding, as a man and a woman came into the courtyard, arguing loudly. As they went into their first-floor dwelling, Neesha realized that the light was on in Eden's apartment. The bedroom window, which looked out over the courtyard, was aglow. But then, as she watched, the light went off and the window went dark.

She almost stood up, almost crept to the stairs so she could climb up them and scratch at the door before they fell asleep, praying that she was right and that they were on her side and would help her.

Instead, some instinct made her wait. Something—the whisper of footsteps, a shift in the air as large bodies moved in the darkness—made her curl even more tightly into herself.

And she caught her breath as her blood froze in her veins because it was the two men from the mall—the bald man named Jake and the man with the hat—and God save her, they were with Todd, whom Mr. Nelson had sent to kill her.

They didn't see her. They didn't even think to look around—believing that they were alone in the deserted garden.

One of them—Jake—spoke. His voice was low, but it carried clearly to Neesha. "The older brother and the husband are military, so shoot to kill. But we want both the kid and his bitch of a sister alive. Are we clear?"

The other two men nodded, and Todd, always eager, started for the stairs. But Jake stopped him.

"Masks," he said. "We want them to think we're going to let them go after they give us what we want."

And Neesha didn't understand what he meant, until they all reached into their pockets and pulled on hats that stretched all the way down to cover their faces.

As they started for the stairs, she knew she had to act. She had to stand up, to shout, to scream.

And then she had to run so that they'd kill her now, quickly, with a bullet to the head. Because if they took her alive, she'd die slowly and painfully.

But she couldn't move, couldn't speak. Terror had her too securely in its claws. All she could do was tremble as she watched.

But then the three men stopped before they started up the stairs. They moved quickly, fading back into the shadows because someone was coming.

God help her, it was Ben, coming swiftly down the stairs, his movement graceful and sure.

And Neesha still couldn't scream through her frozen throat, not even to warn him.

As he reached the bottom, one of the men—Jake—said, "Jesus, it's the kid," and Todd and the other man moved toward him.

Ben realized he wasn't alone, realized who they were, and he scrambled back toward the stairs, even as he opened his mouth to try to scream. The first came out as little more than a squeak, "Help!" But then he drew in air and let loose. *"Hel—"*

One of them must've hit him in the head, because his shout was silenced and his body went limp.

But lights went on in the apartment nearest to that set of stairs, and Jake and Todd and the other man with the hat grabbed Ben and ran.

Neesha could see the entrance to the street from where she was hiding, and she watched as the three men hustled Ben into a waiting car, being driven by a fourth man. They took off with a squeal of tires, even as that downstairs apartment door opened and an elderly man leaned out.

"Keep it down out here," he called crossly. "People are trying to sleep!"

He slammed the door shut, and the sudden sharp sound freed Neesha, unfreezing her.

She stood up, careful to stay in the shadows, as she moved down that entrance toward the street.

It was deserted. There were no cars idling, no one there.

And even though she knew the right thing to do was to run upstairs to Eden's apartment and hammer on the door, terror still coursed through her veins.

And when she ran, it was down the street, away from the apartment, as fast as her trembling legs could carry her.

SATURDAY, 9 MAY 2009
OH DARK HUNDRED

Izzy awoke with a start, and a very solid sense that something was wrong.

He was instantly alert, and even though it was dark, he knew immediately where he was: on the cheap foam mattress on the floor of the living room in Eden's Las Vegas apartment.

He also knew that he was, absolutely, alone in that bed. *And* that it had been his choice that put him out here, and not with Eden, in her bedroom.

No doubt about it, he was a fucking idiot. And yeah, *that* was wrong. If he'd caved and gone in there with her, *then* he would've been a fucking idiot. Instead, he was a decidedly *non*-fucking idiot, but an idiot just the same.

Over by the window, the air conditioner was roaring, working desperately to cool the place down and not quite succeeding. The clock on the ancient VCR told him that it was four minutes after midnight. He hadn't slept that long—only about two hours—but he'd slept hard, and he already felt more like himself, i.e., significantly less angry and enormously more horny, which was dangerous, considering Eden was in the next room.

Still, he had to take a leak, so he pushed himself off the floor and headed toward the bathroom, careful not to bump the air mattress where Ben was fast asleep, a silent, motionless lump beneath the covers.

He didn't bother to turn on the light—there was plenty coming in from the streetlamp outside the narrow bathroom window, so he just pushed the door closed and locked it.

It wasn't easy to whiz with a boner, but Izzy didn't believe in having to think about death and destruction simply in order to keep from spraying the bathroom floor and walls—even though he'd witnessed more than his share during his adult life. He'd been there, done that, and had learned to process it ASAP, so bringing it back into his focus was never an option.

He hadn't yet, however, processed his current problems with Eden and it shouldn't have taken more than a quick replay of the way she'd driven the rental directly into that truck to give him a total freak-out softie, but that didn't work, either. So he set to work alleviating the problem the old-fashioned way, with a little bit of soap and water from the sink on his hands, and a fantasy of Eden running like a silent movie through his brain.

His fantasy version of Eden looked like Eden and smiled like Eden and moved like Eden and fucked liked Eden. And as long as he kept her in the imaginary apartment in his mind, where she could cook and clean and perpetually wait for him to come home so she could rock his world, like some kind of a Stepford wife, he didn't have to imagine her putting herself into harm's way to create a diversion that would save the littlest hooker-with-a-heart-of-gold in Vegas.

Except the problem was, when he tried to imagine that version of Eden? She wasn't Eden.

And Izzy recognized with a flash of insight that came from no longer having a completely sleep-deprived brain, that he hadn't been angry with Eden merely because she'd put her life in danger by behaving foolishly and impetuously. Because Jenn had been right. What Eden had done was incredibly courageous. And while it wasn't what *he* would have done had he been behind the wheel of the rental car—he would've gone after Neesha, gotten her into the car, and gotten them all the hell away from the bad guys—it was pretty damn close.

No way would *he* have left a little girl at the mercy of two men who were hunting her, even if he didn't know why. So really, why be so angry with Eden for doing what he would have done?

No, she didn't have his training or his experience or his size or his strength. But her choices had been limited. Stand there, wringing her hands and watching while Neesha got grabbed or gunned down? Run to get him to help, which would've come too late? Or do what she'd done—act and, yes, put herself at risk, because not to act was unthinkable, despite her lack of training, experience, size, and strength.

Although as far as strength went? What Eden didn't have in muscle mass she more than made up for in sheer will.

And the truth was, when it came to the real Eden versus his appallingly unattractive and plastic Stepford wife version? It was her very impetuousness and crazy-ass courage that had attracted him to her, right from the start. No shrinking violet, she. She was who she was—with plenty of swagger and attitude, and damn, just thinking about her—the real her—made him hot.

Hotter.

And yes, while watching her take those crazy risks tonight had damn near given him a stroke, the real problem here was his, not hers.

"Whoops, sorry—*whoa.*"

And...fucking fabulous, it was Eden—although if Izzy had to make a choice between Eden or Ben, as to who was the better candidate to walk in on him in the bathroom while his dick was in his hand...? Well, it was probably best that it was Eden.

Of course, being Eden, she didn't beat an immediate retreat. She just stood there, looking at him through the now half-open door. Any other woman on the planet would have been embarrassed for both of them—yes, mostly for him, the masturbating loser—and would've at least averted her eyes. Not so much Eden. She was absolutely checking him out, probably because—Izzy being who he was—he refused to try to hide what he'd been doing and fumble himself back into his shorts. Instead, he just stood there, temporarily on pause, and stared right back at her.

"You really should learn to lock the door," she told him.

"I *did* lock it," he whispered back. "Do you *mind?* I'd like a little privacy...?"

He turned his back on her—conversation over—but she didn't take the social cue, assuming social cues worked in this situation. Although yes, she eventually closed the bathroom door, but only after she put herself on his side of it. She locked it, checked that it was securely latched—a step he'd apparently missed when he'd first come in—and then sat up on the sink counter. "Do *you* mind if I watch?"

He laughed his surprise. "This isn't exactly a spectator sport."

"I'm curious," she said. "Plus, it's unbelievably hot."

"You think that me, jerking off in the bathroom, is hot," he said, lacing his voice with his disbelief.

"I think that you, anywhere, is hot," Eden told him, which was such a freaking line, especially coming out of a woman who looked the way she did. She was wearing an old T-shirt and a pair of boxers, with her face scrubbed of all makeup and her hair back in a braid, and she *still* managed to be hotter than ninety-nine-point-nine percent of all human beings who walked the earth. "Plus, I couldn't sleep, either— and maybe I can get some pointers. I mean, your technique must be pretty good if you'd prefer this to . . . being with me."

And just like that, all of her cockiness and badass attitude vanished, leaving her vulnerable and uncertain. Izzy could see her hurt in her eyes—she didn't try to hide it as she gazed at him.

And looking at her like that triggered something in him—a wave of sorrow so intense, he had to sit down. So he put himself away and he lowered the lid of the toilet and he sat.

Of course, she immediately apologized. "Sorry," she said. "I didn't mean to—"

"No," he stopped her. "Don't. Because it's me, Eden. It's all me. And I'm the one who's sorry."

Her face caught the light from the window, and he could tell from the way she was looking back at him that she knew exactly what he meant. But she didn't want to understand, so she shook her head. "I don't—"

"I can't be who you want me to be," he told her honestly. "I just can't do it anymore."

She leaned forward. "I don't want you to be anyone but—"

"Yeah, you do," he said. "You only want the happy fuck-me guy."

Eden laughed at that—a burst of disbelieving air. "You think I want—"

"I'm leaving," he interrupted her. "Tomorrow. You don't need me here, so . . . I really should get back to the base."

Now she was looking at him and nodding as if in agreement. But her lips were pressed tightly together, like a little kid who was trying desperately not to cry.

"So that's it, then?" she said. "I mess up, *once. One time.* And you leave . . . ?"

"That's not why I'm leaving," he told her quietly.

"You *said* you'd *stay*," she started hotly.

"For as long as you needed me," he finished for her. He sighed.

"Sweetheart, let's be honest here. You *don't* need me anymore. Dan and Jenn are going to help Ben and...He's going to be great with them. It's better this way, not just for Ben, but—"

"For *you*," she said, sliding down off the sink. "Yeah, okay, I get it. Sorry to have inconvenienced you. I'm glad I don't have to do that anymore."

Izzy stood up, too. "*Not* for me," he said, moving to block her path back to the door. "For *you*. This way you don't have to sacrifice—"

"Yeah, sorry, I think you're projecting—"

"And this way"—he raised his voice to speak over her—"Ben gets to live in a home that isn't so goddamn dysfunctional for a change, where we don't have to keep *lying* to him about why we're together. He's still innocent enough to believe that people get married because they love each other—"

"Oh, like Danny and Jenn?" Eden countered.

"Exactly like Dan and Jenn," Izzy shot back. "You *know* she loves him. You can't spend more than two seconds in a room with her, without feeling it—the Force is strong in that one."

"So what?" Eden said. "She loves him. Big whoop. Doesn't it fit your definition of dysfunctional if it doesn't go both ways?"

"I'm sorry, weren't you there tonight?" he answered her stupid question with a stupid question of his own. "Have you ever, in your entire life, seen Danny that happy? I thought he was going to shit himself with joy. And believe me, that wasn't about Ben. That was *all* Jennilyn. If that's not love? I don't know what is."

Eden was silent at that, because he was right, and she damn well knew it.

"It's better for Ben this way," Izzy told her, quietly now. "And yeah, okay, it *is* better for me—"

"Because you don't want to be *Happy Fuck-Me Guy*," she said. "Glad we worked that out. Sorry to have put you through all that inconvenient sex."

"*And* it's better for you," he finished. "Eden, you can have a life."

"Getting rich from stripping," she said, "because screw you, you can't tell me what I can and cannot do if you're...leaving me." She started to cry then, with huge gulping sobs, as if something had broken inside of her, and she couldn't keep her emotions hidden any longer.

Izzy was caught by surprise. She was usually so stoic that a single escaped tear was, for her, the equivalent of an emotional explosion that needed to be immediately brushed away and hidden.

She turned and ran—no doubt horrified by her outburst—flinging the bathroom door open so that it hit the wall with a bang.

She escaped into her bedroom, slamming that door, too, and as Izzy prepared to follow, to apologize and—holy shit—to try to talk her out of the stripper thing, which was clearly a knee-jerk reaction, he stuck his head into the living room, to reassure Ben that everything was okay.

He expected to see the kid sitting up. There was no way he could've slept through those door slams, but he hadn't moved. In fact, he wasn't even stirring, and Izzy went toward him to investigate, concerned that he was sick. The whole diabetes thing was a little scary and he didn't know enough about it, other than the fact that kids with it sometimes went into comas.

Another good reason to leave the parenting to Danny and Jenn. Izzy would be tempted to check on the kid twenty times each night. God help him if he ever had a baby of his own...

"Yo, Ben," he said as he bent down to look. He found himself face-to-face not with a face, but with one of the sofa pillows. He pulled the covers back and, hell yeah, it was classic high jinks from overnight camp. Ben had put pillows beneath his blankets to make it look as if he were in bed, asleep.

Son of a bitch.

Izzy slapped on the light both in the entryway and in the kitchen, but the kid had definitely left the apartment. In fact, he'd left behind a note on the kitchen table.

Ran to the drugstore on the corner. Be right back.

Son of a bitch.

"Eden!" Izzy grabbed his cargo shorts, and on his way back to the bathroom, he hammered on the bedroom door. "I know this is bad timing, but Ben's gone AWOL."

She opened the door immediately, eyes red, and he thrust the note at her, then headed into the bathroom, stepping into his shorts as he went.

This time, he had no problem with the mechanics of taking a leak.

And also because, this time, he'd left the door open, it wasn't *that* big a surprise when Eden came in, too, to splash water on her blotchy face.

"Do you think he left because he heard us fighting?" she asked as she dried herself on one of her faded pink towels.

"I don't know," Izzy said as he flushed and zipped, moving past her into the living room to jam his feet into his boots. "But I'll ask him when I find him. *After* I kick his ass."

"Yeah, well, you can't kick his ass until *I* kick his ass first," Eden said, hopping as she slipped her feet into her sneakers, even as she fastened the button on her cutoff shorts and stuck a baseball cap onto her head. She scooped up both her cell phone and her keys and was out the door before Izzy.

SATURDAY, MAY 9, 2009
1:06 A.M.

Jenn wasn't sure which woke her up—the sound of Danny's cell phone ringing in the darkness, shrill and persistent, or his whispering, "Shit, shit, shit..." as he tried to pull his arm out from beneath her without waking her.

But he couldn't find his phone and he let loose with a whole string of creative sailor words—all sotto voce—until she told him, "Your pants are over the back of that chair...? By the window...?" as she sat up, turned on the light, and reached for her glasses.

"Damn it!" he said as the moment he dug his phone from his pants pocket, it stopped ringing. He turned to look at her. "God, baby, I'm *so* sorry that woke you."

"It's all right," she said, because there were plenty of bad things one could find when turning on the light in the middle of the night. Her naked new husband was not one of them. "I know you're not supposed to turn off your cell phone, but...Was that...work?"

She knew that, as a Navy SEAL, when he got the call, he had to go.

"No," he said. "I'm not...It would have to be World War Three for them to call me in while I'm out on medical leave." He shook his head as he glanced down at his phone, then looked back at her, trepidation in his eyes. "This is a different World War Three. That was my mother."

Jenn glanced over at the clock on the hotel bedside table to find that it read 1:06. What kind of mother returned her son's phone call after one o'clock in the morning? And okay, maybe that was unfair. Maybe a mother who was used to her son being in exotic time zones would call whenever she could, hoping he'd be available. Plus, the messages he'd left *had* stressed how urgent it was that she call him immediately...

"You could call her right back," she suggested.

Danny nodded, looking down at the phone somewhat expectantly. "I could," he said. "But I'm waiting to see if..."

The phone beeped.

"Jackpot," Dan said. "She left a message." He dialed his voice mail as he came over to sit on the edge of the bed. "I know this is probably reading as really cowardly but—"

"Baby, you know I don't think that," Jenn told him.

He put his hand on her foot, holding on to her through the blanket as if he needed that contact as he listened to Ivette's message. Jenn couldn't hear what his mother said, but he made a face as he listened, then winced again and said, "Jesus," as he hung up.

"I gotta call Zanella," he said, already redialing his phone. "Apparently Ivette didn't lose her phone, it just ran out of juice and she didn't have her charger. She's home now and..."

Izzy must've picked up—no doubt thrilled to be awakened at this ungodly hour—as Danny said, "Yeah, Z, it's Gillman. Sorry to wake you, man, but I just got a call from Ivette. She's back and she left a message saying that Greg's got a bender going—she doesn't sound all that sober herself—but she said he's threatening to go over to Eden's to get Ben and..." He paused, then replied, "Yeah. Apparently CPS contacted them and Greg went bullshit. I don't know how he did it, but he found out where Eden's been living and..." Another pause and Dan's body language changed, and his voice went up a full octave. "What the hell? *When?*"

He looked at Jenn, and put his phone on speaker, so she could hear what Izzy was saying.

"...Eed and I were just having an argument about whether or not to call you. We really don't know when he left the apartment, but we're pretty sure he never made it to the CVS. The clerk there's been on all night, working the register by the door. He says he didn't see Ben come in."

"Hang on," Jenn said. "Wait. Are you saying that—"

"Ben's gone," Dan finished for her grimly.

"Eden's spitting fire," Izzy reported. "She's ready to go grab Greg by the balls and twist 'em off..."

"Yeah, well, tell her to hang on," Dan said, "because from what Ivette said, Greg's only in the nefarious plotting stages and—"

"I don't think she's going to buy it," Izzy said. "Ivette isn't exactly the most trusted source in news. Besides, there's no saying that Greg didn't already call the posse from Crossroads and... Seriously, bro, I'm not going to be able to stop her from going over there. She's already starting to walk it, and, well... I thought you might want to be there for the impending family reunion. I know the timing sucks, wedding night and all, but—"

"It's okay. We'll meet you over there," Jenn said as she got out of bed and started searching for her underwear.

"Thanks, your bride-ness," Izzy said. "But, Danbo? I haven't said anything to Eden yet because I didn't want to freak her out, you know, *more* than she's already freaking out? But I keep thinking that this might not be Greg. Eden's address was also on that police report that got filed tonight. If the goon squad who's after Neesha has someone in the local PD in their pocket? They could've been watching the place. And when Ben went out for his little late-night walk? He could've walked right into their hands. And if they think he knows where Neesha is...?" He exhaled loudly, his breath making a rushing sound against his phone's microphone. "Sorry to be going all *Charlie's Angels* episode on you—you know, heavy with the overblown drama with the diabetic kid being tortured for information he doesn't have—but I already went back to the apartment and got Greg's weapon. Just in case. I'm locking it in the trunk for now, because guns and Greg don't mix, but I wanted you to be aware of what I'm thinking. That maybe we should ramp it up to DefCon three or even two. Shit, I say that and it sounds nuts, but every instinct in my body is screaming that we shouldn't leave Jenni or Eden alone at the apartment until we really figure out what's up."

"I hear you," Dan told him as he watched Jenn hang up her rented wedding gown and slip it into the plastic garment bag that the Fudds had given her. "And crazy or not, I agree. Maybe you should bring Eden over here, to the hotel, while we go talk to Greg and Ivette."

"Yeeeeah," Izzy said, drawing out the word. "That's not going to happen. Look, I gotta go chase after her. See you in about fifteen?"

"I'll be there." As Danny ended the call, Jenn glanced over to find him looking at her, as she finished putting on the clothes she'd been wearing before they'd gotten married.

I'll, he'd said.

"No," she told him. "Nope. I *won't* stay here, so don't even bother suggesting it. There's no way I'm letting you attend *that* circus parade on your own. Nuh-uh. No way. Not a chance in hell, Gillman. Wear your uniform, by the way. Full-on white power ranger—in case it gets noisy and the police show up."

Dan smiled at her, but it was rueful. "In case?" he repeated. "I think you mean *when*. This is really going to suck."

"It's nothing that we can't handle."

He kissed her—hard—before he went past her to find his shirt and shoes. "Circus parade is a good way to describe it. In the rain, with a serious outbreak of diarrhea among the elephants, a squadron of evil clowns, and a lion or two on the loose." He paused to look at her. "Still sure you want to go?"

"Positive," she told him. "Evil clowns? Can't wait. Throw in Greg, the dancing douchebag, and some cotton candy...I wouldn't miss it for the world."

He laughed as he tied his shoes. "I love it when you say *douchebag*."

"I know." Jenn smiled back at him as she gave up trying to make her hair look as if she hadn't just gotten out of bed. Instead, she simply pulled it back into a ponytail. "Hey, I'll make a deal with you. Make it through this without killing anyone, and when we get back here?" She paused dramatically. "I'll let you be on top."

He laughed, but then asked, "You really think we're coming back here?" Because, in silent agreement, they'd gathered up all of their things.

"A woman can dream, can't she?" Jenn hoisted the wedding gown over her shoulder as she smiled at him and led the way out the door.

CHAPTER
TWENTY-FOUR

If someone had designed a level of hell especially for Eden, this would be it.

Stuck in a car with a man who'd just announced that he was leaving, heading toward a showdown with her jellyfish of a mother and ugly-mean dick of a stepfather, anxious that Dan was going to blame her for losing track of their little brother, and worried sick about Ben.

Izzy broke the strained silence. "I didn't think to check Ben's blood-sugar-meter thing before we left the apartment. You know, to see when he did his last reading." He glanced at Eden. "Did you?"

She shook her head at yet another fail. "No."

"How often does he need to do that, you know, check his insulin levels?"

"Before meals," she recited, "before things like tests at school, before driving—although he doesn't drive yet, before and after strenuous physical activity, in times of high stress, or if he's just feeling wonky."

"So...Not so much before running out to the store."

Eden stared at the road. "Nope. And especially not if he left quickly—to escape the screaming."

Izzy made an exasperated sound. "We weren't screaming."

"Yeah, well, he didn't know that we weren't going to start—did he."

Izzy sighed. "Eden—"

"Chht!" she said, making the hissing sound that the Dog Whisperer used on his TV show, to discipline an unruly animal.

"I don't—"

"Chht!"

He had the audacity to laugh. "Well, *that's* fucking productive."

She couldn't let that one go. "Productive? There's no more *productive*. You're leaving. You're done. And that's fine. That's *great*, actually. I'm glad you're finally being honest with me. But what I *don't* get is why you're still here. In fact, you should just drop me off and go."

"Yeah, that's not going to happen."

Eden turned to face him. "Why?" she asked hotly. "Because with Ben gone, I suddenly 'need' you again? According to *your* definition— forget about what *I* really feel, what *I* really need! Because I couldn't possibly be sincere or honest. I couldn't possibly be anything but mercenary. If Ben's in trouble, I need you, but if not, I don't, so get lost so I can have my *freedom* to go screw an entire football team!"

"That's not what I meant," he argued.

"Isn't it?" she asked. "Because it sure sounded like that to me. And why do *you* get to decide when I do or don't need you, anyway? Why does it have to be life or death, if I need you or I don't? Why can't I just…*need* you—on an average, I don't know, Saturday morning, when the sun is shining and the biggest challenge is deciding whether to go to the beach or the park for a bike ride? Why can't I need you just to make the sun shine a little more brightly or to make the sky be a little more blue?"

Izzy glanced at her again, his face somber and mysterious in the glow from the dashboard, as he pulled up in front of Greg and Ivette's house.

And Lord, Eden's stomach twisted, because she didn't want to do this. She didn't want to see her mother, to watch as her lips tightened disapprovingly. And wasn't *that* covered in irony—the fact that Ivette could disapprove of *anyone*, considering her own track record?

Eden wanted to throw herself into Izzy's arms and beg him to drive away, to just go—anywhere but here.

But it was possible that Ben was in that house or worse—that Greg had had him picked up by the god squad—lowercase g on *god*, because any so-called god who approved of those idiots' decidedly non-Christian actions didn't deserve the respect that came with a capital letter.

Besides, Izzy had been adamant that he didn't want her throwing herself at him again, for any purpose. So she folded her arms across her chest and held on to herself instead. She could do this. She *had* to do this . . .

Over in the driver's seat, Izzy cleared his throat after her little outburst. "You really expect me to believe—"

"No," Eden said, cutting him off. "I don't expect *you* to believe *any*thing I say. You've made it more than clear that you don't trust me, and maybe I deserve that. Maybe I earned it. And maybe you won't ever love me—maybe you can't. Maybe it's entirely my fault, maybe I broke that in you, too. But you are *not allowed* to tell me that I don't love you. You can reject it. You can discount it. You can be a total dickweed and laugh in my face and mock me for it. But you *cannot* tell me that I don't feel what I feel."

And with that, she pushed open the door and climbed out of the car on legs that were shaking. And great, now she was going to throw up, but she closed the door and briefly bent over, hands on her knees, closed her eyes, and breathed.

Izzy being Izzy, he refused to give her space, crossing quickly around the front of the car, in case she needed a hand.

She pushed him away as she started for the walkway to the hellhouse. "You're not allowed to touch me anymore. Just . . . go back to California."

He stood in front of her, blocking her path and making her pull up short. "We're supposed to wait for Dan and Jenn."

"Danny's not the boss of me."

"And he's not the boss of me, either," Izzy told her evenly. "Sometimes he's an asshole, and sometimes he's right, and this is one of the times that he's right. And you know it, too."

He glanced down the street, where, yes, those were headlights approaching. It was Dan and Jenn's rental car, and both he and Eden watched as it approached.

Or rather Eden watched, because Izzy was still gazing at her as if he were trying to read her mind.

"You're not allowed to *look* at me anymore, either," she told him. "So just stop."

He glanced over at the approaching car. Jenn was driving and she pulled up in front of the house and parked, waving at them as if they'd gathered for a family picnic.

But then Izzy touched Eden's arm and looked at her, both actions clearly meant to be in-her-face violations of her latest rules. His words, however, were dead serious. "Eden, do you really...love me?"

And for a half a heartbeat, as she looked up at him, she thought maybe—just maybe—he was finally starting to believe her. But then he added, "Or do you just hate to lose?"

She jerked her arm away. "Screw you."

"Sorry," he said, wincing. "*Sorry*. I didn't mean it the way it sounded, like it was a bad thing, because I've got it, too, you know? This inability to accept that it's time to quit. And that's what I'm trying to do here. With you. Be a grown-up about the fact that we're together for all the wrong reasons." He glanced over to the other car as Jenni and Dan got out. "And I just wanted you to think about that and... You're right—I *don't* get to tell you how you feel, but...I just want you to know that...Well, shit, I'm eleven—ten and a half—years older than you, and most of the time *I* don't know what the hell this is that *I'm* feeling."

"Well, right now I hate you," Eden said. "About as much as I ever have. I'm very clear about that."

He nodded, still somber, as if he were actually taking her at her word. "There have been times that I've hated you, too," he told her. "I've tried, but I just can't manage to make myself feel indifferent."

What was he saying? "Look, if you're really going," Eden said, wiping away the tears that kept springing into her eyes, "please, just *go* already."

"Hey." Jennilyn greeted them, looking from Eden to Izzy and back again, clearly picking up on the tension between them. "So *this* is going to be hard, huh?"

"Izzy's got to go back to San Diego," Eden told her new sister-in-law, who turned to Izzy with surprise.

But he was shaking his head. "Are you kidding? And miss this episode of *Dysfunction Junction*? I call dibs on hog-tying Greg. Assuming Greg's gonna need to be hog-tied, which . . . is a pretty sure bet."

Jenn was the only one who laughed. Dan was already grimly starting up the stairs, leading the way—taking the point, as it was called in the SEAL teams. He was still wearing his dress uniform, which was a nice touch when dealing with their mother, who'd always loved shiny things.

"We're going to get through this," Jenn told Eden, pulling her in for a quick hug. "Maybe it'll be easy. Maybe Ben's inside, and together we can get your mom to agree that living with Danny and me in San Diego is a good solution for everyone—because it is. We can do this. We *will* do it."

It was all Eden could do not to cling to her, weeping. But Dan was already knocking on the door—the buzzer had stopped working a long time ago.

She let Jenn hold her hand and lead her over to the foot of the cracked and broken steps, with Izzy—who hated her, too—in the rear, clearly not going anywhere.

Eden and Dan's mother came to the door with a drink in one hand and a cigarette in the other.

"Whozat, Ivy?" someone—Greg, had to be—shouted from the back of the house.

"It's Danny," Ivette shouted back in a voice heavy with nicotine-laced Southern sugar. She didn't let them in, she just looked out at them through the screen, leaning close to whisper in a drunk's version of sotto voce, "Why'd you bring *her*? You know seeing her makes Greg go all apeshit crazy."

The *her* in question was Eden, and as Izzy watched, she stood a little taller, chin high. *Sticks and stones can break my bones, but words* . . . He knew damn well that words could hurt pretty fricking badly.

"Nice to see you, too, Ivette," Eden said as Dan spoke over her. "We don't want any trouble. I know it's late, but I got your message and . . . We're looking for Ben. Is he here?"

"Benjamin?" she said as she took another sip of her drink, as if that would improve her memory.

It was pretty freaking amazing, seeing her in the flesh.

Eden had described Ivette to Izzy, back when they'd gotten married. He'd always thought she'd been exaggerating, but in truth she'd been pretty damn accurate. The woman was in her late forties—some years younger than Dan Gillman the elder, which made sense, because she had been his second wife. They'd married out of necessity when she was still a teenager, after he'd gotten her pregnant. She was formerly, fadingly pretty in an aging porn-star way. And if Izzy looked hard enough, he could see traces of Eden's beauty in the shape of her face.

But the similarities ended there. Ivette's eyes were a watery, washed-out blue and her hair was bottle blond, and her lips had been recently collagened, giving her a solid whiff of Stiffler's Mom, if Stiffler's Mom had been both ill-educated and a substance abuser. She was high on whatever meds she'd stolen from her most recent client. Izzy could see the drugs, along with the blurring effects of alcohol, in her out-of-focus eyes.

The woman didn't open the screen to hug Danny or Eden, despite the fact that it had been well over a year since she'd seen either of her children. Of course, her hands *were* full.

Yeah.

"Is Ben here?" Eden pushed.

Her mother turned to scream back into the house. "Greg, is Benjy here?"

Just what they needed—Greg adding his personal brand of crazy to this nightmare.

Izzy stepped forward, reaching out to nudge Danny, who was clearly overwhelmed, and not in a good way. "Hey, man, why don't we just go in and look around?"

Danny snapped back to life. "Yeah, I'll do it," he said, opening the screen. "Excuse me, ma'am."

His mother stepped back, gesturing with her drink. "Knock yourself out."

"You're not letting them in, are you?" Enter Greg, limping out of the kitchen, with a bottle in his hand. He was wearing the same clothes he'd had on back in the hospital, days ago. Classy, all the way.

Eden took an involuntary step back, and Izzy stepped toward her, putting a hand on her back, even as Jenni refreshed the grip she had on Eden's hand.

"You," he said, peering out through the screen at Eden, his eyes narrowing. "You fornicating slut—"

Izzy didn't need to move, because Dan was already there, on the same side of the screen as the dirtbag.

"You're not allowed to call her that," Dan said as he grabbed Greg by the front of the shirt and pushed him up against the wall. The bottle fell, but it didn't break, and Ivette—another class act—went scrambling for it, apparently unwilling to waste a precious drop. "Not in my house."

Greg was too skunked to know when to S-square, because he neither sat the fuck down nor shut the fuck up. Not that he *could* sit down, with Dan's arm against his throat. Still, he could've managed the second S. Instead he sputtered and flailed and said, "This isn't...You can't...This is *my* house!"

"Daniel Gillman, you stop that, right now," Ivette chimed in as if he were an unruly kindergartner, but the sudden parental tone simply didn't cut it.

Dan ignored them both as he turned to Izzy. His face was composed, but his voice was tight and his eyes betrayed his soaring levels of stress. "Zanella, do you mind...?"

"I'm on it," Izzy said, going up the steps and pulling open the creaky screen.

"And who is this?" Ivette asked, moving to block Izzy, shades of Mrs. Robinson radiating from her body language as she apparently noticed him for the first time.

"I'm your son-in-law," Izzy said. "Mom."

The M-word made her recoil, and Izzy moved past her, even as Greg chimed in with another chorus of, "I don't want him in here!"

"You're welcome," Izzy told him because the bottle Ivette was now holding was one of the ones he'd sent.

He searched the house quickly and thoroughly, but none of the rooms were locked and all of them were empty. Still he checked every closet and even sifted through piles of laundry.

No Ben. No sign of him, even. No used vials of insulin in the trash or out on the counter in the kitchen—no insulin in the refrigerator at all.

There was, however, a mysteriously cleared-off kitchen table—odd because every other surface in the house was filled with clutter.

Hmm.

Izzy started opening cabinet doors, and hit the jackpot when he opened the cold oven to look inside. There was a rusted cookie sheet on the top rack, upon which sat a vast pile of pill bottles, all prescribed to one George King—presumably Ivette's former hospice patient. Someone—probably Greg, crafty devil that he was—had started transferring the various medications into snack-sized zipper-shut baggies, where they would be, no doubt, easier for him to sell on the street.

Felony drug charges, anyone? Possession, perhaps, with intent to distribute?

Izzy took out his cell phone and snapped a few photos, careful to get pictures that clearly showed both the labels and the fact that the bottles were nearly full. Then he took one of the bottles and one of the baggies and slipped them into the pocket of his cargo shorts, because sometimes photographic evidence simply wasn't enough.

Then he closed the oven door as quietly as possible, acutely aware that while *his* childhood had been unconventional, and while his own parents had been woefully inattentive, and his brothers had often been overly rough and frequently less than kind, he'd never had to deal with addicts and their ensuing criminal activity. And maybe Ivette hadn't always been this way, at least not while Dan was growing up. In fact, she probably hadn't.

Yes, his and Eden's older sister, Sandy, had been a real mess, which had to have been hard to live with. And they'd all constantly dealt with the stress of Ivette's cheating while their father was away.

But from what Izzy could tell, Ivette's drug problem hadn't started until after the loss of their home and their livelihood from the post-Katrina flooding. Danny had long since gone into the Navy by then, but Eden had still been a young teenager, and Ben? He'd been just a little boy.

And somehow, Ben had managed to remain one of the nicest, sweetest kids Izzy had ever met, despite his having to live day-to-day with *this* kind of bullshit horror show. But maybe his sweetness *wasn't* such a mystery because despite that hell, he'd had Eden to love him, to protect him, and to raise him right.

Even though, through most of that, she'd been just a kid herself.

Out front, the conversation was growing more heated.

Get your dirty hands offa me! Greg.

Why would Ben be here, anyway? Ivette. *Greg said he was staying with you!*

Jenn's voice, an indiscernible murmur.

Then Ivette again, louder: *Danny! You got* married, *and you didn't even* tell *me! You couldn't wait for me to come home so I could be there?*

Izzy exhaled hard, resisting the urge to rush out there and offer Jenn a thousand dollars to slap the bitch for him, knowing how badly it must sting for Eden to hear her mother say that—after Ivette had flatly turned down their invitation to attend Eden's own wedding.

The best thing Izzy could do was finish up quickly so he could get Eden the hell out of here.

He continued to scan the kitchen, and he finally saw what he was looking for—a cell phone out on the counter. He couldn't tell if it was Greg's or Ivette's, but when he flipped it open—it was a fairly standard low-budget model—he could access the phone's recent history, where there was a list of calls that had been either made or received. The phone wasn't sophisticated enough to differentiate between the two, but he quickly deduced that it was Greg's phone, because there was no record of any calls to or from Danny.

But there *were* quite a few calls—dozens, in fact—made yesterday, before midnight, to the same four numbers—one of them identified with Ivette's name—starting in the midafternoon.

He's gay, Mom. Eden's voice from out front. *He was* born *gay. You can't change that. You can only make him hate himself and really screw him up. I think he's perfect.*

Jenn: *I do, too. He's really a terrific kid, Mrs. Fortune.*

It was nearly 0130, but hey. It was no skin off of Izzy's nose if the peeps on the other end of those numbers woke up thinking Greg was drunk-dialing them.

He went down the list of mystery numbers, hitting TALK.

The first got him an automated message system for the State of Nevada's Child Protective Services office. The second was an answering machine for the Church of the Righteous Redeemer. The third?

Bingo. But bingo in a really bad way.

You've reached Crossroads youth counseling center and school for positive values. This outreach helpline is open twenty-four hours, three hundred and sixty-five days a year, so please stay on the line for our next available life coach . . .

Life coach, his ass. Brainwasher, was more like it. Not to mention hate monger. Izzy cut the connection and went to Greg's voice mail, to see if, like many people, he failed to delete his messages after listening to them.

But out in the entryway, Ivette and Greg were both getting shrill—

more shrill—so he pocketed the phone to listen later, and went back to join the big show.

"And you honestly think"—Ivette was damn near screaming at Eden, who still stood with Jenn outside on the stoop, her face pale but determined in the glow from the porch light—"that Ben would be better off with *you*?! Look at how well you take care of him—you lost him. Again. As if what happened during the hurricane—you abandoning him at the Superdome—wasn't disgraceful enough!" Ivette turned to Dan, who still had Greg against the wall, as tears streamed down her anger-twisted face. "Honey, your sister Sandy and I didn't tell you this—you were under enough stress as it was, being over there in Iraq at the time—"

"I *didn't* abandon him," Eden interrupted. "I went to find insulin. Ben was *dying*! What was I supposed to do?"

"Maybe that would've been for the best," Greg intoned. "Considering..."

"—but if you're actually thinking about sharing a home with her"—Ivette spoke over them both, talking earnestly to Danny—"you really need to know the type of person she is—that she was screwing her own sister's husband, right under the same roof."

"That's *not* true," Eden said hotly. "And oh, my God, didn't you hear what Greg just said about Ben?"

"*I* heard," Izzy said, and she met his gaze—just long enough for him to see her fear. She was afraid—terrified—that he was going to believe the stupid shit her mother was spouting.

"Ron said it was going on for months," Ivette shot back.

"Yeah, great," Eden said. "Trust the crack addict. Because he'll *never* lie."

"Eden was *fifteen*," Izzy said, and Eden looked at him again, even as Ivette countered.

"Going on forty," she scoffed. "He had disgusting pictures of her on his cell phone."

"Because he used to walk in on me in the bathroom," Eden countered.

"Oh, so now you're back to saying that it never happened?" Ivette sucked furiously on her cigarette. "Because that's not what you told Sandy—"

"I told Sandy the *truth.*"

"That you sucked her husband's cock," Ivette shot back. "That he *made* you. How does that work, exactly? Without him holding a gun to your head?"

"Oh, my God," Jenn said, putting her arms around Eden, as if trying to protect her.

"Jesus Christ," Dan said. "You make me sick."

Out on the stoop, Eden flinched, as if she were certain her brother was talking to her.

But he wasn't—he was looking at his mother like she was some kind of monster. "Do you even hear what you're saying?"

"You don't know what she did," Ivette implored him. "What she's capable of. She was home with the kids, babysitting. After Ron relapsed, Sandy and I had to get second jobs, waitressing. We were working that night—"

"With a hurricane coming...?" Dan asked. "You left Eden home alone with three kids with a category-five hurricane—?"

"We didn't have a choice. If we didn't go in, we'd lose our jobs. Besides, they weren't alone. Ron was there."

"A relapsed crack addict?" Dan gave voice to Izzy's own disbelief.

"He was clean," Ivette said.

"He was *not*," Eden countered. "He was using again. He was high, and when the time came to evacuate, I was *not* going to let Ben and those little girls get into his car with him."

"Ron said they had a lovers' quarrel," Ivette countered, talking to Danny, "and she left him behind to die."

"We argued," Eden said. "And he hit me and he knocked me down and he tried to *rape* me, but Ben hit him with one of our cast-iron porch chairs. I grabbed his keys, and we got into the car and locked the doors, and he started trying to smash the windows—with his own daughters inside!—so Ben got us the hell out of there."

"Except Ben conveniently doesn't remember that," Ivette said.

"He doesn't remember much about any of it," Eden said. "The hurricane *or* the Superdome . . . And I thank God for that!"

"He also conveniently doesn't remember you abandoning him," Ivette accused her. She turned to Dan. "She left him and Sandy's girls with a *stranger*, so she could go meet Ron at the store."

"Yeah," Eden said. "Right. I left my brother, who was going into a *coma* from lack of insulin, and I waded through water that was up to my *shoulders*, so I could meet Ron at the store and give him a blow job. What planet do you live on? Although you're right about one thing. I sucked him off. And I *didn't* have a gun to my head." Her voice shook. "Okay, *Mom*? Are you happy to hear me admit it? You're right, I didn't *have* to do it. I could've left the store without the insulin—I could've just walked away, and let Ben die."

"Ah, Jesus," Dan breathed. "There was insulin at the store."

Eden nodded. "We went there, every day, after school. There was a minifridge in the back. I knew the power would be off, but I thought maybe it would still be cool enough. And I figured it was better than nothing. But when I finally got there? Ron was already there. And at first, I thought maybe he'd be sober and, I don't know, maybe just a little bit glad to see me—to know that Kimmie and Kendra were alive. But he was still high, so he didn't give a shit. You can relate to that, huh, Ma?"

"I've heard this sob story before," Ivette started, but Izzy stepped forward.

"Shut up."

There must've been something in his eyes, something dangerous, because she shut her mouth, fast.

"Sweetie, you don't have to explain anything," Jenn told Eden, who was still standing there, defiant, chin high, and ready for them all to side with her mother and call her a liar. "You did what you believed you had to do—"

Eden looked through the screen, directly at Izzy, and whispered, "He said I could have the insulin if I gave him a blow job. And I figured, I'd done worse with John Franklin, and it didn't kill me, you know? It didn't mean anything. It was just...sex. I just kept telling myself that. That it was nothing. It meant nothing. Except it did. It meant...that I was exactly what everyone said I was." She looked at Danny then. "What *you* said I was, when you came home for Charlie's funeral."

Danny looked ill, but he didn't get a chance to say anything, not so much as an *I'm sorry,* or a *God, Eden,* because Greg couldn't keep his mouth shut.

"We don't speak his name in this house," he said.

"Who? Charlie?" Dan asked, his disgust dripping from his words. "He was a hundred times the man that you are—*you're* not allowed to speak his name." He turned to Eden. "Eden—"

But she didn't let him speak. "It *didn't* mean nothing, but it *got* me nothing," she told him, told her mother, told Izzy with eyes that were resigned and devoid of all hope that any of them would believe her. "Because I never made it back to the Superdome. I got picked up by a boat that took me to one of the highway overpasses, and I couldn't get back to find Ben or the girls. I tried, and I *tried,* but I kept getting stopped by all these men with guns and...I offered them what I gave to Ron—you didn't know *that,* did you, Mom? Come on, let's hear you condemn me for that—for doing anything—*anything* to try to save Ben. But I failed."

"Oh, honey..." Out on the stoop, Jenn tightened the hold she had around Eden. "But he was all right. Ben was..."

"He survived. Barely. Because a stranger gave him insulin. He *was* all right." Eden shook her head, rigid in her self-hatred. "No thanks to me."

"You tried," Izzy whispered, through a throat that was tight. He'd imagined the hell that she'd lived through in the aftermath of the hurricane, but he hadn't come even remotely close.

Eden looked right at him. "There is no try," she said. "Remember?"

"This time," Izzy told her, "Yoda's wrong."

"Ben *was* all right—no thanks to you." Ivette couldn't keep her mouth shut. "And, for the record? That's *not* the story Ron told us, and he was *very* convincing..."

"What the hell is wrong with you?" Izzy didn't have to say it, because Danny did.

"Don't you talk to your mother that way!" Greg said as Ivette gasped and then burst into a fresh flood of tears.

Dan ignored them both. "Get Eden away from this poison," he ordered Jenn tersely. "Get her into the car."

Jenni nodded, but Eden wasn't ready to go anywhere. She stood her ground, still thinking first and foremost about her little brother. "Was there any sign of Ben?" she asked Izzy.

"I don't think he's been here," he told her, but he couldn't withhold the potential bad news. "But I found Greg's cell phone, and he was talking to the people over at Crossroads earlier this evening. There were three different calls."

"Oh, my God," Eden said as Dan tightened his grip on Greg.

"You had *no* right," he started.

"I have every right," Greg countered. "No son of mine—"

"He's *not* your son!" Eden shouted.

"Okay," Jenn said, "sweetie, this isn't helping." She raised her voice to be heard inside the house. "Mr. Fortune, did you make arrangements for Crossroads to pick up Ben from Eden's apartment?"

"I did," Greg said. "And there's nothing you can do about it."

Eden stood there, stricken, and Dan looked like he was damn near ready to choke the life out of the bastard as both Greg and Ivette continued to make a shitload of useless noise. Greg was proclaiming that he also had the right to call the police after they left, and have them all arrested for home invasion and assault, and Ivette chimed in with a still-teary and incredibly misguided belief that Crossroads was like a great, big camp, where "Benjy" would go and have fun, maybe meet some nice girls, because maybe he just hadn't met any nice-enough girls...

Izzy had had enough. He put on his deadliest war-face, and

stretched himself up to his full height. "Everyone! Shut!" he shouted. "The fuck! Up!"

The sudden silence was deafening—there was definitely fear in both Greg's and Ivette's eyes. Good. He pointed to Greg. "Fuck you," he said, and then he turned to Ivette, "and fuck you!" Back to Greg. "I always knew you were a worthless piece of excrement, but you?" Back to Ivette, whose eyes were wide. "I always thought that there must've been at least *some*thing halfway decent in you, because you brought Dan and Eden and Ben into the world. I thought you were somehow responsible, but it's clear that they became the outstanding human beings that they are not only without your help, but with your hindrance. So thank you for showing me this, for this little display tonight. Because now my respect for all three of them is completely off the scale." He turned to the door, where Eden and Jenn were staring at him, too. "Ladies, to the cars. Danny, my friend, I'll take Greg from you, from here. I want a few words in private with your asshole pseudo-parents before I join you at the cars, where we *will* go—immediately—to Crossroads to pick up Ben, where he *will* be waiting for us."

Izzy had it all figured out. Illegally obtained drugs, plus addictive behavior, plus threat of arrest and incarceration . . . ? He was going to use what he'd found in that oven in the kitchen to buy Danny and Eden everything they wanted—Ben's release from that prison of intolerance, *and* a signed letter granting the fifteen-year-old permission to go to San Diego and live with either his brother or his sister.

Izzy had it all figured out, until Greg opened his ugly-ass mouth, and smugly informed them, "He won't be there. Crossroads has a half a dozen sister organizations, all across the country, used when certain family members are uncooperative. Benjamin is on his way to an undisclosed location right now. Even *I* don't know where he's going. All I know is he won't come back until he's cured."

"You *son* of a *bitch!*"

If Izzy had had to put money on which of the Gillmans would lose their shit first on account of getting that kind of bad news about Ben, he would've picked Eden. But it was Danny who went over the edge as he tightened his grip on Greg. The older man flapped and flailed, but he didn't stand a chance as his stepson choked the jumping bejesus out of him.

And maybe Danny was just trying to scare him. Maybe he was intending to stop before the old dude actually stopped breathing, but it sure as hell didn't look like it.

Ivette didn't think he was going to stop, either—her screeching started up again.

Jenn, too, was on that bus. "Please, Danny, don't," she said. She looked at Izzy beseechingly in a silent *do something* as she opened the screen door, stepped inside, and tried to pull Dan back. But all she succeeded in doing was hugging him—there was no way she could manhandle him away from Greg.

There was no way Izzy could do it, either. Not by force. Well, he *could* do it by force, but not without seriously damaging Greg in the process.

So Izzy did the only thing he could. He took Jenn's lead, and just put his arms around Dan, too, holding on to him from behind.

"Don't do this, brother," he said quietly as Ivette wailed from where she'd fallen, prostrate on the floor. "This doesn't make it better, it only makes it worse."

And then Eden spoke up from her place of exile, still out on the stoop. "Danny, Ben needs you," she pleaded. "And...I do, too."

And with that, Danny finally released Greg. Izzy caught the old man and kept him from falling as the asshat gasped for air. Damn, he smelled bad.

"I'm done," Danny told his mother. "Sending money, answering your calls...It's over. And I'm taking Ben, even if I have to drag you to court to do it."

"Don't say that," Ivette sobbed. "You're my son, and I love you!"

"No, you don't," Dan said. "You only love your alcohol and your drugs. You want to be part of my life? You lose this asshole, and you put yourself through rehab. If you do that? Then we'll talk."

He put his arm around Jenn and went out the screen door, where, on the stoop, he stopped and roughly pulled Eden in for a hug. "Eedie, I'm so sorry," Dan said, his voice breaking.

And Eden—tough, resilient, screw-you-attitude Eden—started to cry, too, with deep, body-shaking sobs.

"Get them into your car, and wait for me," Izzy told Jenn, who was the only one who wasn't weeping—okay, well, she was, too, but she looked as if she could still see well enough to navigate the stairs. "I'll be out in a sec."

As they moved away from the house, Izzy turned back to Greg and Ivette.

"So," he said. "I'm betting *some*one, *some*where, knows where Ben is . . ."

CHAPTER
TWENTY-FIVE

B en wasn't waiting for them, back at the apartment.

Danny knew that that had been a real long shot, but he'd been hopeful just the same.

Whatever Zanella had threatened his mother and her scum-sucking husband with, it had worked like gangbusters—to a degree. He'd returned to their car with signed letters stating that both Ivette and Greg gave their full and complete permission for Ben to move to San Diego to live with either Danny or Eden. *And* they'd promised, under threat of...whatever—Izzy wouldn't say—to both appear at CPS in the morning to give a similar statement in person.

But getting Ben released from Crossroads was apparently another thing entirely. When pressed, Greg was foggy about the details of the arrangements he'd made with the Crossroads staff, for picking up Ben. He'd been under the impression that it wasn't scheduled to happen until the morning. But maybe he'd been confused, and it was the transporting Ben to Utah or Alabama part of it that was scheduled for the morning.

In which case, Ben could well still be at the Las Vegas Crossroads compound.

After failing to raise the facility via phone, Izzy had offered to make a little in-person visit. Dan had expected Eden to volunteer to go along—but she didn't. And then he found out that Greg was going, too, as Izzy's unwilling and belligerent copilot.

It was then that the three of them—Danny, Jenni, and Eden—headed back here.

"Ben's last blood sugar reading was after we got home from the wedding," Eden reported now, coming out of the kitchen with the device. "Around ten o'clock."

"And we think he left the apartment...when?" Dan asked. He'd changed out of his uniform and was digging through his pack for a clean pair of socks.

"We don't really know." Eden sighed as she sat down next to Danny on the couch. "Izzy and I had a fight—it must've been around, wow, midnight?" She sighed again. "We got loud. I think it might be my fault—Ben's leaving the apartment the way he did."

"Or maybe it wasn't anyone's fault," Dan suggested. "Maybe it was...just Ben being Ben."

Jenn had been sitting across the room, in the easy chair, with her eyes closed, but now she stood up. "I'm going to make some tea," she announced, but she came over—no easy feat with all of the mattresses on the floor—and she kissed Danny before she went into the other room. Not because she wanted tea, but because she wanted to give them privacy to talk.

Dan smiled at his sister. "She's training me and I just got a kiss, so I must be doing something right."

"Training?" Eden repeated.

"Yeah," Dan said. "That's not what *she'd* call it, but we Gillmans are so messed up, we need to be reminded, frequently, how to be human. For example"—he raised his voice so Jenn could hear him from the kitchen—"I managed not to kill anyone tonight."

Jenn laughed. "Yes, I made special note of that," she called back.

"Even though I wanted to," Dan told Eden. "I had my arm against Greg's throat, but it was really Ivette I wanted to..." He sighed, still feeling sick from all he'd learned tonight. "How come you didn't tell me? About Ron and...the insulin?"

She looked up from her examination of Ben's meter. Her answer wasn't really that much of a surprise. "Because," she said simply, "I didn't think *you'd* believe me, either."

Ouch.

He tried to imagine how awful it must've been, to have survived all that Eden had—the hurricane, the flooding, her courageous quest to save Ben, and her assumed failure despite all of her sacrifices—and then have her own mother believe Ron's lies.

"She's damaged," Dan told Eden now, talking about Ivette.

"I know."

"I'm damaged, too," he admitted. "But…I'm getting better."

"Is that an apology?"

He forced a smile. "I kind of feel like I should start every sentence I ever say to you with *I'm sorry.*" He sighed. "I know it's lame to make excuses, but growing up in that house, with Sandy? I used to go out, looking for her, late at night, so she wouldn't spend the entire night passed out on the neighbor's lawn—or worse, in the street—"

"You don't have to explain," Eden said. "I was there, too."

"You were so much younger."

"But I knew what you were doing."

"I *am* sorry," he said. "Because you were right when you said… what you said. You're *not* Sandy."

Eden nodded. "And you're not Dad. I know that, too."

She was talking about his accidentally hitting Jenn, and he had to look away so she didn't see the tears that leaped into his eyes. Or maybe it was okay to let her see. "Thank you," he said.

"Thank you, too," she whispered back. "Although, for a while, I thought I was. Sandy. After…I think maybe I tried to be just like her, since everyone thought…And I made a lot of bad mistakes, I'm well aware of that. I also owe you a lot of money—I want to pay you back— I've got most of it—"

"From stripping?" he asked, looking at her, and she didn't disagree. "Like *that's* not a mistake?"

"I quit," she told him. "Working at the club. Izzy asked me to, so…"

"Good," he said. "Because you have plenty of other options."

The look she shot him was not one of agreement.

Dan sat forward. "You do," he said. "You're good with kids—weren't you working as a nanny for a while?"

"For a single mom," she said. "But the women with the husbands? They don't want to hire me. Believe me, I've tried."

"You know, Jenk and Lindsey are having a baby," Dan told her.

Eden's face brightened. "I know. Izzy told me. That's so great."

"Jenk was telling me that there's such a baby boom going on, over where Lindsey works, at Troubleshooters, they're talking about setting up child care, right on the premises."

"Seriously?" Eden asked.

"One of the pregnancies is Tommy's wife, Kelly," Dan said. "And since he owns the place..."

"Well, that's really great," Eden said.

"Sophia's pregnant, too," Dan said. "You remember her, right?"

"The Sophia you have a mad crush on?" Eden lowered her voice to ask, her eyes wide.

"Had," he corrected her, glancing toward the kitchen. "Past tense. Very, *very* past tense."

"How did *that* happen? By immaculate conception? While she was flying around on her perfect angel wings?"

Dan had to laugh. "No, I'm pretty sure it happened the good old-fashioned human way. She's married now. To Dave Malkoff."

"What?" Eden said, her mouth dropping open. "Wow, I missed a lot. It's like I went away for a while, and came back to some kind of weird alternate universe where Princess Sophia *married* the grumpy troll."

"Dave's not so grumpy anymore."

She laughed. "I bet."

"If you want," Dan said, "I could check with Tommy, maybe get you a job interview. If they're actually gonna go ahead with the child-care thing..."

She was silent, so he quickly added, "Unless it's too soon, you know, for you to work with, um, infants. And I'm sorry if that's a touchy subject—"

"No," Eden said. "No. It's not. I just...need to think about it a little bit, before..."

"Just let me know," he said. "Okay?"

She nodded and they sat in silence for a moment, but then Dan had to ask, "Do you, I don't know, want to press charges? Against Ron? I don't think it's too late. Statute of limitations and everything. We could—"

She was shaking her head. "Ron's already in jail."

"But not for what he did to you," Dan pointed out.

"You and Izzy are so much alike," Eden told him. "Always ready to rush in and slay the dragons. Ron's in jail—he can't hurt anyone else. And me? I'm...okay."

"Are you?" Dan asked.

She didn't answer him directly. She just said, almost wistfully, "Do you think maybe things would've been different? If Charlie hadn't died?"

"Maybe," Dan said, smiling as he remembered the one man that their mother had hooked up with that he'd actually liked. Loved, even. "I don't know, Eed. Ivette seemed to be the happiest she'd ever been when she was with him, so...Yeah. Maybe."

"He was teaching her how to be human," Eden told him, using close to his own words. "But he ran out of time." She laughed, but it wasn't because she thought anything was funny. "Do you know he was the *only* person who told me that I was going to be okay, after John Franklin dumped me? Everyone else told me I was going to hell, that *you reap what you sow*, but Charlie told me that making bad choices was a part of growing up. I'd made the mistake of believing John, and...*Live and learn*, Charlie said. But then, just a few days later, he was gone. And then Katrina happened, and the thing with Ron, and...I started making bad choices on purpose. Because I didn't think I deserved anything better."

"Is that why you were fighting with Zanella?" he asked her quietly. "Because you don't think you deserve to be happy?"

"No, actually, I'm good with being happy these days," she said, and she looked away, but not before he saw the misery in her eyes. "Izzy, um, told me he was leaving. For good."

Shit. "Eden, he sometimes drives me nuts, but he's..." Dan laughed and rolled his eyes. "I can't believe I'm saying this, but... beneath his outer asshole, you were right. Zanella *is* a good guy. I mean, tonight? When he went off? *Fuck you and fuck you!* That was pretty beautiful. And if there's one thing that I have absolutely no doubt about? Even when he's pissing me off? It's that he loves you."

"Yeah, well, great. He's got a funny way of showing it." She stood up, clearly not wanting to talk about this. "We need to focus on finding Ben. If he *is* at Crossroads, the stress is going to be intense. When Izzy calls, we should be ready to meet him with this"—she held up the meter—"and some insulin."

"Maybe he's not there," Dan suggested. "Maybe he went out looking for his freaky little friend. Neesha. Or...maybe...Do you know if Ben has a, you know..." He cleared his throat. "Boyfriend?"

Eden shook her head. "I don't think he does, no. He really hasn't had any friends at all, since Deshawndra. Seriously, Dan, Neesha's the first person his age that he hasn't shut out."

"Are you sure?" he asked. "A boyfriend might be different. Maybe he wouldn't tell you. I mean, I don't think I told anyone about my first girlfriend..."

"There's this homophobic kid, Tim," Eden said. "At school. And this boy, Bo, he's got a crush on. Ben, not Tim. But Bo's so far in the closet...How did Ben put it? He can't even see the door."

"Maybe Bo turned on the closet light," Dan said. "Jenn said Ben spent a lot of time earlier today doing something on Facebook."

Eden didn't look convinced. "I think he was trying to track down the boyfriend of that kid he met at Crossroads. Peter something, from Connecticut. He wanted to make sure Peter's friends knew he was at the facility here in Las Vegas. I didn't quite get it when Ben first told me—how could this boy's friends not know where he was, you know? But now it makes sense. If they ship kids across the country..."

"It's twisted," Dan agreed.

"It's worse than twisted," Eden said. "Jenn said she thinks it's illegal. Transporting minors across state lines...? She's going to talk to Maria and that other lawyer, Linda Thompson."

It was then, before Dan could say, *that's good,* that it happened. There was a knock at the door.

They were both startled, and they both looked over to check the time on the VCR. It was 0213.

"Maybe Ben forgot his key," Dan suggested. "Maybe all the drama is going to end—right now."

"Please, God," Eden said as she stood up.

Dan stood, too, relentlessly cautious. "Don't just open it—check the peephole first."

Eden pointed to herself. "Female, living alone?" she said, shooting her brother a *you better believe it* look as she went to the apartment door and peeked out through the peephole.

She'd expected it to be Izzy, but there was no one there. Or rather, there was no one there of his height. But when she looked down toward the concrete walkway...

"It's Neesha," she said to Dan and to Jenn, too, who'd come to stand in the kitchen doorway. She pulled the door open and it was, indeed, Ben's freaky little friend, as Dan had so aptly called her.

The girl was a mess. She was still wearing the clothes she'd had on when Eden had spotted her near the Starbucks—a T-shirt beneath which the sequined straps of a hot-pink halter top peeked out, and a pair of black pants that were dusty and torn at the knees. Her hair was a matted, sweaty mess, and she had dirt mixed in with the streaks of perspiration and tears on her face.

"Oh, dear Lord," Eden said. "Get in here."

The fact that the girl came swiftly inside, and even helped Eden close the door securely behind her was telling. She was terrified and exhausted. And had probably been running, full speed, since Eden had seen her last.

In the living room, Danny had gotten to his feet, but he sat back down as Neesha eyed him nervously.

Jenn, meanwhile, had gone back into the kitchen and she now brought Neesha a glass of water. "Honey, here," she said, handing it to the girl. "Drink this. You're okay now. You're safe with us."

But Neesha looked up after taking only a sip from the glass. And as she looked from Jenn to Eden and over to Danny in the living room, she said, "But I'm not. And you're not safe here, either. They know where you live. They were here, in the courtyard."

"Who was?" Jenn asked as Eden glanced over at Dan. Like her, he already knew what Neesha was going to say before she said it.

"The men who are chasing me," Neesha said. "They were *here*. Four hours ago. I saw them. They took Ben."

Danny snapped instantly into Navy SEAL mode, getting very decisive, very quickly, after Neesha told them, in pretty specific detail, what she'd seen and heard—*and* a condensed but no less horrific version of precisely why those men were chasing her.

The man from the mall, whose name apparently was Jake, had been in the courtyard with two other men—one of them named Todd, whom Neesha knew not only because he'd worked as a guard at the brothel where she'd been a slave, but because he'd also been one of her "visitors," or clients, for years.

Jenn didn't want to think about what that meant. And there really wasn't all that much time to focus on that aspect of the nightmare—because Neesha had overheard Jake telling the other two men to shoot and kill Dan and Izzy on sight. He had somehow known they were in the military and therefore a threat.

The girl had also overheard Jake telling his cohorts to wear masks—so their abductees would believe they would survive their kidnapping.

Which meant that the men who had taken Ben had every intention of killing him—no doubt immediately after he divulged Neesha's location.

Except Ben had no idea where Neesha was hiding.

And this time, Danny didn't need his uniform to become larger and commanding.

"Get your things," he ordered both Jenn and Eden, "your handbags, whatever. Grab Ben's insulin, too. We're leaving. In about thirty seconds."

"I need to call Izzy," Eden said, her phone already out in and in her hands.

"You can call him from the road," Danny told her, checking to make sure he'd put his own cell phone into his jeans pocket.

"I'm calling him now," Eden told him.

"Kill the light in the hall," he said as Jenn stayed over by Neesha, giving the girl what she hoped was a reassuring smile as the light went out so that Dan could go into the bedroom and look out the window and into the courtyard without being seen.

"He's not picking up," Eden said. "Come on, Izzy…Answer your phone!"

"Doesn't it seem really unlikely," Jenn said as Dan turned off the bedroom light, "that they'd come back here? They got what they wanted, right? When they took Ben? I mean, I know it's not safe for us to stay here, but to have to rush away?"

Dan stopped there in the bedroom doorway to grimly say, "If they've had Ben for four hours, they know by now that he's got no information that'll help them find Neesha. So yes. They'll come back. To get Eden, who helped Neesha escape. They'll think she knows something, and they'll come while it's still dark."

"Oh, my God," Jenn said as he went into the bedroom.

"Eden, shit, come here," Dan called in a rough whisper, and Eden followed him.

"Oh, crap," Jenn heard Eden say. "That's him. The man with the gun, from the Starbucks. Izzy, where *are* you?"

"Oh, my God." Jenn said again, her heart in her throat. "Are you serious?"

"Keep watching them," Dan commanded Eden, adding, "Jenni, put the chain on the door and throw the bolt." He limped out of the bedroom and over to the window in the living room—the one that looked out over the street—as he dialed his cell phone. "*Shit.* There's a van idling on the street. That's not good. Neesha, were you followed? Did anyone see you come here?"

The little girl was shaking her head, terrified. "I was careful. I waited and watched—even after I saw you come home."

This little chain on the door wasn't going to keep anyone out for long. Not if they wanted to get inside. Jenn turned back to Dan.

"There are two men in the courtyard," he told her, even as he held his phone to his ear, "and one of them is the man Eden tried to run over earlier tonight. They look like they're waiting for someone. Whether they're here for surveillance or...something else, they're sure as shit not even attempting to be covert—No, I can't hold—God *damn* it."

"If we try to leave," Jenn started.

"They'll see us," Dan confirmed, holding out his phone and glaring at it. "There's no way we're sneaking out without that happening. And with my fucking leg, we can't outrun them—"

"Yeah, sorry," Jenn said, looking around for something to push in front of the door, since leaving wasn't an option. "But I'd bet big money you can *still* run faster than me, even with your 'fucking' leg. So we hunker down. Shouldn't we call the police?"

In the bedroom, Eden was finishing up leaving a detailed message for Izzy, with a *Call me back, now—we need you!*

"Already doing that," Dan said, "but the 9-1-1 operator just put me on hold. Neesha, get into the bedroom. In the closet. They may not know you're here."

"They'll find me," the girl said. "In the closet."

"It's better than just standing here," Dan argued. "Except...Wait a minute..."

While they were talking, Jenn had gone into the kitchen—the refrigerator was the only thing heavy enough to barricade the door. When Neesha saw what she was doing, she quickly came to help. She was stronger than she looked, and they moved the refrigerator across the linoleum floor with a screech. Although, to be honest? Even with it in front of the door, it was only going to slow down an assault by a minute or so, at the most.

Out in the living room, Dan had started pulling the cushions off the sofa as Eden called from the bedroom, "Danny, where's Greg's gun?"

"Zanella has it," he said tersely as he pulled up the metal-and-canvas bed frame that was folded into the body of the sofa. Normally, when it was closed, the folded mattress would occupy all of the space inside the furniture's outer shell. But with the mattress on the floor . . . He pulled his phone from his ear again, to look at it now in disbelief. "Jesus Christ, they cut me off." He redialed. "Neesha, forget about the closet—I need you over here. *Now.*"

Jenn took out her cell phone, and dialed 9-1-1, too. "Maybe I'll get through."

"I should just go out there," Neesha said. "Give myself up."

They all spoke at once. "Like hell," Dan said as Eden called from the bedroom, "Yeah, *that's* not going to happen," as Jenn said, "Honey, we're not going to let you do that."

"But they'll kill you," she told Danny, fiercely, turning to look at Jenn, too. "Maybe they'll kill all of you. And they're going to find me anyway."

"I'm calling Izzy again," Eden said, as if, like Superman, he could instantly swoop in and save them, despite being all the way on the other side of town.

"Neesha," Dan said to the little girl. "Look at me. If you really overheard them talking before they took Ben—"

"I did!"

"Then you have to climb in here and hide. Whatever happens, whatever you hear, you *have to* be silent. Because once they find you and kill you?" Dan looked from Neesha to Jenn, his face grim. "Ben's dead, too."

On the way to Crossroads, just to add insult to injury, Eden's wicked stepfather Greg did the glorious Technicolor yawn and vomited all over himself in the front seat of Izzy's rental car.

"Really?" Izzy said, pulling hard over into a deserted strip-mall parking lot as the malodorous smell assaulted him, full force. *"Really?"*

His night had already been a suckfest, and he'd been driving with his full focus on the task at hand—going to Crossroads to free Ben— trying *not* to think about Eden.

And yet he couldn't stop himself from seeing her face and hearing her crying after the truth had come out about the hell she'd survived after Katrina.

She cried, but not because of the injustice and abuse she'd endured at her brother-in-law Ron's despicable hands. No, the outpouring of emotion had come when Danny'd put his arms around her and said, *I'm sorry.*

And not just *I'm sorry you had to go through this,* but also *I'm sorry that no one believed you.*

As Izzy jammed the car into park, his cell phone started doing its happy little vibrating dance in his cargo-shorts pocket. But there was no time to reach for it and answer as he unlocked the doors and burst out into the heat of the night as fast as his legs could carry him. He knew some guys—some of them SEALs or former SEALs—who reacted to someone's barfing by immediately barfing, too, like the most disgusting call and response in the history of the planet. But his stomach was made of iron, so that wasn't the reason for his speed. He executed the front-hood slide-over in a mad rush only in order to open the passenger-side door and pull out Greg the human volcano before he erupted again.

Although, *damn* Skippy. The damage was done and the car was now a frakking stank-mobile of vomitous doom. And even with his cast-iron innards, it was hard for Izzy not to gag.

He had Greg-puke on his hands from grabbing the man by his shirt, and there was no way he was reaching into his pocket to pull out his phone with those fingers, so he let the call go to voice mail as he strategized his next move. It was probably just Danny, anyway, calling for a sit-rep. Izzy'd call him back, after there was better news than *Hey, the inside of my rental car—the second car I've rented because the first one was totaled—is now a new color, and it's not a pretty one.*

Holy shit.

The splatter factor was off the charts—the passenger-side dash was sprayed, as was the floor mat and part of the seat, which was fabric of course, here in the land of molten-lava heat. Vinyl, in Vegas, could deliver third-degree burns, but it sure as hell would've been easier to de-puke. As Izzy stood there in the oppressive heat, he wished he'd been given an option at the rental-car counter.

Although, he could just imagine that conversation. *I understand you'd prefer the ball-burning but easy-to-clean vinyl, sir, because you anticipate driving passengers who'll regurgitate regularly. Please initial here, here, and here, acknowledging that you've been properly warned of the potential danger to your nether regions. A barf-scraper and absorbent towels come with the vehicle. Would you care to rent a cooler for an additional ten dollars a day so you can ice your scrotum after being scalded?*

He wished Eden were here, because she would think that was pretty funny, too, and . . .

Yeah.

Izzy pulled out the floor mat and deposited it next to Greg. The man was down on his knees, in the classic position of acquiescence and prayer, bowing to the gods of substance abuse and overindulgence, and making another loudly yukatatious offering right there on the pitted pavement.

"Fuck," Izzy said in disgust as he wiped his hands on the back of Greg's shirt—which wasn't all that clean, but at least was vomit-free.

And hey, it could've been worse. Dude clearly had been on a liquid diet for days. He could've been blowing chunks.

There was nothing for Izzy to do but take off his own T-shirt and use it to wipe clean the interior of the car—at least as much as he could. There was surely a convenience store open somewhere between here and Crossroads, where he could stop in and pick up a T-shirt. And? If he were really lucky? It would have Siegfried & Roy on it.

Eden had left half of a bottle of water in the car door, and Izzy was using it, with his shirt, to clean up as best he could, when his phone jiggled again.

He checked his hand—clean, okay, clean-ish—before he dug for it and... Shit, it was Eden, and she'd called before, left a message, too. Izzy hit talk. "Hey. I haven't made it to Crossroads yet—"

"Izzy!" Eden sounded almost out of breath, as if something was terribly wrong. "Thank God. Ben's not at Crossroads, he's been kidnapped. The men, from the Starbucks—that I hit with your car? They're here!"

What the fuck...? If he'd spoken aloud, Eden didn't acknowledge it. She just kept going.

"Neesha—she was hiding and she saw them take Ben, but now they're back, and she said they were going to kill you and Danny because they know you're military, but Danny won't hide—Jenn wants him to hide, or to go out the window, but he *won't* and—"

"Whoa," Izzy said. "Whoa, Eden, slow down. Where *are* you?"

"At the apartment," she told him. "Izzy, please, you have to get over here. Now."

Greg had collapsed in a puddle of puke, his cheek against the pavement and his eyes closed, and Izzy tucked his phone between his shoulder and his ear as he grabbed the man by the belt and hauled him up, moving him onto the sidewalk in front of a dark and shuttered nail salon, as Eden kept talking.

"They're down in the courtyard, but Danny's sure they're just waiting for backup before they come in," she told him as he ran to the car and climbed in, then peeled out of the lot with a squeal of tires. "We can't leave without them seeing us, and there's no way to stop them. You have Greg's gun."

Shit, he did—and it was locked in the trunk. He squealed to a stop, popped the trunk, and grabbed the case, bringing it up into the front seat with him, as he pulled back out into the street

"I'm on my way," Izzy told her, pushing the pedal to the metal on the deserted streets, as he keyed Eden's address into the car's GPS, then focused on unlocking the case. "But I'm—shit!—at least fifteen minutes from you." If he didn't get stopped for going ninety in a forty-five-mile-an-hour zone... But maybe it would be a good idea to get a police escort over there. "Sweetheart, stay on the phone with me, okay, but tell Jenn or Dan to call the police."

"We've been trying," Eden said. "We keep getting put on hold. Danny's been disconnected, twice."

Shit-fuck. "Tell Danny to call Mark Jenkins," Izzy said as he blew through a second red light, then slipped the weapon and several magazines of ammo into the pockets of his shorts. "His wife, Lindsey, has a contact in the FBI, but shit, whoever we call is going to take time to get to you, too, and... Listen, sweetheart, do you know any of your neighbors? Is there anyone you can call, maybe have everyone open their doors and go into the courtyard and just scream and yell and wake up as many people in the complex as you can? I'm thinking there's safety in numbers."

"I don't know anyone here," she told him. "I don't have anyone's phone number." And then she gasped words that made his heart damn near stop: "Izzy! Danny! Oh, my God, they're coming!"

Eden came out of the bedroom, still on the phone with Zanella. "Danny," she said again.

"I heard you the first time," Dan told his sister as he put the cushions back on the sofa, with Neesha hidden safely inside.

"Dan," Jenni said. "Please. Just go out the living-room window. I *know* you can make it up onto the roof without them seeing you..."

"I can't do that." He took her face in his hands and kissed her, briefly, on his way over to the door. His plan was to throw his weight against the refrigerator, try to keep them out as long as he possibly could, while hoping one of them would be foolish enough to stick a hand with a weapon inside, to fire it indiscriminately.

At which point Danny would gain possession of said weapon and kill the bastards. Provided he was still alive . . .

"Please," Jenni said again. "If Neesha's right, they're just going to kill you. No questions, no warning."

"I can't just desert you," he told her, told Eden, too.

"What do you think you'll be doing when they kill you and you're *dead?*" Jenn asked.

He had no good answer for that. "Just get in the bathroom and lock the door," he ordered them. "Now."

"Izzy says that if *he* was the bald guy from the mall, and he suspected that you were military—forget about SpecOps," Eden said. "He'd kill you straight off, too."

"Thanks so much, Zanella," Dan said loudly enough for Eden's phone to pick up his voice.

"Uh-huh," Eden said, into her phone, still talking to Zanella as she went into the kitchen. "Okay, I got it, yeah . . ."

"Danny, please," Jenni begged him, moving away from Eden and not toward the bathroom, where they'd be safest should the attack come through the bedroom window. "I love you."

"I love you, too," he told her, right before—what the *hell?*—someone—Eden, damn it—hit him hard over the head with something heavy. The room spun and he fought it as he hit the floor with his knees, but she hit him again, almost gently this time, and he lost the battle and the world went black.

Eden picked up the cell phone that she'd dropped, in order to drop her brother with the heaviest thing in the apartment—a metal statue of

Buddha that had been sitting on the kitchen counter when she'd moved in.

"Oh, my God," Jenn said. "I can't believe you did that. Is he okay?" She searched for his pulse, fingers at his very unconscious throat. "Okay. All right. His pulse is strong and steady. But now what? Do we hide him?"

"I hit him where you told me to," Eden told Izzy as she shook her head no at Jenn. "But I had to hit him twice."

Izzy exhaled hard on the other end of the phone. "Damn, he's going to kill me," he said, his voice rich and warm in her ear. "Okay, get his cell phone, Eden. Get it now, hang up, put your phone—this one that you're talking on right now—in your pocket, and call me back on *his* phone."

"What?" she said as she found Danny's phone. "Why?"

"Do it," he said. "He's got a better phone, it's got GPS—it'll be easier to track you, but please, sweetheart, don't question everything—we don't have that much time."

"You better pick up," she said as she cut the connection and quickly found Izzy's number in Danny's phone book, in the Zs.

"Eden," Jenn said, from her place on the floor next to Dan, his head in her lap, "please don't make me regret trusting you..."

"You're not trusting me," Eden said. "You're trusting Izzy."

He answered almost before it rang. "Good," he said. "Now *run* and find a shirt with long sleeves, something with cuffs that'll be tight around your wrists."

Eden ran to her bedroom and grabbed a shirt from her closet and pulled it on as Izzy said, "Put *this* phone with the signal open and on, put it up your sleeve, close to your wrist. They're going to search you, but they'll probably start at your forearms and work down, so they're more likely to miss it. Please, sweet Jesus..."

"Eden?" Jenn called from the living room.

"I'll be right there," she called back.

"Eden," Izzy said. "This may get far worse before it gets better. I need you to brace yourself, because if they've come back to grab you, it could mean that something bad has happened to Ben."

"Don't say that!"

"I'm sorry," he said. "I just... I need you to be strong. Even if Ben is—"

"Don't!" Ben wasn't dead. He couldn't be dead.

"You *have* to be strong," Izzy said. "For Danny and for Jenn, too. I know you can do that, sweetheart. Can you do that?"

"Yes," she managed.

"Eden, someone with a key is unlocking the door," Jenn called from the living room.

"I'm going to find you, okay?" Izzy told her. "Whatever happens. Even if this cell-phone thing doesn't work? I am. Going. To find you. Believe that, Eden. I need you to believe me."

She nodded, but realized he couldn't see her. So instead of saying yes, she whispered, "I love you."

"*Eden!*" Jenn called from the living room.

"I love you, too," Izzy told her, his voice rough. "Come on, do it, sweetheart. Now. And remember what you're going to say, before they even get inside...?"

"I remember," Eden said, and put Dan's cell phone, signal on, up her sleeve.

Please, sweet Jesus, indeed.

"My brother is unconscious—don't kill him—he's the only one who knows where Neesha is," Eden said, loudly, to the men outside, right before they broke through the chain on the door. "He's the only one of us she trusted. And if you kill *us*? You'll have nothing to trade him for the girl."

Whoever was out there was big, and just by pushing the door, the refrigerator moved across the floor with a scraping sound.

Jenn put her hands up over her head, the way Eden had done.

Eden—who'd moved protectively in front of Dan, and who'd

shown Jenn in a quick flash as she'd rushed out of the bedroom that she'd hidden his cell phone up her sleeve—kept talking, repeating the same information over and over. "Don't kill him—he can't hurt you—he's the only one—"

The first man in was carrying the biggest gun that Jenn had ever seen, and he waved it almost wildly, pointing it from Dan to Eden to Jenn. "Down on the floor, hands on your head, move away from him! Move *away* from him."

Jenn didn't want to move. Dan's head was in her lap, and she didn't want to leave him there, with his head against the worn carpeting.

"Jenn!" Eden said sharply. "Do what they—"

Jenn didn't hear the rest because another man, a man who was wearing a hat despite the heat, hit her. It was only a backhanded blow, but it caught her by surprise and it pushed her, hard, away from Dan, whose head hit the floor and bounced.

His eyes didn't open—he was out cold. And fear slid through Jenn, because people died of head injuries, even seemingly mild ones.

But Izzy was coming. Izzy was on his way. And Izzy had saved Dan's life once before. He'd do it again. She held on to that thought as she lay on the floor.

"Don't you hit her!" Eden was saying as third man searched the apartment, looking for Izzy, or maybe Neesha.

"There's no one else here," that man reported, coming out of Eden's bedroom. "No sign of the bigger guy."

"The bigger guy," Eden said, "is my bastard of a husband, and he left me. For good. Okay? He went back to the Navy base in San Diego this morning."

"Good to know. Shoot the fuck out of this other sailor if he so much as moves," the bald man ordered, and now Jenn was praying that Dan would *not* wake up. Not too soon. "Either one of you tries anything funny"—he was talking to them now—"he's dead. You understand?"

Jenn nodded, and rough hands touched her, searching her—it was the man with the hat. He went through her pockets, pulling out her cell phone and the set of keys to their rental car—it was all she had on her. That didn't stop him from searching for more, his hand lingering on her breasts and between her legs.

But that didn't matter. Nothing mattered more than helping Eden keep Dan's cell phone hidden from them. As Jenn watched, Eden was searched by the bald man, who'd kept his gun securely in his right hand—as if he didn't trust her enough to tuck it in the top of his pants, the way the man with the hat had done when he'd searched Jenn.

It meant that the bald man's search of Eden was less thorough, although he was heavy with the inappropriate touching, too. Not that she'd expected anything less from men who worked for a crime boss who ran a child prostitution ring.

Eden tried to distract him further by talking. "My brother Ben is missing. Do you have him? Is he safe?"

"The kid's a junkie," the bald man told Eden as he pulled her phone—not Dan's—out of the top pocket of her jeans. "Going into withdrawal...He goddamn puked on my new boots."

"He's a diabetic," Eden said sharply. "He needs insulin. Where is he? I want to see him!"

The bald man flipped her over onto her back, holding her by her right arm—the arm that had the cell phone—and she squeaked in alarm. He shoved his gun up under her chin.

"You have a lot of questions and demands for someone who doesn't appear to have the power here," he said.

"He's just a kid," Eden said. "A sick kid. He doesn't know where Neesha is. He *doesn't*."

"And you don't, either," the man said, clearly not believing her. "Only this one knows." He gestured with his head toward Dan. "Mr. Conveniently Unconscious."

"I knocked him out," Eden said, "because I knew you'd come in shooting, and he *is* the only one who knows where Neesha is. If you killed him, I'd never get Ben back—and I *want* my little brother *back*."

"Heartwarming," the bald man said. "But someone's a liar. When I told Ben that unless he talked, I was going to come and kill *you?* *He* told *me* that *you* knew where the girl was, and that I better not kill you or I'd never find her. Now *you're* telling me that your *other* brother knows where she is. What would you think if you were me?" He moved his gun from beneath her chin, but turned and aimed it now at Dan's head. "I'm thinking you *do* know, and you're going to tell me where the girl is, in about three seconds. Three..."

"No," Jenn said. "Please. No—" even as Eden said, "I *don't* know! I don't!"

"Two..."

"Please, *please,* I honestly don't know," Eden said, her voice shaking. "But Danny does. He *does.* And if I were you? What I'd do is I *wouldn't* kill him, because what if I'm right, and he's the only one who knows?"

"Shit, Jake," the man with that hat said, holding out Jenn's cell phone. "This bitch put in a call to 9-1-1."

"Shh," the third man said. "Listen..."

Sirens. Way in the distance.

"The police are coming," the man with the hat said, shifting his weight toward the door. "Let's just kill them and go."

"No," Izzy said. "No," as he led the police car, siren wailing, on a crazy chase toward Eden's apartment.

"No, don't—please, don't!" he heard Jenn say through that still-open cell-phone connection. "I called them, but I never got through."

Izzy was still a good five minutes away, and he gunned the little car faster, straining to hear the conversation that was going on in Eden's living room, more frightened than he'd ever been in his life that the next sounds he might hear would be gunshots. Three of them.

But now Eden was talking again. Her voice came through more clearly than the others, probably because she was talking toward the phone in her sleeve, because she knew he was listening.

"If you kill us, you'll never find Neesha," she said. "But if you leave us alive? We'll get Danny to tell us where she is, and we'll make a trade. Her for Ben."

It was unbelievable. Eden was trying to talk them into leaving, to just walk away and let all three of them go free. Izzy held his breath as he blew past the turnoff that would have taken him to the apartment complex. The last thing he needed to do was lead the police and their siren over there now.

There was a brief silence in the apartment, but then the man the other had called Jake, the one who seemed to be in charge, said, "No." He laughed. "No, we'll play your little game, but by our rules. You're coming with us. Both of you. You're worth more to us alive than dead, anyway. Nathan, get the big girl."

Thank God, thank *God* . . .

But then there was a shuffling, bumping sound, and Izzy held his breath again, well aware that if Eden dropped Dan's cell phone out of her sleeve, they were back to being dead again.

Instead she said sharply, "Don't touch me there."

Jake laughed. "I'll touch you wherever I want, bitch."

"What about Danny?" Jenn asked.

"Todd's gonna keep an eye on him," Jake said. "He's going to watch the place, make sure *Danny* doesn't do anything besides answer his phone when we call him, and then go get the girl so we can make the trade. So let's hope you were telling the truth about your *bastard of a husband*, I believe is how you referred to him." He must've been talking to Eden now. "He shows up? Todd'll be watching your front door, and he'll shoot them both dead, and then he'll call me, and I'll kill you, too."

"I told you the truth," Eden lied. "He left. He was so mad at me when I wrecked his car—trying to ram you and Todd?"

The woman was brilliant. She'd just told Izzy exactly who he had to look for—and possibly take out—before going into her apartment to revive Dan.

She was still talking. "I believe the words he said when he left were *the fucking I'm getting is no longer worth the fucking I'm getting.*"

Ah, Eed, no, don't bring sex into it. These guys were animals, and it never, ever paid to put the idea of sex into an animal's brain.

Unless...Damn, it was possible Eden was giving them that message on purpose. *Here's what I'll do to protect my family. Anyone interested in making a trade...?*

The thought of it made Izzy sick. But he knew why she was doing it—for the same reason she'd given her sister's husband what he'd wanted in trade for Ben's insulin, after New Orleans flooded. Because there were things worth dying for, and face it, sex wasn't one of them.

Back in the apartment, Eden wasn't done talking. "You better leave my cell phone here for Danny. He forgot his charger, and his battery's dead. I mean, unless you want to wait to contact him until he can get to the Sprint store tomorrow."

Without a doubt, Eden was on top of everything. Somehow she knew not to say that Dan had lost his phone—that would have seemed too coincidental and would have sent up a signal that something was off. But a forgotten charger when visiting from out of town? That had happened to everyone.

There was talking that Izzy couldn't quite make out, then Eden said, "That one. Leave it where he can find it."

There was more random noise—movement—and some more conversation that Izzy couldn't hear, something about insulin, and then...

"Quiet, both of you," Izzy heard Jake command Eden and Jenn. "You make any noise at all as we get out to the van? And Todd will kill Danny."

"Make it fast, Jake," someone said—had to be Todd—clearly unhappy about being left behind.

Although dude had absolutely no clue about the raging shitstorm of unhappiness that was barreling toward him.

No doubt about it, Izzy was going to leave his boot print on the son of a bitch's face.

But first he had to make sure he had both his cell phone and Greg's. Because he had to ditch this car. Once he did, he could lose the pursuing police officers far more easily—whoops, there were two cars behind him now.

Yeah, he was going to have to do this on foot. He reached over and erased the GPS device's memory, and took a hard turn into a neighborhood that was more middle class than the poverty-stricken street where Greg and Ivette lived. He could see from the map on the GPS that this entire development was less square little blocks and more winding, looping roads. For someone with his skill and training, it was an E&E playground. Most of the houses had fences around them, but nothing that he couldn't get over easily.

Thirty seconds after leaving the car, he'd have successfully escaped and evaded, and he'd be in the clear and on his way back to Eden's.

He found a cul-de-sac on the map, and as he turned the corner he did a quick visual. There were no other cars on the street, no people around. There was going to be some property damage, but it couldn't be helped. He'd pay for it—he'd be happy to—if he were still alive after this goatfuck was over.

He kept the car in gear as he steered to the left, then opened the door and rolled out onto—shit!—not a plush lawn like the yard before it, but desert-style zero-scaping. Little stones and bigger stones and yes, that *was* a cactus he'd just gotten intimate with. But he kept his mouth shut, internalizing his disbelief and pain—needles in his ass could wait while Eden could not—and kept moving silently in the darkness as the car kept on its path, with both police cars in hot pursuit.

He was over a fence and into a backyard, and over the next fence into the neighbor's yard, too, before he heard the crash and scraping of the rental car hitting someone's palm tree.

He heard the shouting of the police officers as they realized that he was no longer in the rental car.

And then, like the good Navy SEAL that he was, he became one with the night, and he vanished.

CHAPTER
TWENTY-SIX

I zzy couldn't kill Todd.

The prick had positioned himself at the window of the apartment directly across the courtyard from Eden's place. He was just sitting there—the guy she'd tried to run over in the street—watching the place, in clear view of anyone who might be looking to take him out.

And even though the range of Greg's handgun wouldn't do the necessary damage from up here on the apartment complex roof—Izzy would need a rifle for that—he could've quite easily worked his way around to that side of the building, without being seen. Then he could've dropped silently down onto the walkway and crept along bent over, down beneath the windowsill, only to pop up right in front of the motherfucker, and shoot him between the eyes at a far more acceptable range of about two feet.

The problem with *that*, aside from the noise from the gunshot and the inconvenience of an impending police visit, was that Izzy had no idea how often Todd was in touch with the mothership, aka Jake-the-asshole-from-the-mall. It also served them better, having Todd here, regularly reporting in that "Danny hasn't left the building," and "Danny *still* hasn't left the building..."

Even though Dan would be long gone, along with Izzy, back the way Izzy had gotten in—via the living-room window that faced the street.

Greg's cell phone shook once, and Izzy glanced down at it—it was Mark Jenkins calling him back. Izzy had already spoken with Mark's wife, Lindsey, and had given her the rundown and had gotten *their* bad news—she'd miscarried—from her.

He answered, speaking softly, moving over to the edge of the roof that looked down on the street, where it was silent in the darkness. "Mark, man, I'm so sorry."

"It happens," Jenk said. "Often, apparently, in the first trimester. I really had no idea, I mean, she's healthy, so I thought—" He broke off. "Look, we can talk about this later. Your problem's more immediate. Lindsey got the software working. According to the computer program, Dan's cell phone is heading south on Interstate 15. If you left right now, and you went the speed limit, you'd be about twenty minutes behind them. They're a few miles north of the exit for Route 161. I'll text you with an update either way—if they take it or go past it."

"Thanks, bro," Izzy said, still watching the street, where no one and nothing was moving. He went back to the courtyard and double-checked Todd, who was still sitting there, and still looking pissed. "I'm going in to get Gillman now."

"Lindsey called Jules Cassidy, you know, from the FBI, and forwarded him the pictures you sent her," Jenk reported. "He ID'd the two men as Jake Dyland and William Nathan, and trust me, you don't want them anywhere near Eden or Jenn."

"Too late," Izzy said.

"Yeah, I know. Cassidy's going to call you," Jenk said. "He's contacting the local Bureau, and he says don't do anything until you talk to him."

"He's not, like, conveniently in town for a conference...?" Izzy asked.

"Not a chance," Jenk said. "I think he's in Boston."

"So whoever he's talking to out here—he has no clue who they are or whether they got promoted because they kissed the right asses," Izzy clarified.

Jenk was unequivocal. "Correct."

"Fuck that," Izzy said.

Jenk laughed, but even that sounded grim. "I knew you were going to say that. Hey, heads-up, Linds says that Danny's cell phone just exited the interstate. It's now heading south on 161, toward a town called Jean with a *J*."

"Keep me posted," Izzy said.

"Will do," Jenk said. "We're picking up Lopez now, we'll get to you ASAP, so stall if you can."

"I can't," Izzy told his friend as he prepared to go over the side of the roof.

"Yeah," Jenk said. "I knew that, too."

Neesha was trapped.

She couldn't get out from where Ben's brother had hidden her, beneath the sofa, even after she heard Todd and the others leave, taking Jenn and Eden with them.

Panic made her heart start to pound and she tried pushing up against the canvas and the metal frame, but lying with her arms at her sides, as she was, she couldn't put her shoulders into it, and it only moved a little bit. She stopped almost immediately, because the fear that Todd might've stayed somewhere close by, where he could look in through the living-room window and see the sofa shaking, was stronger than any claustrophobia that she felt.

And she believed what Ben's brother Dan had told her. That if they found her—Todd and the others—then Ben, too, would die. Of course, she wanted to believe that. It was very easy to believe such an outcome when the alternative was to give herself up and face her own demise.

"Dan," she called softly, praying that he would hear her and wake up. "Danny!"

But he didn't answer, and she lay there in silence for what felt like a very long time, but was quite possibly only minutes.

And then, finally, she heard a sound, something scraping, something rustling—was it Todd, coming back inside?—and she held her breath.

Except then she heard a voice whisper, "Neesha? Don't freak. It's me, Izzy. I'm going to open up the sofa now."

And she started to cry, because Mr. Nelson's men—Todd, and the others—had made it quite clear that if Izzy came back? Then Eden and Jenni and Ben were as good as dead.

But he somehow knew what she was thinking, because as he held out his hand to pull her up and out of her hiding place, he added, "It's okay. Todd sucks at surveillance. He's watching the door from an empty apartment across the courtyard. I went up on the roof and spotted him sitting at the window, what a dickweed—which is good for us."

He wasn't wearing a shirt, and his back and shoulders were all scratched up and bleeding slightly, plus he had a huge scar on his chest. It should have made him look scary, but to Neesha, it made him seem impossible to kill, which was a good thing. He was self-conscious about it, though, and he quickly unzipped a bag that was over on the floor, and pulled out a T-shirt and slipped it on even as he kept reassuring her.

"He didn't see me come in," he continued. "No one did. I came through this window, on the other side of the building, down from the roof."

She'd looked out of that window before, and it was way up high, on this second story, and she went over to it now, wiping her eyes, afraid that someone passing by would see the rope he'd used to climb down.

But there was no rope. And he hadn't broken the window. Everything looked normal—it was tightly shut.

The only thing out of the ordinary was that he'd taken the screen off, and it was leaning against the wall, near the air conditioner. But from the street? No one would ever suspect he'd entered the apartment that way.

She wasn't quite sure how he'd done it.

"Let's keep that closed," he said, talking about the blinds, and as she turned back, she saw he'd already gotten down on floor next to

Dan. "Be a good girl and get me some ice—" He stopped himself and glanced up at her, his dark eyes filled with both an apology and understanding.

"Shit," he said. "Sorry. I bet you heard that a lot. *Be a good girl . . .* I wasn't thinking."

"It's okay," she said. "You didn't mean it the way they did."

"Still."

"I'll get the ice," she told him, and went to do just that.

The light hurt his eyes, and his head was throbbing, and it took Dan several long seconds to remember where he was—and what had happened.

The freaky little girl—Neesha—was out of the couch and was peering at Dan over Izzy's shoulder as the other SEAL knelt beside him.

"You're okay," Izzy told him as he helped Dan sit up and put the ice where it would help the most. Jesus, he was dizzy . . . "That must've been some fight—you're lucky they didn't kill you."

It was then it came back, and he looked around wildly, but Jenni and Eden were both gone. And Dan pushed Izzy away from him, hard.

"You can't lie for shit, Zanella," Dan said, "so don't even bother. I *know* you told Eden to hit me—"

"And a fine job she did of it, too, Buddha be praised. You're not badly injured, and you had just the right-length nap."

"I should fucking kill you!" Danny swung for him again, but the world tilted and he had to stop and press his forehead to the floor in order not to get sick.

"You could try," Izzy said. "But I'd like to remind you that you wouldn't be *able* to try, if Eden *hadn't* hit you. You wouldn't be able to do anything. Eden's and my goal was to make this very conversation— to kill me or not to kill me—possible. It was to keep you undead. And I mean the good kind of undead, not the creepy vampire kind, regardless of any lovely, sparkly—"

Danny lifted his head and substituted the floor for the bag of ice that Izzy had given him. "Jesus Christ, they have Jenni! Do you have any idea what those men are capable of?"

"I'm sure Jenn would agree," Izzy spoke over him "She doesn't seem the type to be into the whole pale, cold skin thing, not to mention the creepy stalker vibe. I'm betting she's far more Team Jacob anyway—"

"Zanella! For the love of God!"

"And yes, I *do* know what they're capable of," Izzy said, "so if you've managed to get your eyes focusing in tandem again, and I've finally got your full attention, with all threats to beat the crap out of me temporarily out of your system, I'm ready to give you a sit-rep. You ready to listen?"

Dan managed a nod and a somewhat civil "Yes. Please."

"We got one man, guy named Todd, last name unknown, watching the front door of this apartment," Izzy said, "with orders to shoot to kill if I show up, or if you attempt to leave without clearing your movement with the boss, the big bald guy whose handle is Jake. So whatever you do, don't go out that door. Eden and Jenn are still in transit, but we're tracking their movement as we speak, because your amazing, incredible sister who saved your life tonight also managed to hide your cell phone up her sleeve."

"Oh, thank God," Dan said, closing his eyes. But he opened them immediately as Izzy continued.

"She also convinced them to leave you *her* cell phone so that they could get in touch with you—they've already sent you a text, telling you to call Jenn's phone, allegedly to set up an exchange—Jenn, Eden, and Ben for Neesha." Izzy looked over at the girl. "We're not going to do that. We have no intention of giving you to them." He looked back at Dan. "Same way they have no intention of giving Jenn, Eden, and Ben back to us. They didn't try at all to hide who they were. Todd and Jake and a dude named Nathan all called each other by name while they were in here."

Dan was still focused on what Izzy'd said a moment earlier. "Tracking them how?" he asked.

"You want the good news or the bad news?" Izzy asked, but didn't let him answer. "Bad news: Lindsey miscarried, but out of the two of them, Mark's the emotional wreck, even though he's pretending to be strong. They just got home from the hospital and jumped on top of this as a major distraction. They're picking up Lopez, and the three of them are looking for the fastest way up here. And with Markie-Mark in the equation, I'm thinking they might be here in about ten minutes, via stealth bomber or maybe space shuttle. But the *real* good news is that he and Lindsey *still* have your cell phone's GPS info in her laptop, from the last time we were war-gaming. He's got the program up and running, so whenever you're ready to blow this Popsicle cart, we can start following the bastards that took our family, because we now know *exactly* where they are—which is now thirty-five minutes ahead of us." Izzy paused. "Unless you want to follow the rules and wait to talk to the FBI. Jenk told me Lindsey called Jules Cassidy—and I agree with her, we can trust him, he's good people, but he's in Boston? And I have no idea who he's going to contact out here to work with us, *or* how long they're going to take to get their asses in gear, so—"

"I'm not waiting for anyone," Dan said. "If we know where Jenni and Eden are . . . ? I say, fuck the rules."

Izzy nodded and held out a hand to help him to his feet. "Welcome to my world."

CHAPTER
TWENTY-SEVEN

SATURDAY, MAY 9, 2009

3:45 A.M.

E den turned and looked at Jenn in the dimness of the back of the windowless van as the vehicle slowed and turned onto a bumpier, less well-maintained road. They'd been traveling for a while, first on what felt like a highway, then on smaller roads, still at high speeds, and then on what may have been dirt at a much slower pace.

This, however, was even more pitted and rough. It was possibly made of gravel—there were pings and clunks from small pieces of rock being thrown by the tires, up against the bottom and sides of the van.

All in all, they'd been on the move for just over forty minutes.

It didn't take much more than that to go from the bustle of downtown Vegas out into the middle of nowhere, as this bumpy road implied.

Eden had checked Dan's cell phone a number of times throughout their journey, and had discovered, very early on, that both the active phone call and the GPS setting generated a glow. She'd had to work to keep it covered and shielded with her body, curling into near-fetal position, which wasn't that odd for a kidnapping victim to do.

Jenn had helped, putting her arms around Eden and spooning together, once she'd realized what was going on. Halfway through the trip, Eden had figured out how to dim the phone's screen, but even then, Jenn didn't let go of her.

Eden knew Jenn was scared—she was, too.

Jenn was also intensely worried about Danny—about how hard Eden had hit him, about him not waking up. She was also worried about him *waking* up and running out of the apartment wildly in his search for them and running directly into Todd's deadly weapon.

Eden was afraid of that, too.

It was entirely possible Jenn was never going to see Dan again. It was possible that Eden, too, had seen Izzy's beautiful smile and heard his infectious laughter for the very last time...

I'm going to find you, he'd said, but he wouldn't find more than her body if she were dead.

But she couldn't think like that. It wouldn't help her.

I need you to believe me, Izzy had told her. So she would. She'd believe that he was going to find her—find all of them—and then, after this nightmare was over, when she was safe in his arms? When she told him, again, *I love you*, he would believe her, too.

"It's going to be all right," she whispered to Jenn, in part because she wanted to put voice to it. It was what she wanted to feel and maybe if she said it out loud, it would help add to her conviction.

"I said no talking!" the man named Jake barked.

Eden had also wanted to test to see if the two men in the front of the van could hear her if she whispered to Jenn.

Apparently, the answer to that was a solid yes.

She cautiously checked the phone, to make sure they still had cell signal out here, and they did. Not for the first time, she was grateful that Izzy had made her take Dan's phone. Hers could well have had zero bars a mile outside of the city limits, depending on where they were.

As it was, they'd lost signal a few times, no doubt when they'd passed too close to cell towers, and Eden had checked to make sure the phone was set completely on silent, which it was, with the volume turned all the way down, which it wasn't—before she'd redialed Izzy's number—just in case the GPS signal wasn't enough, and she needed to be in direct contact for him to track them. It would've been bad for

the thing to boop and beep or the phone to ring, and then have Izzy
pick up with an amplified *Hello?*

Not that he would have, but still.

But now here they were, with the van's tires crunching on more of
that gravel as they made another turn and—maybe they weren't at
their final destination, because the gravel turned back into pavement,
smooth beneath the tires. And they sped up, but only briefly before
they slowed down even more.

One of the two men up front spoke—it was the man with the hat
who'd wanted to kill them back in the apartment. "Pull close to the
building so the plane can land—"

"Shut up," Jake cut him off loudly enough for Eden to risk a whisper to Jenn, as he said, "Jesus, what are you? A goddamn moron?"

"We need to ditch this," Eden breathed, even as she wondered who
was coming here via airplane. "We can't let them find it." When Izzy'd
been giving her rapid-fire instructions, he'd warned her that wherever
they were being taken, they could well have electronic detection de-
vices in place—and it would pick up the signal from Dan's phone if
they brought it inside.

And that would be a very bad thing. Because Jake and company
would then take her and Jenn somewhere else. Somewhere that Izzy
and Dan wouldn't be able to track them. That is, if Eden and Jenni
weren't just killed right then and there.

Izzy had also warned her against hiding the phone in whatever vehicle they were transported in. If it was found in there, there'd be no
doubt as to whom it belonged.

Jenn nodded.

And as the man with the hat—Nathan—shot back with, "Yeah, *I'm*
the moron. I'm not the one always thinking with my dick," Eden whispered, "I'll pretend to faint and toss it under the van. Do whatever you
can to help."

"Just keep your mouth shut," Jake said as Jenn nodded again. "This
is almost over."

"It better be," Nathan said.

Except, wait, what if they moved the van? Eden didn't have a chance to ask the question aloud, because the front door opened and the interior lights came on—further proof that they were in the middle of nowhere. Their abductors knew that there was no one around to see them.

Eden squinted in the sudden brightness as they sat up as Jenn looked at her again, and moved down toward the back doors of the van so that she would be the first one out.

Eden pointed to herself—let her go first—as she ended the open call to Izzy, and sent a text message that she'd already prepared.

Arrived. I love you.

Be careful, she mouthed, and Jenn nodded briefly, but the look in her eyes was steely, and Eden knew she didn't expect either of them to live to see the dawn.

The doors swung open with a metallic screech, and Jake and Nathan the hat man were there, weapons drawn.

Please God, let this work . . .

"We should've taken her with us."

Izzy was driving the car that they'd hot-wired from a hotel parking lot not far from Eden's apartment complex, because they didn't want to risk taking Dan's rental car on the off chance that Todd was keeping an eye on it, too.

Izzy suspected that Dan had never before hot-wired a car for his own personal uses, and had certainly never done it for any other reason here in the States. Under other circumstances, he would've been ragging on the fact that Dan had popped his grand-theft-auto cherry, but seeing how they were both a little preoccupied with the task at hand, they'd been following the signal from Dan's cell phone in relative silence.

But now Dan was starting to second-guess the extremely correct choice they'd made in leaving Neesha behind, in Eden's apartment.

"We couldn't take her with us, man," Izzy said, telling Dan nothing he didn't already know. But sometimes it helped to be reminded. "If something goes wrong, we'd be delivering her right into the hands of the people who want her dead."

And okay, *that* was stupid to say. *If something goes wrong...* Definitely not a good strategy to add to Gillman's doubts and fears. This was a success-mandatory mission. Failure was *not* an option.

"Nothing's going to go wrong," Izzy continued. "*Because* we're not going to be dragging a kid around with us, right? You know if we took the time to get her out the window and then down from the roof? We'd still be up there, bro."

Dan nodded at that. "Yeah," he said. "I know. I just..." He exhaled hard. "I'm having second thoughts about having to leave Greg's hand-gun behind."

"We couldn't leave Neesha there alone," Izzy reiterated. "Not without it." He glanced at Dan again. "You saw the power it gave her."

Dan nodded. He'd given the girl a crash course in firing and re-loading the handgun while Izzy had scrounged in Eden's kitchen and bathroom, gathering whatever homegrown bomb-making supplies he could find. There wasn't much. And the closest thing to weapons he could find—aside from that heavy-ass Buddha—was a collection of kitchen knives of various sizes and types.

He'd tossed all of it—a roll of aluminum foil, rubbing alcohol, nail polish remover, and a bottle of Drano—into his bag with the knives.

"But what if she falls asleep?" Dan asked, still talking about Nee-sha.

"She's not going to fall asleep," Izzy said. "She knows what's at stake." Probably more than any of them...

"If that guy Todd gets impatient," Dan said, "and comes in to wake me up..."

"She'll blow a hole in him," Izzy said, "and when he's good and dead, she'll call us and give us a heads-up." They'd left her with Greg's cell phone, too.

They passed several more miles in silence, then Dan spoke again.

"Ben's probably dead."

Izzy glanced at him again. "That was my conclusion at first, too." Because why else would Jake and his posse come back to Eden's apartment? If they had someone—Ben—that they could use to offer in trade for Neesha, why did they need to come back and grab Eden and Jenn? Why not just call and threaten?

One obvious answer was that Ben had tried to escape, and they'd shot him. Another was that they got too rough with their interrogation, and had accidentally killed the kid. And then there was all of the potential life-threatening dangers that came with Ben's diabetes...

"But I've been thinking about it," Izzy continued, "and there *are* other possibilities. Maybe they wanted the women as leverage, to get Ben to talk. Or—and I think this is the one I'm going with—I heard Jake say he thought Ben was a junkie. Apparently the kid threw up on his shoes. Maybe Ben's faking it. I mean, he was fine at the wedding, right? And his blood sugar reading when we got home was also excellent. That was just a few hours ago. What's the likelihood of him having an incident so soon? I mean, in all honesty, I don't know that much about the disease, so maybe it's possible..."

"I don't know much about it, either," Dan admitted.

"We're both going to have to learn," Izzy said, purposely acknowledging a future in which they all survived, Ben included.

Dan went with him, willingly, into that world of Everything's-Going-to-Be-Fine. "Yeah," he said. "I know. It's pretty complicated, but...We can get Ben to tell us how it all works. Or Eden. She's... done a good job taking care of him." He glanced at Izzy. "Thanks for... doing whatever you did to get Ivette and Greg to write those letters."

"*De nada,*" Izzy said.

"Yeah, we both know it was fucking huge," Dan said. "What did you threaten them with?"

"You don't want to know."

"I already do," Dan countered. "You found something incriminating. I'm guessing drugs. Although you're right, what it was really doesn't matter. The important thing is we win. We get Ben." He paused. "If he's alive."

Izzy sighed and tried, again, to bring Dan back to a more positive place. "He's alive. You know, there are high schools in San Diego that have solid gay-straight alliances in place. We should do some research, see where they are..."

"Jenni already started doing that," Dan said. He laughed a little, then said, "I tried to get her pregnant tonight."

"Shut the front door!" Izzy looked at him in genuine shock. It was such a personal and private thing to share. Of course, maybe Dan believed they were all going to die, and he wanted to tell *someone*—even Izzy—before he kicked. "Seriously?"

"Yeah," Dan said. "We just...You know."

"I'm familiar with the act."

"I've never done that before." Dan quickly added, "I mean, without the condom."

"Yeah, yeah," Izzy said, "I got that, bro."

"I just didn't want you making any stupid virgin jokes, because I'm being serious here."

There was definitely something that could've been said there, about stupid virgins, but Izzy let it slide. "I, um, fully recognize your seriossitude."

"I thought I'd flip out after," Dan continued, "like, holy Christ, what have I done? But..." He shook his head. "I just...I want her in my life."

And okay. That was a very future-tense statement. It didn't sound as if Dan was planning his own funeral just yet. Maybe...he just wanted to talk.

"You really don't have to knock her up to do that, man," Izzy pointed out. "I mean, she kinda married you."

"I know," Dan said. "But I want it all. I want a family and...Jesus, I'm turning into Jenk."

"Maybe you're turning into me," Izzy suggested. "It's far more likely, considering you've got a shitload of my blood in your veins."

Dan laughed. "Yeah, no, Zanella, see, Jenk's married to the love of his life and—" He stopped himself. Looked at Izzy.

Who looked back at him like, *and . . .?*

For once, Dan was speechless.

"For me, it was love at first sight," Izzy told him, as long as it was true confession time, "that was completely cemented when your sister started to talk. Every day I love her even more—it's crazy." He glanced at Dan again. "And you'll note that *I'm* not afraid to use the L-word, unlike some pussies, one of whom might be sitting next to me in this very car."

"I'm not afraid to say it," Dan scoffed, but he was smiling, too. "I love Jenni. See? Unlike some douches who say it, and then have to make sure everyone knows *they're* not a pussy *because* they've said it."

Izzy glanced over at him. "It's scary as shit, huh?"

"Hell, yeah." Dan paused. "If those assholes hurt them . . ."

"Why don't you dig into my bag and see what you can make that'll give us some flash and bang," Izzy suggested, still trying to distract.

And Dan was about to do just that, when Izzy's cell phone beeped from its place, front and center, in the cup holder between them. Dan picked it up.

"Signal's cut," he announced.

"On purpose?" Izzy asked, which was stupid, because how would Dan know? "Use Eden's phone to call Jenk and Lindsey and ask."

"Already on it," Dan said, but then said, "Whoa, you're getting a text. From me. *Arrived*," he read. "*I love you.*"

Izzy glanced over, and as he met Dan's eyes, he knew that the other SEAL was thinking the same thing he was. That that *I love you* was terribly final sounding. That Eden thought they were going to die.

And *that* kind of thinking wasn't going to help any of them. So Izzy swallowed past the lump in his throat, and tried to change the gloom-and-doom mood by saying, "I love you, too, man."

But Dan didn't take the bait. He didn't roll his eyes or *Zanella don't be an asshole* him, the way he would've done in the past. Instead, he just kind of nodded and said, "Eden can't let them find my phone."

"She knows," Izzy said. "She'll ditch it."

"She better."

"She's Eden," Izzy said, trying to feel as confident as he sounded. "She'll get the job done."

It wasn't easy to lie, naked, in a puddle of his own vomit.

But Ben knew that he had to do it, if he was going to continue to convince his kidnappers that he was not only unable to respond to their questions, but unable to move or otherwise put up a fight.

He'd made himself lie still, even when the bald cop from the mall—who wasn't a cop after all—told Ben that they were going out to find Eden.

Find was better than kill, and the man had already threatened to kill Ben's sister, in an attempt to force him to reveal Neesha's location.

"I don't know where Neesha is!"

Ben had said it, over and over and *over* after waking up here, head pounding, on the floor of this hot little empty room. With its too-high-to-reach drop ceiling and the in-the-wall air conditioner chugging ineffectually away, with the single door leading out to who knows where, Ben could have been anywhere in Las Vegas or outside of the city, for that matter.

And the men who had grabbed him from the courtyard of Eden's apartment complex made it very clear that where he was didn't matter. It was who he was with and what they wanted from him that counted.

And they hit him and they kicked him, and he still couldn't tell them where Neesha was, because he honestly and gratefully didn't know. And finally, when the bald cop said that unless Ben told him— immediately—where the girl was, he was going to go and kill Eden, Ben had lied and said that if he did that, he'd be screwed, because only Eden knew where Neesha was hiding.

Which wasn't true, but he would have said anything to keep his sister safe.

And then he made himself shake and he made himself throw up, right on the bald cop's boots.

Which had gotten him another kick, but he let himself flop back from it, as if he'd fainted.

The bald cop—who wasn't a cop—was cursing and shouting at him, "Tell us where Neesha is!"

But Ben didn't move.

It was then that he thought they were testing him, because two of them grabbed him and pulled him away from the mess that he'd made, and started taking off his clothes. They weren't very gentle—so much so that after they pulled off his T-shirt, his head bounced against the cheap tile floor so hard that he saw stars beneath his closed eyelids.

But he still didn't fight them, didn't speak, didn't move. Not even when they yanked off his boots and stripped his jeans and briefs from him so that he was buck naked.

He almost gave himself away at that point, because there was no way he was going to lie there and let himself get raped without fighting back.

But no one touched him, other than to grab him by the ankles and straighten his legs—a move that shifted him completely onto his back—and to roughly push his hair out of his face.

It was then he heard the unmistakable sound of a digital camera.

The pervs were taking pictures of him naked.

Someone—the photographer, apparently—said, "Turn him over."

Again the hands that touched him were impersonal and not at all gentle. The camera clicked and whirred, clicked and whirred.

And then someone tossed something—his shorts and his jeans— over Ben's bare butt, and even though the message was clear—he could get himself dressed now—he still didn't move because he wanted them to think he was helpless.

"I wonder if he speaks Korean," one of the men said.

Another laughed. "Yeah, that's where I was thinking he'd be going. Good old Mr. Kim. Poor kid."

"Maybe there'll be a bidding war. Maybe he'll end up in Turkey, instead."

"Could happen. The boss is the only guy I know who can turn a profit from a threat."

One of the voices faded. "Provided Jake gets his ass in gear and finds the girl."

The remaining man called after him. "If he doesn't? Boss is going to ship *him* off to Korea or Turkey, too."

And Ben almost opened his eyes as he realized what they were saying.

But then the last guard left, too, closing the door behind him with a solid-sounding thunk as a bolt fell into place.

Ben did open his eyes then, looking around cautiously to see if there were cameras watching him. But if there were, they were invisible, and he sat up, and then stood up and looked around.

Shit, if he put his pants back on, they'd know that he'd moved. He held his briefs up to cover himself as he explored the windowless room, searching for a way out.

They'd taken his picture, because they were going to ship him out of the country, and sell him to the highest bidder.

And his solid faith that, wherever he was, Eden and Dan and Izzy and Jenn would come after him, shifted and stirred and cracked with doubt.

Not that they wouldn't come for him. Ben believed that, absolutely.

But he now was afraid that they wouldn't come quickly enough.

And once he disappeared, the way Neesha had, from her family, all those years ago? They might never find him.

Neesha sat on the sofa in Eden Gillman's living room with the gun that Ben's brother Danny had given her on the cushion beside her.

It was heavy.

She'd held it in both hands, aimed at the door, for quite a long time after Izzy and Danny had gone out the window. But the muscles in her arms and shoulders had started to shake, so she'd finally put it down.

Aim for the chest, Dan had told her, *for the largest body mass. And don't just pull the trigger once. Keep on pulling it, steadying yourself with your left hand. You got that?*

She'd nodded.

Leave the light on in the entryway, light off in the living room; that way, if he comes in, you'll see him clearly and he won't see you.

Another nod.

He probably won't just come walking in the door. He'll push it open and he'll poke his head around the frame, really quickly at first. Don't take the bait. Hold your fire. He'll come in along one of the sides of the door, weapon leading. Again, wait until you have a clear, close shot of his chest—until you can't possibly miss.

Neesha had nodded.

You gonna be okay?

It was a good question, and one she managed to avoid answering.

Her cell phone rang now. She could tell from the number that it was Danny. She answered with her left hand, her right resting on the grip of the gun.

"Yes."

"I'm just checking in on you," Dan said. "You okay?"

"Yes," she said.

"Good," he said. "You, um, have—I don't know—any questions?"

"May I move the couch so that I can hide behind it?" That way, when Todd came in, she'd be able to let him get *really* close. And she could brace the gun on the back of the thing. "I don't have to move it much to get back there."

"Yeah," he said. "Sure. Knock yourself out. Whatever you want to do, to feel more secure. You go ahead and do it."

"Thank you," she said.

"We're getting close," he told her. "It's all going to be over soon. I'll call you again, in a bit."

They both said good-bye, and Neesha hung up the phone the way Dan had showed her before he'd left.

She moved the couch—just a little. Just enough to squeeze behind it. And she took the gun back there and practiced peeking over the top, gun aimed at the door.

Whatever you want to do, to feel more secure—you go ahead and do it, he'd told her.

After all that she'd been through, Neesha wasn't sure she'd ever feel completely safe, not ever again. Although, at the same time?

She found herself almost hoping that Todd *would* come in.

"Come on. Move it." The man with the hat—Nathan was his name— held out his hand in an impatient offer to help Eden down from the back of the van.

But she made herself recoil from him, shaking her head in a very strong but silent, *No, I don't want you to touch me.* She turned around, onto her hands and knees, as if she were going to climb down that way, Dan's cell phone concealed in the palm of her right hand.

Please God, please God . . .

"She said she was feeling dizzy." Jenn dared to speak despite their previous order to be silent. She also moved closer as if to try to help Eden. "Can you get her some water?"

"I want to see Ben," Eden chimed in. "Do you have the bag with the insulin?" She'd insisted that they take it when they left her apartment—when they'd left Danny unconscious on the floor and Neesha hiding in the sofa. The man with the hat had carried the bag out to the van, but he didn't have it with him now. Maybe he'd go and get it from the front . . .

But Jake had had enough. "Let's go," he said as he grabbed Eden by the back waistband of her shorts.

Eden screamed and shot a wild look at Jenn, fearing that he'd pull her too far from the van. Jenn moved quickly and grabbed both of

Eden's arms, which both slowed her down and pulled Jenn out of the van with her.

The additional weight proved too much for Jake, who had his weapon in his other hand, and Eden and Jenn both went down into a heap on what appeared to be concrete. It was. It was some kind of landing strip, with a warehouse-type structure nearby.

"Get off me!" Eden cried, even as she pulled Jenn more completely on top of her. "I can't breathe!"

Jenn played along beautifully. "My knee! My knee!" she sobbed. "I think I just broke my knee!"

And Eden did it. She scrambled toward the van, as if trying to crawl out from beneath Jenn, flailing both her legs and arms—and tossing the cell phone into the darkness beneath the van's chassis.

It was then that the world slowed down into a series of nanoseconds that seemed to take forever, as Jake turned away in disgust, as Nathan, with his hat, reached down and grabbed Jenn by the wrist, pulling her up and onto her feet.

And as neither of their captors said, "Hey, what the hell did that bitch just throw beneath the van?" or "What was that scraping sound?"

In fact, neither of them said anything at all that wasn't a four-letter word or a plea for help to whatever twisted god that killers and kidnappers believed in.

Eden pushed herself up onto her hands and her knees as Jenn wiped her eyes and her nose and said, "No, wait, I'm okay—I think I'm okay. I can walk. I'm okay."

And they were good—or at least as good as they could be as they were marched at gunpoint into that warehouse, here on the edge of an airfield, in the middle of nowhere.

The phone rang.

Izzy's phone. The one he hadn't been able to use for quite some time, because it was holding open the line to Eden and Jenn.

It wasn't Jenk or Lindsey, because Jenk was already talking to Dan. Jenk was confirming that the signal from the cell phone Eden had been using had stopped moving. He was verifying the directions they should take to arrive at the same location.

And he was reassuring Danny that everything was going to be okay—that he and Lindsey and Jay Lopez were on their way. If everything went *just* right, they'd travel most of the way via helo, and arrive in two and a half hours.

Izzy didn't recognize the number that was on his cell phone's screen. But it had a 6-1-7 area code, which was... "Good morning, Boston," Izzy said as he answered, one hand on the steering wheel as they continued to zoom through the night. "Jules Cassidy, I presume. How's it hanging, bro?"

"It's... hanging with no small amount of trepidation," Cassidy, a high-ranking agent in the FBI, said. "Where are you, Zanella?"

"Approximately twenty-five—twenty-four—minutes now from the place where my wife, her little brother, and a dear friend are being held hostage," Izzy said, "by some very nasty people."

"You have *no* idea how nasty," the FBI agent told him. "Do me a favor, and put me on speaker so that Dan Gillman hears this, too."

"Is that necessary?" Izzy said, lowering his voice so Dan, who was finishing up his call with Jenkins, wouldn't hear him. "He's... wound a little tight. Understandably so. He got married tonight and... Someone stole his bride."

"I know," Cassidy said. "But really, Zanella. You both need to hear this information."

Dan had ended his call with Jenk, and was ready to listen in as Izzy pulled his phone from his ear and punched a button. "You're on speaker, Cassidy."

"Hey, Gillman," Cassidy said. "Congrats—I heard about the wedding. I've met Jenn, you know. She's great. You're a lucky man."

"Yeah," Dan said. "*Lucky* might not be precisely the right word to use at this exact moment."

"I hear you," Cassidy said. "And I understand your anxiety. There's something you both need to know, and you *also* need to know that I've been encouraged *not* to divulge some of this information to you and there *are* definitely things that I cannot tell you. As it is, I'm going out on a bit of a limb by telling you this, so...factor all that in, okay?"

Izzy glanced at Dan in the light from the dashboard. This was *not* going to be good. That was one hell of a cryptic message, and Jules Cassidy was usually a straight shooter when it came to telling it like it was.

"With that said," Cassidy continued, "I first want to inform you that I've been in contact with Field Agent Kathy Gordon, who's been working a case there in Las Vegas. That picture you took on your cell phone, Zanella? That one of the two men who came to Ben's house, looking for him, because they were trying to track down the girl, Neesha? They allegedly work for an organization that specializes in international sex trafficking. We're talking the sale of women and children to buyers who are...Well, they're in the market to *buy* women and children, so that pretty much tells you all you need to know. Except maybe that some of them are snuff enthusiasts, which is pretty much just another name for serial killers who happen to be really rich men, who can purchase victims who won't be missed."

"Jesus," Dan breathed.

"That's just one branch of this booming business, but it's one I thought you should know about, in terms of the danger that Ben, Eden, and Jenn could well be in."

Izzy couldn't believe what he was hearing and he drove a little faster. "Are you freaking kidding me?"

"I wish I were," Cassidy said. "But there's a whole nother side to this, and it's the more immediate subject of this FBI investigation, because this organization also deals in the sale or trade of girls—and I'm talking *really* little girls, seven, eight years old—to brothel-type businesses, here in the U.S. One of those esteemed establishments is believed to be northwest of Vegas, just over the Clark County line. The children are nearly all brought here from outside of the country. Most of them are sold by their families, some of them thinking that they're going to work as maids, others knowing exactly what their daughters are going to be doing. Others are orphans. Some are kidnapped — some are from families of illegals who are living here in the United States. They can't go to the authorities to report the disappearances and... Well, bottom line, these little girls are easy to exploit, because they don't exist. And when they grow up or if they cause trouble, they're sold at a discount to one of those snuff fans who'll kill them and dispose of the body. Neat and tidy, two birds with one stone."

Dan spoke. "So you're telling us that Neesha's one of these girls."

"We believe so," Cassidy said. "Yes. And securing her as a witness, to testify against the men who run this operation? That's the priority of the AIC of this investigation. I've been asked to obtain from you the girl's location, so that she can be brought into custody as quickly as possible—"

"We do that," Dan interrupted, "and those very dangerous people who have Jenni and Eden and Ben? They're going to know it, and they're going to kill them. They've got a man watching—"

"Neesha doesn't go anywhere," Izzy cut *him* off. "Until we get our family out of harm's way."

"I suspected you'd say that," Cassidy said evenly. "And, in anticipation of that, I've been instructed to inform you that an FBI task force is being created to rescue your family members, if possible." He paused so his words could sink in. "We have access to the GPS signal from Gillman's cell phone, too, and have pinpointed their location. From satellite images, they appear to be in some kind of storage-type structure, alongside an airfield."

"An airfield?" Dan's voice cracked.

"Correct," Cassidy said. "The belief is that this is one of the locations where the children are transported into the country. And where... others are transported out. If you arrive at the airfield and there is an aircraft on the runway?" He paused, again very deliberately, and then said, "Report that information immediately. But I am to insist that you remain back, out of danger, until the authorities arrive. At which point you will be taken into protective custody—"

Fuck you, Dan started to say, but didn't get more than the *F*-sound out before Izzy reached over and whacked him in the chest. He shot Izzy a *what the hell* look, and Izzy answered with a hard look and the hand signal for *silence*. This man was *not* their enemy.

"—while the team determines the best option for apprehending the suspects and rescuing the hostages."

It was no mistake that he'd again mentioned the apprehension of the suspects as being the FBI team's priority.

Izzy had to work to keep his voice even. "Task Force ETA?" he asked.

"Best guess," Cassidy said, "is they're about thirty minutes behind you." He paused again. "Do you understand what I'm telling you, Zanella?"

"Sir, yes, sir, absolutely I do. Any other info you can share from the sat images?" Izzy asked. "Any infrared?"

"You don't need that information," Cassidy said. "Unless you can reassure me that you'll limit your participation to surveillance only." He cleared his throat rather loudly.

"Cross my heart," Izzy said, "and if I lie, sweet baby jeebus can poke me in the eye."

"Fabulous," Cassidy said dryly. "I'm completely reassured. And in that case, there are what appears to be four guards outside the structure, eleven people inside—but it's difficult to discern which are the prisoners and which are the bad guys. Sorry. I know you have concerns about Ben's health and safety, but I don't have access to moving images and can't begin to speculate which green dot belongs to Jenn, Eden, or Ben. If this information changes, I'll...text you."

Text, not call. Because Cassidy knew damn well that Izzy wasn't going to be able to pick up while he was dispatching those four guards and kicking down the door of that storage facility.

"Thank you, sir," Izzy said.

"I thought I was your bro, Zanella."

"No, sir," Izzy told the man. "You're the kind of leader I would follow into hell, should the need ever arise."

Cassidy cleared his throat. "I'll keep that in mind," he said quietly, then added, "Good luck, guys." And with that he ended the call.

Dan looked at Izzy. "Did he just say what I think he said?"

"He certainly did, and he could lose his job for it." Izzy glanced back at Dan. "But if there's a plane on that runway? Shit, even if there's not... He just told us we shouldn't wait for anyone. As soon as we get there? We're going in."

CHAPTER
TWENTY-EIGHT

Izzy and Dan knew where they were.

Jenn held on to that thought as the man named Nathan held her tightly by the arm as he half pushed, half dragged her with him into what looked like a warehouse.

There was a sign—a small one—on the side of the building: A&B STORAGE AND DISCREET PEST CONTROL.

There were windows in the structure, but they were up along the roofline. They were more like air vents that opened to keep the building, with its nearly flat metal roof, from getting too hot in the daytime.

Although, *that* was an impossibility. When the sun was out, this place would literally cook. It was crazy. The construction looked new. Who would build something like this, out in the middle of the desert, and expect to be able to store anything here at all?

Although there were large garage-bay-type doors all along the side of the building—large enough to accommodate a small plane or a fleet of trucks.

The place had what looked to be a relatively low-tech security system. There were two cameras—at least that Jenn could see—each mounted at a corner of the building, but they were fixed in place. They were seemingly consistent with the type of security at a storage facility—enough to lower the insurance, but not enough to break the bank. But, incongruous with a typical storage facility's security system, there was also a very large guard out front, carrying a very large assault rifle.

"You need to get the bag with the insulin and the needles," Eden was saying again, but then she screamed, and Jenn turned quickly back to look at her.

Jake had her arm twisted up behind her back as he told her, "What *you* need to do is to shut the fuck up."

She didn't. "Ow! He could die without it! *Ow!*"

"Keep it moving." Nathan gave Jenn a nudge that nearly knocked her over.

"Do I look like I give a shit?" Jake asked.

"You should," Eden gasped. "Because Danny's going to ask for proof of life."

"And you're going to tell him that you're all hunky-dory," Jake said.

"He's not an idiot," Eden argued. "He's going to ask to talk to Ben."

Jenn was pushed again, past all the bay doors, past that very large guard, who spoke into a cell phone. "They're here."

There was a large metal door down at the end of the building, and it opened before they reached it, before Nathan knocked.

The man who opened the door could have been Nathan's twin, they looked so much alike, with those same blue-gray eyes and lean faces. This new man greeted them without any words, and barely even a glance. He just stepped back to let them in.

Nathan gave Jenn another nudge, so she stepped inside.

And yes, it was a warehouse, and absolutely, it was extremely hot in here.

A large thermometer on the wall advertised the fact that it was 120 degrees Fahrenheit. Despite that, a series of fans up in the high metal rafters moved only very slowly, and only a few of the window vents were open.

And yes, there was a fleet of trucks inside—if you could call one truck and two vans a fleet. They, too, bore the name A&B Storage on their sides. No doubt the discreet-pest-control part of the business was *so* discreet that it wasn't advertised on the trucks.

It was weird in the warehouse, though. Most of the big dimly lit room was empty, but there were huge wooden crates, wrapped in plastic and perched on pallets, distributed haphazardly throughout the vast, shadowy space.

One would think they would've been stacked neatly, in one corner, but they weren't.

It made the place look spooky.

"Bedbug remediation," Nathan told her as he saw her confusion. "It's a growing business. Heat over a hundred and seventeen degrees kills 'em dead."

"Bedbugs," she repeated. She knew they were a problem, particularly in urban areas... Still, it was mind-bending. An organization that ran a child prostitution ring and dealt in the purchase and sale of human beings also managed a bedbug remediation service...?

Although it gave them a reason to be here—to have trucks and a warehouse in the middle of the desert.

Or maybe the people who owned A&B Storage were similar to Jenn and Eden and Ben. Maybe they'd also gotten involved in a bad situation purely by accident.

Eden was still pushing Jake about Ben. "We want to see him. And there's a device in the bag? That you didn't bring in from the van? It'll test Ben's blood sugar levels so I'll know how much insulin to give him."

Jake pushed Eden, hard, at Nathan's brother. "Get them photographed and secured in the back. And someone call Todd. Tell him to get back inside that apartment—find out why the sailor hasn't called us yet."

By *sailor*, he meant Dan.

Oh God.

Jenn met Eden's gaze. The younger woman was terrified, too—Jenn could see it in her eyes. But she was fighting it—and she was going to keep on fighting it. Jenn could see that, too.

"He's probably not calling because he was drunk before I hit him," Eden lied. "You better let him sleep it off, or he's going to be useless."

"Todd just called to check in," Nathan's brother volunteered. "He says the sailor didn't leave, so he couldn't follow him to find the girl. He says nothing's moving, no lights have gone off or on, nobody's come near the place."

Jenn raised her hand. "Excuse me," she said, trying, like Eden, to distract. But she couldn't keep her voice from shaking. "I'm so sorry, but I need to use the bathroom."

Jake had had enough. "Forget the photos, just take them to the back," he ordered Nathan and his brother and two other men who'd come from somewhere to join them. "And call Todd, and tell him to get the hell over there and wake that asshole up. We are running the fuck out of time." He looked at Eden and Jenn. "We're not going to give him proof of life. If he doesn't tell us what we want to know, we'll give him proof of death. Flip a coin, girls. One of you, or the kid, is going to die."

They'd gone as far they could risk going in via car, but they still had about a half a mile of ground to cover before they had to slow their pace and move covertly.

Normally, a half-mile run would've been a piece of cake. But Dan hadn't done more than very short spurts of fast movement for quite a few weeks. Running half of a mile seemed as daunting a task as running a full marathon immediately after eating a huge Thanksgiving dinner.

Izzy was on the phone again with Jenk as Dan hauled Izzy's bag out of the backseat of the car that they'd driven off the dirt road and down into a gully, where it wouldn't be seen by any casual passersby.

The sun was going to come up soon, and the sky to the east was already giving off the start of a predawn glow.

It was actually a good time to approach a guarded facility. If the guards had NVs—night-vision glasses—they'd have to take them off. Even just that little glow from the sky would prove to be too bright and would distort their vision. But without the NVs, the desert would seem otherworldly. Heat would stir and shimmy. And darkness and shadows would prevail.

Now, if the guards had infrared glasses, able to pick up the heat signal from a human being... Then they were completely screwed.

Because Izzy and Dan had, between them, a series of kitchen knives, each blade duller than the last.

Dan would have preferred an M16 or a grenade launcher.

Izzy snapped his phone shut as they headed briskly south. "You know Tess Bailey? She works at Troubleshooters with Lindsey? She's their comspesh. She's got mad hacking skills."

"I've met her," Dan said. "Yeah."

"Jenk says Tess is using her home setup to try to access those satellite images, give us a better read on how many tangos we're up against."

"She can just hack into a high-clearance FBI—"

"I'm not asking questions," Izzy cut him off. "When people want to help, I say thank you. If *you* want to be a Boy Scout—"

"No," Dan said, working hard to keep up. "I'm just impressed. I didn't think anyone besides WildCard could do that." Navy SEAL Chief Ken Karmody, nicknamed WildCard for obvious reasons, was currently OCONUS, with most of Team Sixteen. So Tess Bailey would have to do.

"Jenk'll send a text when she gets through. Dude. Gimme that." Izzy took the bag from him. "You should've reminded me."

"I'm okay," Dan said. "But if you've got the bag? I'm good to run."

Izzy looked at him hard, but then nodded. "Your pace," he said. "Save something for when we get there." But then he softened the implied *I'm reminding you because we both know you're an idiot* of his words by adding, in his best Groucho Marx, "And save a little something else for even later, to throw to Jennilyn."

"Zanella, you're an asshole." Dan started to run, slowly at first and then faster. Jesus, his leg hurt. And after all those weeks of sitting on his ass, his wind was for shit.

"What?" Izzy said as he easily kept up, bag and all. "I'm just saying. I got *my*self a post-mission plan..."

"TMI," Dan gasped.

Izzy ran closer and put his free arm around Dan's waist. "Arm around my shoulder, bro."

And with much of Dan's weight transferred to Izzy, they could both punch up the pace:

Izzy, of course, started to sing, because *he* clearly had wind to spare. *"The road is long, with many a winding turn..."*

The song was "He Ain't Heavy, He's My Brother." Through the years that they'd worked together, Dan had heard Izzy singing it plenty of times, along with a whole playlist of similarly themed tunes. He'd always thought Izzy'd done it to purposely annoy and just generally be an asshole.

But it was entirely possible that Dan had been wrong—and that Izzy sang the sappy lyrics because he meant them.

"Actually," he gasped now, cutting Izzy off mid-*brother*. "I'd prefer 'Lean on Me.'"

Izzy laughed his surprise. "I was trying to piss you off," he admitted. "Get a little stamina-building rage burning."

"I got plenty of rage," Dan told him. "Those assholes have my family." He corrected himself. "Our family."

"Not for long," Izzy said. And he started to sing. *"Sometimes in our lives, we all have pain, we all have sorrow..."*

He really did have a nice voice.

The entire back section of the warehouse was air-conditioned.

It was separated from the main area by a heavily insulated wall with a single door in the middle that opened into a significantly cooler but still-warm hallway.

The hallway was windowless and ran the entire length of the back of the building, with one of those white acoustical-tile drop ceilings overhead and cheap linoleum tile in an industrial shade of speckled tan underfoot.

Eden's heart was pounding as the two men who were escorting her and Jenn led her to the left, past two, then three, then four doorways, all of which opened into dark rooms. She didn't get more than a peek inside. Two had typical cheap office setups, with desks and chairs and file cabinets—she couldn't see if there were phones on the desks—and one was simply empty.

"I really need to use the bathroom," Jenn said again.

"I'll get a bucket," the man holding Jenn told her as he pushed her toward the very last room at the end of the hall. The door was shut and locked with a big thumb bolt on the outside, and he opened it and shoved Jenn in.

"Oh, my God, and towels, too," Jenn said. "And that bag, from the van!"

Something was wrong—Eden could tell by the tone of Jenn's voice, and as she, too, was pushed forward, into the open doorway, she saw... "Ben!"

Her little brother was lying on the floor, on his stomach, with Jenn beside him, checking for his pulse.

"What did you do to him?" Eden cried as she scrambled down next to him. He was naked—his jeans and briefs draped almost modestly over his bottom by whoever had left him there—and she imagined the worst. "No, oh, no, Boo-Boo..."

"He's alive," Jenn told Eden, her hands in Ben's hair. "I'm not feeling any lumps or bumps. I don't think he's got a head injury."

But he'd definitely thrown up, and he'd absolutely been hit. Repeatedly. His lip was bleeding and his face was scraped and swollen. He had a bruise already forming on his rib cage, too, as if he'd fallen and then been kicked.

Jenn leaned close as if whispering to him, murmuring something that Eden didn't hear—as if beseeching him to be all right—as she started to cry.

Eden reached for his pants, dreading what she'd find beneath them, but to her surprise, Jenn reached out and caught her wrist, stopping her.

"Come over here," Jenn said. "You need to..."

"I thought you said he didn't have a head injury," Eden said as Jenn physically moved her closer to Ben's head.

But then she gasped, because his eyes opened.

Ben looked directly at her, and it wasn't the unfocused, hazy look of a diabetic going into shock. His eyes were clear and filled with apology and understanding.

And as Eden turned her gasp into noisy pretend crying, as she shifted slightly to make absolutely sure that the guards couldn't see Ben's face, she understood why Jenn had been whispering and murmuring. She'd been talking to Ben, who was faking his unconsciousness.

"I'm okay," he told her silently.

Was he, really? She had to ask. "Did they...?" She couldn't say it.

He knew what she was asking, and he shook his head, furtively, barely moving at all. Still, he was definite. "I'm okay. I made myself throw up. Did you bring insulin?" But then he closed his eyes again, because the second guard was coming back into the room with a bucket and a sorry-looking pile of rags.

"There's a bag," Eden told the man—it was Nathan—as she wiped her nose on the sleeve of her shirt, "outside in the van. It's got insulin and needles in it. I need it in here, or my brother's going to die."

"One of you's gonna die anyway," Nathan told her.

"Yeah, well, it's not going to be him," Eden said fiercely. "You get us that bag, or neither one of us"—she looked at Jenn—"will talk to Dan. Without proof of life, he'll never give you Neesha. *Never.*"

Jenn nodded her solidarity as she used the rags to wipe Ben's face, as well as the arm that he'd convincingly let fall into his own vomit.

"We'll see about that." Both guards left them then, pulling the door closed behind them and locking it with a thunk.

Ben sat up, talking softly but quickly, as he pulled on his shorts and his jeans. "This is all my fault. I couldn't sleep, so I went out. They grabbed me in the courtyard. Eden, God, I'm so sorry—"

"They were planning to kick in the apartment door," Eden told him. "If they hadn't bumped into you the way that they did? Izzy

would be dead right now. They would have killed him. So no blame."
She hugged him, hard, then pulled back to look him in the eye. "They
really didn't...?"

"No," he said. "I'm okay. They took pictures of me. That was it."

"Pictures of you naked?" Unlike Eden, Jenn still hadn't figured it
out.

"They're going to auction me off," Ben told her.

"Oh, my God," Jenn said.

Jake had originally said that Eden and Jenn were to be photographed, too. Until he'd decided he was going to kill one of them.

Ben looked at Eden. "Are Danny and Izzy—"

"Coming," Eden said. "They're going to get you out."

"Us," Jenn said sharply. "All of us."

Eden didn't look at her. "I've already decided. If it comes down to
it? It's going to be me."

Ben looked from Eden to Jenn and back. "What—" he started.

"We're *all* getting out of here," Jenn said again. She turned to Ben.
"Ben—"

"Don't scare him!" Eden said hotly.

"He's not a child," Jenn countered. "Not with *that* mother. So
don't treat him like one." She turned to Ben. "Jake—the skinhead—
said that if Danny didn't tell him where Neesha was? One of us was
going to die."

Ben turned to look at Eden, his mouth open, as he realized what
her words had meant.

"None of us are tied up," Jenn continued, "so I say, if it comes to
that, we..." She took a deep breath. "We go for it. We jump them. We
try to get their guns. In fact, why wait? The next person who opens that
door—"

"Unless he's got Eden's bag from the van," Ben interrupted her. He
turned back to Eden. "Did you bring only the insulin, or the glucagon,
too?"

"I brought everything," Eden told him. "The meter, too. We didn't
know what you'd need."

"I don't need anything," Ben reassured her as Jenn looked up at the ceiling, which was too high for them to reach, even if Eden stood on Ben's shoulders. "I was thinking we could try to use the glucagon on the guard."

"That's the drug that raises your blood sugar?" Jenn asked, turning her attention to the air conditioner that was set into the wall.

"Yeah," Ben said. "Unlike the insulin I use, it's super fast-acting."

"What'll it do to him?" she asked.

"I don't know," Ben said, "but I'm pretty sure it'll mess him up. When I take it? When I *need* it? It knocks me to my knees. Total puke-city."

Eden said, "At which point, we grab his gun."

Jenn smiled at her. "That's a much better plan. Not that I didn't appreciate your selfless sacrifice, but... You're not expendable."

"Still," Eden said. "If it comes to it..."

"It won't," Jenn insisted, back to gazing at that air conditioner.

Ben nodded up at it. "It's in there solidly. Believe me. I've been in here for a while—the only way out? Is through that door."

Neesha had to pee.

She'd been crouched there, back behind the sofa for such a long time. And even though she hadn't had anything to drink or to eat, nature called.

She considered relieving herself right there, but it seemed ungrateful and impolite.

So she took the gun and the cell phone that Dan had given her, and she went into the bathroom. She left the door open and the gun on her lap. It was cold against her knees, so she pulled her pants up a little bit farther than she normally would and kept the fabric between the metal and her skin.

She didn't hear it over the sound of her water. That was what her mother had called it—*making water*.

And because she was making water, she didn't hear the sound of the key in the lock. She didn't hear the sound of footsteps in the entry-way, or even down the hall.

He just suddenly appeared, standing right outside the bathroom doorway, with a gun of his own in his hand, aimed directly at her, and she froze.

Todd.

He smiled when he saw her.

Neesha couldn't keep her terror from her face, from her eyes, and his smile grew into a grin and then a genuine laugh of amusement. "Well, isn't *this* a lovely surprise," he said.

And instead of sending a bullet into her head and killing her right then, right there, he slipped his gun into a holster that he wore beneath his left arm, and he locked it into place. At first she didn't understand, but then he reached for the buckle of his belt, because he thought he had the power, because he hadn't seen her weapon. "I don't have to call the boss *right* away," he said.

And she didn't wait a second longer.

Neesha picked up the gun from her lap with her right hand, brac-ing it with her left the way Danny had demonstrated.

And now Todd's were the eyes that were widened in fear, as she didn't hesitate. She aimed for the center of his body, and she pulled the trigger and pulled the trigger and pulled the trigger and pulled the trigger as he fell back against the closed bedroom door, leaving a smear of blood behind him.

The noise was incredible and someone was screaming—not Todd, though. He'd screamed his last. When he'd fallen, one of her bullets had connected with his head, and she had no doubt that he was dead.

It was Neesha, herself, who'd made that noise like a wild animal, high-pitched and rough in the back of her throat as the trigger clicked and clicked and clicked—her gun long emptied.

So she put the weapon down on the counter and finished her busi-ness, carefully washing her hands in the sink.

She took the gun with her as she went back into the living room, stopping first to lock the door, and even push the refrigerator in front of it again. She could already hear police sirens—one of Eden's neighbors had no doubt reported the ungodly noise.

Neesha took a can of soda from the fridge, and went back to the couch. No need to crouch behind it anymore. She set the gun on the cushion beside her and took one of the full clips that Dan had left on the end table, and replaced the one she'd just emptied.

And then she took out the cell phone that Dan had given her, and called him, reporting what had happened in a clear, even voice.

Dan kept saying, "Are you all right? Are you sure you're all right?"

And she kept saying yes.

He told her that some friends of his were on their way—friends who worked for the FBI, friends that she could trust, friends who would take her someplace safe. But she asked him if it was okay if she stayed right there and just waited for him and Izzy and Eden and Jenni and Ben to get home.

And he said yes.

It was only after she hung up, only after she opened her soda and took a sip, that she started to shake and she started to cry. And she remembered the fear that had bloomed in Todd's eyes—fear and a dark despair as he realized that he was doomed—the same fear and despair that she'd felt every day for eight years, three months, and thirteen days.

And she couldn't imagine ever getting pleasure from making another human being feel that way.

Although with Todd? When she'd given him her absolute and final *no* in the form of those bullets barreling out of that gun?

She'd come pretty close.

Ben barely made it down onto the floor before the guard unlocked the door and pushed it open.

Jenn and Eden quickly snapped to it, dropping to their knees beside him as if they'd just finished dressing him, and were tying his sneakers, looking up at the door as if surprised that it was opening.

"Oh, thank God," Eden said, and Ben heard the crinkling sound of a plastic grocery bag before the door thunked shut again, and the bolt slid home.

Jenni poked him. "Door's shut. We're good."

"We're more than good," Eden said, taking out both of his glucagon kits, and tossing one to Ben. "We're ready to get out of here. Or at the very least improve the odds for Izzy and Danny. I counted seven of them—including the ones called Jake and Nathan."

"I got six," Jenn said. "Five inside plus the one out front."

"No," Eden said, "I saw two outside, plus those same five..."

"Wow," Ben said, mixing the powder with the liquid in the vial as Eden did the same with the second kit. "I have no idea how many bad guys there are."

"Your eyes were closed." Jenn gave him a good excuse.

"So it's Danny and Izzy against seven men with guns," Ben repeated.

"At least," Eden confirmed. "But maybe we can lower that by one." She moved back behind the door, where she'd be hidden from the guard's view when it opened. "If I'm standing *here*, and you're *there*, with Ben on the floor..."

"He's not going to come in if he can't see you," Jenn pointed out. "Maybe you should just stand more in the middle of the room, like, Ben's choking and you're distressed."

"I can do distressed," Eden said.

"If I'm the one who's choking," Ben said to Jenn as he got into position, "*you* should have the second syringe." He handed it to her.

"And we hit him with both," Eden said, "right at the same time."

"While I go for his gun," Ben said.

Jenn and Eden looked at each other over the top of Ben's head.

"Come on," Ben said. "If we're doing this, we have to do it. All of us, together."

"If you get yourself shot," Eden told him, "I will kick your ass."

She hugged him hard, hugged Jenn, too, and Ben knew what his sister was thinking. It was do-or-die time.

And they were probably going to die.

"We have maybe five minutes," Izzy said as Dan ended his call with Neesha, "before you need to call Jake."

"We're not ready for me to call Jake." Dan was shocked—Izzy could see it in his eyes, on his face. Neither one of them had expected Todd to come back into the apartment, although now that he had, it made perfect sense.

Whoever was down there in that big white warehouse that seemed to glow in the predawn darkness had gotten tired of waiting for Dan to call, and had sent Todd in to wake him up.

But instead of moving forward, Danny was still struggling to compartmentalize the idea that the sweet little girl they'd left behind had needed to defend herself with deadly force. Instead of giving himself a pat on the back for successfully teaching her to fire the weapon that had killed her attacker, he was mired in the horror of it all.

They'd reached the point in their approach where they had to move in more slowly, more cautiously, and if Izzy had more than five minutes to spare, he would have sat there for at least thirty, just watching the place and observing the patterns and check-in procedures of the various guards. He also would have traversed the building's perimeter before making that phone call to Jake. He glanced at his watch. Or maybe not. Once that sun came up, they'd lose their advantage. So maybe this was fate plus common sense giving them a friendly nudge.

While Dan had been on the phone with Neesha, Izzy'd spoken briefly to Jules Cassidy, who was probably going to get his ass fired for helping them this way. But that was another thing that Izzy couldn't worry about right now.

"The witness your AIC is looking for just killed a man in self-defense," Izzy had reported, giving Jules the address of Eden's apartment. "You might want to get someone over there, pronto, because the police are on their way, and it could get ugly if they try to kick down the door. She's inside with the body, and she's armed and understandably tightly wound. She's also got a cell phone." He rattled off Greg's number so the FBI could at least contact her.

"Bless you," Jules said. "I'll make sure she stays safe."

"Roger that, sir," Izzy said. "I'm betting you grok how the fact that their man being dead makes him unable to communicate with the mothership via cell phone, which shortens the time line for our"—he cleared his throat—"surveillance. I need a little help, ASAP, from our friendly eye in the sky."

"I'm on it," Jules had said, and cut the call.

Izzy now got a text from the FBI agent: *4 out, 11 in, believe 3 of those 11 are Hs in sm rm NE.* It was followed, immediately by a text from Troubleshooter Tess Bailey, verifying those numbers.

Yes. "Fifteen life-forms—twelve tangos, three H's," Izzy told Dan. "Cassidy just told me they believe the three hostages are being held in a small room in the northeast part of the building."

That information brought Danny back. Or maybe he'd just got his second wind. Because he nodded and took out Eden's cell phone as he said, "I have to call Jake. We have to give him a reason for why Todd's not answering his phone or calling to check in."

"Wow, what a good idea," Izzy said. "But hold up there, Skippy, I already got it all figured out. Here's what you're going to say."

CHAPTER
TWENTY-NINE

S ome kind of serious situation is going down," Dan said as he
spoke via Eden's cell phone with Jake, who was inside of the
very building he and Izzy were watching. Jake, who was holding
Jenni and Eden and Ben at gunpoint. Jake, who started this conversation with a threat to kill one of them if Dan didn't tell him what he
wanted to know. Dan had interrupted *that* shit midsentence. Control
the conversation, Izzy had advised him. He was trying. "Right here, in
an apartment directly across the courtyard. The police are all over the
place—squad cars are everywhere. They've got a guy cuffed and three
uniformed officers are taking him out of here. Don't tell me—you left
a man behind to follow me. One of the neighbors must've spotted him,
knew he didn't belong here, saw his weapon, and called it in."

On the other end of the phone, Jake swore, but Dan didn't let him
take control of the conversation.

"I know you want the girl," Dan said as Izzy, who was listening in,
nodded his approval, "but the cops have already knocked on my door,
no doubt looking for information, and I didn't open up because I had
blood in my hair and I thought it might raise eyebrows. If I come walking out there now..."

"Well, you figure out a way to get it done," Jake told him.

"No," Dan said. "*You* fucked this up by leaving this idiot here—

you're going to have to wait. And while you're waiting? I want proof of life and I want it right fucking now. I want to talk to all three of them, and then I'm going to want to talk to them again, after—"

"Which one do you want me to kill?" Jake asked, throwing Dan's own words back in his face. "Right fucking now?"

And Dan couldn't help himself. He hesitated. Just a second or two, but it was enough. Izzy made *keep going* motions, but it was too late. He'd dropped the ball.

"You'll go to the girl," Jake said, "and you'll get the girl. And then you'll call me. Because *I* want proof that *you* have *her*. You have ten minutes, or one of the hostages is dead."

"Ten minutes isn't—" Dan said, but the call had been cut. "Jesus!"

"That's okay," Izzy told him, tried to reassure him. "You did okay. Well, maybe not okay, but we both knew it was a long shot and . . . We can do this in ten minutes."

"Maybe we can set up a conference call," Dan said. "You know, with Neesha?"

"I'm betting Jake wouldn't recognize her voice," Izzy said as he started toward the building.

Dan followed. "But that's great. That means we can call back in, like seven minutes, and I say that I have her, and *you* pretend to be a frightened little girl."

Izzy looked back at him with an odd mix of sympathy and disgust in his eyes. "And if he wants a picture? You gonna put me in a dress with a little pink bow in my hair?"

Dan was grabbing wildly at solutions and he knew it, but he couldn't stop himself. "We pretend we lose connection and then we get Neesha to send me a picture, which I send to him."

"What if he wants a picture of her dead body?" Izzy said.

"We fake it."

"She's alone in that apartment," Izzy pointed out. "Even if you could get her to take out the ketchup and squeeze it onto herself, how's she going take the picture of herself lying there, dead?"

"So...we talk her into letting the FBI in there," Dan said, but even as the words left his lips, he knew *that* would never happen. Not in the next ten minutes.

"We're doing this the simple way, bro," Izzy told him, not unkindly. "We're going in there and we're getting them out."

Armed only with kitchen knives, except okay, there were four men outside that building who were in possession of a variety of weaponry. It wouldn't take much to make a transfer of all that firepower into the two SEALs' hands.

The plan was a relatively simple one that they'd already established. Izzy would take out the security cameras and the guards in the front. Dan would dispatch the other two, and they'd meet up on the roof and play it by ear from there.

Except...

"I'm giving you an order to use deadly force," Dan said to Izzy as they moved closer to the structure.

Izzy looked at him like he'd gone mad. "Who died and made you admiral?" he asked.

"If one of us is going to burn for this," Dan said, "I want it to be me."

Izzy made a raspberry sound. "You're the career Navy man," he pointed out. "Dude, look at you—you have master chief written all over you. If you really think there needs to be an order, *I'll* give the order. These assholes just threatened to kill someone we love. They are dead fucking serious, and we are, too. If you have a problem eliminating those guards in a permanent fashion, you tell me now—"

"No," Dan said. "I just didn't want..." He stopped. Started over. "You're an asset to the Teams, and I'm planning on getting out anyway."

"No, you're not."

"Yeah, I am."

"Dude, you're suffering from marriage madness. You don't know what the hell you're saying, because you're too busy trying to find words that rhyme with love so you can write Jennilyn a freaking sonnet.

Above, okay? It's moon above, stars above, either work equally well. Problem solved, move on."

Dan shook his head. "That's not—"

"Zip it, Chatty Cathy, it's go time," Izzy said, shooting Dan the hand signal for *ready* along with *shut the fuck up*.

They were just going to make it before the sun burst, in its full glory, over the mountains to the east.

Except there was something . . . a light in the sky, coming from the west, shimmering slightly as it moved toward them . . .

Izzy saw it, too.

A light—and a noise. Getting bigger and louder and . . .

"What the fuck?" Izzy said exactly what Dan was thinking. He turned to look at him, shouting over the deafening roar. "Okay, bro, change of plans . . ."

Eden took a deep breath, about to pound on the door and scream, *Help! We need help in here*, when a sound started, distant at first, then louder and louder, a high-pitched whine accompanied by a low rumbling.

Ben and Jenni were both looking at her, confusion on their faces. And she knew that she was looking back at them the same way.

It was Jenn who identified it first. "It's a plane," she said, and even though Eden couldn't hear her over the rattle and roar, she could read her lips. "A jet—it's landing on the airstrip outside."

And Eden's first thought was that it was Izzy, even though she knew it couldn't possibly be. She had to close her eyes for a moment, because she was filled with such a rush of hope and longing at the idea that, in just a few short moments, she'd be safe in his arms.

But then she realized that if it *wasn't* Izzy on that plane—and it wasn't, it couldn't be—then it was someone, or a lot of someones, who worked for or with Jake. Two against seven was dangerous enough odds. This plane was definitely adding to that number by at least one, and quite possibly doubling or even tripling it. Shoot, big enough planes could carry hundreds of men.

And Eden knew that Izzy and her brother were SEALs, and that they were good at taking care of themselves, good at what they did. But they weren't invincible.

Still, she also knew no matter how many additional men came in on that plane to provide backup for Jake, that Izzy and Dan weren't going to let that stop or even slow them. In fact, it was likely that they'd use the incoming plane as a diversion.

And she found herself waiting, heart in her throat, listening for the sounds of gunshots or shouting—sounds that would let her know the battle had begun.

Izzy had done everything but kiss Dan good-bye.

"Okay, bro, change of plans." After that initial *what the fuck*, Izzy'd taken the landing jet in stride. And they needed a change in plan because they both realized that their new priority one was to make sure that Jenn, Eden, and Ben did *not* get on that aircraft.

"Go around back," Izzy said, "take out those two guards, ammo up, and get inside through one of the air vents—think you can do that, Gimpy McBaby-Man?"

Dan laughed as he said, "Fuck you!"

"I'll take that as a *Yes, Mommy*. Once you're inside, locate the women and Ben. Stay put if you think it's safe; if not, get them out of that northeast room, but I want you to *avoid* the front of the building. Do you hear me? Stay back from the airfield."

Dan nodded, because he knew what was coming.

Izzy said it anyway. "Because I'm gonna disable the plane, and if I have to, I'll make it go boom."

"How the hell are you going to . . . ?" The words were out of Dan's mouth even though he knew the answer.

"I'll improvise." Izzy held out his hand to Dan, and what started as a handshake turned into a tight hug. "Fuck you, asshole. I hate you and your ass face. Keep Eden safe for me," he said, and it was the closest the irreverent SEAL would ever come to a *should I not return* type appeal.

"Make sure you improvise an escape while you're at it," Dan said, past an inexplicable lump in his throat.

Izzy pushed Dan away. "*Go.*"

Dan went.

Whoever was in charge of security here was a total fool.

As Izzy watched, the two guards in the front of the building went to meet the plane with another two men, who came out of the building with a portable set of metal stairs, after pulling up one of the garagelike bay doors and leaving the damn thing wide freaking open.

He wanted to call Dan on Eden's cell phone and say, *Come on back, bro, lookie here, you can sneak right in.* Thing is, Dan needed the firepower he was going to borrow from the guards around back—except, oh, *sweet!* The guard who was built like a linebacker actually set his AK-47 down, leaning it against the side of the building so he could help move the stairs.

Izzy helped himself to the weapon donation and ducked inside—and nearly ran into the guy with the hat he'd seen visiting Greg's house with skinhead Jake. The guy's gun went up in a classic gangbanger sideways hold, and Izzy opened both hands in a gesture that said *Whoa, Nellie,* even though he was still holding tight to the linebacker's weapon.

"Who the hell are *you?*" the guy asked.

Jesus, what *was* Hat Guy's name?

"Nathan," Izzy said, pulling it out of his ass. "Damn, you scared the shit out of me, man. I just came in from the plane. I'm looking for Jake . . . ?"

The fact that he used their names worked like a charm, and Nathan lowered his weapon just enough for Izzy to hit him in the face with the butt of that AK-47—no, wait, it was an AK-74 with a slightly smaller-caliber bullet, but the same grand Kalashnikov design.

Nathan went down, his lights out, and Izzy dragged him back

behind a conveniently parked A&B Storage truck, relieving him of his various weapons—that very nice Smith & Wesson 9mm pistol that he'd held like a dipshit, and a backup SIG Sauer with the same caliber; okay, so maybe he wasn't a total dipshit. Maybe he just liked the drama of an unconventional handgrip. Maybe he found that holding his handgun like that got him laid.

Although, truly? What it had gotten him this morning was laid out.

Nathan was carrying magazines for his weapons in his pockets, as well as a set of keys—one of them bearing the symbol for a Ford, and no doubt belonging to the van that was parked outside, near a fucking Volvo.

Hi, my name is Bob, and I'm a security guard for an organization that sells children as sex slaves, and yeah. I drive a Volvo because I'm into auto safety.

Right.

Nathan also was carrying a set of plastic restraints—no doubt because they had cargo that needed to be restrained, aka Eden, Jennilyn, and Ben, due to be shipped out on that plane. Izzy hummed a few bars of "Bohemian Rhapsody"— *Mama, just killed a man*—as he opened the back of the truck and used one of the pieces of plastic to restrain Nathan, hands behind his back, to one of the anchors on the floor that was inside of the truck, rather than breaking the motherfucker's neck the way he kinda sorta wanted to.

But in the aftermath—at least the aftermath Izzy was envisioning— it was good to have one of the bad guys still be capable of communication. And someone relatively far up the chain of command was particularly likely to start communicating effectively; i.e., confessing to all of his evil boss's sins, when faced with life in prison or worse.

So Izzy yanked off the guy's sneaker, stripped off his smelly-ass sock and jammed it into his mouth, then gave him one more tap on the head to make sure he stayed unconscious, before closing and securing the truck door with another of those handy plastic restraints.

Outside on the runway, the sun had risen, and the metal stairs were in place as the plane's door popped opened. And as the two guards stood there along with two of the men from inside, like neatly lined-up little ducks in a shooting range, Izzy knew he'd never have a better opportunity to take all of them out.

And whether they drove a Volvo or not, they *did* willingly work for an organization that sold children—internationally—as sex slaves.

So Izzy did what he had to, knowing as he did it that all hell would break loose at the sound of that AK-74, but that the dirty dozen that they'd started with—if Danny'd done his job, and if he knew Danny and he did, Danny *had* done it quickly and efficiently—would drop down to a far more manageable five.

Not counting, of course, the potential army that awaited him in that plane.

The climb up to the air vent on the north side of the warehouse was a bitch and a half.

But Dan did it, because he had to.

Because he could not fail.

Because he'd trained and trained and *trained* for this. For getting the job done despite the pain.

So he made it up and he made it inside, and he swung himself onto a series of catwalks that crisscrossed the ceiling, up near a set of big, slow-moving fans.

Jesus, it was hot in here, but there was no time to rest or congratulate himself for making it this far. Gimpy McBaby-Man, he was not.

Infrared images had put the three hostages—his potentially pregnant wife, his brother, and his sister—in a small room in the northeast corner of the building. He found it easily. The entire back of the building was partitioned into a row of rooms, with lower ceilings covered by rolls of insulation, probably because those rooms were air-conditioned and the rest of this place sure as hell wasn't.

As Dan made his way over in that direction, he could see the tops of the walls that segmented the rooms, and he saw there was a long hallway that connected them all.

It was then that he heard it—the unmistakable sound of gunfire.

And five men burst out of the single door in that long wall that separated the warehouse from the back rooms.

One of them—a man with a shaved head—stopped a second and snapped out an order as the remaining three ran for the airfield. "Go to the prisoners and get one of them."

The man who'd been given the order hesitated. "Which one?"

"I don't give a shit! Just *do* it! Now!"

They were too far away, and outside of the range of the weapons that Dan had acquired from the obviously inexperienced guards—which was a shame, because if he had more than this stupid lightweight room broom or these small-caliber pistols, he could've taken them all out when they'd come through the door.

And as the skinhead followed the other men toward the open warehouse bay and the brilliant morning light, and as that last man ran back toward the partition door, Dan ran, too, heading for that northeast corner of the building.

There was no ladder down. He was going to have to jump, counting on the ceiling's tile-and-metal framework and that insulation to break his fall.

Dan swung himself over the edge of the catwalk and let himself drop.

Eden and Ben were both talking at once.

"It's Izzy!"

"It's Danny! It's got to be!"

They both started yelling. "Hey! We're in here! We're back here!"

Jenn, too, had heard what undeniably sounded like gunfire. She'd heard shouting, too, but none of the voices belonged to Dan, and that worried her.

But then she heard the sound of footsteps running down the hall.

"Here comes the guard," she said. "It sounds like only one . . ."

Ben and Eden both moved into place.

The door opened with a crash, and the guard—the man Jenn thought of as Nathan's brother—was standing there, waving a gun at them, shouting, "Get back from the door!"

They couldn't get close enough to stick him with the glucagon. At least not yet. But maybe if he ordered them out of there...

"Down on your knees, hands on your heads," he shouted. "You! The big girl! Get over here!"

He was talking to Jenn—she was larger than Eden—and she was going to have a chance to do it.

It was then that the ceiling exploded and Jenn threw herself down on top of Ben, who was still pretending to be unconscious, only to find that Eden had done the very same thing.

But it wasn't an explosion, it was an entrance. The ceiling tiles had shattered from the force of a man plunging through them, bringing insulation and pieces of the metal framework with him, and God, it was not just any man, it was...

"Danny!"

The jet was one of those personal-sized baby jets that richie-riches or celebrities with pilot licenses used, to flit from L.A. to Palm Springs.

Izzy charged up the stairs and hit the door to the plane with his shoulder before the frightened-looking man standing there could swing it all the way shut.

The guy was a flight attendant, or maybe the copilot—either way he was unarmed—and Izzy pushed his way past him into the cabin, which was wonderfully empty, thank you, baby Jesus, for that lovely surprise.

It had been stripped of seats—all except for the very front row on both sides of the aisle—to make room for the kind of sturdy cages that could be used to transport dangerous animals.

Or human beings.

And shit, he was wrong about the cabin being empty.

There was one little girl locked in the cage in the back. She poked her head up to look at Izzy with brown eyes that were wide with alarm, but then ducked back down, as if trying to hide.

Behind the cages—there had to be a half dozen of them—was what looked like a bar setup.

Just in case the slave traders wanted a gin and tonic midflight.

Izzy tossed the flight attendant into the plush leather of that single row of seats after the guy went unconscious due to his head connecting solidly with Izzy's elbow. He was definitely a flight attendant, because the copilot was up with the pilot in the cockpit, both of them fumbling for weapons as they gazed at Izzy with alarm through the open cockpit door—which had a pre-9/11 design, seeing as how it swung open into the cabin so they couldn't kick it shut.

If the cages and that little girl hadn't been there, Izzy might've tried a *Freeze!* or a *Hands where I can see 'em!*

But that child made it so clear that these assholes knew *exactly* what they were doing. They'd chosen to dance with the devil.

So Izzy sent them to hell.

Dan hit the ground hard amid the rubble and dust from the ceiling, but he rolled, and as he rolled, he brought up his weapon and he fired, and the man in the doorway fell.

"Is Ben badly hurt?" were the first words out of his mouth as he reached for Jenn's hand, to pull her up to her feet.

She was shaking, she couldn't help herself—that man was *dead*— and she wanted to throw herself into Dan's arms, but she knew there was no time. She settled for looking hard into his eyes—that fall had hurt him, but he'd never admit it—as Ben answered for himself. "I'm fine. I was just pretending—"

"Good," Dan cut him off, even as he squeezed Jenn's hand and released her to help Ben up, because there was no time for even the briefest of kisses.

"Is Izzy here?" Eden asked.

"He's out there," Dan said, crouching next to the dead guard as if he were no more than an unpleasant pile of trash, and taking what looked like a rifle and a smaller handgun off the man's body.

"By *himself*?" Eden asked, her worry radiating off of her.

He nodded. "Yeah."

"Oh God," Eden breathed.

"We counted seven of them," Jenn told Dan. "Two outside and five in."

"We got an infrared head count of twelve from the FBI. Who are on their way, but it's going to be a while before they get here," Dan told her as he handed what looked like a small machine gun to Eden and the handgun to Ben. He offered a similar weapon to Jenn. "Baby, I know you don't like firearms, but—"

She didn't, it was true, and she'd discovered she liked dead bodies even less, but she took it from him willingly. It was heavy and solid. "I've never even held one before."

"Don't point it at anyone you aren't willing to kill," he told her, told all of them. "And if it comes to it, aim for the biggest body mass— you'll have a better chance of hitting your target."

"I'll show Jenn how to release the safety," Ben volunteered.

Dan looked at him hard. "I'm not sure I want to know how you know that, but good."

"Please. You need to go help Izzy," Eden told Dan. "We'll be all right here. If the FBI's coming..."

Jenn wasn't sure she was in agreement. She herself would certainly be far more all right with Dan safely beside her, but she couldn't be so selfish as to make him stay. "I love you," she told him.

And he did take the time—a fraction of a second—to kiss her. And then he was gone.

Izzy couldn't get the freaking cabin door to close.

Which meant that the three-man assault team that lurked just inside the warehouse bay door could easily get inside and take him out.

Except they weren't exactly an assault team. They weren't even close. They were more like three petty criminals who'd graduated to more serious crimes and hooked up with some really evil men with a ton of money and international connections. They obviously had some knowledge and experience when it came to handling firearms. But it was limited to the tune of *keep your head down so it doesn't get shot off,* and *point the barrel of the weapon toward the target and squeeze the trigger until said target doesn't move anymore.*

Two of them were doing just that, their wildly inaccurate bullets bouncing off the concrete and only occasionally pinging into the fuselage of the jet—which was helping Izzy make the damn thing unsafe to fly, thanks very much, boys.

They were clearly a little freaked by the display of death at the bottom of the portable aircraft stairs—so much so that one of them squirted.

As Izzy watched, the guy squeezed out of the cover of the warehouse and ran not toward the plane in an heroic attempt to end the battle, but rather toward the parked van and that Volvo. He was fleeing the scene as squirters were prone to do, and Izzy saw no need to take him out, since he was removing himself from the equation.

One of his co-workers, though, apparently had a problem with his desertion, because he leaned out of the doorway to shoot the guy square in the back.

Izzy took the opportunity—and the clean shot—to take out the shooter, who fell, too. Which brought his magic number down from five to three.

He had the location of one of 'em pinpointed. It was the other two he was worried about.

He had to get the hell off this plane so he could find them and take them out.

Danny came back—almost right away—into the room that had changed from their prison cell into their fortress for this impending siege.

"I can't leave you here," he said. "There's a cache of weapons in a room down the hall—these guys must be gunrunning, too. It's a freaking munitions dump and Izzy was talking about blowing up that plane—"

"*What?*" Eden said, not quite able to believe her ears.

"*Possibly* blowing up the plane," her brother corrected himself as he took out a cell phone—it was hers—and hit the speed dial. "I don't know what he's doing, not yet, but whatever it is he does, I don't want you to be trapped back here." He led the way out into the hall. "Stay close to me. We're going to head over to where there's a bunch of crates." He looked at Eden and shook his head. "He's not picking up."

She took the phone from him. "I'll try him again."

"Do it when we get there," Dan said. "Right now I need eyes open and top speed. If someone starts shooting, don't run in a straight line. Zig and zag. Got it?"

They all nodded.

"Let's go."

Izzy used his feet and kicked the stairs away from the plane, which was another step in the right direction in terms of surviving an assault, but several steps back in terms of getting his ass off the plane and taking out the final three.

It wasn't until he was completely back inside and he'd shut the door—Jesus Harvey Christ on a pogo stick, so *that* was how it latched, wow, he was an idiot—that he realized his pants had been shaking because his carefully silenced phone was ringing.

Of course, he wouldn't have been able to hear it over the sounds of the little caged girl in the back of the plane, who was crying rather loudly at this point.

"Hey, I'm the good guy," Izzy told her as he took out his phone, but of course it had stopped. A missed call from Eden, who was really Dan, since Dan had Eden's phone. But it *could* actually be Eden, because Dan should have found her and Jenni and Ben by now. "I don't suppose you speak any English . . . ?"

If everything was going *just* right, Izzy's wife, her two brothers, and his new sister-in-law should be hunkered down in that back northeast corner of the building, waiting for Izzy to take out the remaining bad guys. Which, okay, maybe he could do while safely ensconced in this plane, as if it were a great big Iron Man–type suit.

As he called Eden's phone back, he moved Dumb and Dumber out of the cockpit, and he could see through the windshield that good old skinhead Jake was one of the surviving baddies. He and another man—skinny with a ponytail—were having an argument right there in the shelter from the open bay door.

It was too much to hope that Jake would eliminate another of the enemy, and sadly enough it didn't happen—nor did Eden or Dan pick up the phone. Which freaked Izzy out just a bit, and made him redo the math in his head. Twelve tangos, not counting the three on the plane, minus two via Dan, minus the one Izzy'd put in the truck, minus four at the bottom of the stairs, minus two was . . . three. Which left one unaccounted for and possibly doing damage to Dan, Eden, Jenni, and Ben, which was alarming.

He dialed Eden's number again.

As Izzy watched, Skinny disappeared back inside, while Jake leaned out of the doorway just a little bit to look up at the plane. As he did, he saw Izzy there in the cockpit, and he raised his weapon and let loose a blast of bullets.

Izzy hit the deck, but the glass was apparently bulletproof, which really wasn't that big of a surprise on a high-end toy like this, particularly one used for nefarious deeds.

But Jake didn't seem all that nonplussed. He smiled at Izzy, and even came out a bit farther from his cover, no doubt because he now believed that Izzy couldn't shoot him, either. So he pointed a finger-gun at Izzy and pretend-shot him, like, *bang*, still with that big *you are so dead* smile on his fugly face.

Izzy was just about to prove how so not dead he was when Eden picked up.

"Izzy," she gasped. "We need help! Danny's been shot!"

• • •

Dan had zigged instead of zagged, taking up the rear as they'd run toward the shadowy crate that was closest to the back hallway door.

He'd seen the man coming—skinny with a ponytail—heading back toward the very doorway they'd just vacated, and he'd fired his weapon, half hoping he'd hit the son of a bitch, and half hoping he'd draw the man's fire, so he wouldn't kill Jenni, Eden, or Ben.

He'd gotten part of his wish.

Right before Dan made it to cover, he felt the bullet slap him, and he went down.

He tried to make it look intentional—like he was sliding into home. And he managed to bring his weapon up and fire back a long burst, so that even if the gunman knew he'd made contact, he didn't think they were defenseless back here.

Jenn knew, right away, that something was wrong. Particularly when Dan ordered Ben to climb up on top of the crate and unload his weapon at anything that moved.

"I'm hit," he then told her, as if she couldn't tell, at this point, from the blood.

Jesus, it was his leg—his left one this time, and it was bleeding like a bitch.

"Tell me what to do," Jenn said, calm and steady, as Eden got on the phone with Izzy.

"Tourniquet," Dan said, "something to slow the bleeding," as Eden asked, "Izzy wants to know how bad is it?" She turned to look and answered the question herself. "It's bad."

"It's not. I'm going to be okay," Dan told Jenn even as she said to him, "You're going to be fine." She was taking off her bra, right out from under her shirt—a feminine talent that had always impressed him.

"Izzy wants to know how many of the twelve you took out," Eden asked Dan as Jenn pulled it free and wrapped it around the top of his leg.

"Three," Dan told her, and she forwarded the info to the other SEAL. "Two outside, and one in."

"He says we're down to two—the guy named Jake and the one who just shot you," Eden reported.

"That's good news," Dan told Jenn. He could see she didn't quite believe it, so he told her, "I'm not leaving you."

"You better not, you bastard," she said. "If you think you can just attempt to knock me up and then check out..."

Dan laughed, but then, Jesus, it started to hurt. "Ben, you okay up there?" he called.

"I'm good," Ben reported. "There's movement, back by the doorway that we came out of. I'm pretty sure I'm too far away..."

"Hold your fire," Dan said. "Good call. But if they come any closer..."

"Yeah," Eden was saying into the phone. "There're all these crates in here. We're behind the one that's closest to the back of the building."

"Closest to the northeast corner," Dan told her, and she relayed that info, too.

"Izzy says to stay put," Eden reported. "To hold on. He says he's on his way."

"Hey, Danny?" Ben called from atop the crate. "The man who came out of that doorway? He's carrying—jeez, I don't know what that is, except...Holy crap, Eed, I think it's that thing that they used against that demon on Buffy. The one in the mall? Where Zander had memories of being a soldier from that Halloween episode, right after Angel becomes Angelus in season two...?"

"Oh, shit," Eden said into the phone, to Izzy. "If Ben's right? I think they've got a rocket launcher."

Driving a plane wasn't as easy as it looked when sitting in coach and traversing the airport runways.

And Izzy hadn't been one of those flip-a-coin-to-see-if-you-join-the-

Air-Force-or-the-Navy kids who loved the water but also secretly yearned to fly. He'd never particularly wanted to learn how to be a pilot, mostly because his goal had been to jump *out* of the plane, and you sure as hell couldn't do that while you were sitting in the captain's chair.

Still, he'd always been curious about how things worked, and he knew enough to finally figure out how to make this particular vehicle move.

And not a moment too soon.

"Hold on back there, little girl," he shouted as he backed that sucker up, his phone tucked up under his chin.

"Little *what?*" Eden said on the other end of the satellite signal, her voice traveling up into outer space and bouncing back down to his phone, even though she was only some mere hundreds of yards away from him, in that gleaming white warehouse.

"There's a girl," Izzy reported as he put that puppy back into the equivalent of drive, "maybe nine or ten, in a cage, in the cabin of this plane."

"Seriously?"

"You think I'd make this shit up?" Izzy asked.

Eden laughed, but then she stopped. "Please, *please* don't die," she said.

"It's two against five," he countered.

"But they have a rocket launcher."

"And I'm about to drive a jet up their ass. Ready or not, here I come." And Izzy hit the equivalent of the gas.

Only Irving Zanella would crash a jet plane through the side of a building. He actually aimed the nose of the thing through the bay door and just kept going, and the sheet metal shrieked and tore. He hit a truck and then another truck, and a wing was clearly damaged, too, before the plane rolled to a stop.

Dan found himself looking up at the fans that were slowly spinning and the catwalk that he'd used when he first came in, and he was glad that nothing was directly overhead, to fall on them.

They were far enough away to be safe.

Except…

"Uh-oh," Ben said, from his perch atop the crate. "The bald guy with the rocket launcher? He's aiming that thing at *us*!"

Izzy'd missed.

He'd hoped he'd hit Jake when he plowed into the building. He was pretty sure that that one bump he'd felt was the plane hitting the dude's very last minion.

But Jake had jumped clear.

And Izzy knew he was screwed. He knew he'd failed—he'd taken too long to figure out how to get this thing to move, because now the bastard was going to blow his shit sky-high.

Except…

Holy crap, Jake was aiming that rocket launcher not at Izzy and the plane, but at the crate where Eden, Jenni, Dan, and Ben were hunkered down. The asshole actually took his time to do it, as he looked back at Izzy, like, *You ready to watch while I kill your family before I kill you, trapped the way you are behind that bulletproof glass?*

Which gave Izzy enough time to bring that AK-74 right up to that glass, because unlike the asshole down there, he knew that bulletproof tended not to work so well when the barrel of a gun with a Kalashnikov's power was pressed against it.

And he squeezed the trigger, and the gun did what he'd expected it to do and blew a hole in that window, which allowed Izzy to send the next round of bullets into Jake, who had turned back to look at him, this time in astonished surprise, before he died.

"Yeah, asshole. That'll teach you to fuck with my family." Izzy picked up the phone he'd dropped when he'd grabbed for his weapon. The line was still open. "Hey," he said, still breathing hard as he watched and waited, but there was no other movement. "You still there?"

"I'm still here," Eden said, her voice warm and steady in his ear.

"Ask Ben if he saw whether I got 'em both."

She put her hand over the bottom of the phone, and he heard muffled voices, but then she came back and said, "He said *yeah*. Jenn says we need a medical kit. And she needs me to get off the phone so we can find out how soon the FBI'll be here."

"I'm on my way," Izzy said as he used the last of Nathan's restraints to lock the still-unconscious flight attendant to the nearest cage before he searched for the plane's first-aid kit. It was in one of the overhead compartments and it was seriously lacking in anything useful like a plasma expander—that would've been too easy—so he punched the bulkhead right over the seats, hard enough to release the oxygen masks.

"I'll be back," he told the wide-eyed and now silent little girl as he grabbed the tubing and pulled it free. "We'll get you out of here, ASAP. But first? I gotta help a friend and go kiss the shit out of my wife."

"Here he comes," Ben announced.

And there, indeed, was Izzy, dropping lightly from the open door of the plane onto the concrete floor of the warehouse, his cell phone to his ear.

As Eden watched, peeking around the edge of the crate, he bent down and picked up the rocket launcher, checking it—no doubt making sure it no longer was a danger.

He also swung past one of the trucks that his plane had pushed over, making sure that the back door was securely closed as he ended his phone call.

And then he was jogging toward them, with that smooth and easy gait that Eden had come to know so well.

"FBI's ETA is approximately seven minutes," Jenn announced,

Eden's phone to her ear as she sat beside Danny. "They're sending a medevac chopper."

"I'm doing okay," Danny reassured her as Izzy came closer and saw Eden and smiled. "This is nothing like the last time."

"I'm sitting in a puddle of your blood," Jenn pointed out as Eden stepped out from behind the crate.

"Yeah, but it's slowed. Look at me. I'm fine. I'm not in shock, I'm alert—"

"You're a terrible liar—I can *tell* you're in serious pain—"

"Well, *yeah*," Dan said. "I've been shot. It hurts—"

They kept talking—Danny obviously knew Jenni was reassured by his ability to have a conversation—but Eden didn't hear any more of it as she threw herself forward and into Izzy's arms.

"You okay?" he asked her.

"I'm so sorry," she started, but he cut her off.

"Chht!" he said, making that sound that she'd made at him just a few hours earlier, like the Dog Whisperer. "Those aren't the three words I want to hear."

"I love you," she told him.

He did his best Han Solo. "I know." But then he ruined it by laughing, except it didn't really ruin it, it made it that much better, because his laughter was pure Izzy, and as he kissed her, Eden knew that he loved her, too.

But he broke the kiss almost before it had started, carrying her with him around the side of the crate so he could take a look at Danny's leg.

"Gimpy McBaby-Man!" he said. "Got another boo-boo?" He held out a length of plastic tubing that he'd brought from the plane as he knelt down beside Dan. "I know we've got some needles, in with that insulin—Ben, you still have that bag?"

"I do." Ben tossed down the bag that he'd carried with him out of their prison cell and Izzy caught it.

"This, along with a little tape and plenty of this fine gravity that planet Earth provides...I kneel before you," Izzy told Eden's other brother as he continued to check his wound, "your walking and talking bag of type O blood."

"We've really got the bleeding under control," Dan told him.

"It looks like you have," Izzy said, not to Dan, but to Jenn, who was looking more pale than Danny. "Looks like the bullet missed the artery."

She nodded, still not completely convinced.

So Izzy looked at her directly, squarely, and said, "We'll keep an eye on it. If it starts bleeding again, well, we've got the tools we need to keep him alive until the helo gets here. Okay? I promise you, he's going to be fine."

And this time when she nodded, she actually smiled, too.

"I just spoke to Jenk," Izzy told Danny. "He and Lindsey and Lopez are heading over to Eden's apartment—to try to talk to Neesha. She's still holed up, inside." He looked at Eden. "She went one-on-one with Todd."

"She *what?*"

"We left her Greg's gun and she kicked his ass," he told her as he wiped Dan's blood from his hands on the front of Dan's shirt.

"Hey!"

"Yeah, what? You're already a mess. Anyway, it got noisy and now the police and the FBI are out in the courtyard, trying to get her to put down her weapon and come out with her hands up. She wants to wait for us to get home. Which could be a while." Izzy reached for Eden, pulling her down onto his lap. "Ben, you're still keeping watch, right?"

"I am," Ben said.

"Good boy," Izzy said as he looked into Eden's eyes. "Because right now? I've got to kiss my wife."

And that he did.

CHAPTER
THIRTY

Neesha waited.

Every so often the phone would ring, and she would answer it, hoping it was Danny or Izzy or Eden or Ben, but it was always a lady whose voice she didn't recognize, and Neesha always said, "No, thank you," and hung right up.

But then the phone rang, and it *was* Ben. He was all right—they were *all* all right, but they were being taken to the hospital. And he wanted Neesha to meet them over there.

He told her that a woman named Lindsey, who looked kind of like Neesha, would come to the door. Neesha should let her in, and she would take Neesha over to the hospital.

And finally, it came.

A knock on the door. A voice, calling from outside. "Neesha? My name is Lindsey. I'm a friend of Ben's. I have a key, may I use it to unlock the door and come in?"

"Yes," Neesha said.

And the woman came in, pushing her way around the refrigerator.

She was short, like Neesha, and she had dark hair, like Neesha, and brown eyes similar to Neesha's. And when she smiled, Neesha was reminded of her mother's smile.

"Hey," she said. "I'm Lindsey." Her hands were empty, and she kept them out and open in front of her. She was also wearing some kind of padded vest that made her look like a baseball umpire.

One of Neesha's visitors had liked baseball, and always tuned the TV in her room to a game.

"Did you get the pictures I sent to your phone?" she asked.

Neesha shook her head. "I didn't know how to see them," she said.

"May I come into the living room?" Lindsey asked. "I can show you..."

"Please close the door behind you," Neesha said, so Lindsey did before she crossed the apartment, still with her hands out.

She sat on the couch, next to Neesha, taking in the fact of that gun on Neesha's lap, the same way she'd glanced down the hall and made note of Todd's body sprawled in front of the bedroom door. She was not afraid, but she was also not a fool.

Continuing to check for Neesha's permission, she reached for the cell phone and opened it, pushing some of the buttons and... She held it out so that Neesha could see the pictures on the tiny screen.

Yes, that was Lindsey with Izzy and Danny and another, shorter man, and another man with darker hair. "That's from my wedding," she told Neesha with a smile. "Izzy and Dan and our other friend, Jay Lopez, they were all best men. My husband, Mark—that's him." She pointed to the shorter man who was smiling broadly. "He couldn't decide who should be his best man, and since he has three best friends, he had three best men. He's very diplomatic." She pointed to the dark-haired man. "That's Jay. He's outside, with Mark, right now. The three of us will take you to the hospital. With a police escort, of course. But you'll be in the car with us. And one of us will stay with you, until you feel confident that you're safe. Is that okay?"

Neesha looked back into Lindsey's eyes, but didn't respond. She wasn't sure yet if it was okay. "Can I keep the gun?" she finally asked.

"No," Lindsey said.

Neesha nodded. "I didn't think so. Will I go to jail?"

Lindsey answered the exact same way, with no hesitation. "No."

"But I'm illegal."

This time Lindsey didn't answer quite as quickly. This time, she said, "Is that what they told you? That you'd be arrested because you're here illegally?"

Neesha nodded. "I saw on the TV news—all the people who hate me."

But Lindsey was shaking her head. "Neesha, you were brought here against your will. You're the victim of a terrible crime—you're not a criminal. And if you want to? You can help the police and the FBI bring charges against the people who hurt you. You can go to court and testify. But only if you want to."

Neesha looked at Lindsey. "I want to," she said.

"Good," Lindsey said. "The first thing you'll do is look at some pictures and point out the men and women that you recognize—if there *are* any that you recognize."

"I don't have to look at pictures," Neesha said. "I can just..." She reached over to the paper and pen she'd been using while she'd waited, after Todd was no longer a threat. It had been a long, long time since she'd had either to work with and at first she was rusty, but then she got better. She handed her drawings to Lindsey. "That's Mr. Nelson, on the top," she said as Lindsey flipped through the pages. "And a man called Karl and another called Ron. I haven't seen them at all in the past few years, so maybe they're dead—"

"They're not," Lindsey said. "Neesha, this is..."

"There's Jake." Neesha pointed at her drawings. "And a man named Nathan. And Todd. When he still had a face."

Lindsey looked back at her. "Now I know why they were so desperate to find you."

"They stopped giving me paper and pencils," Neesha told her, "when I was twelve. It was the same year I first... met Todd."

"God." Lindsey held up the last page. "Who's this?"

Neesha pointed to the woman she'd drawn. "That's my mother," she said, "before she got sick and died. And the man is her father—my grandfather."

Lindsey nodded. "We can help you find him."

"He might not want me anymore."

"If he doesn't," Lindsey said, "he's an idiot. Whatever happens, though? You'll be safe. I can guarantee that." She stood up. Held out her hand. "Why don't you give me that weapon so we can get over to the hospital, get you checked out. You can say hi to Ben..."

Neesha looked up at Lindsey. And handed her the gun.

CHAPTER
THIRTY-ONE

Danny needed surgery, because the bullet that had hit him hadn't exited his leg.

It was supposed to be quick and easy, but Eden knew that Jennilyn was anxious. She and Izzy had volunteered to sit with her in the waiting room, even as Ben was being given a thorough examination just down the hall.

Mark Jenkins had gone to get food from the hospital cafeteria, and had brought it back with him—burgers and salads and fries. Izzy dug in—they were all hungry—while Eden went to see what was taking Jenn so long in the ladies' room.

She bumped into Lindsey—Mark's wife—who was also on her way in to use the facilities.

"Oh, hi, Eden," Lindsey said. "Neesha's in talking to Ben, and Lopez is with them. I've had a lot of coffee this morning, so..." She made a face.

"It's been a long night," Eden agreed.

Jenn was over at the sinks, washing her hands, and she looked up at Eden in the mirror. "You can say that again."

"It's been a long one for Lindsey, too," Eden told her. She looked at Lindsey. "Danny told me about your miscarriage. I'm so sorry."

Lindsey sighed. "Yeah," she said. "It still hasn't really..." Tears flooded her eyes, but she blinked them back and smiled. "The really stupid thing is that I was really scared, you know, at first? At the idea of having this baby. But Mark was so happy and . . . I *just* finally started to really get into it and . . ."

"The *really* stupid thing isn't that," Eden told her as she gave Lindsey a hug. "The really stupid thing is that you miscarried. It's *not* fair, and it sucks, and I am so, *so* sorry."

Lindsey laughed through her tears as she hugged Eden back. "Yeah, it really does suck, doesn't it?"

"And everyone goes, *well, I guess it wasn't meant to be* and you just want to bitch-slap them," Eden said, and she felt Lindsey nod.

"Mark's really upset," Lindsey confessed. "You know, we're buying this house, and now he's talking about just fixing it up a little and turning around and selling it right away. And I know what he means, because it just feels so pathetic and sad."

"But you can try again," Eden said, pulling back to look at her. "Can't you? I mean . . ."

"Well, yeah," Lindsey said, wiping her eyes. "Except, we weren't exactly trying. It was kind of accidental, so . . ."

"So now you get to try," Eden said. "I mean, if you want. If you don't, that's okay, too, you know? And you move into the house, because you weren't buying it for the baby—that's crazy. You don't buy a baby a house. You buy it for your family. And your family's just going to be a little bit smaller than you'd thought, at least for a little while. You've still got Mark and he's still got you."

Lindsey nodded. "You know, you're right." But then she laughed. "Am I the only one aware of the irony of this wisdom coming from the crazy woman who ran away to Germany after losing *her* baby?"

Eden laughed, too, as she wiped her own eyes. "Guilty as charged," she said. "I *was* crazy. But I got better. Eventually, it starts to suck a little less."

Lindsey hugged her again. "Thanks," she said. "You know, Izzy really loves you."

Eden smiled. "I do know. And I love him, too."

"Good," Lindsey said, "because if you mess with him again, I'd have to beat you senseless, regardless of how nice you are to me."

"You won't have to," Eden said.

And as Lindsey went into one of the stalls, Eden looked over at Jenn, who'd been standing there quietly, by the sink. "You okay?"

Jenn nodded. "I'm just..."

"I know," Eden said. "The doctor should be out soon. And then you can go in and see Danny."

"That'll be good," Jenn said.

And together they went out and sat with Izzy and with Mark Jenkins. And they were even joined by Ben and Neesha and Jay Lopez and finally Lindsey, who came out of the bathroom right before the doctor appeared and said the words they all were waiting to hear.

"He's going to be just fine. He's alert—you can go in to see him now."

The first thing that Dan said to Jenn when she went into the room where he was recovering from his surgery was, "The doctor said the bullet didn't even so much as nick the artery. Recovery's going to be much faster and easier."

She laughed because she knew that he was thinking about sex, but then she started to cry, because she was just so overwhelmed.

"Hey," he said, trying to sit up to put his arms around her, but the nurse started making noise, so Jenn came to him, so he could hold her. Even though he was the one in the hospital bed.

"I'm sorry," she said, but he stopped her.

"It's okay," he said, his hands so gentle in her hair. "It's all right. Everyone's all right..."

"I know," she said, "and I'm so grateful. And it's all working out just perfectly. You know, we missed the meeting with CPS, but even that's okay, because Ivette and Greg didn't. Izzy really must've had some kind of come-to-Jesus meeting with them, because they convinced the social workers to let Ben live with either you and me or Eden and Izzy, either is fine, so maybe we can share him, you know? He can have a room in both of our apartments, like joint custody, so we can all have some alone time, too. And I was talking to Eden and we figured when you and Izzy go overseas, the three of us can live together, I mean, we'll try it, you know? It might make it easier. And all the charges against Eden have been dropped, and the FBI is going to help Neesha find her grandfather, and everything's going to be *wonderful*, except Mark and Lindsey just want to crawl away somewhere so they can cry, because it *didn't* work out perfectly for them. They lost their baby and what if I really am pregnant and won't that be rubbing their faces in it? I mean, *God!*"

"Wow," Dan said. "Okay, I'm glad I opted for the local anesthesia, because if I were on something heavy-duty right now? I'd start crying, too. That would've been a mind-bender. But I'm pretty sure I followed. And really, Jenni, I don't think you're gonna have to worry about—"

Jenn wiped her face as she sat back to look at him. "I threw up. Before. In the bathroom."

He laughed. "Are you shitting me?"

"Maybe it's a bug. I really didn't think you could get pregnant that fast."

"Well, *I* can't get pregnant at any speed," he pointed out.

"You *know* what I mean."

"Wow."

"Yeah."

"I'm *good.*"

Jenn laughed her disbelief. "That's your response? That you're *good?*"

"Well, obviously I am."

"Maybe *I'm* good," she said. "Maybe I'm just, like, so fertile, we're going to have twenty kids. Ten sets of twins. One a year for the next decade."

Dan was unfazed. "Only one a year? We can do better than that."

She laughed again, and he said, "I meant what I said. I love you. I also meant what I said about leaving the Teams. I think it's time."

Jenn shook her head. "You don't have to do that for me. I know that I was scared when you got injured—"

"It's not just about that," Dan told her. "It's about... Well, you having to leave your job. But if I don't reup, we can live in New York, and you can keep doing what you're doing. Your work with that shelter for homeless veterans—Jenni, that's so important—"

"And what you do isn't?" she countered. "As important as it is to make sure homeless vets have a place to go, what *you* do, as a SEAL, keeps regular soldiers out of harm's way. What *you* do reduces the need for homeless shelters." She smiled. "Dan, trust me, I'll find an important job—something that I love doing—in California. And if I am pregnant, well, I hope I don't shock you, but if I have a baby? I'm going to want to work, part-time, from home, if I can. At least until, I don't know, preschool? Like I said, please don't do this for me."

"How about if I do it for me?" he said quietly.

Jenn gazed into his eyes, and nodded. "I've already given Maria my notice, so... Whatever you do, I think we should stay in California, at least for the short term. Until Ben graduates."

He looked back at her. "You're serious."

"I meant it, too," she told him. "When I made those vows."

He drew her in for a kiss. But then he started to laugh. And when he pulled back to look at her, Jenn expected a variation on the "Damn, I'm good" theme.

Instead, he smiled at her with such warmth in his eyes, and he said, "Baby, you have no idea how very much I love you."

"Actually," Jenn said, smiling back at him, "I think I do."

By the time Dan was moved into a regular hospital room, Lindsey and Jenk and Lopez had left to bring Neesha to an FBI safe house, along with the little girl who'd been on the plane.

Jenk and Lindsey were going to be staying with Neesha for a while, until she felt more secure in her new surroundings.

So it was just Eden and Izzy and Jenni and Ben hanging out in Danny-Danny-bo-banny's room, mocking the contents of his dinner tray, complete with runny Jell-O.

Actually, it was Izzy who was doing the mocking as Eden sat on his lap. Jenn was still looking a little peaked, and Ben was curled up on the other empty bed, taking a nap.

There weren't a lot of chairs in the room, but that wasn't why Izzy had pulled Eden down on top of him.

He wanted his arms around her for another few hours. Okay, days. Weeks? Years. Damn, it would be okay with him if they could just sit like this for the rest of their lives.

Of course, having her there made it hard to concentrate on the quiet conversation that Jenn and Dan were having, across the room. Until Izzy heard Dan say, "... two bedrooms—it's really nice. It's close to the base, too, and ... I talked to Jenk, and he said it would be great if we rented. He thinks it's unlikely they'll be able to sell in this market—"

"Are you talking about Jenk and Lindsey's condo?" Izzy asked. "Because I just talked to Linds, and *she* said that Eden and I could rent it."

"No, no," Dan said. "Uh-uh. We got first dibs."

Izzy sat up, making Eden grab him more tightly around the neck, which was very nice. "How do *you* get *first dibs*? What are dibs, anyway, and why should you get them?"

"Maybe we should flip a coin," Jenn suggested, ever the voice of reason.

"Flip a coin?" Izzy asked, "for the greatest apartment in San Diego?" as Dan chimed in with, "Ah, babe, seriously, their place is *awesome.*"

"Cool," Ben said, opening his eyes. "If I'm living with both of you guys, I get to live there no matter what, right?"

"The kitchen's amazing." Dan waxed poetic. "And the living room has this huge slider that opens up the entire wall to this screened porch. At night, when the sun sets...The view...It's gorgeous."

Izzy was nodding his agreement when Eden kissed him on the side of his face. "It's just an apartment," she whispered into his ear. "We can find someplace else."

And as he pulled back to look into her eyes, he realized that she was right.

"Tie goes to the man who was shot," Izzy said as he held Eden's gaze. "The man who has to stay overnight in the hospital instead of renting a fabulous hotel room with his wife, on the government's dime."

"Are we seriously renting a fabulous hotel room on the government's dime?" Eden asked with a smile.

"Kinda gotta, sweetheart," Izzy reminded her. "Dead guy in your apartment."

"Yeesh," she said. "I forgot about that."

Izzy stood up, with Eden still in his arms. "In fact, I think we're going to go out right now and make those arrangements. Ben, we'll be back for you a little bit later, dude."

"I'll be here," Ben said.

"Wow," Izzy heard Dan say as he carried Eden out of the room, "I think Zanella just let me win, but how come it doesn't feel like I won?"

Eden was laughing, so Izzy put her down in the hallway, and they walked, hand in hand, to the elevators. It wasn't until they were out front, at the taxi stand, that she turned to him and said, "Thank you for believing me—and not giving up on me."

"You're welcome," he said.

"I love you," she said, "and I need you. You make the sky more blue."

"You do the same for me," he admitted.

She nodded. "Good. And—I just want you to know that, the next time something in my life is hard and painful, I'm going to run toward you, not away from you, okay?"

Izzy nodded, too. "That would be most excellent."

"And about the apartment," she said. "I just thought since Danny seemed to really be into it, and . . . That sort of thing doesn't matter that much to, well, to either one of us and . . ."

"Eden," Izzy told this woman who was his wife, his lover, and his best friend, "we'll find someplace perfect. I know we will, because as long as you're there? I'm home."

Eden smiled and kissed him.

And the sky was very, very blue.

ABOUT THE AUTHOR

SUZANNE BROCKMANN is the award-winning author of fifty books, and is widely recognized as one of the leading voices in romantic suspense. Her work has earned her repeated appearances on the *New York Times* bestseller list, as well as numerous awards, including Romance Writers of America's #1 Favorite Book of the Year and two RITA Awards.

Brockmann divides her time between Siesta Key, Florida, New York City, and Boston, Massachusetts. Visit her website at www.SuzanneBrockmann.com and find her on Facebook by searching for Suz Brockmann's Troubleshooters World.

ABOUT THE TYPE

This book was set in Electra, a typeface designed for Linotype by W. A. Dwiggins, the renowned type designer (1880–1956). Electra is a fluid typeface, avoiding the contrasts of thick and thin strokes that are prevalent in most modern typefaces.